Broken Angels

Ben pointed again to the snow-covered Chilkats and told Kris about winter in the Brooks Range. How it comes sooner than you expect, before you had thawed out from the last one. How one day, while you are still enjoying the warmth and greenness of summer, you look up and see the faint, almost transparent powder of snow on the distant mountains. You look at it with dread, almost exhaustion, knowing too well the months of cold and darkness that lie before you. Relentlessly, winter creeps down from the mountaintops and seeps into the flats and river valleys. It settles in the streams, and soon, clear ice rims the rocks, reaching each day a little farther outward until its frozen fingers clasp in the middle of the stream and imprison the racing waters, stilling them until breakup, a lifetime away.

Bill!
WELL MET #7
EXPLORERS CLUB
Russell Heath

Broken Angels
A Novel

RUSSELL HEATH

Alatna Works
Juneau, Alaska

First Alatna Works Edition, May 2015

This book is a work of fiction. References to real people, events, establishments, organizations, or locales are intended only to provide a sense of authenticity and are used fictitiously. All other characters, and all incidents and dialogue, are drawn from the author's febrile imagination and are not to be construed as real.

ISBN: 0692379681
Library of Congress Control Number: 2015904517
Alatna Works, Juneau, AK

ISBN 13: 978-0692379684

www.alatnaworks.net

Mom and Dad

WEDNESDAY, NOVEMBER 11

The plane dropped out of the clouds into the afternoon dusk. Rain streamed across the window and Kris pressed her face against the cold glass, shielding her eyes with a hand to see past her reflection. Below her was a dull sea and opposite, not far off the wing, were steep mountains, their tops hidden in the clouds and their sides blanketed with spruce, dark and still in the fading light. Snow clung to the trees on the upper slopes and cars streamed along a road cut into the mountainside above a line of houses standing at the water's edge.

The jet banked into a sharp dogleg turn and its flaps whined into their full position. The trees cut away and the plane raced low over a salt marsh matted with dead and broken grasses. The wheels touched the wet runway, rainwater exploded in a cloud of spray, and the plane braked hard, pressing Kris against her seat belt. The brakes released and, as they taxied toward the terminal, the cabin speakers hummed and a voice, indistinguishable from the others that had herded her north, welcomed them to Juneau and thanked them for flying Alaska Air. The plane stopped, seat belts clicked open, people stood, murmuring among themselves and unloading bags from the overheads before filing slowly forward.

Kris sat. She stared without seeing at the men in industrial raincoats outside the plane unloading baggage with silent efficiency. What was her mother doing in Juneau? She'd been south of Fairbanks only a few times in her life. And only once as far as Anchorage, which had been too big, too spread out for her. "You've got to have a car just to take a piss," she'd said. Juneau, even farther away, was another world.

Evie's letter had appeared in her mailbox a month ago. Kris turned it over in her hands, disbelief mixing with muted fear. How had she found her? Evie's clumsy scrawl stared up at her and Kris stared back, awash in uncertain currents of feeling and memory. Nine years. And she was still alive? Her fingers worked the envelope open. Nine years since she'd last seen Evie—nine years since she'd stepped over her mother's unconscious body and walked out the door of their two-room apartment into the sub-arctic night, leaving, she'd promised herself, Evie and Alaska forever.

The cabin had emptied. The cleaning crew was moving down the aisle gathering trash, checking for left bags, and tucking magazines back into seat pockets. Kris reached into the overhead and pulled out her canvas duffle. She stepped out of the plane and felt the sting of the cold air spilling in through the crack between the plane and the jet way. The lights in the arrival lounge were bright and harsh; night-blackened windows looked blankly at the empty seats, the glass display cases of stuffed animals and the retreating backs of people bunched up around the exit.

She moved off to the side and searched the mass of people talking loudly, laughing, and touching as they moved through the glass doors. They drained quickly out of the lounge and in another minute she was alone. She heard a click, and the sign announcing the arrival of her flight turned off. A uniformed woman stepped from behind the counter, flashed Kris a smile, hiked the strap of her bag higher on her shoulder, and hurried out. Kris waited, her back to the lounge doors, and stared out the big windows, lightly pocked with rain, at the blue lights rimming the runway.

Returning to Evie and to Alaska was like picking at an old scab; even the letter had irritated sores she was upset were still there: "I'll be so happy to see you!" Yeah, Mom.

A security guard, reflected in the lounge window, stared through the glass doors behind her, hesitating briefly before moving away. Taking a breath, she turned and walked out of the lounge, pushing through the security doors, into the greeting area where the last of the arriving passengers were hugging friends and relatives. She retreated into a corner next to a glass case with a yellowish polar bear standing in it and scanned the crowd.

There was no black-haired woman waiting for her. No lady with the dancing, unreliable eyes that would slide from yours to a burst of laughter across the room. No one with the silvered laugh that cigarettes had begun to darken even before Kris had left. Evie wasn't there, and Kris wasn't surprised.

She walked downstairs to the baggage claim area. A single carousel snaked into the room. Not much was left on it: a pack, some suitcases, and a cardboard box wound with duct tape. Already a uniformed man was pulling them off and stacking them in a corner.

Her mother wasn't here either. Kris walked past the Alaska Airlines ticket counters to the other end of the terminal. It was tiny; it looked like only Alaska Air flew jets into Juneau. The other counters were for local airlines flying charters and small planes out to the villages. She climbed the stairs back up to the restaurant. The man behind the bar glanced up from his book without interest. All the tables were empty. It wasn't Evie's kind of place anyway; too bright, too clean.

Irritation masked a rush of relief that the meeting had been put off a few more minutes. She walked slowly back down the stairs to the baggage area. Nine years ago Kris had walked out and not once in those years had she sent Evie a note or a postcard letting her know where she was or that she was OK. Nine years had dulled Kris's anger and now, in grudging moments, she allowed some excuses for Evie. Evie had grown up hard. Her father, an Athabascan who'd wandered out of the bush and into Fairbanks in the late sixties, had been killed when she was a teenager. He'd rolled his truck one winter, crushing the roof, trapping himself inside. When they found him, he was frozen hard as river ice. Evie's mother, Kris's grandmother, had left her Athabascan village just before she married and Kris remembered stories she'd told of her first ride in a car, her first taste of an orange—which she'd spat out and never tried again—and her fear of the white men who ran the shops in Fairbanks with cold indifference to anything except the coins in her pocket. It was a rough way to grow up—raised by a mother with bad English in a city that had, only a few years before, taken the "No Natives" signs off its hotels and restaurants, and who's only offered comfort was whiskey.

Alcohol had racked their lives. It had killed Evie's mother when Kris was still a girl and Kris was surprised it hadn't killed Evie by now. Evie's first drinks—the ones that started an evening—vaulted through her. They lifted her, flushing laughs from her throat, igniting sparks in her eyes, which teased and flirted and pulled people—men—to her until she was circled by bodies lured by her glow. She would be gone, lost like a queen bee in her swarm, and Kris, when she was still a kid, would slink into the shadows at the edges of the lamp light and pick at the gum stuck to the undersides of the tables or play with a bottle-cap, an empty cigarette package, her resentment brushed by fear, knowing that Evie's drinking would end with a man in her bed, usually drunk, sometimes violent, and always a stranger, even if he stayed for a month. Evie attracted them, helplessly. "You're a bitch who doesn't know she's in heat," Kris had yelled at her when Kris was older and anger had scabbed over the hurt and resentment.

Kris's father had been one of those men; Evie didn't even remember his name.

She stepped off the stairs and back into the baggage area. No Evie.

"Damn," she whispered.

The only people left in the baggage claim area were a couple poking through the bags and boxes stacked in the corner, a short man in jeans leaning against a counter by the exit, and a girl behind the Hertz counter.

The man leered at her. She glared back. He smiled and touched his hat. Kris turned away and went up to the girl at the Hertz counter. She was young and pale with fading spots of red on her cheeks.

"May I help you?" the girl asked. Her fingernails were painted purple.

"Can I get a bus to town?"

"You sure can. There are bus schedules right over there." She pointed to the counter against the far wall where the man was leaning. Kris walked over. On it was a sign saying Juneau Chamber of Commerce and next to it was a rack of hotel and tour brochures. Off by themselves, lying on the counter, were two stacks of bus schedules, one red the other blue. She took one of each.

"Need a ride somewhere, missy?" the man asked her.

"Not from you, buddy," Kris said and walked away, trying to make sense of the schedules.

"Suit yourself," he said.

She ignored him and went back to the girl, pulling out Evie's letter from her jacket pocket. The return address was a post office box.

"I need to get to the AWARE shelter," she said. "Does the bus go near it?"

"Right past it." The girl took the schedule, pointed her pen at the map, and traced a long blue line. "This is Glacier highway and the shelter is just outside downtown. Ask the driver where to get off." Scanning the schedule, she said, "The next bus leaves in about forty-five minutes."

"You're joking." In L. A. they came every few minutes.

The girl's face went blank. "No one rides the bus here."

Kris tucked the schedule into her pocket, picked up her bag, and walked toward the door. The man in jeans had disappeared. Her face, hollowed by shadows, was reflected in the glass doors as she pushed them open and walked into the night. The air was cold and heavy with moisture. She stopped at the curb and lit a cigarette. She drew in the smoke; then held the cigarette down by her thigh to let her eyes adjust to the darkness.

The airport terminal looked smaller from the outside. No cars were parked in front of it. Across the street were a couple of flagpoles and a small parking lot with a few scattered cars. Overhead, the airport strobe pulsed rhythmically. She could see a distant glow of lights and hear the slick of car tires on a hidden road, but nothing else.

Unseen clouds pressed down on her. A drizzle fell out of the blackness and into puddles crowded with rain-rings. A breeze slapped the ropes against the metal shafts of the flagpoles and pushed itself, cold and slimy, through her clothes and against her skin. She shivered, took another drag on the cigarette, and stepped off the curb. Only fucking lunatics would live here. She tossed her butt and walked toward the glow.

Behind her an engine coughed and revved briefly before fading into the night.

■ ■ ■

That same afternoon, Ben Stewart drove his truck the five miles down to the end of Thane Road. It was as far south from Juneau as he could get in a vehicle with wheels. He parked, slid stiffly out of the cab, lifted the door slightly to align it with the frame, and leaned into it until the latch clicked. The rusted panel rattled loosely.

It wasn't cold enough to snow, but the air was so heavy with moisture his breath misted. He sidestepped cautiously down the muddy slope at the beginning of the trail. The hoarfrost that had been there a few days ago had melted away in the rain. Point Bishop trail ran along the steep side of the mountains fifty feet or so above the slate water of Gastineau Channel. It ran under great trees of Sitka spruce and hemlock, trees monstrously larger than the sticks of black spruce that grew in the interior. He straightened his curved spine and gazed up through the drizzle at their distant tops, black against the clouds. Their size seemed unnatural, as alien as the arctic spring seemed when it came to the south slopes of the Brooks Range, creeping northward up the Alatna. After eight months of the black and white of winter, the fresh golden-green of the new aspen leaves and the first spikes of sedge poking through the snow didn't look like they belonged to this world.

Ben straightened and headed down the trail, glad to feel the wet bite of the air and the scent of the spruce in his nostrils after a day indoors. He liked the Point Bishop trail. It was close to town, and not that crowded; few people hiked it once the fall rains started in September. And it was flat; most of the trails close to Juneau climbed up the mountains that pressed against the town and, at this time of year, disappeared under snow before they broke the tree line twelve or fifteen hundred feet above the channel.

The trail went all the way to Point Bishop; farther than he'd ever been able to go. This late in the day, there wasn't enough light left for him to make the mile and a half to Dupont Point where the AJ mine had stored its dynamite before the war.

It was dryer in the forest; the trees soaked up the drizzle. Ben moved slowly, alert to any movement, but the woods were quiet. In a patch of mud, he bent to study the tracks of a squirrel; each print delicately traced in the mud: four toes on the forefeet, five on the hind. The prints disappeared under a shallow footprint, partly filled with water. So someone else had been down here recently. It was a small print, a woman's perhaps, or a child's, without any tread on the sole and with too much weight in the toes, as if the person had stumbled.

The path turned a corner into the cut made by Little Sheep Creek. The water crashed into the rocks as it fell down the slope. Ben had never seen it so full before. It seemed strange to have the streams high in November, instead of in the spring when the June sun melted the snow. A wooden bridge crossed the stream; he leaned on its railing, watching the water tumble out from beneath it, rushing toward the channel. The stream flattened here; the steepness of the mountains gave way to an easier grade before leveling out at the beach. His eye followed the water down to where the stream tumbled around a curve. It caught on something.

He watched it for a few seconds. It was too green for this time of year. He ran his eyes along the opposite bank. A little upstream, the brown and leafless stalks of the brambles were bent and broken. Something big and clumsy had moved through there, and not long ago. The inner piths of the broken stalks, not yet weathered brown, were still tan and yellow.

The slope down to the stream was too steep by the bridge. Turning back, Ben searched for a way down to the water. He stepped between the thorny stalks of devil's club as he climbed down to the stream and then walked along its edge until he came to the patch of green. It was a piece of material snagged on a branch that was stuck under a rock. The tip of the branch had pierced the cloth. It needed some force to do that; more force than the driving power of the current. He looked downstream.

Below him, thrown into the shallows by the pounding water, lay a body.

Ben scrambled down the stream, his feet slipping off the rocks and into the water. He grabbed at the grasses on the bank for balance. He came to it, his feet wet and his heart thudding against his chest.

It was a woman.

She lay on her back, legs twisted in the rocks, her head bobbing in deeper water. An arm fished back and forth in the current. Under her open coat was a bright green dress, shapeless in the water. Over her face floated long black hair.

Squatting at the stream's edge, Ben reached out and lifted the hair. He started, inhaling through his teeth. Her face was gone. The flesh was chewed and mangled; only ragged edges of skin and shards of broken skull stuck through. It was fungus-white, washed bloodless by the stream.

He dropped the hair, which filled and floated back down over her face, the longer strands reaching past her chest. She had been shot with a shotgun. Both barrels at close range, no more than a couple feet away, the shot string had still been tight. He lifted an arm out of the water. The fingers were shattered stumps. She'd held them in front of her. For protection? Mercy?

The water washed over her rhythmically, like a pulse. Slowly, as he watched her, sitting on his heels in the water, his face tightened and the roar of the stream faded away. Ben let the arm slip back into the water. With great care, he lifted the hem of her dress, pulling it up against the current over her twisted legs to her waist. High on her left thigh was the scar, thick and puckered against her bloodless skin. The dress dropped from his fingers. It tangled in the current. After a moment, he gently tugged it back down over her knees.

Water had seeped into his boots and his feet were cold. He waded back up the stream until he reached the spot where she and her killer had stumbled out of the brush. He studied the tracks carefully, moving aside the broken stalks and soggy brown leaves. Then, working his way back up to the trail, he slowly and methodically erased all sign of their passage.

■ ■ ■

Kris stepped off the bus into a puddle of black water. Behind her, the bus whined and drove away. The blocky building of the AWARE Shelter was bigger than she'd expected. Off to the side was an addition still sitting in the mud of new construction. The driveway down was steep and the front door locked. She pushed a bell and it was opened by a woman about her age, but shorter and with a softer face.

"Can I help you?" she asked, glancing up at Kris.

"I'm looking for Evie Gabriel."

The woman pursed her lips. "We can't release the names of the people who are staying here."

"She's my mother." Kris pulled Evie's letter from her pocket and pointed at AWARE's address in the corner. "She told me to meet her here."

The woman fingered the letter, reading the address. "Come in." She left Kris standing inside the door while she disappeared into a side office. A minute later she was back following an older woman with probing eyes, white, clean skin and a blouse with shoulder pads.

"So you're Kris," she said. "Evie talked about you." She came forward, smiling, and shook Kris's hand, speaking her name, which Kris immediately forgot.

"Is she here?" Kris asked.

"No, she left about a month ago."

"Do you know where she went?"

The woman's eyes became assessing. "When was the last time you saw your mother?"

"I know she's a drunk," Kris said.

"Yes," the woman said carefully as if there were more to it than whiskey. "I don't know where she is. She'd been staying at the Glory Hole before she came here."

Kris shook her head.

"It's a homeless shelter downtown," the woman said.

She came back to Alaska for this? "Where is it? Can I call from here?"

"Of course." The woman pointed to a phone on the desk that faced the entrance.

Kris punched the buttons as the woman recited the number. She talked to the man who answered. In the background people were talking, chairs scraped on linoleum and knives and forks clinked on plates. He yelled into the noise without putting his hand over the receiver. "Anybody here named Evie Gabriel?" A couple of voices answered and the man said to her, "No one's seen her for a while. More than a couple of weeks, I think." Kris hung up.

"I wrote my mother at this address," Kris said. "Did she get my letter?"

"Letters are kept in the advocate's office." The women picked up the phone, punched a button and spoke briefly into the receiver, waited and then thanked the person before hanging up.

"We have nothing here for her," she said. "If the letter got here, either she got it, or we sent it back to you. We only keep letters a few weeks."

The woman regarded Kris with concern and Kris stared back, not wanting any part of her pity. She reached down and picked up her duffle.

"Do you need a place to stay tonight?" the woman asked.

"Yeah," Kris said.

"There's a hostel in town. It's not expensive and it'll be fairly empty this time of year. It's on the corner of East and Sixth."

Kris climbed back up onto Glacier Avenue and turned right toward town. It probably wasn't seven yet, but the street was empty. Yellow streetlights shone through the drizzle and reflected off the wet street. Cars sped by on a highway partly hidden by trees to her right, on her left were houses. Her sneakers were wet; the cold was starting to sting her toes and the strap of her duffle cut into her fingers. She switched hands, balled the cold one in her jacket pocket to warm it up. She was on the next plane out of there. She wasn't going to piss away one minute trying to find Evie. It's not like you can look a drunk up in the phone book.

The sound of tires came up behind her and she moved off the road onto the gravel shoulder without glancing back. Suddenly, the vehicle dropped a gear and wheels screeched against the asphalt. Headlights pinned her, throwing her shadow into the night. Kris jumped to the side; the truck's mirror hit her shoulder, spinning her onto the ground. The truck skidded, reversed, and roared back at her. She threw herself off the embankment and rolled down the steep slope into wet leafless bushes.

The truck door slammed and a man, short and stringy, ran around the front through the lights. He paused at the top of the slope looking down into the darkness. She sank into the shadows. He hesitated only a second and then raced down the slope. Kris leapt to her feet and tore into the trees. Bushes slapped her face and grabbed at her clothes. The body crashing through bushes behind her came closer. Then his hand was in her hair; he grabbed it and yanked her back. The bones in her neck popped, her feet flew forward, and she fell hitting the ground hard. He jerked her head back and a blade snicked open.

Kris pivoted away, her hair twisting hard in her scalp. Digging her toes into the ground, she rammed her head into his gut. He rocked back a step, dropping her hair. Before he could swing his knife, she fell to the ground, wrapped her arms tight around his ankles and slammed her shoulder into his shins. The man toppled backwards. He grunted, swore, and kicked free of her grip. Kris clambered into the wet brush, struggling to escape. His body hit her, she twisted, and then he was on top of her his cheek pressed against hers, his breath hot and harsh on her neck.

He lifted his head to gloat. Kris rose up and snapped her teeth into his lip. He stiffened and wrenched his head back. She held on, grinding her teeth into the flesh. Blood ran into her mouth. A fist pounded into the side of her head. Where was the knife? Hands locked onto her throat. She heaved and they rolled over, she was on top, her knees between his legs. She stretched a leg and slammed her knee into his balls. He blubbered, spraying hot blood and spit into her face; his legs scissored against her knees. She hit him again. He convulsed; through his lip, her teeth touched.

Kris let go and raced back through the trees. She struggled up the slope, slipping on the wet grass. The truck was there, lights on and engine idling. She ran to the driver's side, flung open the door, and searched wildly for the parking brake. With both hands, she twisted it; it snapped in. Pushing against the door frame and twisting the wheel with her hand, she turned the back end of the truck off the road. The rear wheels found the slope and it accelerated down the embankment, crashing into the bushes below. The lights shot up into the trees across the street.

"What happened to you?" the woman behind the desk asked.

"Nothing. Got lost in the woods," Kris said. On her way into town she'd sneaked into a gas station bathroom to clean the blood and dirt off her face and change her shirt, but she was still a mess. The marks of his fingers were purpling on her throat. In the morning, they'd be ugly.

"Lost in the woods?"

"I thought I could cut across to Glacier from the highway," she said. She let her eyes drift toward the common room where four or five people were slouched on a sofa and in chairs, talking. A radio sitting on a book-case was tuned to a station playing old rock.

"Oh. Well, you can take a shower after I check you in."

An hour later, clean and warm, Kris burrowed deep under the weight of the extra blankets she'd stripped from the bunk above her. She hugged her knees to her chest and tried to push away the lingering fear of the chase through the bushes and the bitter, unnamed feeling that hovered at the edge of her awareness. Her mother had forgotten her, again.

After a while, the air under the covers became stale and her hip began to ache. She stretched, pushing her feet into the cold sheets at the end of the bed, and poked her head out of the blankets for fresh air. Only a fool would have expected something different from Evie; nine years weren't long enough to make any difference.

Nestled in the bed, her fear and hurt quietly slipped away. It was going to be a chore to get that guy's truck back up on the road. He probably worked for AWARE; its way of keeping business coming through the door.

Voices drifted up from the common room accompanied by the tinny sound of the radio. In the fog of near sleep, Kris heard a pause in the murmur and then a man's voice say: "Whoa. The cops found a body in Sheep Creek."

THURSDAY, NOVEMBER 12

"Name's Barrett." The detective motioned her to a chair.

"Barrett," Kris repeated without interest. The title wasn't there, but it was understood. He had dark hair clipped short, brown eyes, and the kind of everyday, standard white man's features that reminded Kris of the missionaries working the streets in L.A.; you couldn't tell them apart. Except Barrett was a big man, a head taller than anyone else and he radiated dominance.

Kris sat warily; she didn't do well with dominance. She broke his gaze and looked around the office. The desk and the chair she sat on were gray steel. A couple of pictures in gilt frames, their backs to Kris, were on his desk next to a model tank; the cannon pointed off at an angle. On a side table was a computer with a screen saver going and against the back wall was a short bookcase with loose-leaf binders and manuals ordered by height. Next to it was a metal file cabinet. Framed certificates or diplomas hung on white, windowless cement-block walls.

She looked back at Barrett who sat watching her silently. His eyes probed the bruises on her cheek, rested on the bandanna around her neck, then dropped for a second to her breasts before rising back to her face.

"Do you like them?" Kris asked.

"Like what?" Barrett lifted his eyebrows.

"My tits."

A file drawer screeched open in another room and someone laughed. "Sorry."

Sorry wasn't a word Kris heard often. She let it hang.

"You found my mother in a creek yesterday." It had been on the morning news. The other people staying at the hostel were hustling around the kitchen, ignoring the radio chattering in the background, as they made themselves breakfast. Kris stood to the side, leaning against a counter, watching them heat water, fry eggs and toast their bread, when her name, "Gabriel," cut through the clutter of kitchen noise. No one noticed when she moved over and stood next to the radio. She caught only the last half of the story, but she heard enough to know why her mother hadn't met her at the airport.

"We didn't, someone else did," Barrett said. "And if we'd known that she had next of kin, we wouldn't have released her name. I'm sorry you had to hear it on the news. You live in Juneau?"

"What made you think she didn't have relatives?" she asked.

Barrett considered her for a moment, as if it weren't his job to answer questions; then opened his hands signaling that he'd grant her control of the conversation. "The person who found her knew her," he said. "An old trapper from Fairbanks and apparently met her there. He told us she had no relatives."

"Who's he?"

Barrett opened a file on his desk. "Ben Stewart; he's lived in the interior since the fifties. Trapping mostly, north of the Koyukuk. He moved down here last spring. May." He looked up, generously waiting for her next question.

"Was she living with him?"

He looked surprised. "No."

"How was she killed?"

"Looks like both barrels of a shotgun. A post-mortem is scheduled this afternoon. We won't have the report until Monday, longer if the ME orders lab tests. I suspect she was killed early on Tuesday; the rigor had already left her body. But it's hard to tell; the water's cold and decomposition won't be normal." Barrett paused. "Sorry; it must be difficult to listen to this."

Barrett went on in a quieter voice. "Stewart drove back in to tell us and by the time we got out there it was dark. We went in with lights, examined the area, and brought the body out. We checked with all the people living down there but no one heard a thing. The stream is loud and the houses are fairly distant and buffered by trees. I'd be surprised if someone inside could've heard a shot."

Kris was starting to hear excuses; he was setting her up for dumping the case. She'd seen it often enough—some colored kid or a Native gets killed and the cops just hang police tape around the blood, shove the body into an ambulance, and leave. Barrett wasn't going to waste time on Evie.

"What happens next?" she asked.

"Tell me about your mother." Barrett shuffled pages in the folder. "Stewart says he didn't have much contact with her here in Juneau. But he would see her around town. Apparently she was having trouble. She spent some time on the streets last summer." Barrett stopped and looked at her expectantly.

The last nine years of Evie's life were a black hole to Kris, though it didn't look as if much had changed. In any case, talking to cops had never done her any good and anything she could tell Barrett would only pump up his white man's view of Natives. She said, carefully, "All I know is that a month ago she was in the AWARE shelter and before that she was at the Glory Hole."

"You didn't see her much?"

"No, I live in L.A."

"Oh. When did you come up?"

"Yesterday." She told him about Evie's letter.

"May I see it?"

Kris pulled it out of her jacket and handed it to him.

"Is this her writing?" he asked, smoothing it on the desk.

"Yeah." She didn't make any excuses for the scrawl and broken sentences.

"So, she thought things were getting better for her," Barrett said.

"She was always thinking that."

"Why did you come up then?"

A constant pressure came off Barrett; she pushed against it and didn't answer. Barrett watched her, waiting. Kris held his gaze then looked at his certificates on the wall. U.S. Army; Purple Heart.

"When did you see her last?" he asked.

"Two thousand six."

"Nine years? You kept in touch?"

"I don't know how she found me," Kris said, getting irritated.

"You wrote back at this address?" He pointed to a spot in the letter, ignoring her tone.

Kris nodded.

"So she knew you were coming up yesterday, the day after she was killed." He began to play with a pencil. "Interesting."

"Who's going to bury her?" Kris was done being interrogated.

"If she's indigent, the city will." Barrett eyed Kris, but she wasn't going to volunteer; it wasn't money she had. Barrett shrugged imperceptibly. "It'll be pretty basic. One of the pastors in town will provide a service. I think it'll be tomorrow; they won't want to keep her body over the weekend. Check with Rick Tyson at the city."

"Where's this stream?"

He told her.

"And the trapper?"

"He's up the Third Street staircase; in the little house on the left. I don't think he gets out much."

Kris stood.

"May I keep the letter for a couple of days?" he asked, tapping it.

Kris didn't want him to, but she wasn't going to haggle. She shrugged.

"Before you go, tell me where you're staying." He pulled a notepad out of a drawer.

"At the hostel."

"When do you go back to L.A.?"

"Sunday."

"I'm headed over to the Glory Hole this evening during dinner to see what I can learn," he said. "But they won't tell me what they'll tell you.

You up for it? Eat there tomorrow or Saturday and let me know what you find out?"

He stood. Kris resented having to look up at him. "I'll see," she said and left.

■ ■ ■

"The trail starts to the left of the guardrail." The woman who'd given her the lift pointed through the windshield.

"Thanks." Kris closed the door; the car turned around and headed back toward town. The drizzle was heavier here. In the hostel's lost and found, she'd found a clear plastic poncho with "Princess Tours" printed on it in aqua blue letters. She pulled it out of her jacket pocket and stuck her head through the center hole. Fed by the drizzle, little beads of water began to cling to it.

The cold air stung and Kris kept her fists balled in her jacket pockets, balancing with her elbows as she picked her way down the trail until it leveled out. Fifty feet in, she found the muddy spot where she guessed the trapper had found Evie's print; it was a low point in the trail and on wetter days, it looked like water seeped across it from the upper slope. When she turned the corner into the cut of a creek, she saw a man leaning on the railing of a narrow wooden footbridge, watching the water crash over the rocks. His face and blond hair were pasty against a high-end purple and green raincoat. As she stepped onto the planks, he caught sight of her and nodded.

Kris stopped a few feet away and he pointed silently downstream. Below them, the water coursed over the rocks, then leveled out for a ways before rushing around a bend. Beyond the turn, Kris saw a sagging square of yellow police tape tied to the stems of bushes on either side of the stream.

The man leaned over and shouted in her ear, startling her. "This is where that woman was killed," he said.

Through the drizzle and surrounded by the naked shrubs, the area bound by the tape looked abandoned and desolate. A sudden loneliness filled and emptied her and Kris dropped her elbows on the railing, letting her weight slump onto them, surprised at the unexpected surge of feeling.

"Hey, you OK?" A tentative hand rested on her shoulder.

She straightened and it fell off. Still looking down the stream she said, "She was my mother."

"What?" He lowered his ear.

"She was my mother," she shouted, turning toward him, angry that he'd intruded and angry that he hadn't understood.

"Oh." He lifted his head and gazed down at her. "I'm sorry." His words were lost in the noise of the stream, but she read them on his lips. He fidgeted, ripping open a Velcroed pocket flap and smoothing it closed again. He looked concerned and started to lift a hand, then let it drop as Kris turned away and leaned again on the wooden rail. Below her, the stream raced out from under the bridge and its mist boiled up into her face, cooling her skin and dewing her eyelashes.

The railing creaked and canted out a fraction; in the corner of her eye, Kris saw the man's arms resting on the rail a little farther down. She wanted him gone. It irritated her that he was staring like a tourist at the spot where her mother had been murdered. She let her anger grow, but couldn't stay focused and she forgot him as she stared at the yellow square of tape. She felt confused. Her mother was dead; why should she care? What had she been hoping for when she came up? A real mother this time? A friend? Or a chance to unload her bottled resentment and anger? She'd fought herself for weeks before deciding to come. And she wasn't sure why she did—some troubling sense that it was the right thing to do.

A finger tapped her shoulder and she jumped. Before she could turn, she felt his head next to hers and puffs of breath against her ear as he spoke.

"Sorry about your mom." He put his hand on her arm. "Let's scout around, maybe the police missed something." He paused, then added. "You'll be warmer if you're moving."

This jerk wanted to play detective. What was Evie—a freak show?

"Come on." He pulled at her sleeve, urging her toward the far end of the bridge.

She gave in and followed him across the gray boards of the bridge and up the trail a few yards to a cut-off that led down to the beach. It was steep and slick with mud; Kris climbed down backwards, holding onto roots and rocks until the trail leveled out again. He beat through the brush and reached the stream below the police tape. She followed without enthusiasm.

"The police have mucked this place up," he said when she came alongside him. The surrounding banks had been churned by heavy boots and rocks in the stream bed had been overturned and pushed aside. "I wonder how well they went over the area before they moved the body out." He ducked under the tape and lifted it for her. On the other side were parallel lines of white twine spaced every couple of feet running up either side of the stream.

"For their search," he said, pulling one; a bush up the hill jerked. "It was dark, they were cold and wet." He looked at her. "Mind if I take a look?"

Kris shrugged.

He crouched and, keeping low, began slowly moving upstream examining the bank. Kris lit a cigarette and watched him indifferently until he disappeared around the bend. She squatted on a rock, tucking her poncho under herself to keep dry and stared at a pool of quieter water ringed by muddy footprints on the other side of the creek.

For no reason, Kris suddenly remembered a snowmobile trip out at Two Rivers that her school had organized when she was fourteen. Evie had promised her the money to go, but when Kris shook her awake that morning the money was gone. This time, Evie hadn't drunk it, but had spent it on a pair of mittens she'd found in the surplus store. "It gets real cold when you get going fast and the ones you got are too thin." Kris pounded the bed and yelled. What good were mittens if she couldn't go? In the end, she managed to hustle the money before the bus left; but, furious at her mother, she'd flung the mittens into the street and the cold and wind had frostbit the thumb that worked the throttle.

Why did her mother still anger her? Nine years and Evie still wasn't out of her head. Tomorrow, she could be on a plane back to L.A. and out of this mess. Let Evie fade out of her mind like mud settling to the bottom of a puddle. But something unseen stopped her and fastened her to that rock. She bent over her lap, squeezing her eyes shut, hugging herself under the poncho, and curling her numb toes in the wet sneakers. Why wouldn't Evie let her go?

"Hey, look what I found." The stream was quieter in front of Kris where it had leveled, but she barely heard the shout above the noise. She edged upstream, trying to keep her feet out of the water. When she turned the corner and he came into sight, he was standing on the opposite bank pointing at something in the mud.

"Can you see this?" he yelled.

"No," she answered, not looking hard.

"It's a footprint. But the sole is wrong. It's a crepe sole, the kind on a cheap work boot." He looked at her as if she'd understand the significance of this. When it appeared she hadn't, he waded over to her side, splashing through water up to his knees. "Damn that's cold," he said. "Look. All the other footprints are either lug soles or Xtratufs. See here?" He pointed at several tracks in the mud. "Lug. Like the Vibram soles on hiking boots. These have to be police prints. But the crepe print belongs to someone else. A cop isn't going to wear boots from Wal-Mart."

Kris tossed her cigarette in the stream; he watched it swirl away.

"Well, it's something. I wonder if the police saw it." He waded back across, climbed the bank, and, dropping to his hands and knees, crawled into the undergrowth. Kris went back the way they'd come, crossing the bridge and hiking up the path toward the road, until she could see him moving up the slope through the bushes. Her clothes were damp; the bandanna around her neck was soaked and she began to shiver as she stood watching him.

"Hey, come down and look at this."

She was starting to feel like a dog; next he'd have her fetching sticks. Kris waded into the scrub, pushing the wet stalks and leafless branches out of her way. Bushes with thorns pricked at her poncho and she gently pulled it free so it wouldn't tear. He was holding back a couple of thick, heavy bushes with one arm and pointing under them with the hand of the other. Under the bush, brown leaves lay flat and matted against the earth—except for a small cluster half the size of her palm that had been twisted and torn.

"Looks like someone putting out a cigarette with his toe," he said. "Somebody's been walking through here," he said. "Too many stems have been broken. Look." He pointed at a stem broken off at knee height. He dropped back on all fours, letting the bushes fall onto his back, and crawled another foot up the slope, shoving bushes out of his way.

"Here's another bunch of twisted leaves." He pointed at it. "This one's bigger, there're two twists." Kris pushed aside the bush and saw two soggy clumps of twisted leaves next to each other. He picked up a leaf and carefully flattened it on his thigh. "This looks normal, don't you think?" He handed it to Kris. It looked normal. Working methodically, he smoothed each leaf. "Nothing weird here. Though the leaves in this clump have holes in them." He held them up; Kris didn't touch them. So leaves have holes.

Crawling another foot up the slope, he found another clump of twisted leaves; it was a single clump like the first. He smoothed out these leaves as well; nothing unusual. The bushes thinned, but he stayed on his hands and knees until he got to the trail. He didn't find anything else.

"What do you think?" he asked. His hair was snarled with dirt and bits of twigs, and his pants were wet, the knees baggy with mud. "This has got to be the way they walked down to the stream, all those broken twigs. Though it's funny there weren't more footprints—just that crepe sole."

He looked at his watch. "Damn," he said. "It's past one; I've got to get back to work."

When they got back up on the road, he glanced around; there was only one car parked there, a blue Subaru wagon.

"How'd you get down?" he asked.

"Thumbed."

"Come on, I'll give you a ride back." He moved a pile of books, tools, paper, and other trash out of the passenger seat and foot well, dumped it in back, and motioned Kris in.

"Justin Palmer," he said after he'd gotten the car started.

"Kris."

He reached out his hand; it was muddy and she wiped her hand clean after shaking it.

"Sorry. Are you local?"

"L.A."

"You got up here fast," he said. "Where're you staying?"

"The hostel."

"If you want a mellower place without so many rules, you can crash on my couch."

"I'm OK."

"You're welcome to the car too, if you want. It's never locked; the keys are there." He tapped the ashtray. "Just let me know when you're taking off with it, so I don't run around trying to remember where I parked."

"Things aren't locked in Juneau?" Kris let his offer ride. She might need a car, maybe an apartment if she stayed much longer; she hadn't arrived with much and only had rent money left in her account back home. But she was wary; she knew what the deal would be.

"You lock your car here and eventually you'll kill your battery," he said. "It rains so much you've got to drive with your lights on during the day. Sooner or later, you'll forget to turn them off when you park. If you leave your doors open, someone walking by will do it for you." He downshifted and accelerated up a hill.

"What did you think about those twisted leaves?" he asked.

Kris hadn't thought anything about them.

"Leaves don't twist themselves," he said. "And they were spaced about a footstep apart." Kris stared out the side window, letting him talk to himself. "Sure looked like someone putting out a cigarette. You want to swing by the police station and tell them about it?" He turned to her. "Have you talked to the police yet?"

"They won't do anything," she said.

"What do you mean?"

"The police have only been trouble for Evie; they're not going to go out of their way to help her now." Kris could tell by the way Justin kept quiet that he didn't believe her; for white boys, cops were the good guys.

"Evie's your mother?" he asked.

"Uh huh."

"So you don't want to tell the cops?" he asked.

Not about leaves.

"What are you going to do?" he asked.

The car bounced, something in back rattled, and suddenly the anger that had been simmering half hidden inside her broke open. "I'm going to find the asshole that killed her," she said, unable to control the heat in her voice. Kris caught herself and forced her mouth closed. This guy, who'd probably never gone to bed hungry, didn't need to know that her mother had been stepped on by everybody who'd come through her life: The police who'd hauled her off for vagrancy when she had no place to go; men who'd promised love but just screwed and beat her; landlords who'd tossed her out of rooms that stank of piss; and social workers who'd nit-picked her with a million chicken-shit rules. Kris never let anyone jerk her around and nine years since she'd last seen Evie it still pissed her off remembering her mother just shrugging when someone dumped on her.

"I'm going to find him," she said again, knowing suddenly that she wouldn't let go.

"Do you think you can?" Justin asked.

Kris hardened, waiting for his laugh.

It didn't come, but she didn't answer him and let the silence grow. They came around a curve, passed a huge satellite dish pointed low in the sky, and a few hundred yards later they drove by a tank farm spread out over a barren flat of gravel that stuck into Gastineau Channel.

"Tailings from the old AJ mine," Justin said, as they sped by. "Someday, in the middle of the next century, maybe something might grow there."

They came into town and passed under cables that disappeared up a mountainside and into the clouds.

"It's a tram that goes halfway up Mount Roberts. Another gift to the tourists. It's kind of like slow-motion rape around here, every year another mountain, another beach gets sold to the tour companies. We had a million people come through here last summer. Only thirty thousand live here full time—you could hardly walk the streets downtown and it's like Iraq with all the planes and helicopters flying around."

"You were in Iraq?" Kris asked, letting sarcasm creep into her tone; she'd had too many self-stuffed blow-hards unload on her to have any patience with them.

"Like Apocalypse Now, then. It's like that from May to September. The city will sell whatever it can to make a buck."

"Where are you going?" he asked a second later, turning right on a wide road that topped out on a ridge six or seven blocks up.

"Third Street," she said.

"What's there?"

"The old man who found her."

Justin shifted down as the road began to rise. Without looking at her, he asked, "Mind if I join you?"

"I thought you had to go back to work." He'd just be in the way.

Justin paused. "I'll call in sick," he said. "I'm late already and I'm a mess. By the time I got cleaned up it would be quitting time."

Kris looked at the passing buildings, considering. She was going to need the car. "Get cleaned up first, then."

"OK. That's Third there." He pointed to the right.

"And be cool; something's off," Kris said.

"What?"

"He knew my mother. He found her body. He told the cops she didn't have any relatives."

"Maybe he didn't know about you."

"Maybe." Probably. Kris couldn't see Evie telling anyone about her.

"So, what are you thinking?" Justin asked.

Kris didn't answer.

■ ■ ■

"I know this house." Justin was behind her, climbing the stairs, ringing its metal grates with each step. "It belongs to a friend of mine. It's tiny. She had to move into a bigger place when she got married. She just rents it now. There're the ashes of an Australian buried under a tree up here. He fell off a cliff on Mt. Jumbo."

They stepped off the stairs and onto a board walk leading to the house. "I think this is the tree." Justin touched a leafless twig on a tree about four feet high. "It doesn't look very healthy." Kris walked past it to the door of the entryway, pushed it open and stepped through. She knocked on the inner door. Finally silent, Justin came in behind her as it opened.

Ben Stewart was a small man, stooped. His head, bowed toward the floor when the door opened, was hairless with ears that wagged out from his skull. When he straightened and looked at her, his eyes, at first welcoming, slackened and dulled. He stared silently at Kris until Justin shuffled his feet and Stewart, glancing at him, turned and walked back into the house.

Uninvited, they hesitated before following him in. Stewart walked behind a wooden chair angled to look through a rain-splattered window at the town below and the mountains that rose out of the far side of the channel. Resting his hands on its back, he watched them come in. The room was unfurnished but for the single chair and a small table under a wall cabinet by the front door. Against the back wall; a steep staircase led to a loft that was too low to stand in and behind Stewart, a wood stove stood on a platform of bricks, bathing the room with warmth. On the other side of the stove was a narrow kitchen. The kitchen sink, under a window in the opposite wall, wasn't five big steps from the front door.

Kris stood awkwardly, wondering why Stewart had retreated behind his chair.

"I'm Kris Gabriel," she said, finally. "Evie's daughter."

"I know." He was wary, like a kid on the wrong gang's turf.

"Can I bring those chairs over?" Justin interrupted, pointing to chairs stacked in a corner that Kris hadn't seen.

Stewart looked startled, shifted his eyes from Kris to Justin, and then nodded.

Justin set them in a semi-circle in front of the window, offering the middle one to Kris. Stewart sat; his hands resting in his lap. They were crooked and gnarled, too big for his body, which was short and bent with the tightness of old muscles. He took a breath, his eyes, blue and nested in wrinkles, were clear.

"She thought you were dead," he said.

"Who?" Kris asked.

"Your mother. One morning she told me she woke up and you were gone."

"Woke up on the floor."

"I wouldn't know," Stewart said, ignoring Kris's sourness. "Where did you go?"

"L.A. I hid in trucks until I got into B.C. Then hitched down the coast." She didn't say more, telling your stories was like handing someone rocks; someday they'd be thrown back at you.

"In the winter, wasn't it? How old were you then?" His voice was scratchy, like a woolen blanket.

"Fifteen."

Stewart studied her. Kris tensed, expecting a dismissive shrug, but didn't yield to his gaze.

"Not many people could've done that," he said. "How–" he started, but Kris tipped her head toward Justin and Stewart changed direction. "The police gave you my name?"

"Yeah. You knew her, didn't you?" Stewart didn't fit. He was too quiet, too comfortable with himself; he didn't have the water-in-hot-oil frenzy of the people Evie hung around.

Stewart shifted his gaze out the window, turning his shoulders as if his neck were stiff. Drops of water beaded on the glass, swelling until they burst and slid down the pane in crooked streams. While she waited for his answer, Kris leaned forward and pressed her finger against the glass, feeling the outside cold pushing in. "I met her five or six years ago," he said, turning back to her. "We became friends." He hesitated, his words didn't come quickly, as if he hadn't had much practice with them. "I ran a few trap lines up the Alatna River. I'd bring the skins in before breakup, combed and stretched, to my buyer. I met her in town one spring."

"Where's the Alatna?" Justin asked.

Kris glanced at him, irritated; she didn't want him taking over.

"It rises in the Brooks Range and empties into the Koyukuk at Allakaket, about a hundred and fifty miles northwest of Fairbanks," Stewart answered.

"I should introduce myself." Justin stuck out his hand, leaning in front of Kris. "Justin Palmer."

"Proud to know you," Stewart took Justin's hand, shifting slightly in his chair, to look more fully at him.

"How did you know who she was?" Justin indicated Kris.

"She looks like her mother."

"I do not," Kris said. She didn't look anything like her.

"What happened to your neck?" he asked.

Kris touched the bandanna. "I was attacked."

"You were what?" Justin examined her neck.

Kris untied the bandanna and pulled it off. When she'd looked in the mirror that morning, the marks had purpled and were rimmed by a pus-yellow color.

"Whoa," Justin said. "What happened?"

Kris felt a flash of contempt at the surprise and shock spread across his face, as if he thought the worst life had to offer was soggy corn flakes.

"I was attacked by a man outside the AWARE shelter," Kris said, retying the bandanna.

"You were attacked? How come?" Justin asked.

Kris let him figure out for himself why women were attacked by men.

"You're OK?" Stewart asked quietly.

"Yeah, it was nothing."

"Did you call the police?" Justin asked.

"No," she said tensing, knowing he wouldn't leave it alone.

"But they might be able to find the—"

"Stuff it. I can take care of myself," Kris said.

Justin straightened in his chair and plucked at his coat pocket.

Stewart stood. "Would you like some tea?"

"Sure," Kris said and followed him into the kitchen. Justin trailed them and propped himself against the refrigerator at the kitchen's entrance; there wasn't enough room for three. Stewart put a pot of water on the stove.

"Only two cups," he said, taking them out of the cupboard. The wrinkles around his eyes multiplied when he smiled. "Not much company makes it up my stairs."

"Barrett said you came down last May."

Stewart wiped the counter top and stuck a loose fork and knife into a drawer. Kris noticed that a seam in the back of his shirt had been hand stitched with a different color thread.

"The interior was getting too cold for me. My joints get sore." He flexed his fingers.

"Why didn't you go Outside?" Any sane person would.

Stewart moved the rag over the counter again. "Nowhere to go."

"But Juneau? All it does is rain."

"It's warmer." He squinted into the steam rising out of the pot, checking for a boil. Kris sensed a struggle in the old man. "I can't leave Alaska— there's the Permanent Fund, the Longevity Bonus, and old folks don't pay taxes here."

"I write your Bonus check then." Justin said from the refrigerator. They looked at him. "I maintain the Longevity Bonus computer system."

"What's that?" Kris asked.

"A state program that gives every Alaskan over sixty-five two hundred-fifty dollars a month; three thousand a year."

Kris wasn't interested. "Did you know my mother was here when you came down?" she asked Stewart.

"No, that was a surprise. We'd gone separate ways. I, ah, she got into other things," Stewart said vaguely. But Kris could guess what they were and let it drop.

"Did you see her much here?"

"Sometimes we'd pass on the street and say hi." Kris didn't push. He seemed awkward talking about Evie and she guessed he was uncomfortable talking in front of Justin. She didn't need to have Justin listening to any of this either. The pot boiled. Stewart poured water into the cups and dropped in tea bags.

"I didn't know people still drank Lipton's," Justin said.

Stewart handed each a cup and they moved back into the other room while he put a log in the stove and fiddled with the damper.

"Where'd you run your trap lines?" Justin asked.

"Upper Alatna. Mostly in the eastern drainages." Stewart's eyes crinkled up. Kris tapped a finger against her cup. Justin was taking over again. But she let him run on; there was a comforting sturdiness about Stewart that quieted her and she watched him as he talked. The tracery of wrinkles around his eyes and the creases in his cheeks and forehead smoothed out and vanished into his bald scalp, which was stretched tightly over his skull. It seemed odd that the face could look so lived in and the rest of his head so deserted. A fleeting awareness of a vulnerability or hurt passed through her as she watched him, but vanished when she tried to focus in on it.

"Good fox and marten, wolf and lynx sometimes; muskrat always." Stewart was saying.

"Did you run dogs?" Justin was leaning forward, elbows on his knees, teacup clasped in both hands. He was lanky and angular, like he'd never filled out when he became a man. Kris guessed he was around thirty; faint lines were beginning to show in his forehead and she could see the blood vessel that bulged over older men's temples.

"I had a team until nineteen eighty or so, then switched to a Skidoo. I kept my lead dog, Kobuk, and sold the rest. Kobuk's gone now."

"Why'd you switch to a snow machine?"

"Don't have to feed it so much fish."

"Yeah, but you got to haul in all that fuel, and they're noisy and they stink."

"A dog yard gets pretty ripe on a warm day and you've got to be real partial to dog poop to work them."

Dog poop? Kris looked into her cup; she didn't like the tea, it needed sugar.

"But there's no romance to a snow machine."

"Romance?" Stewart's brow wrinkled. "I'm just trying to get a job done. Skidoos are easier than dogs."

Kris let them talk. Justin was like a dog worrying a rag with his questions, but she couldn't tell whether he was bothering Stewart. When men were together, she had trouble knowing what they wanted; when they were with women, it was obvious. Kris had grown up watching Evie and her men. Pushed into the darkness, hiding against a wall or under blankets on a sofa that smelled of stale beer, she'd watch her mother. Evie glowed, as if only she reflected the lamplight. Men leaned toward her; the other women at the table sunk into the shadows, the whiskey beginning to bypass them—the bottle short-cutting back to Evie. "Suck, Evie." Her head cocked back, her lips opened and slid over the glass neck, the neck entered, her tongue darted into its throat teasing the whiskey into her mouth. Laughter, a groan. She swallowed, exhaled, passed the bottle on. Later, a hand emerged from the darkness and worked the buttons of her shirt, slipped a finger into her bra; slipped it around the cup. Her breast fell out; quivered. Evie looked down at herself. "Oh my," she said, the nipple hard and erect.

Kris was certain Stewart had never been there; that he'd never circled Evie in the shadows, playing cowboy and Indian sex. He'd said they'd been friends, but Evie never had friends—not with men, and Kris couldn't see where Stewart could have fit in.

She watched him. Behind the clouds, the sun must have set; the light coming through the window was weak and his face was becoming less distinct. He was telling Justin how to blacken traps and boil off odors using a dye made of peat and spruce bark. What did Justin care, he'd never trap, there wasn't enough edge to him to get him out of an office and into the bush.

Justin interrupted Stewart and Stewart glanced at her, smiling fleetingly. He was getting tired of Justin too.

"We better be going," she said. She'd come back without Justin to find out what she needed to know.

Stewart rose and walked them to the door.

"When was the last time you were up there?" Justin asked, unwilling to quit. Kris opened the door and stepped into the entry. Old cans of paint, cans of nails, and tools were neatly stacked on shelves or hung from nails pounded into the wall.

"The winter after the Koyukuk flooded Allakaket. Whenever that was," Stewart said.

"The cabin is still there?"

"Kindling by the stove."

Kris reached her hand past Justin, and Stewart took it.

"Come back," he said.

■ ■ ■

"Did you see his boots by the door?" Justin asked, following her down the stairs. It was lighter out of the house, but still dusk. The drizzle had quit; Kris pulled off her poncho and wadded it into a pocket.

"They had crepe soles," he said. "Which makes sense, since he found her. But it's funny there weren't any other prints around."

Kris kept her eyes on the steps in front of her.

"And did you buy that story about his joints?"

"That they hurt?"

"That he came down here because they hurt. If you've got arthritis, you want to be somewhere hot and dry. Moving to a rain forest doesn't make any sense. If he had to stay in Alaska, Homer'd be a better spot than here. It's a lot drier and about as warm."

Kris stepped off the stairs onto the start of Third Street, which sloped steeply downhill from the bottom of the stairs to Franklin before leveling out.

"We should call him on that," Justin said, coming up alongside her.

Loose stones rolled under Kris's shoes. She skidded and Justin caught her arm; she pulled it free.

"Can I buy you a drink?" He asked when they got to the bottom of the hill.

"OK." Dinner would be better. That morning, after everybody'd left the kitchen, she lifted some bread and peanut butter someone had left in a cabinet, but she hadn't eaten anything since.

They turned left onto Franklin, passing the Baranof Hotel and some tourist shops that were lit but empty. The downtown sidewalks had overhead covers to keep off the rain and snow, and signs hung from them, naming each shop. They walked along a level stretch until they came to the Alaska Hotel.

Justin held the door for her. Black and white photos of sailing ships tied up in front of Juneau and of miners working mules hung on the wall, stained glass lampshades covered the lights, and a crimson rug lay in the short passageway into the bar. There were no pool tables, Miller signs, or moose antlers nailed to the wall.

"You drink beer?" he asked when the waitress arrived. "Try an Amber; it's made here."

"I want a Bud." She had started drinking beer a few years ago to prove—to herself, to Evie?—that she could handle the alcohol.

Justin ordered the Amber and leaned forward on his elbows, hunching his shoulders. Kris had to look up at him. His face was open, soft like he'd never had to fight for much. There were still bits of twig or dirt tangled in his hair and in one ear, an earring hole had healed up leaving a pinprick scar. He didn't look too bad and his nose was small enough for an Anglo.

"So how come you stowed away on trucks to get to L.A.?"

"I wanted out."

"Of Alaska? You were born here?"

"Fairbanks."

"I used to wish I was born in Alaska instead of some white bread American suburb. But then I realized if I'd grown up here, Alaska'd be normal. When I was a teenager, Alaska was the last frontier, a wilderness where life was real. If I'd been born here, Alaska'd be just another place. I'd probably be living in L.A. now."

"L.A.'s OK. Less chance of frostbite."

"Hard to have a good adventure though."

The waitress put their drinks on the table.

"Adventure," she said. It sounded like something you had when you were used to regular meals. Kris counted the change the waitress handed back to him.

"Coming to Alaska, canoeing the Yukon, climbing in the Alaska Range, rafting, mushing. Homesteading in the bush."

"You've done that?" Why go out of your way to be cold and wet when you could live in a place where the sun always shone and a couple of bucks would take you anywhere you needed to go?

"I came to Alaska," Justin said.

"Anybody can buy a plane ticket."

"You got to get yourself ready. Put the gear together; find people to do it with. Other things come up. It's hard to leave the job," Justin said.

"You just go and do it," Kris said.

"It's not that easy."

"Why not?"

Justin watched her sip her beer. "For me, it's just not. Seems like I get so far and then stop, can't go any farther," he said.

Kris backed off; she wasn't interested in a heart-to-heart. His easy admission of weakness startled her. Do that on the street and someone would take immediate advantage of it.

"As soon as I got up here, I got a job with the state running the Longevity Bonus computers. It was good money—too good to leave."

"Good money?" she asked. Kris would take home maybe nineteen thousand that year.

"More than I'm worth."

Kris let her eyes wander to the people sitting at the other tables. The after-work crowd was starting to filter in. There was no background music, just the noise of people talking, chairs scraping against the floor and jackets and raincoats being unzipped. The room and bar had been redone to look turn of the century Alaskan—fancy woodwork, mirrors, and stained glass. Disneyworld.

"Huh?" she said.

"I said what do you do in L.A.?"

"Dispatch short-haul rigs, for a delivery company owned by some Mexicans."

"Mexicans?"

"Most are legal."

"Do you speak Spanish?"

"No."

"Do you like it?"

"I do it. They pay me. They leave me alone."

The waitress came by and asked if they wanted another round. Kris nodded, as long as Justin was paying. "You got any peanuts or anything?" she called after her.

"Did you get this job when you got down to L.A.?"

"No, I lived on the street."

Justin's eyes got serious and she could tell he was going to worm the story out of her. To head him off, she told it her way.

"I lived on the street. Sometimes in shelters. I sold dope, shoplifted, stole from drunks, and fenced stuff. But I wasn't anybody's whore, people left me alone. Then I got caught lifting a bra out of Target and they prosecuted. I had some coke on me I'd forgotten about and I spent four months in the can. When I was in there, these women started coming around and talking to me. I blew them off, but when I got out, they caught up with me, cleaned me up, and got me this job. I've been there maybe four years now."

"That sounds really rough." His voice softened.

"You get by," she said. She had fought those women hard; no way she wanted to come off the streets. She got what she needed there and was good at it. And she never would have left, if Mariah hadn't wrapped her arms around her one day, crushing her against her chest, and whispered harshly in her ear that the reason why Kris didn't want off the street was because she was scared, because she secretly didn't believe that she was good enough to make it, because she was frightened that the real world would reject her, would throw her back into the street. Like it had often enough, Kris had said to herself. But at some level, she knew that Mariah was right and Kris had let herself be pushed into the job.

Now she could see how carefully Mariah and the other Sisters had planned it, placing her in a company run by Mexicans, outsiders, people who, like her, lived on the edge of society, although not quite as far. She and they had an enemy in common and for Kris it was the unspoken basis of a camaraderie that had allowed her to slip sideways into the world of work, regular meals, and a bed of her own.

"So were these women religious or something?"

"Dykes."

"What?"

"Lesbians. Save Our Sisters. They worked with girls living on the street. Trying to get them fixed up. They were good people. The first ones to go out of their way for me without wanting something back."

"Hey, I don't want anything from you," Justin said.

"Bullshit." Everybody wanted something. She wanted dinner.

"No, seriously."

"When was the last time you got laid?"

Justin laughed uncomfortably. "You think I bought you a drink because I want to have sex with you?"

Kris snorted.

Justin pushed back against his chair, lifting it on its back legs, and studied her. Kris stared back. Finally, he came down and planted his elbows on the table. "I'll tell you why I bought you the drink," he said. "You've got something interesting going on and I want to be part of the action."

Bullshit. If she had a face full of zits he'd be in front of his computer right now making good money.

"And I can help you out," he said. "I know Juneau, I have a car, money, and an apartment. The hostel will only let you stay three nights."

"You're Nancy Drew." He grinned.

"Who?" Kris asked. His smile looked condescending.

"Famous detective."

Kris glared at him. Was he making fun of her? Did he think she and Evie walked out of the TV or something? "This isn't some damn game," she said.

"Calm down," he said.

"Get a life." Kris drained her glass. "I'm out of here." So much for dinner. She stood, pulling her jacket off the back of the chair and headed for the door, shrugging into it as she went. It was raining again. The city lights danced in the black puddles of water as the raindrops rippled their surfaces. She turned up the street toward the hostel, walking fast. A car crept by with kids staring out the window looking for something to do; a bunch of shaggy drunks were knotted in a doorway across the street by the Liquor Cache.

Justin caught up with her when the street started to climb the hill. After a few steps, she turned on him. "What the hell are you following me for? Hanging around me isn't going to do you any damn good."

Justin stood looking down at her, his hands stuffed in the pockets of his raincoat. As he watched her, his expression slid from defensive to calculating. "Maybe," he said, "because I want to have sex with you."

Before she could explode, he laughed and, taking her arm, said, "Lighten up. I'll buy you dinner.

FRIDAY, NOVEMBER 13

The lower limbs of the spruce had been lopped off, leaving behind knobs that leaked sap like gray pustules. Ben Stewart moved quietly, unobtrusively, in under the tree and out of the rain. A hundred feet across the yellow grass a small group gathered around a muddy hole in the earth; a neat pile of dirt had been left at one end. Over the hole was a casket. Plain, brown, short. Ben couldn't see it well from where he stood, but the rainwater, collecting from the light drizzle, beaded on a better finish than he'd expected on a pauper's coffin.

A movement off to the side caught his eye. From the parking lot, a tall man strode briskly across the grass. He shimmered as he walked and when he neared the hole, Ben saw that he had a clear plastic slicker over his black robes. Tucked out of the rain in one of the sleeves was a small book.

The group opened and eddied around him when he reached the grave. His head stood above the others and swung around taut with impatient authority. A woman Ben did not recognize made a discreet motion with her hand and the priest's head turned toward Kris, who was standing off by herself. The priest beckoned her over, taking her wrist when she approached, and pulled her to his side. He surveyed the gathering again and then opened his Bible.

Heads bowed and the priest's lips moved, but Ben could hear nothing. Kris stood on the far side of the priest from Ben. She was tall, almost his own height; her hands were thrust into the pockets of her jeans and her head grudgingly bowed so that her black hair, flat and stringy in the rain, swayed forward to hide her cheek. Her skin was browned by the Athabascan blood of her mother and perhaps by the southern sun as well. She wore the same dull red jacket she had worn the day before when she'd come to visit. It was the only spot of color among the somber clothes surrounding her. Over the jacket was her plastic poncho. The previous summer, Princess Tours had passed them out by the thousands each time one of their cruise ships arrived in the rain.

Ben wondered how Kris had gotten out to the cemetery. It was in the Valley ten or eleven miles from town. He cast around and spotted Justin sitting in a Subaru in the parking lot. This was odd. He'd have expected Justin to be leaning over the grave, peering into its depths. Had Kris made him stay in the car? Ben understood keeping one's pain to oneself.

Other than Kris, there was no one Ben recognized. Two women on Kris's right looked like they belonged there. The one who had pointed out Kris to the priest had the nervous manner of a person in charge but not in control. Next to her was another woman standing with the deference of an employee.

Across the hole, their backs to Ben, was a couple that did not belong. The woman was tall, thin, and very erect. She stood with her head bent stiffly at the neck, her shoulders square and unbowed. Below her calf-length raincoat, her legs stood rigidly in a pair of black high-heels. As he watched, she raised her head and glared sharply at Kris and then again at the ground.

The man at her side stood more piously, with deeply bowed head and rounded shoulders. Under his black raincoat, he bulged at the waist and rear. It was an expensive coat; even at this distance Ben could see the luster in the material. Like the coffin, it was not a coat he had expected to see at Evie's funeral.

As Ben watched the bowed heads, Kris slowly lifted hers and their eyes met. No sign of recognition flashed in her face and she lowered it again. The priest closed his Bible and made some motions in the air over the casket. There was a small whine and it sank into the grave. The group stepped back from the edge and milled about uncertainly. There weren't enough ties among them to bring them together. Ben saw the priest bend to talk to Kris. Her brown skin glistened amid the pallid whiteness of the others who circled her at an uneasy distance. The priest straightened, glanced at his watch, nodded to the circle of faces, and left.

The two women offered their condolences and hastened away, leaving only the erect woman and the man in the expensive raincoat. The woman acknowledged Kris and then stood off while the man approached her. As he moved toward her, Ben felt his attention sharpen, his old eyes squint. It was a movement he had seen before. He watched carefully. The man in the suit bent over Kris. But unlike the priest, whose posture had been distant and superior, this man lowered his shoulders like a dog curling its tail between its legs.

He talked longer than he needed to for a condolence from a stranger. When he'd finished, he reached into his breast pocket and, pulling out a wallet, he offered her a card. She took it in her fingers without looking at it. He straightened, said a final word, and touched her shoulder before glancing around for his wife. Reaching out an arm, he steadied the tall woman as she walked on her toes to keep her heels from sinking into the soft earth. When they reached the pavement, she dropped his arm and, shoulder to shoulder, they walked across the lot to a black Mercedes.

Kris walked to the grave and looked down. She stuck her toe into the dirt at its edge. Ben stepped behind the tree leaving her alone. When he looked again she was gone. In the distance, he heard an engine kick to life and in a moment a small backhoe lumbered across the lawn. The operator climbed out and disassembled the winch, fastening it to the backhoe. In a few short minutes the pile of dirt had been dumped back into the hole. With quick and careless precision, the operator squared and smoothed off the mound with the bucket of the backhoe. Then he curled up the hydraulic arm and the machine headed back the way it had come.

Ben waited for the noise to fade away. In the silence, he could hear the soft hiss of the rain as it fell through the air. Turning to the spruce tree, he pulled out his pocketknife and in his slow and methodical way, began to collect the beads of sap that oozed from the wounds left by the severed limbs. He warmed the pieces of sap in his hand and then slowly rolled them into a ball. When the sap began to stick to his skin, he scraped bark dust from the tree and worked it into the sap as he would work flour into sticky sourdough.

He stopped adding sap when the ball was the size of a ptarmigan egg. He brought it to his nose and inhaled. The scent of spruce had filled almost every day of his last sixty years. It evoked the sparse black spruce forests, the racing clear water streams, the winter sky ablaze with the frozen fire of the northern lights and the silent mountains. Ben breathed in deeply and felt the vastness of Alaska. And then, because it was lost to him now, he felt a melancholy too bitter to bear.

Ben had plenty of time.

He walked slowly in the rain across the yellow grass and knelt at the head of her grave. He placed the ball of spruce sap on the muddy, rain-pocked earth and gently patted it below the surface.

"Oh Evie," he said, saying good-bye.

■ ■ ■

"Do you want a glass with that?"

Kris nodded without looking up as she slipped into the chair. A minute later, the waitress put an opened bottle of beer and an empty glass in front of her. Kris pulled out a few ones and let the waitress drop the change onto the table.

The glass was wet and she made circular patterns on the table with it until they swarmed together into a senseless mess. She wiped them away with the flat of her hand and poured a few inches of beer into the glass. Behind her came the crack of billiards and a rise in the background murmur as the balls found their places on the table.

When she was small, her mother would take Kris with her when she went drinking. If the bar help wasn't cool with a kid sitting next to her mom, she'd be tucked in a corner of the booth, hidden in the dark. She knew the drift of blue smoke; the enfolding clamor of raised voices, of jukeboxes and unwatched TV's. She knew the sour yeast smell of beer and the comfort of pressed bodies.

When Kris grew older, her mother left her behind.

Bubbles clung to the inside of the glass, let go, and streamed to the surface. She swirled the beer, wiping them away.

Damn. Damn. Damn.

Behind her, balls clattered into pockets, someone cheered, voices rose and then sank again into the embracing murmur.

■ ■ ■

The Glory Hole served dinner at 6:30. The meal line had already curved around the dining room and doubled back on itself when Kris arrived. Homeless shelters begin filling up in the fall in Alaska when people drift into town from fish camps or a summer's smoke jumping, though maybe in Juneau, they began filling when the tourists leave.

The line moved slowly forward. Eyes rested on her curiously, but darted away when she caught them staring. Up ahead, two women moved through the line together; one was older, maybe in her mid-forties—after a while it gets hard to tell. They loaded their trays and sat at a table in the back. A few minutes later, Kris picked up a tray and was handed a plate of mashed potatoes, stew, old bread and something pink. It looked familiar, not much different from shelter food in Fairbanks or Los Angeles. Kris headed toward the back table weaving around people hunting for a place to sit.

"Hey, can I squeeze in here?" Kris asked. The table was filled up. "I'd like to talk to you." She looked at the older woman.

"We can do that," said a scraggy man with thick glasses. He scraped his chair to one side and waved at the others to squeeze down. Kris pulled a chair over from another table. The woman across from her was probably closer to fifty. Black framed glasses hid her eyes and the skin of her face was chalky and lifeless; the victim of bad food and sunless summers. She stared blankly at Kris as if all interest in the world had drained out of her. The woman at her side was younger, though her hair was flecked with gray. She scrutinized Kris, leaning close to the older woman as if for protection.

"I'm looking for someone who knew Evie Gabriel," Kris said, flattening the mashed potatoes with her fork. The table quieted and eyes turned toward her.

"The police have already been here asking about her," someone said.

"What'd you tell them?"

He shook his head.

"She was my mother," Kris said.

"Oh," said the woman across from Kris.

"Did you know her?"

"Kind of. She was in and out of here most of the summer up until October. I only started coming in when the weather turned. But I'd eat with her when she was here. She said you might be coming. What was your name?"

"Kris."

"Yeah. Kris."

"Bad deal her getting killed and all," said the younger woman.

"So what do you want to know?" asked the first.

"Who killed her."

The young woman sniggered. A man on Kris's side of the table, who had been leaning over his plate to listen, clanked his knife against his glass and yelled, "Anyone here know who killed Evie?" The room quieted and heads turned to look at the table for a moment and then the murmur rose again.

"It was that man she went away with," said the younger woman.

"What man?" Kris asked.

"Vern," said the other.

"What was his last name?"

"I don't know nothing about him."

"Do you know where he lives?"

"All I know is what she told me," she said. "She came down from Fairbanks with this guy last spring. Maybe he had a job or something, but I think it was a scam he had going. She was certain they would do OK by it.

But you know, she was the type that's always thinking things will get better."
The woman had fixed her eyes on Kris and spoke without much inflection.
She stopped and took a bite. A few of the men from the other tables had
come over with their plates and were standing around listening as they ate.

"So what happened?"

"This is what she told me," the woman continued heavily. "She told
me that this guy, Vern, got picked up on a DUI and since it's not his first,
he pulls time, four or five months, in Lemon Creek."

"So she's lost her sugar-daddy and she's back on the streets," a man
said who was standing behind the younger woman. He lifted his plate to
his mouth and scraped food into it.

"Shut up, Joe."

"Yeah, it's true." Joe looked down at the head of the old woman and
nodded at it.

"So shut up." The old woman looked at Kris. "You know, they only let
you in here," she circled her fork once, "if you're sober. She wasn't always
sober. She'd sleep in Vern's pickup, which she had parked down at the
Indian village. It never moved; she didn't have any money for gas."

"Regular hotel it was, too," said Joe.

"Shut up, Joe."

"Flophouse," he said.

"You telling me she was turning tricks in the truck?" Kris asked.

Joe grinned, the teeth he had left were gray and there were sores on
his lips.

"Christ, she was in her forties," Kris said.

"She was OK."

"Oh yeah, so you know?"

"Yeah, I know."

"So you fucked my mother." Kris put down her fork, her face
hardening.

"She got paid for it."

"Get away from me, little shit."

"Did her a favor; kept her in whiskey for a couple of days." He lifted
the plate to his mouth and scraped a piece of meat into it with his fork. He

chewed with his mouth open smirking. The room quieted and Kris felt the pressure of eyes build on her back. She had spent lots of nights huddled on the floor under thin blankets while some man did his thing to her mother in the bed. It's how you get by. Sex buys you liquor, drugs, food, a place to crash, sometimes clothes, and protection. It takes only a couple months on the street before your own cunt isn't part of you anymore. You lie there and count the cracks in the ceiling while some wine-soaked body grunts and grinds on top of you. After a while, you don't even whimper.

So it was Evie. So it was her mother. Who was dead, lying at the bottom of a muddy hole in a gray city hundreds of miles from home. What did she care?

Kris glared at Joe. "Get out of my face."

"Nah. I got my rights," he said, pointing his fork at her.

Kris stood. She picked her fork off her plate. She was beginning to tremble. "Out of here."

He laughed.

Kris leapt on the table, scattering plates and glasses, and lunged at him. Joe lurched away, dropping his plate. Kris jumped off the table, fork low, aiming for Joe. Somebody grabbed her, wrapped his arms around her from behind and held her tight. "Back off," he whispered. "They'll kick you out." Kris struggled, but the arms didn't give. Two men seized Joe, doubling him over, and marched him down to the end of the tables and out the front door. Kris relaxed; the man behind her dropped his arms. The shelter's den mother bustled out of the kitchen, but someone intercepted her. There was sharp whispering and after a hard look at Kris, the woman retreated to the kitchen.

Plates and silverware were picked up and straightened. Kris walked around the table to her chair and scraped the food that had spilled onto the table back onto her plate.

"She did it, though," the old woman said without sympathy.

"I don't need my face rubbed in it." Kris pushed her fork into the potatoes and stared down them, unable to look at the old woman across from her or at the other faces crowded around the table staring at her. Turning tricks in a pick-up. There had been a hundred men like Joe, more maybe, but suddenly the shame and desolation that Evie must have felt seeped through the anger that Kris carried toward her mother. Evie never fought for herself and she had no one to do it for her—not, at least, when she'd been alive.

"She got beat sometimes, too," the old woman said. "A couple times it was bad enough the cops took her to the AWARE shelter."

Kris picked at a chunk of meat.

"What else do you want to know?" the old woman asked.

"What did you tell the police?"

"Nothing. That she was here during the summer. That she came and went."

"Did you tell them about Vern?" Kris looked up to watch the woman's eyes.

"No."

"How come?"

The old woman looked around at the other faces. A man spoke up. "The cops don't work for us." Some heads nodded.

"So which one of you guys beat her?" Kris asked.

There was an uncomfortable silence.

"It wasn't nobody here," the woman said. "And it wasn't him what killed her. It was too complicated a thing for him, to think about it and to take her all the way down to Thane. When a drunk kills you it happens in the middle of the street and he's too stupid drunk to run."

"Is Vern still in jail?" asked Kris.

"No, he got out in October. Evie quit coming around then and the truck wasn't in the village anymore. I didn't see her for a while. Then one day, she comes in and has dinner here, just to visit. She has this new dress—"

"Green?" Kris asked.

"Yeah. She looked good, real good. Like a million. She's got this new dress and shoes. She's cleaned up, her hair cut. She says they got a regular place out on Montana Creek. After dinner, he pulls up in the truck." She pointed out the window into the street. "And she takes off. Last I ever see of her."

"What'd the truck look like?"

"Just a truck."

"Well, was it big or small? Was it a Ford, or Dodge?"

The woman watched Kris through her thick lenses. Her face hadn't changed expression all evening. "This is important, right?"

"Yeah, it's important," Kris said. "How am I going to find this guy, if I don't know what his truck looks like?"

The old woman shook her head. "It wasn't a big truck, but not real small either. It could have been blue, or maybe it was green. It was old, though." She looked up, certain. "It was rusted around the wheels, I remember that."

So were half the trucks in Alaska. Most were so rusted they wouldn't be street legal in California. "Any dents, or marks?"

"I remember now. The glass was gone. It was patched with plastic."

"Window glass? Which window?"

"He was going up the street." She made a swinging movement with her hand pointing up Franklin. "So the passenger window."

"It was him what killed her," said the other woman, leaning over her empty plate toward Kris.

The other woman gazed somberly out at Kris from behind her black frames. "She looked good," the old woman said. "Like a million."

■ ■ ■

Kris stopped halfway up the stairs to finish her cigarette. The city lights reflected dirty orange on the black clouds hanging low between the mountain ridges that walled the channel. The rain was cold and the drops, thickening with ice, were larger and heavier now than they'd been during the funeral. They spattered relentlessly on her plastic poncho, gathering in its creases and running off the hem in little streams. She shivered, dropped the butt through the metal grating of the stairs, and hurried up the rest of the steps to Ben's.

He was smiling when he opened the door and the light in his eyes didn't fade as she walked in. He got another chair from the corner and set it opposite his at the window. The woolen shoepack liners that hung loosely from his feet whispered against the floor as he shuffled back into the kitchen to fill the pot and put it on the stove.

Kris had wanted to ask Ben about Evie, whether he knew about Vern, and what he remembered about her body in the creek. But when he pushed the warm cup of tea into her hand and turned off the overhead light, and lit a kerosene lantern, which threw a golden softness into the room, a quietness settled over them that she didn't know how to break. They sat sipping the tea; looking out the window at the shadows cast by the city's hard yellow lights and listening to the gusts of wind tap the window with pellets of rain and the crackle of the spruce in the wood stove.

Her tea was gone and the cup cold in her hands when Ben said, "It'll clear tomorrow."

Kris laughed.

"It'll clear off by daylight and get cold," he said quietly. "Let's pack some food and have lunch out the road."

"I thought you said it would get cold."

"It will."

"What fun is it shivering in the cold and eating frozen peanut butter and jelly sandwiches?" Kris demanded.

"We'll keep you warm." Ben smiled.

"What do you mean we?" Kris snapped, surprised he'd hit on her.

"All my cold weather gear is here," he said.

Kris relaxed. "I've got to go to dinner with some people tomorrow night."

"We won't last more than a couple of hours," said Ben. "You're eating with the couple who was at the funeral?"

"How did you know?"

"I saw him give you a card."

Kris fished the card out of her pocket. It was creased and crumpled now. She smoothed it out on her thigh; it read Loren Lambale, vice-president, National Bank of Alaska.

"Some rich guy who put together the money for a new extension at the AWARE shelter. He paid for Evie's funeral."

"It looked like more than the city would pay for."

"Yeah. So dinner wasn't something I could get out of." Kris laughed uncertainly. "I'm not good at saying please and thank you and answering a lot of questions."

"It'll probably be a good meal."

Kris squeezed the tea bag against the side of the mug with a finger. "He's phony. Right at the funeral he was telling me how much he'd done for the shelter. Justin says he's sanctimonious."

"Justin knows him?"

Kris shook her head. "No, that's what he said when I described him. Anyway, I've got to meet him at the parking garage tomorrow evening."

"Tomorrow's Saturday."

"He said he'd be working in the afternoon." Kris stood, leaving her cup on the chair. "So when should I come by tomorrow?"

"Eleven? It's an hour drive out to the beach. We can be back by three."

"OK. You're sure you got enough clothes for me. too?"

"Yes, I think they'll fit."

When he stood, he was about her height, though he'd be taller if he stood straight. She put on her jacket and tugged the poncho down over her head. Ben followed her to the door. She hesitated, not knowing what to do with her hands, then jammed them in her jacket pockets.

"See you tomorrow," she said, stepping into the night.

SATURDAY, NOVEMBER 14

Barrett's door was ajar. Kris pushed it open. His head was bent low over a newspaper spread on his desk. A circle of pink scalp showed through thinning hair on the back of his head. As she watched him, she felt her defenses close around her. In her experience, cops were men who hid their criminality behind a uniform. Kris tapped her fingers against the door and Barrett looked up.

"Come in." He motioned to the metal chair in front of his desk and folded the paper. "How are you?" Barrett sat back in the chair, clasping his hands together at the back of his head; the shirt stretched over his chest. No suit and tie today; he had on jeans and a flannel shirt; black hair curled out of his open collar and his sleeves were rolled part way up muscled forearms. He was larger than he'd looked in the suit.

"Working hard," Kris said, glancing at the newspaper.

"Saturday. Paperwork day." He pointed his chin at the forms piled on the desk behind his model tank. Its gun was cocked higher; he must play with it. "It's relentless."

"Paperwork's more important than a murder?"

Barrett grinned; maybe he thought she was being cute.

"How was the funeral yesterday?" he asked. "It was in the paper." Barrett brought his arms down and reopened the newspaper, putting his finger on a small paragraph on an inner page.

"I need to find out about a guy named Vern," she said. "He did time in Lemon Creek last summer on a DUI. My mother was with him."

Barrett's eyes pinned her, his face instantly intent. "How did you find this out?"

"Glory Hole."

"Good job," Barrett said. "I knew if I sent you in there, you'd find something I couldn't."

"You didn't send me."

"Do you have a last name?"

"No."

"Not a problem. Anything else?"

Kris wasn't going to tell him about the truck or Montana Creek—she wanted to get to Vern first; Barrett could talk to him later. "Yeah, they said that he treated her good. New dress, haircut, she was happy." She didn't want him to get cocky; to think he was getting close.

"Right. The dress she was wearing was new." He pulled the file out of the cabinet behind his desk; it was thicker than the last time she'd seen it. He shuffled through loose papers. "It had been purchased at Fred's," he said, reading from a sheet. "The stock manager said they'd received a shipment of those dresses about three weeks ago."

Kris kept her face blank, but she was surprised. Evie had to be murdered before a cop did something for her? Before she'd left, Kris remembered Natives in Fairbanks getting harassed so much that they couldn't drive across town without being pulled over; they called it being picked up on a DWN: Driving While Native.

"What else?"

"A fair amount," he said and flipped back to the front of the file. "First, the footprint the old trapper found in the mud was your mother's. Right foot. We found no other prints in either direction on the trail. We did find fibers on the bushes they crashed through on the way down to the stream. Some matched your mother's dress; the others were a high quality wool. Dark blue. It appears the killer was wearing a very expensive suit."

Next page. "As I suspected, she was hit with both barrels of a side by side. Somebody didn't want her easily identified, or was very angry at her. Ballistics says it was number two shot from Remington Nitro-Steel Magnum cartridges. They identified the cartridge from the wadding blown into the wound and the powder residue. But this is strange; it was a ten gauge. The ME dug out all of the pellets – over four hundred; the only cartridge Remington manufactures with that many pellets is a ten gauge. Two hundred and eighteen number twos apiece.

"Unless you're hunting turkeys, no one uses ten gauges any more. A hundred years ago they were common because the black powder used then wasn't very explosive and so you needed a bigger gun."

He looked up at her. "With modern powder, you can use smaller gauges and lighter guns. In fact, only one place in town stocks cartridges that size and it hasn't sold any in months, which probably means they were mail ordered. And unfortunately, most of the mail order outfits are NRA folks who hang up on out of state cops without a subpoena, so tracing the cartridges is probably a dead-end."

Another page. "Your mother's blood alcohol was zero, no detectable drugs or controlled substances."

Kris stayed quiet. Why was he telling her this?

"What is interesting," he said, "is that apparently Stewart was down the trail twice as long as he claimed. We found a carpenter who was working on one of the houses up the side of the hill. You can't see it from the road, but the staircase to it takes off from the cul-de-sac there where you park your car. The guy was ready to quit; he was cold and wet and he looked at his watch when he heard Stewart's truck come in. He said it sounded like it had holes in the muffler. There are, I checked. It was 3:20, thereabouts when he looked at his watch. He packed up at four, carrying his tools down the steps. It took him several trips and in between trips, he heard Stewart's truck take off. That's forty minutes. Stewart had told us fifteen or twenty. We can corroborate the time the carpenter said Stewart left. It's a ten-minute drive back into town and Stewart came in here at ten after four."

"He lost track of the time," Kris said.

"I doubt it, but count the minutes: Five minutes to the bridge if you move really slow. Five minutes to find the body and five minutes back. That's fifteen minutes max, twenty is generous."

"He's an old man."

"Can't be too old. He climbs those stairs to his house."

Kris hadn't thought of that. Justin had counted the steps: ninety-eight and Ben had to haul groceries and firewood up them.

"He didn't do it," she said.

"Are you two friends now?" he asked.

"I can tell."

Barrett pulled another sheet out the file. "Stewart had your mother's age wrong. He'd thought forty-two, but she was thirty-seven."

"No. She was forty-two," Kris said. Evie'd had her when she was eighteen.

"Vital Stats has her born on April 4, 1978. Parents: Claude and Katrina Gabriel. Sometimes a birthday gets off by a day or two when it's registered, but never by five years," he said.

Thirty-seven. Kris felt a chill settle in her. That made Evie thirteen when Kris'd been born. The family had still been doing well then—house, regular meals, no one drinking. But it was the year their lives started coming apart. Evie's father had rolled his truck and had been killed and, with no income, they'd lost the house. Thirteen; Evie'd been just a kid. Was she screwing at twelve? Sex had been a staple for Evie since the earliest days that Kris could remember, but Kris'd never seen twelve year olds go looking for it. Usually it came to them and they didn't have a lot of choice about it.

And why would she lie about it? Why'd she want people to think she was older than she was?

"We also got a positive ID on her," Barrett said.

"What do you mean you got a positive ID?" Kris said, suddenly confused.

"She had three fingers and a thumb left. We sent the prints up to Fairbanks and to the FBI in DC. The report from Fairbanks came in yesterday. Nothing on file with the FBI."

"She was buried yesterday." Kris's voice hardened. "How could you bury her without a positive ID?"

"We were certain enough. Stewart ID'd her. Margie Shaker, at the AWARE shelter, also identified her."

"Who are these people? What the hell do they know?"

Barrett sat back in his chair. "Kris," his voice deepened and smoothed. "I didn't want you to have to ID her. She wasn't a pretty sight."

Kris stood and leaned over his desk, her voice cold and hard. "Who the hell are you to tell me what I can see?" She could've seen her mother again.

"I thought it best," he said quietly.

"You thought it best?" Kris stared at him, stunned. Then she exploded, grabbing the tank by its gun and flinging it against the wall. It bounced and crashed on the floor, its treads in the air like a dead roach.

"Don't ever fucking think for me." She steamed out of his office pissed that he hadn't looked upset.

■ ■ ■

Ben heard Kris coming up the stairs, each foot landing on the metal grates with more force than the climb required. He smiled as he let her in, ignoring the anger stamped in her face, and pointed to a pile of cold-weather gear heaped on a chair. She shrugged into his parka, patched where it had been torn by a sled runner—back when he still used steel—and still smelling of the smoke of trail fires. Its skirt hung almost to her knees and her face vanished in the shadows at the back of the hood when she pulled the metal zipper from the bottom of the skirt up to the ruff. The ruff was wolf, from a bitch he'd trapped so late in the season her pelt was too worn and mangy to bother selling.

Kris kicked off her sneakers and stepped into his shoepacks, but refused his wool pants. They looked, she said, too dorky. He asked if she would be warm enough and she said, pushing her bare hands out of the sleeves, her anger fading, that she might be, if she had mittens. Ben pointed to a cabinet by the door and then turned back to the kitchen to finish packing lunch. It was a standard for him, pea soup and potatoes; both pre-cooked since he wasn't certain how long Kris would sit in the cold before she rebelled.

"What's this?" Kris came into the kitchen holding his pistol. "A .38." She opened the barrel. "It's loaded. Why's it loaded? Is this for bear?"

"No," he said. "It's too small for bear and besides, bear are reasonable folk." He watched her click the cylinder closed and check the safety. He wasn't surprised that she could handle a gun; Evie'd told him about their life in Fairbanks—and he'd lived there once himself. Kris looked at him and he said, reaching into a drawer for forks and spoons, "Cities are dangerous places."

"This is for people?"

"That's what makes cities dangerous," he said without sarcasm, pulling out a couple of forks.

"Did you ever have to use it?"

"No," Ben lied.

As he began packing the rucksack, Ben watched Kris return the pistol and pull out his pair of mittens. They were Athabascan. Abbie Jane, from Allakaket, had made them for him from a caribou hide he'd given her back when he still needed a good pair of mittens. He watched Kris trace the beadwork with her finger, smell the leather, and brush it against her cheek. Ben turned back to the rucksack, leaving her alone. He'd had Abbie Jane make Evie a pair, too.

Kris took the pack from him after he'd cinched it closed. He shouldered into his jacket and they stepped outside. It was well above zero, their breaths were only faint wisps of steam, like tails of an arctic hare, which disappeared quickly in the dry air. Juneau's winter might be too mild for his cold weather gear. In front of him, Kris pulled up her hood and burrowed deeper into the parka. Ben stepped carefully down the grated steps while Kris clanked on ahead. She waited at the bottom, an unaccustomed smile working across her face, as she looked back up at him. He led her to his truck and she scrambled in from the driver's side. A couple of years ago, he'd had to bolt the passenger door shut when it began flying open on left hand turns.

Ben drove up to Fourth, cut behind the governor's mansion, and dropped down to Willoughby. Saturday mornings were busy at Foodland but Ben found a space between two other trucks. They walked into the store and Ben asked her if there was anything special she wanted. Kris shook her head; so he led her back to the fish section and pointed to the sockeye fillets. A treat, he told her.

The clerk handed them to Ben, wrapped and bar coded, and they went and stood in the express line.

"Where's your hat, young man?"

Ben looked at the cashier in surprise. She had gray hair, stood taller and straighter than he, and held him with bright, indomitable eyes.

"It's cold out there. You'll catch your death," she said. "Nineteen sixty-eight."

While Ben fumbled in his wallet the woman said to Kris. "Does he talk?"

"I don't think he knows how to flirt," Kris said and the woman laughed.

Ben handed her a twenty and counted his change before filling out the tax-exempt form. Back in the truck, they pulled onto Eagan and headed north, trailed by the snorting of Ben's rusted-out muffler.

Ben had driven all of Juneau's roads; it can be done in a morning. Eagle Beach is thirty-two miles north of Juneau on the city's longest road, which dead-ended in a spruce forest just eight miles past the beach. No one was at the beach when they drove in, but Ben ignored the shelters and fire pits and carried the fish down to the water's edge. The tide was high but falling; little waves lapped the pebbled beach, which left behind a glaze of ice on the stones as the tide fell. In a few minutes the water would race into the distance, baring acres of lumpy mud flats.

He found a spot at the high-water mark, dropped the pack, and headed down the beach gathering firewood. In a few minutes he was back with an armful of driftwood. He disappeared again, this time into the scrub across the road, returning with a handful of alder and spruce twigs.

Ben gathered several larger rocks and placed them in a loose triangle.

"Want to light the fire?" he asked.

Kris dropped to her knees and slipped off her mittens. Ben took the lace-like spruce twigs, broke them into tiny lengths, and handed them to her. She laid them in a haphazard heap between the stones. When she had a little pile, she lit a match and stuck it into the middle. One or two twigs caught, turning dull orange and twisting in the small flame. The flame shrank and died. She struck another match and thrust it into its center. It went out. She struck another, but only the top twigs lit and the flame burned through them without dropping into the sticks below. Kris picked up the knot of sticks and cocked her arm to fling it into the water.

Ben touched her, stopping her, and, with his blunt fingers, gently helped her build a delicate pyramid of twigs. He handed her another match and pointed to the base of the pile. She struck the match and slid it under the twigs and the flame leapt quickly up through the pile. With unhurried care he handed her larger and larger sticks to place on the growing fire and in a few minutes the sticks were crackling and the heat of the flames played across their faces.

The smoke rose straight in the still air and Ben breathed in the tang of the spruce and the unfamiliar smell of the salt-water driftwood. He let the fire burn while he wove the salmon into the "Y" of a green alder branch with other sticks of alder. He opened and poured the pea soup into a pot and balanced it over the flames on the stones. When the fire had begun to lay down, he buried two potatoes in the fringe of ashes at its edge.

Kris sat, buried in her parka, staring into the flames. Once the soup and potatoes were cooking,

Ben stretched out his hands to the flames and after a moment quietly told her of the fires that had cooked his beans and moose. Of their warmth and crackle, the only heat and sound in his frozen world. Of the light their flames had given him during nights too long to sleep through. Of how that dot of dancing light had anchored him beneath the black star-ridden sky alive with the green fire of the northern lights. And to himself, he remembered how, for many years after he'd given up his dogs, that handful of light was his only companion on the trail.

Bubbles began to erupt in the thick soup. Ben poured it into mugs and handed one to Kris. He turned the buried potatoes with a fork, lifted his mug and blew into it, blowing billows of steam into the air.

Lynn Canal lay before them, its waters slate blue and still in the low winter sun. Scattered randomly in the water were rocky islands carpeted with shaggy spruce. An eagle soared on the air and in the distance were the white dots of wheeling gulls. Across the Canal, maybe five or six miles away, the snow-covered Chilkats carved out the edge of the sky.

"You can forgive Juneau weeks of rain for a day like this," Ben murmured. He ran a finger along the jagged horizon and Kris lifted her eyes from the fire and followed it.

"It's like Mom," she said, blowing into her soup. "Some guy'd beat on her for months. Then one day he'd give her a kiss or a trinket, or some nice word, and she'd be all over him. Nicest guy in the world, she'd say. And then the next day, he'd beat her again." Kris touched her lips to the mug and risked a sip.

Ben poked at a stone.

After a pause, he pointed again to the Chilkats and told her about winter in the Brooks Range. How it comes sooner than you expect, even before you had thawed out from the last one. How one day, while you are still enjoying the warmth and greenness of summer, you look up and see the faint, almost transparent powder of snow on the distant mountains. You look at it with dread, almost exhaustion, knowing too well the months of cold and darkness that lie before you. But it comes. Relentlessly, winter creeps down from the mountaintops and seeps into the flats and river valleys. It settles in the streams, and soon, clear ice rims the rocks, reaching each day a little farther outward until its frozen fingers clasp in the middle of the stream and imprison the racing waters, stilling them until breakup, a lifetime away.

"Then one day," he said, "sometime late in the fall, you look at those distant peaks, now white with snow, and you're..."

Ben reached forward and stuck a fork through the ashes into a potato.

"They're almost done," he said to Kris and then to himself he continued, and you're reborn. Alive again to Alaska. Like God had lifted you, struck and rung you like a bell.

"Anyway," he said out loud, "Alaska is winter. The other seasons are just pauses, place markers to keep track of the years. If you don't look forward to winter, if you don't get that thrill when the snows come, then you'd have to leave. It would be too long to bear." He checked the other potato, then carefully placed some green alder on the fire. When it was smoking, he lifted his makeshift grill and lowered the fish into the alder smoke over the coals, glowing orange now through a dusting of ash. Kris said nothing and Ben sat uncomfortably in her silence. Not even to Evie had he told what the mountains and streams, the long arctic nights had meant to him. He kept his eyes on the fish.

Kris toyed with a smoking stick she'd pulled from the fire and then she asked him what had brought him to Alaska.

Ben'd come up with the army after the war and had helped build the DEW line, a line of radar stations pointed over the pole at the Soviet Union. He'd worked with the surveyors out in front of the construction crews battling the cold in the winter and mosquitoes in the brief summer. When the project was over, he stayed. He wandered around the state with a gold pan for a few years, but when he was working the streams that flowed into the Alatna, it felt like home and he quit prospecting, built his cabin, and started trapping.

"Been there ever since," he said, "Until my joints ran me out." The fish was sizzling, the white streaks of fat had melted, making the orange flesh glisten; grease dripped slowly, bursting into low flames when it hit the coals. Ben lifted it off the fire and cut into the thicker meat that had encircled the backbone and peered in. Another minute; he returned it to the fire.

"That was five winters ago," he said, almost to himself. He dug out the potatoes and put one on each plate. A minute later he sprung the alder twigs holding the fish to the branch and dropped the fillets next to the potatoes.

"Five years. Do you miss it?"

Ben spoke to the fire. "Life goes on."

"Didn't you ever get lonely out there?"

Ben shook his head and cut open his potato. Only the last time, he thought. Then he told her about his spruce tree at the top of the little hill behind his cabin, where in the summer he would sit in the evening watching the water chase itself down river, the ravens popping and corking in the air overhead and the whiskey jacks flitting through the trees and hopping boldly around his feet impatient for the crumbs he let drop. In the winter, just days after solstice, he would snowshoe up to the tree at midday to cheer the sharp edge of the returning sun cutting above the horizon.

Ben chewed slowly, letting the salmon fall apart in his mouth and coat his tongue with its oils.

"Did you have any friends there?" Kris persisted.

Ben wondered why she was so curious. This girl, so independent, so unconnected, what did she care about friends and loneliness? He told her about Ezekiel who'd moved into the Sixtymile in the early '60s. One of Ben's trap lines had run up Mettenpherg Creek, which was only fifteen miles or so over a low pass to the Sixtymile. Every couple of months during the winter one of them would cross over for a visit. There would be the times mushing back to the cabin, cold and tired after a week out on a line, when the dogs would start yapping and pulling harder in their traces and he'd wonder what they'd scented. Soon, he'd smell wood smoke and know that Ezekiel was at the cabin waiting for him to come off the trail. It meant a cabin already warm, hot water on the stove, biscuits ready to go, and a hand feeding and watering the dogs.

Ben set his plate to the side and put another piece of driftwood on the fire. They crouched close to it; the flames were small and the heat did not carry far.

"He doesn't trap anymore either."

"Too old?"

"Too crowded," Ben said. The Sixtymile flows into the John and there's a winter trail that goes up the John from Bettles to Anaktuvuk. Lots of snow machines come and go all winter. Then in the summer, ever since they made the National Park, there are canoers and kayakers coming down the John. A couple of times his cabin was broken into even though you can't see it from the river. The streams and the river were his home. Ezekiel'd almost never come out and the hordes of people coming into his country inflamed him. In the end, it was easier for him to move out than to watch his land be overrun.

"Were you ever married?"

Ben didn't answer for a while, uncertain why she was probing and uneasy talking about things other than his dogs, trap lines, or the winter's wood. With a smile he told her that she reminded him of the weasel that used to live around his cabin who wouldn't give up once he'd gotten scent of something. He'd come right in the door when it was warm enough to be open and when the bugs weren't too bad and pillage any food Ben had forgotten to lock away. He'd gnaw at the cupboard doors, break glass jars by rolling them off the counter, and climb into the rafters to attack the jerky hanging from them. Ben would run him out of the cabin with a broom, but the weasel'd be back in a flash unless he shut the door.

"Why didn't you trap him?"

"Oh, we were buddies." Ben's eyes crinkled and he set another stick on the fire.

"So what did you think of Martha?"

"Who?" Ben asked.

"The cashier, at Foodland, who checked us out."

Ben looked at her blankly. Then he remembered the name tag pinned to her apron.

"Well, was she cute?"

Ben turned back to the fire. "Kris," he said. "Let me tell you about my women."

For years, there had been a grizzly sow that had shared his river valley with him. Regular as breakup she'd have two new cubs every third year. Ben would watch them chase the retreating snow up the mountainsides in the spring and then run before it as the snow came back down the slopes in the fall. He and the bears shared the blueberries and crowberries on the hillsides, the wild celery roots and cranberries in the river bottoms. And the fish in the bright streams—she putting on fat for winter and he—running willow wands through their tails and hanging them on fish racks by the hundreds—putting up his winter dog feed.

Ben paused a moment, his plate empty; wondering how much he should tell her. He rinsed the soup pot, poured in fresh water for tea and, feeding the fire more sticks, set it on the stones. He watched her. She was staring quietly into the fire, waiting for him to continue. The tunnel of her hood was folded back and he could see her face. It had the same sharp chin as her mother's; and like Evie's, her nose didn't dip as deeply from her brow nor were her eyes as dark as a full-blooded Native. Her face was ringed by Evie's halo of coarse black hair—so black that blue shimmered in it, like the blue in gunmetal. Her eyes, though, were different; Kris's were harder, sharper—guarded and more impatient. Evie's had been alive, coy and, sometimes, hungry. And Evie laughed, bubbling like a stream gurgling around rocks, while Kris was silent or angry like the mountains when the snow avalanched off them.

Ben looked again at the snow-covered Chilkats across the water and finished his story. One fall, coming back along the Alatna with a sack of fish tied to his pack frame, he stumbled into the sow's cubs. They squalled in terror and crashed into the brush. Before Ben could move, he heard the old sow galloping through the bushes behind him. He spun around, firing his rifle from the hip. The bullet ripped out the back of her head killing her instantly, but her momentum carried her into him, knocking him onto the ground and pinning him underneath her.

"I thought bears were reasonable," Kris said.

"She was. It was my mistake; I got between her and her cubs." As Ben saw it, all nature asked of you was your utmost attention. She had her laws, and if you knew and abided by them, then she would support and sustain you; if you failed to learn and follow them, you would die. Those were nature's only terms, and she didn't offer many second chances—almost never in the arctic—but in return she gave you life, a home, and the opportunity to touch or be touched by something beyond your day-to-day existence.

Ben finished his story. The cubs didn't survive the winter and the valley didn't have any bears in it, other than the odd bull that roamed through, for several years. Then one spring, when ice still rimmed the river's banks and heavy corn snow lay in hollows hidden from the sun, a sow with a single cub appeared on the mountain slopes across from the cabin. She was an inexperienced mother, not quite sure how to handle the energetic cub that bounced and tugged at her.

"I knew she'd stay and it was good to have a bear in the valley again."

"How'd you know she'd stay?"

"It was her home. She'd grown up in the valley. Her mother had been the old sow."

"How could you tell?"

"I knew that old bear like I knew Kobuk. I'd watched her for fifteen, sixteen years. And this one, she walked, she fished, she woofed and sniffed the air just like her mother."

Ben had finished his tea and the mug was getting cold. He put it in the pack and started to collect the dishes.

"Ben?"

Her tone had changed; it was softer and maybe there was something plaintive in it. Ben looked at her; she was squatting on her heels, gazing into the little flame, prodding a coal with a twig of alder.

"Tell me about Evie."

Ben kept gathering up the dishes, the empty soup can and scraps of food from around the fire. This is what she had been working up to all day; skittish as a fox around a baited trap Ben'd left his scent on. She'd used her questions to him to carve herself a space of safety so that she could ask this one. His silence grew, and he didn't know how to break it. Finally, sitting back down beside her, he said, "She was a good person, Kris."

"She was a drunk," Kris blurted, her bitterness raw.

Ben pulled back, surprised at the anger that burned so near her surface. He fell silent, not knowing how to respond, and watched the dying flames flicker weakly. Then, not wanting to fight her, he asked gently, "What are you going to do now, Kris?"

"Find out who killed her." Her bitterness had been replaced by a harder edge.

"Why, Kris?" He hadn't expected this; her anger at Evie was so great that he'd thought she'd pack up and leave, returning to her life in L.A. glad to bury her mother, to put her last connection to her life in Alaska behind her.

"What do you mean why?" she turned toward him, angry, frustrated. "You want to let the shit that killed her get away?"

"What about Evie?"

"She's dead."

"What would she have wanted?"

"Ben, what's with you?"

"Sometimes winning your fights is worse than letting things lie. Think of the pain in her life, in yours, why pick at it, why make the wounds bleed again? Let her be."

"Because people jacked her around her whole life." Kris jabbed the twig into the fire. "It's enough. I'm not going to let them get away with it anymore." The twig snapped and Kris flung it away. "I'll find out who did it. Evie's dead, it won't make any difference to her, and I don't care who gets hurt."

"Nine years, Kris. Why now?"

Kris looked at him, stunned. Then she whispered, "Damn you, Ben."

The fire had died and the cold was working in around his jacket. He took a breath. He released it. And he dropped into a great emptiness and watched Kris shrink away from him. With the certainty of the coming snow he knew that she would find what she was searching for; no one could keep her from it.

"Well, let's go," he said heavily, rocking forward to lever his legs under him. As he rose, he twisted to pick up the pack and something tore; he gasped as pain ripped through his back. He stood, staggered, took a breath, and then looked at Kris. She was kicking pebbles into the coals, her back to him. He forced himself to walk up the beach, barely lifting his feet. At the truck, he opened the door and waited, leaning on it with his eyes dropped, for Kris to slide in. They didn't talk much on the way back to town. At the bottom of the Third Street stairs, he told her not to bother coming up. Kris looked at her feet still in Ben's shoepacks, and kicked at the gravel.

"OK," she said, "See you." She turned and Ben watched her walk down the hill.

■ ■ ■

Kris did not look back. She kicked a stone and watched without interest as it bounced down the street. Nine years. She kicked another, it lifted and put a dent in somebody's Honda. Was the old man accusing her of abandoning Evie? Of walking out on her, of leaving her to fight the world alone? Kris turned left onto Fifth. Hadn't she? Nine years without a note, a card, nothing, to let Evie know that she was even alive.

She turned right on Gold and hiked up the steep slope to Chicken Ridge. At the top she stopped and looked down at the cold, still water in the channel. She'd come back, she thought defiantly. Back to Alaska. That counted for something. But only after she'd spent a month making up her mind. If she'd come back right away, as soon as she'd gotten Evie's letter, would her mother still be alive? Was that her fault, too?

She turned away from the water and walked up Seventh, her eyes on the pavement in front of her feet.

Justin's apartment was in the basement of a house that overlooked the park around Gold Creek; outside stairs led down to his door. Through it, she heard the murmur of a TV and, after she knocked, a thump. A second later Justin pulled opened the door. He hadn't shaved and he was wearing glasses that had fingerprints on the lenses.

"Hey great, come in." He stood back and Kris stepped in. Clothes, magazines and toys—roller blades, skis, an ice ax, a hundred-dollar pair of sneakers—littered the apartment; dishes were piled in the sink and on the TV Jean-Luc Picard was lecturing something that wasn't human. Justin picked up a pile of clothes and loose CDs from one end of the couch and dumped them on the floor behind it.

"Here," he said. "Sit down." He pointed the remote and killed the sound. In a kitchenette that lined the back wall, he clicked on the stove and put on a kettle. "Sorry, no Lipton's." He sat at the other end of the couch, lifted his leg and with a stockinged foot touched her parka at her thigh. "Where'd you get the parka?"

"It's Ben's," Kris said, pulling her arms out of it and throwing it on the back of the couch.

"He gave it to you?" He rubbed her jeans with his toes.

With her thumb and forefinger, she pinched his big toe, lifted his foot and dropped it over the edge of the couch. Justin grinned, and in spite of herself, she grinned back, forgetting for a moment, the pain and loneliness she'd felt standing on the ridge. "Just for the day. We had a picnic, out the road." She told him a little about the picnic; then about Vern and wanting to look for him out on Montana Creek.

"That's all you've got? Just a pickup with a busted window?" he asked.

"Is that a problem?"

"Well maybe. Not too many people live back there, but everybody there has a pickup with a broken window."

"So it'll take a while."

"Do you want to go now?" He glanced at his watch, then at the TV before looking back at her.

"No, I got that dinner with the Lambale's tonight."

"Mr. Sanctimonious."

"Let's do it tomorrow."

"Tomorrow's Sunday."

"You going to church?"

"No. I just thought…well, what're we going to do if we find him?"

"I don't know. See what happens."

"Do you think he murdered her?"

"How should I know?"

His eyes shifted back to the screen. "What about Ben?"

"I don't know. He was acting pretty weird today. He doesn't want to find out who killed her."

"Why not?"

She hesitated. "He thinks it would be better just to leave her alone. You know, not dig up her past."

"What does he care?" Justin asked. The kettle whistled.

Good question. What did Ben care? Kris watched Justin search his cabinets for tea. "I don't know why. But he got real quiet after I told him I was going to find out who did it. He hardly said anything all the way back to town."

Justin grunted.

"Yeah, and that cop told me that he was down the trail twice as long as he said he was."

"Really?" He handed her a mug with a picture of a skunk cabbage on it.

Kris pulled her feet out of Ben's shoepacks and tucked her legs underneath herself. "I don't think he did it, though."

"How come?"

"I just don't. Is there anything else on TV? I've got a couple hours to kill before that dinner."

■ ■ ■

Lambale was late. Kris stood on the sidewalk in front of the door to the parking garage trying to sink deeper into Ben's parka. Patches of dirty ice stuck to the sidewalks. Yellow light from the street lamps seeped into the night, hiding the stars overhead. Skinny, leafless trees grew out of square holes in the sidewalk in front of her. Off to her left were the black waters of Gastineau Channel and behind her, an occasional car turned out of the parking garage and drove past, heading out of town.

The cold cut in around the edges of the parka. Ten years ago, it would have been sweater weather, but L.A. had thinned her blood—and that was OK, this place wasn't home anymore.

She raised her eyes and saw Lambale come out of the alley by the Sealaska Building. About time. He had a briefcase in one hand and a couple of plastic bags that swayed with each step in the other. It was Saturday; he didn't have his fancy coat on, but he was still dressed like he thought he was important. His gloves were leather. Kris looked away.

"Sorry I'm late," he said when he walked up. "I forgot I had to pick up my wife's shoes." He shook the plastic bags. "She lost a heel and she also wanted me to pick up some fresh basil and a red onion at Rainbow." He looked into her hood, trying to see her face in its shadows. "Come on," he said, opening the door to the garage and ushering her through. "This will be fun!" Lambale followed her into the small room, reached around her, and pushed the button for the elevator; it opened right away.

This will be fun! Christ, why is she putting up with this? Kris stared at the stainless steel door, trying to ignore the weight of Lambale's presence behind her. The elevator bleated at every floor it passed, and Kris wondered irritably why they couldn't have given it a more reasonable sound. At "C" level it opened. Gently touching her elbow, Lambale directed her toward a Mercedes, black, unblemished, and reflecting the overhead lights. They got in without speaking and he let the car coast down the ramp, turned left, passed the spindly trees, and got on the expressway heading out of town, the same road she and Ben had taken that morning. Kris let the silence hang.

"I'm sorry about your mother, Kris," he said. "What a tragic thing to have happen." On the edge of her vision, she saw his pale face turn toward her and then back to the road. Warm air blew against her legs and began filling the compartment. Kris unzipped the parka and pulled her arms out of the sleeves, leaving the coat bunched up around her. A faint smell of vinyl came out of the vents.

"I met her at the shelter," he continued when she didn't answer. "She was in twice last summer. Unfortunately, things weren't going well for her." He glanced sideways at her again. "I tried to help her some."

He paused, waiting for her. The car was quiet; Kris couldn't even hear its tires running on the road. The broken white lines sped toward them and vanished under the car. What did he want from her? Was she another trophy, another hard luck case he could rescue and add to his collection of good deeds? You are a good man, Mr. Lambale. She could hear them cooing, the women with tasteful pearl earrings and hundred dollar bras supporting shapeless puddles of flesh, while writing checks for his next project. Looking out the side window, away from him, she saw the lights of the city bus flashing through the trees as it wound around the curves on Glacier Avenue. The shelter was around here, somewhere.

Kris roused herself. So, did she play the game too? Or just ignore him, hoping he'd lay off? She laid the flat of her hand on the upholstery. Leather.

"Thanks," she murmured and felt him swell.

"How long will you be in Juneau?"

"I don't know," she said. Then took a breath. "I should be back in L.A. on Monday. For work." she added, pushing it out.

"So soon? What do you do?"

She told him and he oohed as if it were brain surgery. It wasn't shit, she knew, dispatching trucks. Kris forced her thumb into the padded armrest on the door until she felt the steel beneath it and kept her mouth shut. A minute later, it was clear what he really thought when he asked her how much longer she'd be a dispatcher and whether she ever thought about going back to school and getting her diploma or GED. Then he started explaining the world to her, that she'd make more with a high school education, that she could work at a bank, he'd help her get a job, how she'd move up, she'd be an account rep in a couple years, then floor manager, who knows, maybe president someday.

Right. Like Ken and Barbie Land. Where men say yes dear, kiss their wives on the cheek, and don't fuck them till they bleed.

"I knew a bank manager in Fairbanks," she said, lying—he'd been a schoolteacher. "Once when DFYS took me away from Evie when she was drinking bad they put me in his home. He and his wife were making money off the foster kids they kept. They didn't give us squat; they kicked us out in the morning, even in the winter, and wouldn't let us back in until night, after they ate—they fed us different food. He was screwing one of the boys. Everyone knew it, but DFYS only busted him when the kid got hurt so bad they had to take him to the hospital."

The car was quiet, then Lambale said, "That sounds horrible."

Anger at his innocence flashed in her. "There was blood streaming out his ass," she pressed, not letting Lambale push it away. "Blood all over the man's pants. His wife was screaming that they'd take us away from them, half the kids were crying, and I had to break into the main part of the house to call the cops." It's not the Cosby Show, Mr. Lambale, Kris finished to herself, rubbing the dent in the armrest with her thumb, feeling it slowly refill.

"What happened to you after that?" he asked.

Kris shrugged and they drove on in silence. After another five or ten minutes, the divided highway ended and the evening traffic squeezed into a two-lane road. When they curved around the head of a little bay crammed with boats, Lambale tried to recover the conversation.

"Do you have many friends left in Fairbanks?"

Kris had never considered it; there weren't many people she wanted to see. "They're probably all dead now," she said, knowing it wasn't that bad. Some would be dead, some in jail, some still on the street, and a few would be working in minimum-wage jobs like hers. Annie, she remembered unexpectedly. She'd been cool in a stuffy kind of way, working with the kids at the shelter, playing board games with them and trying to get them to brush their teeth. She'd be doing all right.

"Honestly?" Lambale broke into her thoughts.

"Yeah. In Fairbanks, it doesn't take a knife or a hit with bubbles in it to kill you. At twenty below, passing out in the snow works good enough," Kris said as if these were things anybody would know.

"I'm sorry, Kris," Lambale said almost under his breath.

Kris looked at a big boat, lights blazing in the darkness, and a line of cars slowly feeding into an opening in its hull.

"The state ferry," Lambale said, following her gaze. "You know you can't drive out of here? We're surrounded by glaciers, mountains, and the sea. Boats and planes are the only way in or out."

"The rain, the darkness, and nowhere to go," Kris said. "Why would anybody live here?"

Lambale laughed, but she was serious.

"So Loren, if the family homestead is in Fairbanks, why didn't you move back there once you'd received your MBA?"

Kris couldn't remember her name, but the woman who'd asked the question, sitting comfortably relaxed across the dinner table from her, was, Lambale had told her, on AWARE's board. Her blouse was whiter than any shirt Kris had ever owned, even one fresh from its wrapper. Her eyes were blue and her graying hair was gathered in a simple ponytail. Whenever she spoke, she would try to make eye contact with Kris to include her in the conversation. She glanced at Kris again, but Kris let her eyes drift over the woman's shoulder to a distant light blinking on and off with irritating regularity in the blackness on the other side of the sliding glass doors. The ocean was that way. Little waves had lapped on the gravel beach when Lambale gave her a tour before dinner. The Lambales's house was on the shore, at the foot of a covered staircase almost as long as Ben's, but leading steeply down from the road instead of up from it. It was the road Kris had seen when she flew in; the one that cut through the trees on the slope above the line of houses pressed against the sea by the mountains.

"We made a deal," Lambale said, glancing at his wife at the other end of a table. Kris shifted to the side as an arm reached past her and placed a cup of coffee on a saucer in front of her. It had a silver rim. "Alvilde agreed to come to Alaska only if we lived in a town which had a tanning salon and where it was above zero at least fifty weeks out of the year."

Alvilde looked critically around the table as the last of the cups, their contents hot and faintly misting, were placed, neatly centered, in front of each person. She made a small movement to the woman doing the serving, and Kris's napkin, which lay in a crumpled wad by her cup, disappeared and a clean one, precisely folded, appeared in its place.

"Lucky you didn't end up in Ketchikan," the woman in the white blouse said.

"She thought she had me. She was certain no part of Alaska had even six months—"

"Bet Loren didn't tell you about the Taku winds," interrupted the AWARE woman's husband, who was sitting next to Kris.

"Actually, it was the art community that attracted us to Juneau," Alvilde said mildly, her English lightly accented. They talked about her art gallery; the governor had come to its most recent opening. Kris let them talk around her. She couldn't understand how Alvilde got so clean; her skin was translucent, like it had been waxed. She had smiled when Lambale had ushered Kris into the house and had made an appreciative comment about Kris's shirt with the "CA-4-ME" logo on the breast pocket.

Delicately and precisely, Alvilde stirred sugar into her coffee and passed the bowl. The conversation had circled around to the dedication of the new wing again. Lambale was telling another story—how the architect had mismeasured the door frames and all the premade doors had to be cut down. Alvilde listened attentively, although Kris was certain she'd heard the story before. Alvilde seemed proud of her husband's project, sharing his enthusiasm in a reserved, understated way.

"We almost missed you," said the AWARE woman.

"I wouldn't have missed the dedication for the world," Alvilde said. "But when I tripped and broke my heel, I had to run back here to find another coat and pair of shoes."

"Your outfit was beautiful."

"Beltrami," Lambale said. "Apparently Italians don't design shoes to Alaskan specifications.

The sugar bowl reached Kris. She stirred a spoonful into her coffee using the silver spoon from the sugar bowl and then stuck it, still moist, back into the white crystals.

Before dinner, Lambale had taken her into his study and shown her the drawings for the newly finished wing at AWARE. None of the other guests followed them in and Kris figured that she was new prey; everyone else had seen and heard enough. Lambale pointed out a picture on his desk that showed him giving the governor a copy of the report of the Governor's Task Force on Domestic Violence. It had been very controversial, Lambale told her. "I didn't pull any punches," he said, as if he'd been the only person on the task force. While he talked, Lambale hovered over her, occasionally touching her arm. Was he coming on to her? Exasperated, Kris stepped away. He laid a hand on her shoulder as he pointed out another one of his prizes. Kris twisted, the hand fell. What a fool. Kris moved toward the door, she'd seen enough.

"Would you like another cup, Kris?" Lambale was mother-henning her again. The serving woman, reflected in the glass doors, hovered behind her with the coffeepot.

"No."

"Sure?"

Leave me alone.

Alvilde shook her hand. "It was very nice to meet you, Kris. Please come again," she said. Her eyes, a faded blue, were amused.

Lambale squeezed her arm and told her he'd call her soon and apologized again for not driving her back—but since Jane and Dave lived in town, it made more sense for her to go back with them. She followed the AWARE woman and her husband up the stairs and sat in the back seat, resolutely answering questions, wondering silently what it was that Lambale wanted from her.

SUNDAY, NOVEMBER 15

It was around noon, but the town was empty. There was a high overcast, the color of old milk, and the sunlight draining through it was pallid and lifeless. The car was cold and Justin had done a lousy job scraping the frost off the windshield.

"How was dinner?"

"What a bore."

"You got to slam the door harder."

Kris opened and swung it closed again. The window glass shook.

"Was the food good?"

"They had a cook, she stayed by herself in the kitchen while we ate. It was weird."

The Subaru stalled and Justin let it cruise down Main Street before popping the clutch. It jerked and the engine caught.

"You got a bad muffler, too." Kris heard the muted puttering of the exhaust.

"Yeah, they don't last around here, too much salt in the air. So what'd you talk about?" The light at the bottom of the hill turned red. Justin slowed but turned right without stopping. The view down the channel opened up between the buildings; flashes of white flecked the choppy gray water.

"He was hitting on me."

"Lambale?" Justin turned his head surprised. "With his wife there?"

"In his study, we were alone. He kept trying to touch me."

"Sure he wasn't just trying to be friendly?"

"Give me a break."

"Where did he touch you?"

"He was touching me, OK? He's not going to grab a tit first thing."

"Just because he touches you doesn't—"

"You don't think I can't tell when someone is trying to get something off me?" she said.

"Why are you getting so steamed?" Justin turned and looked at her.

"Why am I being interrogated?"

"Maybe he was feeling sorry for you," Justin said. "Maybe he wanted to give you some support."

"Why would he feel sorry for me?" Kris turned in her seat and faced him, pissed that he questioned everything she said.

"Maybe, just maybe, because your mother was murdered Tuesday," Justin said.

"Why the hell would he care?"

"Just because. Why would he want to hit on you?"

"What kind of bullshit question is that? You guys are slaves to your pricks. Everything you do, you do to keep them happy."

Justin laughed. "That clears up a lot of my confusion about God, Ben and Jerry's, and the World Series." A bright yellow McDonald's cup skittered in the wind across the pavement, bounced off the curb, and rolled back into the street. Justin swerved and flattened it. "You don't think he's getting any off his wife?"

"It'd be like fucking an ice cube," Kris said, calming down and settling back in her seat.

"Crevasse."

"What's that?"

"Big crack in a glacier."

"Yeah." She laughed, feeling some tension drain away. Kris toyed with the zipper on her parka, remembering how exposed she'd felt following the AWARE woman up the stairs in Ben's big shoepacks. Behind the closed door of the house, she imagined Alvilde saying to Lambale, "Did you see that child's shirt, dear? I'm quite certain Nordstrom's doesn't carry it." Kris wrenched the zipper.

"Pick your nose and she'd fry you. Everything was silver and china; Normal beer wasn't good enough for her."

"You had to drink Amber? What'd you think?"

"No, something Danish. She's Danish. She's got an accent and their kids are named Hansel and Gretel."

"Really?"

"Something like that." The kids hadn't been there. Both were Outside at boarding schools. Alvilde had told them that her daughter's photographs were almost good enough to hang in the gallery.

Justin nodded and Kris fell silent letting the hum of the tires on the pavement fill the car as it sped along the expressway. The road ran north between Gastineau Channel on the left and mountain ridges coming down perpendicular to the water on the right. It cut across the mouths of the valleys that lay between the ridges. Kris looked into the valley they were crossing now. It looked industrial. Big heaps of mud and gravel had been bulldozed out of the valley floor. Tucked far up the valley, was the crystal blue of a glacier.

Justin drove on another few miles and then turned right. Spread before them above the trees, only a few miles away, was a glacier. It stretched, a mile wide, across the end of the valley and rose massively, twisting and curving back up between the mountains to the distant ice field. The rains of the last few days had washed its lower reaches and the ice showing in its cracks and folds was a blue so deep and rich that it glowed in the dull daylight.

"Isn't it bizarre?" Justin asked. "To have something so beautiful, so extraordinary, so colossal looming over an ordinary, banal American suburb. It's like a giant Aztec god living in Westchester County. And everybody just scurries around shoveling their walks and walking their dogs like it was normal. Walt Whitman said something once about being blown away by the miracle of a mouse; it's kind of distressing how fast miracles become part of the background."

Kris stared out her side window wondering how much longer she'd have to be up here. Tomorrow was Monday. She'd promised Manuel that she'd be back to work in the morning. They were probably in a mess down there now. None of them could dispatch like she could. And Christmas was coming, their busiest time. She'd better call.

"This is Montana Creek." Justin pointed to a stream the road crossed. "The turnoff is right up here." A few seconds later, he turned right onto a road that cut through a thick forest of spruce. When it forked a ways down, Justin kept left. The trees thinned out, the road turned to gravel, and there were dirty patches of snow tucked under bushes and in hollows alongside the road.

"OK, this is it. What do you want to do?"

"We stop at each driveway and look for a pickup with a missing window."

"You want to drive to the end, just to get a lay of the land or something?"

"What for?"

"Just to see what's there."

"What good's that going to do?"

"Nothing, I suppose." Justin tapped a finger on the wheel. "Stop here."

Justin pulled past the first driveway and stopped. "There're going to be dogs."

"I can hear them." Kris opened the door and slid out. A second later, Justin followed.

"We should take notes, to keep track of the vehicles at each house," he said.

Kris walked up the short driveway. A couple of dogs heaved against their chains. The pickup parked before the mobile home didn't have any rust and had all of its windows. As she turned, someone opened the door. She waved and walked back down the drive.

Back in the truck Justin said, "That was easy enough."

"What'd you expect?"

"Like trick-or-treating." He laughed nervously.

They worked quickly down the road. Most of the houses were owner-built shacks or house-trailers and were widely-spaced in the trees and scrub.

The yards were littered with rusting vehicles, old construction material, and other junk.

"Wouldn't be an Alaskan homestead without a truck carcass and a couple of fifty-five gallon drums in the front yard," Justin said, pulling up to another driveway. Kris slipped out; he'd barely gotten out of the car before she ran back and whispered: "This is it."

"You're sure?"

"Yeah, I'm sure. The passenger side window has got plastic and duct tape, no glass. Looks like the kind of truck Evie'd be around. Pretty beat up."

"So, you want to go get the police?"

"What do you want the police for?"

"He might have a gun."

"Of course he's got a gun. This isn't Kansas."

"You want to get shot?"

"All we're going to do is knock on his door. He'll think we're missionaries or something."

"I don't think this is too smart."

"I thought you wanted some action."

"Yeah, but this is serious."

"You wanted it in Disneyland?" Kris glared at him. Her heart was beating hard against her chest, but she fed off his fear. "Come on, Justin. It's no big deal."

"OK." He put the car keys in his pocket and followed her around the Subaru. The driveway was about fifty-feet long, but the pickup was parked only midway up because the upper end was littered with junk. A rusted washer, bedsprings, and a rotting mattress, a stack of bald tires, a warped pile of lumber, a differential, and other car parts cluttered the driveway and the dirt yard in front of the house. It was more of a shack: small and square and started years ago and never finished. Siding covered only about half of the weathered exterior ply on the front. Shredded pieces of Tyvek stuck out from under the siding and flapped in the spotty breeze.

The place looked empty but there was smoke coming from the stack. Kris picked her way through the junk, her eyes intent on the black windows; no light shone through. Behind her, she heard Justin falling slowly behind.

"Hey Kris," he whispered loudly. "Look at this."

Kris turned. Justin was squatting on his heels, trying to lift a couple of rods of rebar off something half buried in the frozen ground. He tugged it free and held it up. It was a four-inch-square piece of steel with one wavy edge.

"It's a piece of the pipeline," he said. "Half-inch steel. See the curve?" He held it edge-on, so she could see it. "The pipeliners used to cut maps of Alaska out of pieces of the pipe. See this." He ran his finger across the wavy edge. "This is the north coast."

"Justin, who gives a fuck?" She walked toward the door. Without turning she waited for him to come up behind her before climbing the two steps. He came up one. She knocked.

Nothing happened.

She knocked louder. Inside she heard a rustle and soft thump. Sweat pricked along her lower back. The door scraped inwards. Kris was standing one step below the level of the floor. When the door opened she looked up and saw a small man standing in the shadows, his hand resting on the inner doorknob. The harsh smell of whiskey settled over her like a damp familiar blanket.

"What do you want?"

Kris started. It was slurred and fuzzy with whiskey, but she knew the voice. She stared up into the gloom and saw the shadowed hollows of his eyes, the curve of his jaw, the straight line of his lips and, looping below them, a red line that glistened wetly.

"How're the balls doing, Vern?" she asked.

Vern grunted and leaned out of the shadows. Kris saw the jagged marks of her teeth in the liquid-looking wound in his lower lip. It was the man who'd been leaning against the counter at the airport and the man who'd attacked her by the shelter.

"Evie's girl," he said quietly. The whiskey hung in his breath thick as cotton. "Come in." His words were limp and slurred. He left the door open and walked back into the murkiness. Kris didn't move; he'd tried to kill her, walking into his shack wasn't what she wanted to do. Justin lifted his foot onto her step bumping into her heel. The touch pushed her forward; Justin followed her in.

"Shut the door."

Justin pushed it closed. Shapes emerged from the dimness. On the right was a kitchen. A battered green camp stove sat on a plywood counter and crusted dishes were piled in a little enameled sink, which drained into a plastic bucket beneath. Some of the gray water that filled the bucket had slopped over and frozen on the plywood floor. A stoved-in sofa separated the kitchen from the rest of the shack. Next to it was the bottle of whiskey. In front was a metal kitchen chair and against the wall a little wood stove and a pile of carelessly stacked wood. Only the front wall had windows and the light that came through them was too feeble to reach far into the room.

Vern went over to the stove and threw in another stick.

"Sit down." He motioned to the chair, dumped kindling out of a wooden box, and upended it for a second seat. Then he moved over to the far wall and pulled open the drawer of a wooden table that had screws, nails, and other bits of junk jumbled on top of it. He reached inside and when he turned around, he had a pistol in his hand.

"Jeez, man," Justin said.

"Sit down, kid." Vern pointed the pistol at him. It didn't waver much. Kris took the seat; Justin walked past her and sat on the wooden box.

"Where're the cops?"

"Why'd you kill my mother?"

The pistol moved over and settled on Kris. It was a revolver; small and cheap looking.

"You know, missy, I'm a little tanked. Best not to mess with me."

Kris stared back at him.

"Where're the cops?"

"They don't know anything about you."

"How's that?"

"They're not my friends."

Vern grunted. "How'd you find me?"

"Evie told a woman at the Glory Hole about you, that you and she were living out here."

"What're you doing here?"

"You killed my mother."

"You ran out on her."

"Her drinking ran me out."

"Ten years is a long time to be gone because of a drinking problem," Vern said distinctly. He was breathing through his mouth and one of his bottom eyelids sagged, showing a sliver of red under the eyeball. "Phones don't drink. She would've liked that, a call."

Vern waited, but Kris didn't say anything. Evie'd never had a phone in her life.

"You came back for the money, didn't you? Your ma writes that she's got a couple bucks and you're on the next plane."

"You're full of shit."

"Remember who has the gun, missy."

Vern sat down on the couch and rested his elbows on his knees, the pistol pointed loosely at the floor in front of her. A week-old beard bristled around his mouth. His hair was pushed up in the middle, like he'd been lying on his side and hadn't combed it down. He wore jeans, a heavy cotton shirt, which looked new but was rumpled and had stains on it, and boots that were unlaced.

"Let me tell you about your ma and me. We had a good thing going. I dried her up –"

"She was so drunk last summer, the Glory Hole kicked her out."

"I was in the pen. I can't keep her straight if I'm not around can I? She sobered up when I got out. First time she ever had someone looking after her. Someone giving her things, making her pretty, making her think like she's special. I treated Evie—"

"Bullshit." Kris didn't need to hear this. "Why'd you try to knife me?"

"You were in the way."

"In the way of what?"

"Me and Evie."

Kris was blinded by an unexpected rush of anger. Who were these men always pushing her away from her mother?

"Fuck you," she said, hardening her voice to hide the bitterness.

Vern grunted. His eyes steadied and held hers. "That can be arranged."

Hair moved on her scalp and Kris straightened in the chair, suddenly nervous that she'd pushed too far. Vern reached over to the side table and picked up a roll of duct tape.

"Here," he said, lobbing it to Justin, who fumbled and had to hunt for it on the floor.

"Tape her hands."

"Hey man, we won't tell anybody—"

"Tape her hands, kid."

Kris looked at Justin, sitting on his wooden box, his face drawn, looking like he was being whipped. He looked at her, uncertainly. She stared at him, giving him nothing. He shuffled over and stood behind her.

"Turn around so I can see," Vern said to Kris.

Kris sat with her hands on her thighs and did not move. Vern stepped forward and tapped the butt of the pistol against her ear, like he was knocking in a tack. Her hands flew to her head; she gasped, then stifled the pain. Slowly, she turned sideways in the chair and put her hands behind her. She heard Justin groping for the loose end of the tape and then a ripping sound as he found it and pulled the tape off the roll. He clasped her wrists in one hand and wound the tape around them with the other.

"Do it tight, kid."

"It's tight."

Vern tugged at the tape. It hurt. Kris took a deep breath and released it quietly, hiding her pain. Vern moved away and she slid back around in the chair and faced him. He pointed Justin back to his box with the gun.

"Hope the kid isn't too good a friend of yours." Vern waved the gun at Justin, looking at Kris. "We don't need him much anymore."

Justin moaned.

Vern glanced over at him and snorted.

"Where'd you find him?" he said, looking back at Kris. She could hear Justin's breathing. His throat worked spastically like he was trying to swallow sand and he squirmed on his box. Finally, as if collecting himself, he sat up straight and crossed his arms.

"Sorry kid. Just not your day." Vern raised his arm off his knee and leveled the barrel at Justin. The pistol was only a couple of feet away. Justin's finger unfurled from his fist and tapped his jacket where his heart was.

"I won't miss, kid."

He pulled the trigger.

The blast exploded in the room. The powder flash lit Justin's face demon-green an instant before he shot backwards, cracking his head against the wall and squirting the wooden box out from under him. Kris screamed. She leapt from her chair and charged Vern. He whipped the pistol around, both hands gripping the butt now, and Kris slammed into the barrel. It stopped her; its heat warm through her parka.

"Careful missy," Vern said, easily holding her weight with the pistol.

His words sounded faint and distant, the shot still echoed in her head. She closed her mouth, swallowed, then stood, taking her weight off the barrel. Justin was buried in the shadows; a single leg emerged from the darkness. It twitched against the plywood floor.

"They do that for a time," Vern said. "But then they stop. Now come over here and sit by me."

Her vision clouded at the edges and she stumbled backwards. The back of her legs knocked against the chair and she collapsed on to it, her head falling forward. Air entered her lungs again and the muscles in her legs started to shake. She'd seen people killed before, but they hadn't been anybody she really knew.

Then she felt him. He was standing before her. She opened her eyes and looked down through her hair at the floor. The toes of his boots were at the upper edge of her circle of sight. His hand slipped into her hair, gently, and lifted her head. His pants were open and his cock was out, stiff and runty, fluid beaded at the tip. She rolled her eyes down to the floor and tried to pull her head away. His hand tightened in her hair, the blade of his knife slid out and the point pricked lightly against her eyelid.

"You were pretty rough with your mouth the other night," he said. "You're going to be a whole lot more gentle now, aren't you?" He pressed the knife into her eyelid and pulled her head forward.

"I'm not sucking that thing," she said, pulling backwards, her hair stinging her scalp.

He tightened his grip and pulled her forward. Kris locked her mouth shut. The head, warm and wet, bumped against her lips.

"Open up."

"Open up."

He let go of her hair, reversed the knife in his hand, and pulled the zipper of her parka down to her waist. Methodically, he cut each button off her shirt with the knife, pulled it apart and slipped the blade behind the collar of her T-shirt and sliced it open to her belt.

"They're small," he said touching her breasts. He lifted one and let it rest in his hand. His face hovered close above her. Kris gathered her spit. He flicked the blade up and pressed it into the underside of her chin forcing her head back. It cut into her and a thin bead of blood rolled down the curve of her throat.

"Swallow it."

She swallowed, the blade pushing into the floor of her chin. He lowered the knife.

"Are you ready?"

"Fuck you."

"That's the general idea."

"No." Kris felt the anger draining from her voice and struggled to keep it there, knowing fear would fill in behind it.

Vern took a nipple between his thumb and forefinger and pulled her breast out. He slid the knife underneath and sliced up.

Kris strangled a cry. There was no pain for a sliver of time, long enough for her to hope that it hadn't happened and then it came at her, like razor teeth, like the arctic cold. She stifled a sob.

"Are you ready now?" Vern whispered.

Distantly, her head nodded and tears clouded her eyes.

He stood up; his hand gripped her hair, and pulled her head toward him. "Open."

Her mouth opened, her eyes clamped shut. He slid in; it throbbed. "Suck."

Beyond the fringes of her awareness, she felt something. A rustle. A presence in the dark. Vern stiffened. It came again. His hand suddenly clenched violently in her hair. His cock softened.

Justin cleared his throat. "Put your hands up."

Vern spun around, yanking her out of the chair by her hair. Kris, her feet not under her, fell forward onto her knees. Vern wrenched her head back and his knife flashed down to her throat. She looked wildly up into the shadows and saw Justin standing by the back table, arms outstretched, both hands gripping the gun.

She screamed.

Justin fired twice, point blank into Vern's chest. Vern's grip flew apart, dropping her to the floor. She fell, twisting to see him stagger backwards, hit the wall, bounce, and then collapse on to the floor.

"No!" Kris screamed again. She rolled to her feet, her hands taped behind her, and slammed her shoulder into Justin. "No!" Terror twisted into rage, her vision crumpled at the edges. She pounded her shoulder into him again. He lurched dumbly backwards, the pistol sank to his side.

"Why did you shoot him?" she yelled.

"Christ," he whispered. Justin's eyes were fixed on the floor beyond her.

"You shit." Kris backed off and stared up at him, her face warped with anger, her blood hammering in her head.

Justin focused on her. "What?"

"Why did you shoot him?" Her voice still clotted with anger.

"I shot him."

Kris barely heard him.

"Dammit Justin!" She was panting, air wasn't getting into her body.

Justin looked down at her and then at the gun in his hand. His hand was shaking. He searched the pistol until he found the safety, pushed it over and laid it carefully on the table, then collapsed onto the sofa, his face, even in the shack's gloom, bone-white.

"You shouldn't have shot him," Her fury began to implode, her legs started trembling. She didn't want to admit to her fear. She didn't want him saving her. She didn't want to owe him anything.

"He was going to kill you," Justin said, his voice unsteady.

"We could have worked out a deal."

Justin had shrunk into himself on the sofa; he was still staring at the floor.

"He was the only thing we had to go on." The anger had drained out of her voice. She took a deep breath trying to keep herself steady, trying to stop the trembling in her legs.

"If we'd brought the police in like I wanted to, this wouldn't have happened," Justin said, his voice small.

"They would have screwed it up."

"Screwed it up?" Justin lifted his head, his voice louder, hardening. "I'm shot, you've got a cock stuck in your mouth, and he's dead. How could they've screwed it up worse than this?" He glared up at her. "You blew it. I'm going for the cops," he said, standing.

"No."

Justin picked up the gun again and headed for the door.

"No." Kris ran in front of him, blocking his way. "Dammit, Justin. He's dead; it won't make any difference. Let's search the place before they come. They'll never know."

"They'll arrest us for tampering with evidence."

"How're they going to know?"

"Fingerprints, dust marks, there's a million ways."

"Get your gloves then."

"No way. I'm out of here."

"Get your damn gloves."

Justin looked at her. "Where's that blood coming from?"

Kris looked down. The open parka hid her breasts, but the skin between them was visible and smeared with blood. Suddenly, she felt the pain. It surged through the tip of her breast every time her heart beat. "Asshole sliced off one of my nipples."

"Jesus Christ." Justin reached toward her.

"Leave me alone." Kris twisted her shoulder, blocking his hand. "Get this tape off me."

He ignored her and opened her parka and shirt. Blood was starting to cake on her breast and belly. "Let's find it. We can pack it in snow and they can sew it back on."

"I don't need it. It's only the tip."

"You don't need it?" He stared at her. "Jesus, Kris, you are mother-fucking crazy."

"Yeah, probably," Suddenly, the last of the adrenaline drained out of her and she felt giddy. She held her breath to keep from giggling; she let it out slowly.

"Doesn't it hurt?"

"Yeah, it hurts. So let's move." Kris turned her back and pushed out her taped hands.

She rubbed her wrists after he'd unwound the tape, then pressed her T-shirt against her nipple to soak up the slow dribble of blood. She'd been cut worse.

Justin watched her. "You OK?"

"Yeah," she nodded. She tucked in her shirt.

They were silent for a minute, then Justin asked, "Look." When she looked up at him, he pulled his jacket tight and stuck his finger through the bullet hole. "Right over my heart. Glad he was a good shot even drunk."

She stared at the hole, then looked up at him.

Justin stepped over the kindling box and began shuffling his feet in the dark corner where he'd been thrown by the slug. Kris heard a clunk and something heavy grate on the floor. He picked it up. It was the piece of pipeline steel. There was a lead-colored scar in it that she'd hadn't seen before. He tucked it into his jacket and crossed his arms over his chest to hold it over his heart. He tapped it through the material with his forefinger.

"Look, this is where the bullet hit," he said taking it out and pointing to the scar. He pulled at his jacket again and found a second hole off to the side. "I'm lucky it didn't ricochet through my arm." He laughed nervously. "I wonder why he didn't hear the ricochet."

"He had other things to think about. I jumped him."

He rubbed his chest. "It's starting to hurt now. It knocked me out, I didn't feel a thing when it hit." He was quiet for a moment, then said, "It was pretty close, wasn't it?"

Kris remembered Justin's foot sticking out of the shadows, twitching. She looked at the piece of dull steel with the gash in it and then she looked away. "You did OK." It wasn't something she often said to anybody, especially a man, and the words made her feel awkward and uncomfortable.

"Yeah, thanks."

"Get your gloves," she said, covering the faint flush of warmth she suddenly felt toward him. She pulled Ben's mittens from her pocket and put them on.

"OK." Justin went out the door. Kris went over to look at Vern. He'd crumpled onto his side; blood still seeped out of his chest. It glistened in the dim light as it flowed slowly across the room and puddled in a low point in the floor. His pants were open and his penis lay shriveled on his thigh like a tumor, like something alien, like something that belonged on ET. Kris wondered at the frenzied, uncontrollable power it had over its owners. It wasn't something she wanted.

She turned away from the body and surveyed the shack. There wasn't a bed and she wondered where he and Evie'd slept. Looking up, she saw a ladder nailed to the wall in the far corner by the kitchen. It led up to a hole in the ceiling. She climbed up, but it was too dark to see anything and she dropped back down to look for a light. Next to the cook stove, she found matches and a kerosene lantern. She took off a mitten and carefully, so she wouldn't leave any prints, struck a match and lighted the wick.

The loft had two thin foam mattresses pushed together against the far wall. On one side was a box of men's crumpled clothes. On the other, Kris found a neater box of women's things. She took them out one at a time, wondering at the changes that must have come to Evie. Was it Vern that changed her? Clothes had never been folded when Kris had lived with her.

Down below she heard Justin come back in.

"Kris?"

"Up here. You look down there."

"All right."

Most of the clothes were new. Wal-Mart stuff, nothing fancy, but still new. At the bottom of the box were some worn, dirt-stained shirts and Kris wondered if Evie had held on to them because she hadn't trusted her luck. What had Vern offered Evie? How had he sobered her up? More than anything when she was a kid, she'd wanted her mother to stop drinking. She cried, she screamed, she bullied; nothing she did made a damn bit of difference. What had Vern done that she couldn't?

Kris lifted the last carefully folded old blouse and there, at the bottom, was a small brown paper bag. Holding it next to the frail glow of the lantern, Kris opened it. Inside was a simple caribou hide pouch with leather drawstrings laced around the open edge. It was her mother's; she had carried it with her all the years, all the drunks, all the nights in jail that Kris had known her. In the last nine years, Kris had not once thought of it.

"Hey, Kris. I found something. Come down and take a look."

"Hold on." She dropped the pouch into the paper bag and stuffed it into one of the parka's inside pockets. Less carefully, she repacked Evie's clothes and with the lantern in one hand, climbed back down the ladder. The movement rubbed the T-shirt over her nipple, and she felt it start bleeding again. The pain was still sharp and she hardened her face so Justin couldn't see it. He was sitting with his feet dangling through a hole in the floor under the sink. The slop bucket had been moved out of the way and half a plywood section lifted out of the floor. In his lap was a red cookie tin.

"Two thousand, four hundred and twenty dollars, all in twenties," he said putting the wad of cash back in the tin. "And a card and an envelope." He turned the envelope over. "Oh, it's from you."

He handed it to her. It was the letter she'd sent Evie letting her know when she was arriving. The envelope had been ripped open across the top and the letter was still inside.

"Why wasn't this with Evie's stuff? Why were they hiding it under the floor?"

Justin looked up, the card in his fingers. "Maybe Vern was hiding it from her. She probably didn't know about the money, either."

Probably not. Kris shook off a mitten and pulled her letter out of the envelope. "How'd he get this? I sent it to the AWARE shelter."

Justin didn't answer.

Suddenly, she realized with a pang that surprised her that Evie had never known she was coming. She'd died thinking that Kris hadn't answered her letter; that she'd run from her again.

"Take a look at this," Justin said, handing her the card. It was a 3 x 5 card and on the side without lines was a number written in a precise script: 95544.

"What's this?" she asked.

"Phone number."

"It's not long enough."

"789-5544. There are only a few exchanges in Juneau, so all you need to do is write the last digit of the exchange. This is a valley number, so it's probably someone's house, though it could be a store too. It's not Evie's writing, is it?"

"God, no."

"It had to be written by someone who knows Juneau's phone system."

"Two and a half thousand." She picked up the cash and riffled it. "Where did they get this?"

"Bet you'd find out if you called that number."

"There's no phone here."

"No."

"So are we done?" Justin asked. "Let's put this back and get out of here. They'll be able to tell how long we hung around by changes to the body."

"I'm taking these." Kris reached for the tin and put the money, letter, and card in it.

"Are you going to give them to the police?"

"No."

"It's material evidence. You take that and you go to jail."

"How are they going to find out, Justin." It was a warning, not a question.

Justin looked uncomfortable. "I think we should tell them. It probably has something to do with the murder."

"It can't have anything to do with her murder; she didn't know anybody with this kind of money."

"They had to get it from someone."

"I'm taking it."

"It's your ass." Justin crawled out from under the sink and replaced the plywood and the bucket.

"See that?" Justin pointed at the slop water frozen to the plywood. "That's how I knew there was something under there—the insulation had been ripped out so the floor here is colder than in the rest of the shack." Justin walked over to Vern's body, pushed one of Vern's booted feet into the light with his toe. "Not crepe," he said. "Ben's the only one, so far, to have crepe soles."

"Did you find anything upstairs?" he asked.

"A caribou-hide pouch that belonged to my mother."

"Did you take it?"

"Yeah."

"What's in it?"

"Used to be some of my hair. Evie cut it when I was born. She said I looked like a bush when I came out. Then I lost it all before it grew back in later."

"Is it still there?" Justin followed her out the door, closing it behind him. It was dusk now, the sun already behind the mountains.

"I haven't opened it yet."

"Let's look."

"Not enough light. Let's get in the car."

They walked down the driveway, weaving around the junk, and climbed into the car. Justin started the engine and clicked on the overhead light. The car was cold and their breath frosted the windshield. Kris pulled the purse out of her pocket. The leather was soft, almost like tissue. Justin leaned across the seat as she worked loose the leather cord. When she had it open, she angled it to catch the light and looked in. She frowned.

"What's wrong?"

Kris reached in and gently pulled out a snip of black hair that was twined with a short length of white beads around the quill of a feather. The feather's barbs were twisted and kinked and separated from the years in the pouch. It was from a Stellar Jay; a big bird that Kris had liked when she was a kid because its call was loud and unafraid.

"It's still there," Justin said.

"There's two." Kris stuck her thumb and forefinger back into the bag and pulled out a second snip of hair twined around the quill of a black feather. The hair was reddish-brown and much finer than hers. Kris laid it on her palm next to the other.

"Strange. Whose is that?"

"I don't know," she said. "But I think, somewhere, I've got a brother or a sister."

■ ■ ■

Kris leaned against the Red Dog Saloon's phony log wall watching Justin lope up the steep slope at the end of Franklin Street toward Chicken Ridge. She'd refused his offer of dinner; she had enough money now to feed herself and she didn't want anything to do with him until he'd quit being a hero. When he started up the staircase at the end of Franklin, disappearing into the darkness beyond the reach of the streetlights, she straightened and walked down to the Lucky Lady. The nub of nipple that she had left and the outer half of her breast were still numb, as if frostbitten. The doctor had given her a shot to cut the pain, but other than a bandage, there wasn't much he could do and, he warned, scar tissue would form that might make it hard to nurse—not a problem Kris was going to worry much about.

The Sunday evening drinkers had already started collecting in the Lady. The crowd was as noisy as in any bar on a weekday, although, instead of wailing or throbbing, the jukebox was playing something smooth that she didn't recognize. Maybe it had a Sunday line-up. Kris headed to the back hallway past the end of the bar and found the holes in the wall where a pay phone used to be. She scanned the room, spotted a sullen looking man staring into an empty glass.

"Buy you another beer, if I can borrow your cell," Kris said.

The man fished his phone out of his pocket without looking up and handed it to her. She signaled the waitress and sat down across from him. She pulled the card with the phone number, which she'd folded into a tiny square, out of her pocket and flattened it on the table.

She was lucky that Justin had kept his mouth shut and didn't tell Barrett about the money or phone number that they'd found under the floor. Barrett had pressed them hard after they'd gotten out of the hospital; worrying at every damn detail. He wanted them back in the station Monday for follow-up questions and to sign their statements. Kris couldn't tell if Barrett suspected they were holding out on him and she was worried that Justin would lose his nerve overnight and crack if Barrett bore down on them again in the morning.

She picked up the phone. How the hell was she going to get the person who answered to identify themselves? Justin had told her to say that the electric company had had a computer glitch that had scrambled some customer accounts and that she was calling to confirm name and address information. But she'd have to wait until tomorrow to do that; no one would buy the story on a Sunday evening.

Kris didn't want to wait. She tapped in the number. It rang four times and then a woman's digitized voice announced: "You have reached 789-5544. Please leave a message and your call will be returned promptly." There was a pause and then the tone. Kris broke the connection. Slowly, she stuffed the card back into her pocket, left a five on the table, and walked out of the bar.

It hadn't rained in two days and the streets were dry and dusty. A tattered sheet of newsprint swirled in the slipstream of a passing car.

Yes.

Kris accelerated up the street, ignoring the bright lights in the Liquor Cache's window and the few people on the sidewalk. It made sense now. She crossed Front Street. Vern must have been blackmailing him. That's where the money under the floor had come from. Franklin Street slanted up and she leaned into the slope. Blackmail. What did the shit do? Kris pulled out a cigarette. Evie. Did he screw Evie? Christ. Worse than that? The sanctimonious shit. She lit the cigarette and drew in the smoke, pitching the match into the street. She'd seen it a million times. Some angel of righteousness preaching holy hellfire to the whores and crack heads on the street and then, when no one was looking, paying some kid, who hadn't had a serious meal in a week, a couple of bucks to jerk him off.

"Promptly." Who talks like that? Kris stopped suddenly outside the Baranof's glass doors and stared into the hotel's lobby. A couple of gray-haired women laughed soundlessly in the warmth and light, and intent men in suits strode purposively past them. Alvilde. Most likely she can't juice up and that's why he had to go looking. Couldn't imagine her on her back anyway. Or maybe she was part of it. Probably her way of keeping him off her. It happened all the time—a woman pushing her man into the street for his pussy so she didn't have to deal with it.

She turned away from the bright doors, hating the people behind them, hating the clean and the wealthy who played with people like Evie, who took what they wanted, and then tossed them back into the pits of their lives. Or killed them. Lambale had killed Evie. It fit. He knew her, he gave her money, he could talk her into his car and down to Thane, he wore expensive suits—the fibers in the bushes were his—only Lambale would murder somebody in a fancy suit. He'd taken what he wanted from her and when she turned on him, or when Vern turned her on him, he murdered her. Kris drew hard on her cigarette, coughed, spewing smoke into the air in front of her.

She turned on Third and suddenly her anger leapt to Justin. That shit. He hadn't believed her. Lambale's just being friendly; he feels sorry for you, he'd said. What did he know? Like having a mother who tucks you in at night teaches you anything about life.

Kris stopped halfway up the steep street, breathing hard, and searched Ben's window high on the hillside. It was lit, but too dimly for Kris to see if Ben was behind it sitting in his chair looking down at her. She flicked her cigarette up the hill in front of her. It arced through the darkness. Its orange tip glowing like an angry eye, it bounced on the gravel road, and rolled down the slope until it was stopped by a sharp-edged stone.

Ben didn't come to the door when she knocked. She knocked harder and heard a muffled yell. She pushed the door open; the house stank of sweat and piss. His chair was empty and the kitchen behind it, dark. Kris stepped into the front room and caught sight of him on a mattress off to the right against the back wall of the house.

"What's wrong, Ben?" She knelt by him. He was lying flat on the mattress in the same clothes he'd worn the day before with a pillow under his knees. His skin was the color of dishwater and had sunk in at the cheeks and temples.

"Not much," he said, forcing a smile.

"You look like shit."

"I'm OK."

"Bullshit. What's wrong?" He smelled. Kris plucked uncomfortably at the edge of the mattress.

"Back hurts."

"Have you been to a doctor?"

"No." Then, trying to make a joke: "Not since the service."

"Why not?"

"It'll get better." He took a breath. Kris looked at him; he looked away.

"What's this?" She reached for a bottle with apple juice or something in it.

"Urine," Ben said, not looking at it. It was full and warm. She put it down and wiped her hands on her pants.

"I'll call a doctor," she said, getting up.

"No."

"Why not?"

"I don't need a doctor." He looked directly at her, his eyes hard. "Understand?"

Kris looked at his bottle of piss; she should empty it. She should get him something to eat, too; if he couldn't make it to the bathroom, he couldn't make it to the kitchen. Maybe he had to take a dump. Kris picked again at the edge of the mattress, confused. On the street, weakness was something you hid; even from yourself if you could, and Ben's pain was so exposed it embarrassed her.

"Let me go down to the store and buy some pain killers," she said. "They probably have some special back medicine there or something."

Ben's face softened; he looked relieved, as if he wanted her out of there as badly as she wanted out. Kris picked her parka off the floor where she'd dumped it and walked to the door. Ben's head was hidden behind a small wooden chest pushed against the side wall. Kris made a racket, dropping a tin can with change in it off the little table on the far side of the door and, at the same time, she opened the wall cabinet and lifted out Ben's pistol. She dropped it into her pocket as she bent to pick up the coins and drop them back in the can. Then she walked back over to Ben, pulling on her mittens.

"I'll be back soon," she said. Ben nodded, his eyes fastened into space beyond the ceiling.

Kris dumped a collection of back pain medicines on the counter.

"Is this for your bald friend who doesn't get cold?" Martha asked.

"Yeah. He hurt his back."

"Has he seen a doctor?"

"He's not that kind of guy."

"I used to be a nurse."

"What are you doing this for then?" Kris pointed at the scanner.

"No doctors. No stress. No bedpans. Standard beef."

"I don't know what to do," Kris said. Don't sound too helpless.

"I'll stop by if you like. He seemed like a nice man."

"He's the nicest man I ever met," Kris said. "I think he's lonely too, but he won't say so."

Martha smiled. "Men usually don't. Where does he live?"

Kris told her.

"I'm off at ten. But Sunday evenings are slow. Maybe I can get out of here early."

Kris handed her the bag of medicine.

"Do you mind if I put some of this stuff back?" she said, picking through it. "It's all the same and all pretty useless."

"Sure."

"I'll find some other things that might work better and see what I can do."

MONDAY, NOVEMBER 16

This one was wild. Barrett had pissed-off women in his office before, but none had wrapped her fist around the muzzle of his M1 Abrams and pitched it against the wall. He watched her now, his face professional, his eyes piercing. She was sitting in the gray steel chair next to Justin, sullen and defiant; refusing to concede she'd made a complete hash of things out at Montana Creek. She needed something in her hand with more meat to it than a toy cannon.

He forced his mind back to Vern Jones. Why did Jones try to kill Kris? How did he know when she would arrive in Juneau? Where did he get the money for Evie's new clothes and the rent on the shack? If he worked, he did it off the books. The Department of Labor had no record of anyone paying UI taxes on him. Nor was there any cash found in the shack, although his forensics team was still taking it apart. Jones's rap sheet, which described a two-bit thug knocking randomly through life, held no clues: Four DUI convictions since he'd come into the state, two dismissed charges for assaults and a nolle prossed grand theft auto. Since there was only one road out of state, and it was a long one, people stole cars because they wanted a ride or because they needed them for another crime, like moving drugs or bodies. But if Jones was involved in anything bigger, it wasn't on his sheet.

Then there was Stewart and his strange coincidences: showing up in Juneau a few weeks after Vern and Evie had arrived, finding her body and the curious fact that they hadn't found any footprints belonging to the killer at the scene. Who else but an old trapper could hide his tracks so well?

Two suspects; one dead, neither likely to own an expensive wool suit, neither with an apparent motive and neither could be placed at the creek on the day Evie was murdered. A charge of adrenaline shot through his bloodstream—murders don't happen often in Juneau.

And this one had an unbroken Native wildcat.

Barrett was in the police business for the chase. When you caught what you were hunting, the fun was over. You could nail the rack over the fireplace, but life grayed if all you had left were stories about the kill. His best days had been in Iraq as tank sergeant of an M1A1 Abrams chasing the Republican Guard in their Soviet T72s towards Baghdad taking hits in the Battle of Basra and running the Karbala Gap just south of the capital. His unit was one of the first in the city, volunteering to road test a bridge over the Euphrates that hadn't collapsed after the Guard had mined it.

Half way through his second tour, a Sunni kid tossed a grenade through the open hatch when they were moving through a secured village south of Fallujah. Barrett, sitting on the lip of the hatch, his feet dangling inside, never saw the grenade coming and only looked into the tank when he heard it bounce onto the floor, watched it for an endless half-second, as it lay there rocking easily to the motion of the tank before it exploded, killing his loader and gunner and shredding his feet and calves. He was medivaced to Landstuhl Regional in Kaiserslautern, Germany and that had been the end of his war.

Juneau, where a simple assault was a big deal, was not an exciting place. He was here because it was home to a woman he'd pursued half way around the world; chasing her from the Baja and up the coast to San Francisco then across the Pacific to Vanuatu and the Marshalls—a woman whose glamour began to wilt the day he slipped a ring on her finger.

Barrett refocused on Kris and Justin. They'd finished signing the statements he'd taken from them yesterday and were waiting for him to speak. It was odd that Justin had gone down to the creek to gawk at the murder site. Sometimes amateurs return to the scene of their crime, but Barrett dismissed him; there was a tinniness to Justin, as if he couldn't dig his paddle into the current and just sort of twirled along on top of it. Though now, after killing Jones, he was a hero. Barrett was not impressed. He figured they'd been saved by dumb luck. And if it made Justin cocky, he'd be killed next time: dumb luck tended not to be reliable.

Kris stood. Barrett had been silent too long; he put out his hand and shooed her back into her chair, careful not to look at her breasts, which were high and unstayed.

"I can't keep you from trying to find the murderer," he said, "but let's make a deal. Let me give you this." Barrett opened a desk drawer and pulled out a cell phone. "Just carry it with you and any time you need help or information, call me. OK?" He looked at Kris.

"You never know when you might need it," he said.

She didn't respond.

He put it back in the drawer. He picked up Evie's leather purse, which had been lying on his desk, and coiled the drawstring. "So, is there anything else you haven't told me?"

Kris held his eyes and shook her head. In the periphery of his vision he saw Justin glance at her and then drop his eyes to the floor.

"Justin?" he asked with an edge in his voice. "You've got something to add?"

"Nope, we've said it all."

Barrett kept his eyes on him a second longer than necessary; he needed to get him away from Kris. "All right," he said. "Let me know if you learn anything new." He handed the purse back to Kris. "Check in later today. Vital Statistics will have gotten back to me by then."

A clerk waited for Kris and Justin to pass through the door before entering the office. He dropped a fax in Barrett's in-basket and left. Barrett glanced at it and then hit the intercom button to the front desk. "Send Miss Gabriel back in here, please."

When she reappeared, he stood and handed her the fax. Her eyes flashed over the sheet and when she glanced up at him again they were darkening.

"Easy," he said. "We don't know the whole story."

She dropped the paper onto the desk and walked out.

Barrett watched her go—he'd give her five, maybe ten minutes—then sank back into his chair, pleased.

Now he had motive.

■ ■ ■

Kris raced out of the police station and into the morning darkness. Justin yelled something about working late. It was raining again; her feet slapped in water puddled on the sidewalks. She rounded the Red Dog onto Franklin and jogged up the street, which was busy with the morning rush of people and cars.

Her eyes had stumbled over the fax, unable to find anything to latch on to. From nowhere, something squeezed her chest. Finally, across the top, she saw and understood: State of Alaska, Certificate of Birth. But none of the names looked familiar, until she deciphered Evangeline Gabriel. And then she knew. Birth of: Corvus Stewart. Father: Benjamin Stewart. Her heart had started beating again.

Kris jogged up Franklin Street. People dodged out of her way. Under her parka, sweat broke through her skin. Why hadn't he told her? Up Franklin, right on Third, slowing as she climbed the hill to his staircase. It was her mother. Her brother, for *fuck's* sake. He was playing with her. She reached the steps and labored up them, ringing the metal grates, losing speed as she climbed, her lungs pulling for air.

The house was dark. She pushed through the door without knocking. The air inside was still and heavy with the smell of piss. Ben lay on his mattress, in the same clothes and with the same pillow under his knees. She stood over him, panting, mouth opening and then she saw his eyes.

"Don't do that again." His voice, cold and vicious, sliced into her. "Do not mother me. Do not send strangers to mother me. Leave me alone. Is that clear?"

It was quiet. A second. Two. Kris started breathing again. Fury, red as blood, blinded her.

"Then lie there in your own stinking piss," she yelled. "What the fuck do I care?" She stormed out the door and crashed down the stairs. She skidded down the gravel street; the pebbles, lubricated by the rainwater washing down the hill, slipped and turned under her feet. At the bottom, she gulped air and thrust her uncovered head into the rain and stormed the sidewalks. Rage—at Lambale, at Ben, at the whole fucking situation—ignited in her head and hammered the inside of her skull and she was lost to the cold, the people, hunched in their rain gear, who ducked out of her way, and the rain that fell on her, wicking down her hair and into the clothes beneath her parka.

Hours later, wet and shivering, her head throbbing, she pushed through the door into the Lucky Lady. The Miller-Lite clock glowed white on the wall behind the pool table: it wasn't even noon yet.

Five hours to kill.

■ ■ ■

Kris peered through the slit between the door and its frame. The black Mercedes sat alone under the harsh lights. It was quiet. No car had drifted down the ramp in the last five minutes. Kris widened the slit with her fingers and checked the row of parking places against the other wall. Only two cars left. She released the door, letting it close on the mitten stuffed between it and the frame.

She straightened and looked away from the door into the night. The rain had turned to snow. Sloppy flakes fell out of the sky, floating into view just above her head, dimming the lights in Douglas across the channel and muffling the slick of tires on the city's streets. The emergency stairs she stood on, at the back of the garage, were rimmed with snow, finger-deep, and it was falling fast.

She put her eye back to the slit.

Ben's pistol weighted her parka.

Her hands shook, a tremor she couldn't still. She felt as if her body were strung together by barbed wire. Too much coffee and beer. And cigarettes; she needed one now. Her mouth was dry and stale. She scooped up a handful of snow and let it melt on her tongue, swishing the trickle of water through her teeth before spitting it over the railing onto the wharf below. It didn't help.

She gathered another handful of snow and rubbed it, cold and rough, against her face.

She didn't know what she was going to do.

Distantly, through the concrete walls, she heard the electronic bleat of the elevator signaling floors as it climbed. She waited. The doors slid open and Lambale walked out. His hat and overcoat were flecked with snow and he was alone.

He transferred his briefcase to his left hand and rummaged in his pocket for his keys with his right. Lambale thumbed the key bob and she heard the locks click open. He opened the door, setting his hat in the back seat, and sat heavily in the car. Kris picked up her mitten, squeezed through the door, and ran across the concrete floor; her legs rubbery and distant and the aftertaste of beer thick in her mouth. The Mercedes' lights came on, the engine muttered, the exhaust echoing hollowly in the empty garage, and the car began backing out of the parking space. Kris ran around the back end of the car and pulled open the passenger door. Lambale rammed the brakes and swung his head toward her, startled.

"Hi Loren," Kris said, ducking into the seat.

"Kris! This is a surprise. What are you up to?" He shifted into park and turned more fully in his seat, resting an arm on the steering wheel, to face her.

"I need to talk to you." She smiled at him.

"Sure." He looked pleased. The fat on his neck rolled over his collar. "Do you want to come out to the house again for dinner? It'd be a little less formal. TV dinners or canned beans. Alvilde is at an Arts and Humanities meeting until eight."

"No cook?" She fought to keep her voice light. Could he smell the beer on her breath?

"No. When the kids are gone, she's only in a few nights a week." He shifted into reverse and finished backing the car out.

"I want to go down to Thane, Loren."

In the dimness, Lambale's eyebrows rose in surprise and then his face became somber. "If you wish," he said. He turned right out of the garage and they sped past the darkened tourist shops, boarded up for the winter, toward Thane. The snow in the street had been churned into transparent slush.

"I read the article in the Empire today about Montana Creek. Sounds terrifying."

"It wasn't too bad."

"Pretty amazing thing your friend did."

"Justin? Yeah." Kris couldn't keep the talk going; she felt closed in and her head rang and her heart was beating too fast.

Lambale glanced at her and drove on in silence. The heater began pumping in hot air, the plastic smell thickened; she needed air, but couldn't figure out the buttons on the arm rest to lower the window.

She wanted a confession. She wanted him broken and pleading.

"Kris," he said. "Your mother and I. Ah..." He faltered.

Kris turned toward him, hardening. *Don't toy with me*, she warned silently. The car sped over a short bridge and began climbing a hill. Snowflakes swirled in the headlights and blew into the windshield. The lights from the dash colored his face sickly green.

"Do you ever wonder who your father is?" he asked not looking at her. His grip tightened on the wheel.

She gasped like a fish sucking air and the anger that flooded into her took seconds to gather. *Leave me alone*. Once, a man had slept with her mother. That's all she knew. When Kris was young, Evie'd told her that he'd been handsome, had brought her a flower and held her hands and Kris, in her prayers, had begged him to come and take her away—away from the cold, the fighting, the booze, from Evie. Later, she realized that Evie was lying; that she'd made him up. When Kris pushed for more, Evie became frenzied and upset; not looking her in the face and crying, "I don't remember, I don't remember." And Kris knew then that her father was just another nameless man who had gotten what he wanted from Evie and, even if he'd known he'd fathered a child, would've tossed it aside as carelessly as a drunk pitching an empty into the street. As carelessly as he'd discarded Evie.

"No, never," she answered him. She stifled her anger, hiding it from him, but it clotted in her mind and she clung to the armrest, unable to think.

"Kris." He glanced at her, his face unreadable in the shadows. She stared back, her face hard, giving him nothing. He released his breath. "Sorry."

The silence in the car grew as thick as the falling snow and when they pulled up to the guardrail at the end of the road, Lambale tried to break it.

"Twenty years in Juneau and I've never once hiked this trail," he said as if the tension between them weren't there. "Wrong end of town, I guess. Are we going to get out?"

Kris nodded and opened her door. The overhead light came on.

"Why, Kris?" Lambale asked.

Kris looked at him; his face was pasty in the weak light. "Remember the pictures and stuff you showed me at your house?" she said. "I want to show you this; it's important to me." She searched his face; it softened.

"Of course," he said. "I understand." He reached down, triggered something on the floor and the trunk sprung open. He walked around to the rear and pulled out a flashlight. "Might be handy," he said, turning it on and shaking it until the light shone.

Wet flakes landed on Kris's cheeks. The snow was falling heavier here and it lay deeper on the ground, deeper than the black rubbers Lambale had over his leather shoes. He picked his way gingerly, waving the light around the trees. Kris took it out of his hand and pointed to the end of the guardrail. Lambale slipped coming down the slope at the beginning of the trail, windmilling his arms to keep his balance. When the trail leveled off, he walked in the yellow oval thrown by the flashlight. Snow collected on the bottom of his trousers and Kris kept her eyes on the whitened cuffs as they flashed in and out of the dim light.

They came onto the bridge and Kris stopped him. Behind them, the stream crashed invisibly down the mountainside. She pointed the light downstream; the beam disappeared in the thick flakes.

"You killed her, Loren." Kris whispered. The stream was too loud to talk here.

Lambale placed his hand on her shoulder and bent his head close to her ear. "Is this where your mother was killed?" he shouted. The light was on his feet, his legs rose out of it into the dark.

"As if you didn't know," she said and lifted the light.

His face was hung with shadows. Did it harden, his eyes narrow?

Kris pointed the light down the path. She heard him say something. Was he whining?

Kris motioned again. He walked toward the far end of the bridge; Kris followed. When he stepped onto the trail, he turned and looked at her. She waved him forward. They waded through the snow, shallow and uneven under the trees whose interwoven branches caught and held the snow high above the trail. They walked, stumbling over unseen roots and slipping when the trail sloped up or down, until the stream's roar faded. Enough falling snow escaped the branches to muffle the sound of their breathing and the darkness beyond the beam of the flashlight was impenetrably black. The night pressed in. She breathed.

"Stop here."

Lambale turned around. "What are you doing, Kris?" There was authority in his voice.

"Loren." Her voice shivered. "You killed my mother."

His face was hidden; the light pointed down at the snow.

"What are you talking about?"

Kris shone the beam into his face. He blinked and brought his hand up, gloved in leather, to shade his eyes. She pulled it down. He squinted, but the light was not bright.

"You screwed my mother, Loren." His eyes widened. No denial.

"You fucked her, Vern blackmailed you, and you killed her." Kris's voice hardened; heat bloomed in her chest, climbed into her face.

"Kris, that's absurd." He waved his hand, dismissing her.

"I know it."

"No, Kris. It's not—"

"You killed her." The words were louder, bitten out of the air.

"I don't know where you –."

"Don't bullshit me."

"What do you want from me Kris?" He straightened, showed his palms: a reasonable man making a deal with a child.

"Say it," she yelled.

"I didn't kill her." He pushed past her, heading back for the car.

"Loren, stop." She shook off a mitten, let it fall into the snow. "Turn around."

He turned. The .38 was in her hand. She put the light on it.

"Put it away, Kris. You've been drinking."

She flashed the light back into his eyes. They blinked.

"Say it." She had him now.

"Kris, this is dangerous. Put—"

Turning the pistol so he could see, she pushed off the safety. He raised his arms and let them drop against his legs. She stepped forward, close to him, the pistol leveled. Her breath was harsh—it bit her throat—she felt herself hurtling.

"I didn't—"

"Your name was with a pile of cash at Vern's."

"No." The air rushed out of him.

Kris shoved the barrel into his stomach. He moved his hand to brush it away and she whipped it against his fingers.

He gripped his fingers. "Kris. Be reasonable."

"Reasonable. Did Evie ask you to be reasonable?"

She jabbed the gun into him again. He jerked back, slipped, fell; a black shape tumbling in the dark. The light followed him down. Scrambling, trying to get to his hands and knees, floundering in the snow. Kris put her foot on his shoulder and heaved. His knees slid over the edge, feet thrashing for a hold on the steep, off-hill, side of the trail.

"Kris," he called from the ground, the authority in his voice breaking.

She knelt in front of him, power surged through her, riding her nerves. His face was yellow and unstable in the light; it twisted, shadows broke across it.

"I-I did some things wrong—" He stopped.

"You did what things wrong?" Her voice was high.

"I, oh God." His head dropped.

"Tell me." Kris pushed the barrel into his forehead and forced his head back. His face came into the light again. She was shaking.

"Kris," he whispered.

"What things wrong?" Her pulse, amped by the beer, thudded in her brain.

"I...Sex." He looked at her, his eyes pleading.

"Everybody screwed Evie. No one shot her." She pressed the barrel into his forehead. His head skidded off it and slumped to the ground. His hat toppled into the snow and strands of hair sagged outward.

"Did you pay her for it?" She taunted; victory swelling in her.

His head, pale under thinning hair, didn't move.

"You shit, you didn't give her anything?"

The head was still.

"You took it?" Suddenly an added tension charged the air.

Then it connected. "You raped her." On her feet; losing control.

His face lifted. Pathetic. "I tried to help her. I—"

"Help her. Mr. Friend to abused women. Get your picture in the paper. "

"No!" Pulling into himself. "No, that's not—" Shouting, now. "That's not the way it was. I tried—" He surged up, a black shape against the night, coming at her. She swung the pistol with both hands, the flashlight tumbled into the snow. He slapped the gun aside. It exploded like a bomb blast, the gun jumping in her hand. She staggered, dazed, the roar striking like a sledge against her ears.

Then she heard Lambale screaming. The scream rushed at her out of the darkness. "No! Kris!" Frantic, she spun, confused, lost in the night; she slipped, fell.

She lifted the gun.

"You don't under—" He was on top of her.

From the snow, she pointed up, pulled the trigger. Ears slammed. Blinded by the muzzle flash. She rolled, jumped to her feet.

He was a black shape in the snow, crawling.

The night warped around her, a voice screeched in her skull, like metal tearing. The gun lifted, tracked, aimed and the night exploded again and again and again.

■ ■ ■

Kris spun, stumbled, fell to her knees. Her chest heaved, straining at air too thin. Nothing to fill her lungs.

She fell onto her hands trying to hang on. Her stomach lifted. Beer and chips erupted into the night. She saw nothing. Breathe. God, it was hard to breathe.

She tumbled sideways into the snow coiling into a knot.

Her cheek melted into the snow and more snow fell before the hammering in her head quieted and the air became easier to breathe. A snowflake landed in an eyelash. Another on her ear. Cold bit at a wrist exposed to the air. Her hip hurt, squashed against the hard ground. The side of her face buried in the snow burned with cold.

"Jesus," she whispered.

She untangled herself and rolled onto her hands and knees. The night was grayer now, not as black as it was when her eyes had been focused on the flashlight's beam. She looked behind her and saw it glowing faint and feeble under the snow. Beyond it, on the edge of the trail, was a motionless lump.

Oh God.

She stood, tottered. A leg had gone to sleep. She shivered. The cold and wet had seeped into her.

What now?

Snow was still falling.

What do I do now?

In the gray-blackness, the snow on the ground around her was torn and chewed. Black stains splattered it. Blood. And puke. Did she puke? She could taste it now, bitter and acrid.

God.

Fear trickled in. She shivered, she couldn't stop, her arms and legs began to shake. She had to get out of there.

Kris began to move. Dimly, hysterically.

Grab the light. God it's dim. Turn it off. Save it. Where's the gun? Fell over here. Kick the snow—got it. Cold. Smell it, the powder. What am I going to do with it? Put it in pocket for now. Mittens, where'd they go? One in my pocket, the other—by the light. Right, stick it in a pocket. Lambale. Raped her. God, I didn't mean to do it. He attacked me. Dusted with snow already. What am I going to do with him? God he's big. Half off the trail. How steep is it? Can't see a thing. Try it. It's going to be a chore. Dig in here, hands on shoulders. Oh shit. Blood. Push. Push. Get over the edge, motherfucker. Push. Jesus, moving fast. Like somebody grabbed him. How far will he go? To the beach? Someone will see it. Can't hear a thing. Did he stop? What else? Blood. Make snowballs and pitch them. What else? Oh shit, puke. Push it over the edge with your foot. His hat, toss it. OK. Still snowing. How much longer? What else? Footprints. Hide the footprints. Even it out, here. Grab some fresh stuff. Looking good. Couple more inches of snow and no one could tell. What else? What else? Am I OK? Forget something now, I'm hosed. This is it. Move. Move. Get out of here.

Kris followed their trail out, reeling, off balance in the dark on the snow-covered ground. Her heart began to slow. Put some miles on it today. She tripped, fell to a knee. The roaring of the stream grew louder. What next? Get the car back to the garage. Dump the gun. Set up an alibi. What do I need? How long have I been gone? Thirty minutes max.

Oh, God!

She stopped, blood icing in her veins. The car keys.

Did he leave them in the car? Does he have a spare hidden in it? The ashtray? Can I leave the car here?

No. It drummed in her brain. No. No. I'm not going back.

She felt herself begin to crumple, the ground under her shifting, the first small pebbles and rocks spilling out from under her feet and spilling into the void. Oh, God.

The night, the snow, the trees made no sound.

She packed her fingers into fists and pressed them against her ears.

Quit jerking around. It's you. Move.

She turned. It was blacker that way, back into the trees and the trail of their footprints disappeared instantly. She lifted a foot.

It took a long time to find the spot. She peered over the edge of the trail where Lambale had been swallowed by the night and saw nothing. Putting her feet over the side, she backed down, her hands, out of her mittens now, floundering in the dark for jutting angles of rocks and crooked roots to hang on to. It wasn't sheer, but it was steep. Lambale had scraped the slope clear of snow and when she veered off his track, her hands found snow instead of spruce needles and dirt.

She stepped onto the body. It gave under her foot. She jerked back, let her breath catch up to her. She turned and squatted above it. It was shapeless; merging without edges into the black night and the black tree trunk it was twisted up against. There was no snow on it. Maybe the ravens would find it faster.

She couldn't make out anything, head, arms and legs were lost in the night. She fumbled for the flashlight zippered into a pocket. She clicked the button. Nothing. She shook it, the batteries clunked back and forth. The bulb glowed, barely strong enough to show the creases in her hand.

Move.

She crouched forward, pointed the beam on the shape. The clothes were ripped and tangled; blood-soaked snow and dirt were packed into their folds and creases. Chest. Leaning on her left hand, she pointed the light up; the beam disappeared. She crawled to the right bringing the light closer. She leaned over him, her eyes just behind the bulb, searching for detail.

Chin. Wrong end. Streaks of black blood, glistening dully, oozed from the mouth. Still flowing.

She pressed her cheek against the light's shaft, its feeble beam barely jutting into the night. She moved it up his face.

His eyes were open. Brown like hers.

They blinked.

She recoiled in terror. The light fell from her fingers, bounced under the body.

Beneath her, the ground disappeared, she fell—

"Kris."

Oh, God.

She froze, still as death, her eyes fastened on the blackness where his eyes had been.

She heard his breathing now. Raspy, faint. It caught, gurgled, then released.

"Kris. I, I'm…" Whisper soft.

She needed the keys. There was nothing else she was going to do. She reached into the dark and touched his far shoulder, his right one. She ran her hand down his side, fast, through blood, sticky and wet, cold snow, and tangled fabric. She found his waist and hopped left on her knees to come down to it. Her fingers found his belt, then pushed and probed at his pants searching for the opening of his pocket. The fabric was tight, stretched by his leg bent off at an impossible angle. Where was it? She found the slit of the pocket. Yanked at it to open it wider and pushed her fingers in. Warmth. His. There was change, loose up near the top. The pocket fabric was tucked under itself. She pulled at it, probing recklessly, digging her fingers past the fold.

He groaned. The sound wavered behind her.

Keys. She had them. Some were stuck, tangled in the fabric. She stood and wrenched. His leg spasmed, his body shuddered.

He sobbed.

She tugged them free.

Move.

She raced up the mountainside, pulling at the roots and rocks, digging her fingers into the soil, her feet struggled for purchase, sometimes slipping, pitching her full length into the slope.

Shit. No!

The flashlight. It was under him. It had her fingerprints all over it.

Oh, God! Get me away from him.

Don't think about it. Just go. Go!

She slid back down, moving fast. Hands, feet, knees, and elbows flailing against the ground trying to control her fall. Avalanches of dirt and needles and snow tumbled and bounced down with her.

Stop. This is it.

She dug in, dragged her weight to a stop.

The glow peeked out from under him.

Don't say anything. Just be dead.

She reached under, closed her fingers around it and pulled.

Is there anything else?

She climbed back up on all fours, slower, panting, the air burning in her throat. At the trail she staggered erect and fled back to the car, stumbling and falling, blind in the snow-ridden night.

■ ■ ■

Her lungs stopped her. She propped herself on her knees and pumped air into them. Above her was the guardrail and beyond that the Mercedes. Up in the trees were houses and people and she knew that she had to do this right. If she blew it, she wouldn't get a second chance.

Why did he have to be alive?

Her breathing slowed. She stood and looked up at the rail, a dark band at the top of the little slope that started the trail. Kris needed a cigarette.

Blood, dirt, what a mess. Can't get this all over the car. She picked up handfuls of snow and rubbed at her pants and parka, trying to wash off what she couldn't see. She shook the needles out of her hair and tied it in a knot. When she was ready, she walked quietly up to the end of the trail. Out from under the trees, the falling snow was still thick and impenetrable. The Mercedes, across the circle of pavement, was invisible. There was no other sound or light.

She stepped onto the pavement, walked quickly to the car pulling out the key ring; which button was the lock, which was the car alert? She guessed, pressing—the door locks clicked. She pulled off the parka, turned it inside out, and laid it on the seat before sitting on it. She pulled her mittens back on, felt for the ignition, and, gripping the key through the thick caribou leather, pushed it in. The car started. She clicked the lights and windshield wipers alive. Not wanting to mess with the seat adjustment, she sat on the edge of the seat, threw the car into reverse, and backed into a turn, pointing the car toward Juneau.

Five miles to town, stash the car in the garage. Once in the garage, she was committed. There were no places to hide.

The snow swirled through the beams of the headlights, reflecting light back at her. The big flakes were starting to pile up on top of the slush in the road. She drove slowly, edging the car into the snow and dark. Both mittened hands were clamped on the wheel; her face was thrust forward, eyes fixed at the limit of the lights, where the night closed in.

The dash clock said 6:45. One and a half hours—too long. It can't be right.

The Mercedes climbed up the hill by the tank farm, its lights hard and brilliant even through the snow.

Why hadn't he been dead?

A pair of headlights exploded out of the night behind her. Light blasted through the back window, ricocheting off the rearview mirror into Kris's eyes. Her fingers locked onto the steering wheel. They were right on her tail; aggressive, pushy.

They stayed on top of her.

Too high for a cop. It was a truck. Four wheel drive and twenty-five miles an hour was too stinking slow for it. She followed the road left, then right down the hill, pass the boarded up tourist shops, and entered town; the truck glued to her rear.

If someone asks him tomorrow, is he going to remember a black Mercedes coming up Thane?

The garage loomed on her left. Brake. Signal. The pickup accelerated past her on the right, it disappeared into the snow. She turned in and drove up three ramps to the top like she belonged there. Four cars were parked there, no people. Lambale's spot was on the floor below. She pulled into a space, shifted to park, and craned her head over both shoulders, checking for people, before getting out. She left the engine running. Behind the driver's seat she found a snow brush and quickly—stay in control— brushed off the snow. Water beaded on the black steel. Leave it. The garage was empty, hollow.

She slid back into the car and coasted it down the ramp to Lambale's level. No cars, no people.

Which spot was his? Each space was numbered and she hadn't a clue. Move—just go for it. She chose one that felt right, killed the engine, and pulled out the key. What else? Look. Think. Shit, the flashlight. She dug it out of the parka's pocket, wiped it down, and opened the trunk stashing it under the spare. Wait. She scrambled for it. Leave it on, explain the dead batteries.

Is he dead yet?

She lowered the trunk and leaned on it. It clicked shut. No noise. Nobody. She turned her head, scanning, probing: the garage was empty. She walked slowly—walk normal—to the emergency exit at the rear and squeezed through the heavy door onto the landing. Her footprints— two hours ago?—were gone, filled with new snow. The door clunked-clicked behind her. She exhaled.

It was still snowing. Good.

Kris backed into the shadows and looked down the wharf. At the far end, under a light, someone was walking a dog. He was headed away. The garage hid the other end of the wharf. She put on the parka, raised the hood, zippering it closed. She walked down the stairs. Kicking at the snow, she walked out onto the wharf. No one but the person walking the dog. She wandered in the other direction, occasionally scooping up a handful of snow, packing it into a ball, and lobbing it into the water. Without breaking her rhythm—scooping, packing, throwing—she pressed the car keys into one and heaved it into the night. It plopped into the black sea water, bobbed to the surface, turned clear as it absorbed water, and then, disintegrated.

She scooped, packed, and lobbed another.

Is he crawling up that hill now?

The wharf ended at a gangplank for driving cars onto ships. She walked over a metal gantry back to the shore, walked around the gangplank and back onto the wharf on the other side. It was darker on this side, fewer lights and no houses up on the hill. She threw another snowball; it curled into the night. She knelt, pulled out the pistol and packed snow around it.

Standing at the edge of the wharf, she lobbed it like a grenade. It broke apart in the air and the pistol splashed sharply into the water a moment before the flying snow pattered into the water around it.

She waited a moment and then lobbed another snow grenade.

Enough.

She turned slowly around. Looking for peeking faces, unwanted eyes. She was alone.

Ben had probably registered the gun. If they found it, it would be traced to him, ballistics would match the bullets and since he was lying in bed pissing in a bottle, it would come straight to her. He would tell them she knew it was in his cupboard.

Damn. Fingerprints. She hadn't wiped it down. Will the sea water wash them off? She looked back at the black water; the snowflakes vanished into it like magic. Was that her first mistake?

What else?

His eyes—they'd blinked.

Had someone heard the shots?

Someone could be walking down that path right now.

Kris walked off the wharf, her head down, tucked in her hood. She cut across the dark edge of the parking lot, crossed the road, and walked toward town. At the first staircase, she climbed up to Gastineau Avenue. The street was squeezed by old houses and a line of parked cars. No one was on it. Cars had chewed the snow gray.

Ten minutes later she pushed open the door to Justin's dark apartment. Empty. Good. She shook the snow off her parka and hung it in the closet.

Alibi.

She had to make it look like she'd been there for hours. Since five. She turned on the TV and DVD player, slid in a disk, and hit fast forward. There was nothing she'd eat in the refrigerator, but the freezer was stuffed with frozen pizza. She stripped the box off one and put it in the microwave. Back to the DVD, she switched it to "play" and men and women appeared on the screen. Laundry. And a shower. Did she have the time? Go for it. Dirt and blood streaked her pants. Damn. Remember to check the parka and the mittens. She followed a hallway back and found a utility room with washer and drier. She stripped, dumped everything in the washer, added soap and kicked it off. Clothes. Check Justin's bedroom for a shirt. She dug a thick blue shirt out of a box in his bedroom. It came to mid-thigh. Most sex he's had in months. Shower. Can't stay in too long. Don't want him to find me here. The water stung; she edged up the hot until it flailed her skin. Pink. Red. Should change the bandage on this nipple. Out. Dry. Yuck, doesn't he ever wash his towels? Shirt on. Socks? Back in his bedroom, a pair of woolen ones in the same box.

Had she over nuked the pizza? She stuck her finger in the cheese. Warm, not hot. A couple more minutes. Can't eat yet. Check the parka for blood. Brown smears on it and smears all over the mittens. Wipe them down: sponge and cleaner under the sink. Ecoshit. Better be strong. Hang parka back in closet. Should dry clean it when get a chance.

After eight. How much longer have I got?

Listen for the washer. Spin cycle.

Manuel!

Call Manuel. Supposed to do that yesterday. Good. That will prove her here at 8:05,

"Manuel? Kris...Juneau...Yeah, I know...What am I, a Buddhist? Yeah, I know it's Christmas...She was murdered...Thanks...Not a clue... The cop's a white boy, you know what that means –...Exacto...Thanks, Manuel...Yeah. Adios."

Hang up. Click. Do what you got to do. Manuel's OK.

Washer's stopped. Throw everything in the drier. Crank it on high.

Find a blanket, reheat pizza.

Is that everything?

The manic energy that had driven her since she'd climbed back up the slope to the trail suddenly exhausted itself. She slumped into the sofa, set the plate of pizza down beside her and, from deep in her core, began to shake.

The screen was blue—Kris couldn't remember when the DVD had ended—and the pizza still uneaten when she heard Justin coming down the stairs. He opened the door, hair and eyelashes snow-flecked.

"Hey, this is great." Justin smiled and shook himself out of his jacket. It was a new one. No bullet holes. "How long have you been here?"

"Since about five."

"Really? I guessed seven-thirty, by your footprints on the steps."

Oh shit.

"Went out for a smoke."

"Should've guessed. Hey, you're wearing my Klondike shirt. Good to see some skin." He looked at her legs showing under the blanket.

"I took a shower and did a laundry."

"Didn't like the pizza?" he said, looking at the uneaten slices on her plate.

She touched one, it was cold. "I forgot about it."

Justin looked at her. "You OK?"

"Yeah, I'm fine," she said. "Where've you been?"

"Work. It took me forever to install the new version of Big Bruiser."

"Big Bruiser?"

"System scheduler. The old one ran in Windows. Talk about antique. The new one runs in Linux. Not any better, really, but at least it's compatible with the rest of the system." Justin picked up her plate. "Mind if I heat this up?"

She shook her head and he stuck it into the microwave.

"Beer?" He poured himself a glass.

"No, thanks."

He emptied the glass and refilled it. "What were you so steamed about this morning down at the station?"

Kris looked at him blankly. This morning was a long time ago. Oh. She considered. Justin didn't need to know about Ben being father to her brother.

"He's such an asshole."

"Barrett?"

Kris didn't answer. Ben. The numbness that buffered her crumbled away and a clammy chill settled in its place. She remembered Ben's voice—cold and angry. Why did he have to yell at her?

"I think he's doing a decent job," Justin said.

"He talks down to me." Kris was dismissive; she didn't want to talk about it.

Justin collected the pizza carton and squashed it into a trash can under the sink.

"Did you ever call that number?"

"What number?"

"The one we found in the cookie tin. At Vern's."

"Oh, yeah." Scramble. "It was disconnected. All I got was a recording."

"I wonder if the phone company would tell us whose it was and when it was disconnected." He glanced at her. She shrugged; she wanted him to forget about it. "Why don't you call me at work with it tomorrow and I'll see what I can find out."

"OK." Shit, he wouldn't forget.

The microwave beeped. Justin pulled out the pizza, picked up his glass, and walked over to the sofa, pushing aside newspapers so that he could sit down next to her. She shook her head when he offered her a slice.

"Did you see my picture in the paper today? Good article, too."

Kris shook her head again and he handed it to her.

"You know. Something's been bugging me. Yesterday, in Barrett's office, near the end when he was asking you about Ben, you said that the last time he'd been up to his cabin was six years ago."

Kris nodded. It was a good picture of Justin on the front page. He had the piece of pipeline in one hand and the jacket with the bullet holes in the other.

"You're sure he said six years?" He looked at her, chewing; strings of cheese connected his mouth to the piece in his hand.

"Uh huh."

"Well, remember when we went up to his place after we'd been down Thane? He said then that he was last out there the winter after the Koyukuk flooded. That was 2013, two years ago. I know the guy who headed up the emergency response and relief effort for the governor."

"So?"

"He didn't tell us how long he'd really been down Thane, either."

He didn't tell her he and Evie had a boy together, either.

"Seems curious. Something you might want to ask him."

"Can't."

Justin had just taken another bite, and she watched him reduce it before asking her why.

"He hurt his back. I went out and got him a nurse and he got pissed off. He jumped all over me."

"Alaska bushman won't take help from nobody."

"Hang on," Kris said and walked down the hall to check her clothes. They were hot. She changed, dropped his shirt in his bedroom, and came back into the front room. Justin was working on another slice.

Kris looked again at the newspaper. The article spelled her name wrong. Chris.

"How old is he?" Justin asked.

"I don't know. He got up here in the fifties, though. Worked on radars on the north slope."

"The DEW line. Mid-nineteen fifties and sixties, which puts him in his mid-seventies today. So he was getting a Bonus six years ago."

Kris looked at him, lost.

"If he was getting a Bonus, we have his address on file. We can tell where he was getting his check sent to."

"What Bonus?"

"Longevity Bonus. Remember I told you I work on the system that sends monthly checks to Alaskans over sixty-five?"

"Oh, yeah." Kris couldn't remember him telling her.

"So you want to go look?"

"Where?"

"At the office. I've got keys to the state office building. If we want to go now, we've got to move. Big Bruiser's scheduled to kick off at nine. It's ten till."

Checking up on Ben was pointless; Evie's murderer was dead. But she couldn't tell Justin that. "OK," she said.

■ ■ ■

It was still snowing. The sidewalks were covered with a foot of snow, so they walked in the streets. Orange trucks, with whirling yellow lights, rumbled in and out of sight behind the city blocks spinning dirty snow off plow blades like breaking waves.

Kris followed Justin into the state office building through a door on a loading dock.

"It's easier, ALB is on this floor."

"What about security?"

"Most of them know me. Any time month-end blows, I'm camped out down here all night mothering it along."

Justin opened the inner door leading from the loading dock into a long, windowless corridor that looked like it had been bored through the belly of the building. They walked down it, turning left into a narrower hall. Justin punched buttons on a panel and a line of light appeared under a door at the far end; he opened it with another key.

"This is it. Home. I probably spend more conscious hours here than anywhere else." He led her back to a corner cubicle packed with manuals, stacks of paper, and the scattered guts of electronics. On the desk were a couple of PCs. "Let me reschedule Big Bruiser." Justin booted a machine and Kris lost interest. Behind his desk, a window blackened by the night reflected her lighted forehead and chin. The night pooled in the hollows of her cheeks and the cavities of her eyes. She ran her fingers through her hair, black and coarse, shaking it out on her shoulders.

What if they find him?

"OK. Big Bruiser's out of the way. Let me fire up the system and take a look at Ben's file." Justin waited while the computer did its thing.

"What was his last name? Stewart, right?" More clicks. "Whoops. We got a few Ben Stewarts. Must be this one, only one with a Juneau address."

Kris watched over his shoulder. She couldn't follow the boxes and windows that leapt around the screen at Justin's frenzied clicks.

"He started getting his checks at the Third Street address here in Juneau last May. Before that, he got them at a P. O. box in Fairbanks. No change of address since 2006. So if he went up to the Alatna, two winters ago, his checks kept going to Fairbanks."

"What about before 2006?"

"Can't say, that was the year we put in the new system and the old system didn't keep historical data. Let's see. No remote status either. Remotes are people who live in the bush and can't get to a post office every month. So we hold their checks until they come out. You figure if he was at his cabin for the winter, he'd be on remote. Let me pull his file." Justin left the cubicle. A file drawer screeched and in a second he was back with a manila folder which he dropped on the desk and started paging through.

"Yup. Here's a remote application for '99. Looks like he was remote every winter through '06. Six years ago."

"What's going on?" Kris wasn't tracking.

"The computer thinks he was in Fairbanks the winter of '13-14, which was the winter after the flood. But I'm sure he said he was last up at his cabin then." Justin looked at her but his eyes were focused in space.

"Maybe they were forwarded. Like up to Allakaket," she said.

He clicked up another box on the computer. "No, look, all his checks that winter were cashed on the third or fourth of each month. No time to forward them north."

"Maybe someone else deposited the checks for him," Kris said.

"Wouldn't do any good. He's still got to sign the stub. Recipients have to attest that they are in state each month they get a Bonus. You can't get a Bonus if you're out of state." Justin riffled through a stack of papers and pulled out a piece of light blue paper about a third the size of a normal sheet. He pointed to the signature line. "They have to sign this and send it back here."

"They have to do this every month?" Kris asked.

"Yeah."

"You check all the signatures?"

"No, only that there's one there." Justin was slumped in his chair, diddling with the mouse. "Shit."

It was the first time Kris had heard him swear. "So, someone else could've signed it," she said.

"Of course" Justin sat up and started clicking again. He wrote down numbers, his finger following them down the screen. "Batch numbers.

We digitize all the stubs and the number tells us which batch a stub was processed in."

Kris followed him to the other side of the office. It was dark; the lights weren't on. Justin opened a file and began flicking through CDs checking their labels against the numbers on his sheet.

"We're old school—none of this is kept online."

"Let's start with the middle of the winter. January." He pulled a disk and went back to his computer.

"Check me. They're five hundred stubs to a batch; we have to check each one until we find Ben's. Look here." He pointed to a name and address printed in the upper right hand corner of the stub as it flashed on the screen. He started scrolling through the batch.

Kris focused on each one as they flashed past. Justin saw it first. Ben's name was in the corner and on the signature line was an angry scrawl.

"Let's make a copy." Justin printed the screen and the printer on his desk came to life. He pulled a green sheet out of Ben's folder and held it next to his copy of the stub.

"Bingo." He handed the pages to her.

The signatures were not the same. Ben's, on the green sheet, was stiff and angular, nothing like the one on the stub. She looked up. Justin stared at the signature, thinking.

"He probably went in in November, just after freeze-up and came out in April before breakup. So let's look at the stubs for November and December and April and May and see if the signatures change."

It took them twenty minutes to learn that Justin had been right. The last stub Ben had signed that winter was in the first week of November; the first stub he signed the next spring was in May. Someone else signed the others.

"Pretty good work, don't you think?" Justin was leaning back in his chair, the messy pile of Ben's file and copies of the stubs on the desk before him. "This would get him kicked off the program, if anybody here found out about it. I wonder why the hell he didn't just go on remote. We'd keep his checks during the winter and send them to him when he came out in the spring. Not like he could do anything with the money sitting in his cabin up the Alatna."

Kris didn't answer. She stood behind him, staring again at her half-hidden face reflected back at her from the window. What should she feel for the old man? What did he want from her? He hadn't told her about Corvus or about his relationship with Evie. If she focused deeper into the night, she could see the outline of the shadowed side of her face. It'd hurt like it shouldn't have hurt when he'd yelled at her and when he'd left her at the bottom of the staircase after their picnic.

What did she care?

"Earth to Kris." Justin was looking up at her. "I said, what do you want to do now?"

"I know who signed his stubs."

"You do?"

"A trapper named Ezekiel."

"Is he over sixty-five? He'd be getting a Bonus then."

"I don't know. Probably; he was a friend of Ben's. He used to trap near him."

"Last name?"

Kris shook her head.

"Shouldn't be too hard with a name like Ezekiel."

Justin clacked away and Kris wandered into the next cubicle. A woman lived there. Pictures of daughters on a shelf. Cute. A couple of years younger than Kris. What had they seen? TV, supper every night, dancing lessons? Next to them was a picture of a bearded man, father probably. With two hands he was holding an enormous zucchini. There was a picture of a kitten on its back in a hammock with its paws in the air; next to it, a poem about feeling good. Who buys into that kind of shit?

Kris put her hands on the desk and slumped over it, her head sagging between her shoulders. She felt sick. Ben was right; it didn't make a damn bit of difference that she'd found Evie's killer; that he was dead; that she'd killed him. Evie was still rotting in a muddy grave.

What happens to her now? She goes back to L.A. and hopes no one finds Lambale's body until the spring; until it's been eaten by the ravens and the worms and there's nothing left that can tie her to it? Will she sit alone in her room jumping every time the phone rings; every time there's a knock on the door? Was running all she had left?

She glanced at the girls again. The pain of Ben's anger cut into her and suddenly she realized that all she really wanted was to be part of something. A family, a home, a real mother. She slumped into the chair at the desk, feeling empty and exhausted; she'd been fighting for too long—thrown out into the world alone, with nothing to come back to, with nobody to stand by her.

Noises of books being closed and paper being shuffled came from Justin's cubicle.

Ezekiel, Fairbanks, Corvus. Kris remembered the lock of hair and the birth certificate. She had a brother.

"There're two Ezekiels in Fairbanks," Justin called.

What happened to him? Did the State take him? Was he in a foster home? He'd be six now, six and a half. Justin called again. Slowly, Kris walked back to Justin's cubicle. What kind of name was Corvus?

"This Ezekiel died in 2007, so he's not our man." He pointed to the computer. Screens vanished and new ones appeared. "This one's alive. Ezekiel Damon. You wouldn't believe the strange names you find in this program. According to this he was in Fairbanks all that winter." Justin went back to the filing cabinets and pulled Ezekiel's file. He opened it on his desk, shuffled through it until he found the green sheet of paper. He set it next to one of the forged signatures.

"What do you think?"

Kris examined the papers. There wasn't much question; both signatures had the same anger in their heavy, crabbed lines.

"Do you have an address and phone number for him?"

"He has a box at the main PO in Fairbanks too. His residence address is on the Sixtymile, wherever that is; no phone number."

"Sixtymile is a river. He doesn't live there anymore."

Justin looked through the paper file and clicked through the computer. "That's all we got. But he's still in Fairbanks; we processed his November stub last week."

Kris pulled a piece of paper out of a pile and wrote out Ezekiel's post office address. "I guess we're done."

"Yeah. Let me fire up Big Bruiser again and then we can get out of here."

Kris waited for him by the front door. Corvus. Were his eyes blue like Ben's? Could she get custody?

Justin pulled out his keys. "Boy, I'm hungry all over again." He opened the door, locked it behind them, and they headed out.

"I've got to get back to the hostel. It'll close soon."

Justin slipped his fingers through hers and turned her wrist so she had to face him. "Spend the night with me?"

"I'm OK," she said and pulled her hand away.

He raised a finger and touched her gently on the cheek. "Sure?"

It's all they ever wanted. "Yeah, I'm sure." Kris started down the corridor toward the landing dock forcing Justin to take a couple of quick steps to catch up with her. The door swept shut behind them. It was still snowing.

"Always snows in the middle of the week," he said. "By the time us wage slaves get up on the mountain, the 'boarders have shredded it. Not an inch of unmolested powder left. Come on then, I'll walk you to the hostel."

They stepped into the snow and walked along Fourth Street.

"So the noose is tightening."

"What?"

"Around Ben. You know it's got to be him. It's always the person you suspect the least. He seems like such a nice old geezer when you first meet him."

"It wasn't him," Kris said.

"Come on, who else could it be?" he asked, as they climbed over a high ridge of snow running down the center of Main Street that had been left by the plows.

"Don't know." She took a chance. "Loren Lambale, maybe."

Justin grunted. "Not possible. Your mother was killed last Tuesday afternoon. That was the day the new AWARE wing was dedicated. It was his splash. He was the man. People and the press were fawning over him every minute of the day and at the party that night. He didn't have a second to himself."

Kris suddenly felt heavy as lead. It had to be Lambale. He raped her. He told me raped her.

TUESDAY, NOVEMBER 17

"Kris. Morning. I tried to reach you at the hostel, but you'd already left." Barrett watched her sit in his gray chair, wondering what'd brought her down to the station. "I wanted to ask you how your talk with Stewart went yesterday."

"It didn't." She pulled her arms out of the parka and swept back her hair, hooking it behind her ears. Her chin lifted and she looked at him defiantly, like a teenager with a new nose ring facing down a parent. The bruises ringing her neck had faded to a duller blue; they didn't look as ghastly as they had Sunday.

"I thought you went up." When she'd raced out of his office after he'd shown her the birth certificate, he assumed she was going to confront Stewart. The evidence was closing in around Stewart; opportunity, motive—jealousy, Evie living with another man—circumstantial evidence, all Barrett lacked was placing him at the scene and the murder weapon.

"He hurt his back," Kris said. "I tried to help him and he got all bent out of shape, so I left."

"He's in the hospital now."

Kris looked surprised.

"I went up after you and found him on a mattress on the floor and called an ambulance."

"He let you?"

"I didn't give him a choice and he wasn't in a position to stop me. But I couldn't ask him any questions; he was too miserable and the ambulance crew got there too quickly. They packed him off to the hospital and I haven't seen him since. I'll drop by later this morning."

Uncharacteristically, Kris dropped her eyes. His senses pricked alert; she seemed subdued this morning, this wasn't Kris. Was she feeling betrayed? Had she been drawn to the old man and then felt deceived when she learned he hadn't told her about his relationship with Evie? It'd be just like Barrett's wife—there'd be a week of cold nights in bed whenever she discovered he'd kept something from her.

"I came by to tell you I'm leaving for Fairbanks today," Kris said.

"Fairbanks?" Barrett hadn't expected this.

"To look for Corvus."

"Kris, I'm sorry. He disappeared two years ago. I checked after the fax came in yesterday."

Her face closed down.

"I called up to the Division of Family and Youth Services and had someone pull his file. She told me he'd disappeared so I called over to the Fairbanks PD. They had a file on him. In November of '13 a social worker from DFYS had notified the police that the boy was missing. Apparently he'd been missing for a week before she found out and called it in. The police investigated. They interviewed the neighbors, searched the area; but there were no leads and the case is still open."

"And forgotten."

"Yes." When Barrett had been on the line with the social worker in Fairbanks, he asked her to pull Kris's file too. It was thick and the woman only skimmed through it, reading him disconnected pieces over the phone: Father unknown, mother an alcoholic, Kris had twice been a ward of the state, in and out of foster homes, "uncontrollable" was the charge of most of the foster parents and after the last one the state gave up on her—another kid dropped through the cracks. But the record picked up again when she apparently moved back in with her mother, making Evie eligible for welfare again. Then a couple years later, she disappeared. There was a perfunctory investigation; but Alaska didn't have a runaway law: it wasn't illegal for a minor to leave home. And there'd been a handwritten note at the back of the file from a volunteer who'd known her from the children's shelter. It'd told them to leave Kris alone, that it was time for her to leave and that she'd come back when she was ready to.

Kris broke into his thoughts. "I've got to be out at the airport in forty-five minutes." She stood, lifting her parka off the chair, and began pushing her hands into the sleeves.

"Will you be back?" Barrett asked.

"Only because my flight to L.A. leaves from here." She picked up her duffle.

"And your mother?"

"This is more important. Corvus might be alive." She looked at him; daring him to deny it. Barrett kept quiet; she'd learn soon enough it wasn't likely.

"OK," he said. "How can I find you?"

"You have my L.A. address." It was on her statement. Kris started for the door.

"Before you go."

She turned, waiting. Her hair came loose from one ear and fanned across a cheek. Her eyes held his; black, somber and unafraid, her wildness simmering beneath this unexpected vulnerability. He didn't want her vulnerable—vulnerabilities meant complications—he wanted her spitting, you didn't feel so guilty afterwards.

"Loren Lambale didn't come home last night."

"So?"

"I thought you might have seen him." Barrett didn't think so; he was just covering the bases.

Kris almost smiled. "Did you try the AWARE shelter?"

"Why there?"

"Maybe his wife beat him."

"I think this is serious," Barrett said, watching the sparks come back into her eyes.

"He's a white man. He can take care of himself."

"He didn't leave on any plane. There've been no ferries since he was last seen. He hasn't used any of his credit cards since Monday morning and his car was found untouched in its parking space. There aren't many places to hide in Juneau."

Kris moved closer to his desk. "All this by nine o'clock in the morning?"

"It was only a couple of phone calls," Barrett said, irritated that he sounded defensive.

"Right. The world stops for a rich fat man. And you haven't a fucking clue who killed my mother."

"We'll find who killed her, Kris," he said.

"Yeah. Like they found Corvus," she said and left.

Barrett gazed out his open office door. She was right, Lambale'd become first priority—he was probably still alive. And Juneau would come apart when it learned he'd disappeared; the pressure to find him would be unremitting. Barrett toyed with the Abrams's muzzle. There had to be a connection too, between Lambale's disappearance and Evie's murder. It was too coincidental for there not to be.

Barrett probed and tested theories until his mind began to wander. Kris's mood had been strange this morning; subdued. Was it Ben or her mother's murder catching up with her? Even though his wife had warned him that she wasn't going to forgive another one, he was disappointed Kris was leaving town.

Suddenly his thoughts snagged. He frowned, looking at the dent Kris had put in his tank; then he pulled the phone in front of him, punched in the old 789-0600 number and, when the line was picked up, navigated through the voice mail until he found a human.

"Thank you for calling Alaska Airlines. This is Julie, how may I help you?"

"What is the price of an open round-trip ticket from Juneau to Fairbanks, if I want to leave today?"

Over the line, he heard her typing.

"Three hundred eighty-six dollars one way. It's cheaper to buy two one-way tickets, sir, if you don't know when you're returning."

"Thanks."

"Thank you for calling Ala—" Barrett disconnected.

Three hundred eighty-six dollars one way. Seven seventy-two round-trip. Plus expenses in Fairbanks. No way she had that kind of cash. Where the hell did she get it? From Justin?

Or Lambale?

■ ■ ■

"You know it's the end when they start hanging your history from the ceiling."

Kris started in surprise. Leaning against the steel rail a few feet to her left was a man with a couple days of stubble on his face and a blond tangle of curls on his head. The curls bounced when he turned to look at her. He pointed a finger at the tiny airplane suspended from the ceiling with wires. "It's a Jenny, first in Alaska. Ben Eielson flew it in the twenties until he was killed in a crash in Siberia. Back then you were living life. Now you're just showing it off. Or selling it.

"Existential kiss of death. Money and tourists."

Kris regarded him with disappointed surprise: Is this what Annie married? "Ringer?" she asked.

"Yup." He stuck out his hand. It was big and meaty and pieces were missing from the ends of a few of his fingers. She hesitated before shaking it and he laughed. "Frostbite." He examined her, his eyes as unrestrained as his hair. "So did I blow it? Are you a tourist? Not likely this time of year," he said. "That first frost in August tends to run most of them out of state. Damn few left by November." He smiled; his teeth were yellowed and chipped. "Used to work on the slope with a bubba named Raymond Abercrombie. First dust on the hills he'd be gone like sheet ice on a hot spring day. 'Goose's head ain't no bigger'n a cotton boll and it knows enough to beat ass south before winter,' he'd say." Ringer was tall, ragged-looking, with a flannel shirt under his light parka and uninsulated leather boots which bunched up the cuffs of his jeans. A silver ring hung from an ear.

"Actually, you look local." He leaned his forearms again on the railing of the balcony which looked out over the main concourse of the airport. "Annie didn't tell me much; just to swing by and pick you up."

"L.A."

"Came up to cool off?" He looked at her over his shoulder; his hair bounced and he laughed again. "So you're going to crash with us? Good," he said without waiting for an answer. "Strays are our trade. A month ago the South Siders were up from Talkeetna and they camped out with us. There were bodies all over the table and on top of the kitchen counters. It's pretty cool on the floor this time of year. They had a gig down at Chilkoots's. And when they got back in the early a.m., they'd plug in an amp—you know, electricity is amazing stuff, we just jacked into the grid this summer: lights, I mean bright lights, regular radio, no more batteries crapping out in the middle of a cut. Anyway, they'd play for hours. The kids loved it, though it was an unholy chore getting them on the school bus the next morning." He paused, maybe to take a breath.

Kris shot for the crack. "Yeah, let's go." She picked up her duffle.

Ringer lifted himself off the railing and reached down for the mandolin case at his feet. "Can't leave this in the truck," he explained. "It'd crack in the cold." Pasted on one side and cut to fit its curves was a bumper sticker that read, "Pot got more votes than Hickel." Without checking to see if she was following, he headed down the stairs to the main floor of the terminal. "We'll have a blast," he said, loud enough for her to hear from five steps behind him. "The boys are charmers. They'll get you laughing. You look like you could use a couple of good ones. Mama –"

Kris tuned him out. She was thirteen or fourteen when she'd last seen Annie Smythe. Annie used to come down to the shelter and play games with the kids. Somewhere in her thirties, she was sweet—not the sickly sweet of people who live in pink bubbles, who think that things are grand and will always work out—but a serious sweetness that believed what you were saying and didn't try to talk the bad stuff away. She'd hug the kids who let her, laugh at jokes, never get too missionary about anything, and she'd lay into social workers who got picky about rules. She could beat the boys in anything—Monopoly, Risk, checkers, chess, most video

games—without starting a fight. Kris didn't play games, though sometimes she'd watch, and, when the games were over, if it weren't too late
Annie'd take her for hot chocolate down to Rexall's where it was quieter
and they could talk.

Because Annie was white, spoke well, and came from a good home,
Kris never really trusted her, but she liked the attention she got from her.
It was Annie who talked her into getting off the street and going back to
Evie. She helped them find an apartment, taught Kris how to control their
money; pay the rent first, then worry about heat, food and everything else.
But after Kris settled in with Evie, Annie got caught up in other things—
school or something—and she didn't come around much anymore. Kris
shrugged her away: just someone else who'd blown through her life.

Kris had remembered Annie when she was sitting in the Anchorage
Airport waiting for the connecting flight to Fairbanks, wondering where
she could stay so that Barrett couldn't find her if he came looking. Annie
Smythe was in the phone book and her answering voice mail message, after listing everyone else in the family, gave her work number. When Annie
took the call—she worked at the Fairbanks Public Library—and heard
who it was, she yelped "Kris"! Reflexively, Kris pulled away. Affection
tended to front for other things, usually demands for sex or money, and
Kris was suddenly sorry that she'd called. She tensed, feeling Annie read
her; Annie quieted her tone and offered Kris a place to stay like she was
making a deal.

"Stay with us, Kris. The kids always like someone new to play with and
it'd be great to have another woman around. I'm swamped with maleness.
My husband's cool. Ringer doesn't have enough testosterone in him to fire
up a fly, and you can be in charge of the dishes and the bedtime story."

Kris clicked her thumbnail down the armored cord attaching the receiver to the phone. Annie would want to know everything and the husband and kids would be a pain in the ass. Maybe, she could check into a
hotel with a fake name.

"Kris, honey, what's the problem?"

Kris ran her nail back up the cord. "Yeah, OK," she said and gave
Annie her arrival time. Annie told her where to wait for Ringer and to give

him an extra fifteen or twenty minutes since it wasn't likely he'd show up when he was supposed to.

Ringer led her across the terminal, scanning the milling mass of people. "Used to be, back when there weren't any airplanes hanging from the ceiling and Fairbanks was a decent size, you'd always meet someone here that you knew," he said. "Even in the Seattle airport, you'd meet friends at the Alaska gate waiting for the flight up. Friends everywhere, it was like coming home." He paused for the automatic doors to open. "Now, almost never. The town is too big. It's like a foreign city." He looked at her. "It's not like home anymore."

The second set of automatic doors whisked open and the cold swept in around the edges of Kris's parka, cutting through her clothes and into her skin. Drier than Juneau's soggy air, it stung any flesh exposed or clothed too lightly. The lights hanging over the parking lot turned the blackness yellow and purpled the exhaust billowing out of the tailpipes of idling cars. The pavement had been plowed, but across the road she saw in the semi-darkness, old settled snow, grayed by car fumes and city dirt.

"I spent the last couple of weeks working a gig with some friends down in Los Anchorage." Ringer slid his mandolin under his parka as they walked down the steps into the parking lot. "What a madhouse; the place is everything you come to Alaska to escape. Cars, people, strip malls and McDonald's. It's one redeeming feature is that it's only a thirty-minute drive from Alaska."

Kris had trouble hearing him; her head was buried in the hood. She looked down as she walked, the hood tunnel and ruff pinched her sight to a small patch of pavement in front of her feet, and if she turned her head the hood wouldn't move and she'd be staring at its inner fabric.

"Hey Kris. This way."

Straightening, Kris circled around until she found Ringer waving off to her right. Without pulling her hands from her pockets, her duffle hanging from her wrist, she jogged over and fell in behind him. He stopped in front of a black pickup with rounded corners, pitted chrome, and a shack of slab wood built over the bed. They climbed in; the doors weren't locked.

"Ole Bess is older than you," Ringer said, gathering wires that hung out of the steering column in one hand while he searched under papers and coffee cups littering the dash until he found a screwdriver. When he touched the blade to the wires, a purple spark flashed and the engine cranked and fired.

"But she always starts. Trouble is, she doesn't heat up too well. Lucky it's not too cold out. We might just get a little warmth out of her by the time we get home. Drive is twenty minutes." Ringer switched on the headlights and backed out.

Kris had never been to the airport when she was growing up and, as Ringer pulled out of the parking lot and onto a road headed toward the city lights, she didn't see anything she recognized. She sat huddled in the parka, staring out of the windshield, which was cracked and pitted with collisions from gravel kicked up by passing cars, not really interested in the roads and the buildings they passed. Distant memories murmured and fidgeted uncomfortably in her. Never once, in the nine years since she had left, had she ever thought she would be back in Fairbanks. There had been nothing to bring her back and everything to keep her away.

Cars whizzed by, their lights punching through the darkness, their exhaust steaming behind them. Dirty heaps of snow, thrown by the plows, lined either side of the road and the pavement was black and dry.

"How do you know Annie?" Ringer asked, raising his voice over the sound of the engine and wind. Kris told him without going into too much detail.

"She's a good lady," he said, after Kris had trailed off. "I met her when I was pounding nails nine or ten years ago. She was punching a cash register at the Gavora Mall."

Kris remembered Annie working at the mall, but she'd never mentioned a boyfriend.

"We got together and decided to build this cabin off Goldstream. Back then it was almost wilderness, now it's mostly suburbs. Annie is one tough lady. We didn't have the place closed in at the end of the season. That's the point most women threaten to evacuate. Ever notice those places that have three or four courses of logs on the foundation and

T-one-eleven from there to the eves? That's a place where the lady said she was headed back to Brooklyn, if she didn't have a warm place to spend the winter, Annie didn't peep, we had all our money in the land and the cabin and couldn't move back into town, so we spent the winter in a baggy. It was insulated, but six inches of glass wool isn't a lot between you and fifty below. And we're at the bottom of a ridge. If you looked close, you could see the slugs of cold air slide down the hill and roost on top us. Walk up that ridge when there's a good inversion and its thirty degrees warmer at the top."

They were outside the city now. The truck clattered along between black walls of spruce sometimes broken by a lighted house or the openness of a frozen marsh. Tiny flecks of crystalline snow danced and twirled in their headlights, lofted by the car whose red lights were always disappearing around curves and over hills in front of them. Air, sharp as steel, knifed in through cracks around the door. The heating fan added no warmth, only pushed the air around the cab making it feel colder. The cold bit the tip of her nose each time she took a breath and the frozen, cracked vinyl seat pulled the heat out of her rear.

L.A., suddenly, was a long way away.

"–ragging on me to have kids. No way. I was a dead set no. It was part of the deal when we got together: no kids. But she was timing out and nothing would stop her. Those were our roughest times. She was right, though. When I caught Murphy, I almost fainted. What an endorphin rush, nothing like it. When things had quieted down and all her lady helpers ran me out of the house, I went out to the brown study and bawled. I couldn't believe I'd waited so long. I was ready to get started..."

A car arrowed past them in the dark, climbed over a low hill and was gone. Kris peered out of her side window, now that the lights of the city were behind them, looking for the northern lights. There was nothing, no lights, no moon, no stars, just an even blackness.

Ringer and his truck rattled on. He told stories about the days before the pipeline. When if three cars passed without picking you up it was a critically bad hitchhiking day. How strangers were friends and crashed whole winters in people's cabins. How the richest were those who'd hustled enough work in the summer to have unemployment checks coming in during the winter. The Everclear and Kool-Aid parties where you'd lose track of the days because nobody was conscious enough during the forty-five minutes when the sun was up to know when one day ended and the next began.

"Then the pipeline came and—wham! Everything was different. People, mountains of money, construction, murders, suicides. What a show. Tent, this guy who lived in a tent, was one of the first to get out on the line. He sent us back a wad of cash to celebrate his birthday. We bought cases of canned whipping cream and sucked laughing gas for two days. Days of innocence. Six months later there was more coke in any given block in Fairbanks than in all of Columbia.

"Oil money ruined this state. Turned it middle class. People come here now to make a buck, not because they want to live the life. Last winter I had a regular job and every morning driving to work, this guy'd pass me in a BMW. A beemer. Send that carpetbagger back to Marin. He doesn't belong—

"Hey! Do you feel that?" Ringer interrupted himself and waved his hand under the dash. "We've got heat. It must be warmer out than I thought."

Ringer turned onto a gravel road and Kris couldn't hear him over the noise of the truck knocking over the stones and bumps. A few miles later he turned into a driveway that curved down into a hollow. At the end of it was a plowed circle, another car and deep snow, pocked everywhere with leg holes. A dog started barking. Ringer popped the clutch killing the engine.

"Home," he said.

■ ■ ■

"Check the slop bucket."

Kris opened the cabinet door under the sink and peered into the bucket beneath. Gray water with bits of food and scum floating on the surface filled it. Lifting it with both hands, she looked at Annie.

"On the other side of the driveway. You'll see it," Annie said. "Take the flashlight."

Kris found the season's frozen dish and bath water in a crater melted out of the snow on the far side of the clearing. Though only the temperature of the cabin, the water steamed in the sub-zero air when she poured it out. Up the driveway she could hear Ringer and his boys taking Wally for a walk. The dog was a husky mix with enough wolf in him to howl when you got him fired up. Murphy and Minto—Ringer's M&M's—had brought him in after dinner to show Kris their Indian war dance. They started howling, Wally joined in, and then they flapped their hands over their mouths and over Wally's howling muzzle to make Indian war whoops. Ringer joined in and at that point the war party got out of hand and Annie had run them out of the cabin.

Kris shook the last drops out of the bucket and turned back to the cabin. It was in a small clearing hemmed in by spruce trees. It had eight sides—the logs weren't long enough to make an adequately sized square cabin—and looked like a chocolate cake squatting in vanilla icing. The snow on the roof had thinned and patches of shingles showed through. Light blazed from the windows and threw golden rectangles onto the snow. Wally's doghouse was in the back next to the woodpiles; one of cordwood, the other, an unstacked heap of cut and split stove lengths. On the left side of the cabin was a storage shed and the brown study, the outhouse. Annie had noted, as she'd given Kris directions to it, that after about twenty below, one tended not to study in it for very long.

Kris closed the cabin door behind her and hung her parka on a peg before repositioning the bucket under the sink's drainpipe. Dirty dishes were stacked next to the sink and Annie poured water that she had heated on the stove into a washbasin. Kris looked around helplessly, this wasn't a chore she wanted to do, but Annie patiently pointed out the soap and found her a sponge and pot scraper and then left her alone.

Annie looked older than Kris had expected. Her hair had grayed and loose wisps, pulled from her ponytail, floated around her face, which was lined and had filled out. Her eyes were warm, but assessing, and at times during dinner Kris looked away, uncomfortable with how much Annie might be seeing. Under baggy sweats, her breasts jiggled loose and heavy, and her belly had grown; it had pushed into Kris when Annie hugged her. Like Ben, she padded around the cabin in worn shoepack liners. She was shorter than Kris, which unsettled her; she remembered looking up at Annie, and now, looking down, Kris realized how much she'd leaned on Annie when she'd lived at the shelter.

They worked in silence, Kris clumsily sponging cups and silverware and Annie, with unhurried efficiency, returning things to drawers and cabinets. Food to be refrigerated, she grouped in a pile. "So I don't spend my life climbing in and out of the root cellar." She tapped a foot on a trap door in the floor. When the counters were clear, she pulled out a ceramic bowl, cookie sheet, and flour, eggs and butter, and started making cookies.

During dinner, Kris had told them about Evie's death. When he heard that she'd lost her mother, Murphy, only five, dropped his spoon on the floor and broke into tears; Minto, three, looked at his brother and began wailing too. Ringer pulled them out of their chairs and carried them back to a curtained bed where he and Annie slept. Kris watched them go in surprise. Annie leaned over and whispered, "Murphy's a pretty empathic little guy."

"I didn't cry when I found out," Kris said.

"Maybe someday you will," Annie said.

When the boys came back to the table, eyes dried, Kris told them she'd come to Fairbanks to find her half-brother and Ringer explained that Corvus—Corvus corax—was the Latin name for raven, which were the smartest birds and important to Athabascan legend. Raven was the trickster, the animal who tricked other animals and man out of their food and treasures.

Kris started in on the plates, sponging off the remains of a casserole most of the ingredients of which, she hadn't recognized.

"Did you have any contact with your mother after you left Fairbanks?" Annie asked as she started measuring and sifting the flour.

"No," Kris said.

Annie silently poured chocolate chips into her measuring cup, waiting for her to continue.

"I didn't know where to write," Kris said.

"You were pretty angry," she said. Annie was impossible to bullshit.

"Yeah," Kris said, letting Annie drag her out. "All I wanted was a bed, regular meals; she couldn't even give me that."

"She didn't have many chances in life, though, did she?"

"What does it take to wait tables?" Kris, feeling the heat rise in her, wondered why it took so little to upset her.

"Self-confidence, knowing how to add, a nice dress, child care." Annie was mixing the batter with a wooden spoon, the bowl in the crook of her arm.

"She never even tried," Kris said. She pulled the casserole pan out of the pile; the rice was crusted on the bottom and in the corners.

"Alcohol is hard to beat."

"Why are you taking her side?" Kris felt deserted; Annie had defended Evie all evening.

"Am I being unfair?" She came over, her mixing bowl still in her arm and stood by Kris. "I guess it's because I've got a hidden agenda." Annie stuck a finger into the dough and licked it off. "I'm a mother, and I want you to love yours."

Kris found a spoon and started scraping at the crusted rice. "It's OK," she said.

Annie cut off a slice of butter and greased a cookie sheet with her fingers. "You know, none of us can help the things that life has done to us. They're done before you realize it, and once they're done they make you do other things until at last everything comes between you and what you'd like to be and you've lost your true self forever. Evie did what she could."

Kris struggled with the dish and Annie dropped spoonfuls of dough in crooked rows on the sheet. She finished and began greasing a second sheet.

"Do you have a sweetie in L.A.?" she asked.

"No," said Kris. The crust wouldn't come out of the corners.

"Men are a problem?"

"Men are scum." Too heated, she thought and tried to back up. "Some are OK. But look at you and Ringer. You have a job, and you work in the kitchen. You've gone backwards; it's worse than when women just did the housework."

"Who's out with the kids?" Anne asked, lightly.

"That's because it's fun for him."

Annie laughed. "It only counts when it's a drudge? But you're right. I do more of the work around here. Not too much more, he puts in eight or ten cords of wood a year, plows the road and fixes the leaks. I whine about it sometimes, but it's more like I married a man without ambition, than I married a monster. Most days, I don't have any regrets.

"What's your problem with men?" Annie asked.

"Are you kidding? Power, control, violence, they take what they want –"

The door crashed open; cold air and bodies tumbled in.

"Are they done yet?" The boys ran over to Annie. Murphy scooped a finger through a raw cookie.

"Hey come back here," Ringer yelled. "You're tracking snow every-where." He got their gear off and their feet into slippers; then came over and, resting his chin on Annie's shoulder, reached around her and shov-eled dough out of the bowl with a finger. "What's our time frame?" he asked.

"Fifteen minutes."

"OK boys, let's get ready for bed. Cookies in fifteen minutes." Ringer herded them back into the shadows. Annie finished the sheet and slid it into the oven. She licked her fingers clean, then came over and stood next to Kris, touching her at the hip and shoulder, and took the casserole dish out of her hands. Kris picked up another pot.

"I can't imagine why anybody'd want to be a man," Annie whispered, "Isn't it the most comical thing you've ever seen? Stretching and shrink-ing, wriggling around like that—like a worm trying to get out?"

Annie laughed. Kris tried to stifle hers and blew snot out her nose.

"Red alert, boys!" Ringer yelled from across the cabin. "That's Mom's men-are-knuckle-draggers snort. Get her!"

Kris looked over her shoulder and saw the boys, naked, streak out of the shadows, making Indian war whoops; Ringer right behind them. They ganged around Annie and paddled her butt. Kris returned to her pot. Just as they retreated, she felt the tentative pat of a small hand on her rear and then they were gone.

"...Niska reared up on her hind legs and"—Kris turned the page—"with a great heave against the traces, broke the sled out of the snow." From the corners of her eyes, Kris saw each boy's pajamaed legs lying motionless on the bed on either side of her. Looking up through her hair, which had fallen forward as she bent over the book, she saw Ringer and Annie in the kitchen, the light behind them. He was hugging her from the rear, his arms under hers, squeezing her breasts, his hands clasped above her crotch. He nuzzled her neck, and as she watched, Annie leaned her head back on his shoulder, her eyes closed.

Kris dropped her eyes back to the page and searched for her place. Soft sucks and giggles came from the kitchen and she pressed her finger harder under each word that she read. "Niska raced the sled down the mountain trail. 'Haw,' cried..." Kris felt a silence, charged and electric, come from the kitchen. Lifting her eyes, she saw through her hair, Ringer and Annie, still in his arms, looking at her, their expressions sharp and intent, like a pair of dogs with ears pricked and senses alert to a movement across a field.

What's wrong now?

Then Kris saw the three of them—she and the boys—stiff and apart, their backs against the wall like thugs in a line-up. She dropped her eyes; her legs were separated from theirs by acres of bedspread. They didn't want to touch her. She found her place and continued reading, awkwardly now.

A few pages later, Minto faded out and fell against her arm, breathing easily in little boy snuffles.

She leaned into his slight weight.

WEDNESDAY, NOVEMBER 18

Annie's taillights ran like red eyes through the blackness ahead of her. It was still dark; the long subarctic dawn would not begin for another hour and the sun wouldn't lift above the horizon until after eleven, three hours away. An overcast blanketed the winter sky and until it cleared off, it would stay warm, not dropping much below zero.

Annie's lights brightened and her turn signal flashed right. Kris slowed and signaled, although nobody was behind her. They had decided to give her the Subaru, since the truck was too cranky. It was a chore day at the cabin for Ringer, so he didn't need a car. Annie had told Kris, as they'd walked out into the dark that morning that she could live without running water, but not without two cars. One car, she'd said, was life threatening— for Ringer. Time and space weren't something he paid much attention to and she'd threatened to cut him up and feed him to Wally if he left her waiting once more on some frozen street corner. Ringer decided it was safer to buy a second car.

Other taillights trickled in from side roads until they were part of a quickly flowing stream funneling into the city. Annie led her past the brilliant lights of the University atop a hill and then onto a highway that took them above the northern fringe of the town. Nothing looked familiar to Kris until she drove across the Chena River into downtown. The traffic moved fast and she caught only quick glimpses of the old buildings that she had grown up with, lit now by yellow lights. She quailed; she felt no thrill of returning home, of walking old streets and seeing forgotten friends. She gripped the steering wheel and concentrated on tracking Annie through the tangled traffic. Suddenly, she saw Annie's arm wave briefly from the window and then her car disappeared in the stream of red lights.

Kris drove on to the south end of the city to the Old Richardson Highway. The state office hadn't moved since she'd last been there, waiting numbly in some line to fill out some form or to talk to some social worker who had already seen fifty hopeless cases that week and wasn't much interested in hers. She scanned the directory for Family and Youth Services, punched the button in the elevator, and got out on the third floor. It hadn't changed either. The same color, the same cubicles, packed in the same arrangement as when she'd last seen it. She stood in front of the receptionist's desk until the woman looked up.

"I'd like to see the supervisor."

"Supervisor? We usually have you go through an assessment first."

"I'm not here for services. I want to ask her some questions; it won't take long."

The receptionist eyed her, then reached for her phone. "Your name?" she asked. Kris told her. She spoke into the phone and then pointed Kris between the cubicles toward an open office door. A gray-haired woman with wire-rimmed half-glasses turned away from her computer when she entered. Kris sat in a seat opposite her desk.

"Kris? Joan Cranshaw. What can I do for you?"

"I have a brother who was born in 2009 and who disappeared in 2013. I'm trying to find him. The police told me that DFYS has a file on him. I'd like to look at it and talk to his case worker."

"Those files are confidential."

"Even to family members?"

"Siblings at least. The police never found him?"

Kris shook her head.

"Let me take a look. What was his name?"

"Corvus Stewart."

"Corvus? Raven? Good Alaskan name." She tapped in a number on her phone and asked the woman who answered to bring in Corvus's file. When it came in, she paged through it carefully.

"There's no mention of a sister here," she said, looking up.

"I'd left home by then. You can pull my file, or my mother's, if you want."

The woman shook her head.

"Your brother's case worker resigned a year ago," she said. "To have a child. Which, given that she worked here, demonstrated an unwarranted faith in the world. You want to talk to her." Cranshaw found the case worker's number and tapped it into her phone. A couple minutes later, after a brief chat, she handed Kris a sheet with an address and a penciled map on it and said, "You can catch her this morning, she'll be home until one."

Half an hour later, Kris pulled the Subaru into a neatly-plowed driveway on the north side of Chena Ridge. Gray had begun to infiltrate the morning darkness. She could see the shape of a house through a leafless stand of aspen and birch. There was no arctic entryway and the woman who opened the door recoiled as a wall of cold air forced its way into the house. Kris stepped in quickly and the woman pushed the door shut.

"Hi, I'm Pat Shannon."

"Kris Gabriel." They shook hands.

"Evie's daughter?"

"You knew her?"

"Of course. Come in. I'm sorry about what happened. I read about her death in the paper."

Kris hung her parka on a peg by the door.

"Sit down. Would you like some tea or coffee?"

Kris shook her head. Pat was short, with sandy hair and eyes that were used to watching. A stylized cross, slung from a gold chain, rested on her chest. She was overweight, her body bulged over its restraints—a bra strap and a belt cinched too tight. The living room had a white carpet, white walls, and sliding glass doors with white drapes. A fancy wood stove stood clean and unused on white tiles in the corner and Kris wondered how many cords of wood it would take to heat the house in the winter if the furnace went out. On the couch, wrapped in a blanket printed with cartoon characters, was a baby with a pacifier sticking in its mouth.

Pat picked up the baby, and sat down.

"Joan said you wanted to know about Corvus."

"I left home in 2006 and didn't know my mother had had him until a couple of days ago. The police said he disappeared and was never found."

Pat pushed up the baby's clothes and drew a circle with her fingernail around its dimpled bellybutton. It wiggled and made sucking noises around its pacifier. "I was assigned to Corvus because I specialize in FAS cases," she said.

Kris looked blank.

"Fetal Alcohol Syndrome."

It didn't help.

"A woman who drinks during her pregnancy can cause acute neurological damage to her baby. That's what happened to Corvus. He was severely mentally disabled. It wasn't diagnosed until he was three because your mother had almost no post-natal care. But by then it was obvious that something was wrong. He had minimal language development, was two years late learning to walk, and had made no progress in toilet training."

Pat tickled her baby until it giggled and thrashed its arms and legs in impotent pleasure. It had good post-natal care.

"FAS is a severe problem, especially in the villages. The percentages are scary. It can't be cured, but there are programs adapted to FAS children that can help quite a bit; especially by taking some of the pressure off the parents. FAS children can be difficult to control and care for. I tried to convince Evie to get Corvus started in one, but she was resistant. So was her partner." She paused.

"Ben."

"That's right, Ben Stewart. But for different reasons. Evie didn't want to lose Corvus. I don't think she trusted us. Stewart, I don't know. It was like he'd given up, or lost interest." Pat unbuttoned her blouse, pulled the pacifier out of the baby's mouth, and levered a nipple into its mouth. It hadn't even whimpered.

"They were doing OK. Ben had a job and had gotten them off food stamps. He still got his Bonus, though. Funny how Alaskans think they are entitled to the PFD and Longevity Bonus, but that food stamps and welfare are government handouts and evidence of personal failure. Their apartment was pretty meager, but they were making the rent. And, as far as I could tell, Evie was sober. I don't think Ben had a drinking problem.

"It must have been about two years ago, I came by to check in on Corvus and he wasn't there. Evie's eyes were red and puffy. Ben sat in the corner with a face hard as stone. Corvus had been gone a week, and I think both of them had worn themselves out. I contacted the police and they spent another week interviewing people, organizing teams to search the patches of forest and the industrial sites in the neighborhood. The police didn't find anything and eventually gave up. There was nothing else they could do.

"Once Corvus was gone, I lost contact with Evie and Ben. But I heard through the grapevine that they'd split up and that Evie had started drinking again. It doesn't take much to tumble a couple that's just on the edge back into the hole. I was sorry, they were good people. They just weren't capable of dealing with life's blows."

Weren't capable? Kris stood up. *You and your kid wouldn't last a day on the street.*

"Kris." Pat rose too, her baby still nursing in her arms.

Kris stared into the righteous light of Pat's eyes and knew she was going to be given a Truth.

"Kris, Corvus is dead. It's been two years and his body's never been found. He was utterly and absolutely incapable of caring for himself. If he had wandered outside, he would have died of exposure in an hour. Less. It snowed that week and the plows probably scooped him up and deposited him in the snow dump on the Chena. He would've washed down the river at breakup."

Kris let the car coast down off the ridge and then squashed her foot hard against the floor when the road flattened out on Chena Pump. The Subaru choked, backfired, then picked up speed. Chena Pump was arrow straight and she let the car race its headlights down it. She came to the Parks Highway and turned right, back toward town. At University Avenue she turned right again, slipping into the ceaseless traffic which she followed left onto Airport Way. A mile later, she turned left onto Barnette, hoping that the police station was still where she remembered it.

It hadn't moved; it looked the same as the last time she'd been there—bailing Evie out of a vagrancy charge. Kris left the car in the visitors' parking lot and pushed through the doors. A woman working through a pile of yellow forms behind bulletproof glass glanced up as Kris approached.

"May I help you?" Her voice came out of a mike. In the room behind her people were working at desks, talking on the phone and bunched up around the coffee machine.

"Two years ago my brother disappeared. They never found him. I want to talk to the officer who worked on the case and look at the file."

The woman pulled a pad of post-its out from under the loose forms. "What was his name?"

"Corvus Stewart." Kris was surprised; she'd expected a fight.

"Take a seat; it'll take a few minutes to pull the file."

Kris sat down and waited.

The door to the inner offices pulled open and a black policeman with a thick, liverish-brown face, grizzled hair, and a potbelly sagging over his belt came out with a manila folder in his hand.

"Ms. Stewart? Hi, I'm Officer Hart." He reached out his hand and wrapped it around hers, smiling. "Why don't we find some place quiet?" He held the door open for her; then led her back to a small room with a table, worn and chipped chairs, and a blackboard. He offered her a seat and pulled out a chair next to hers, laying the folder between them.

"I wasn't on this case. The man who was is a lieutenant now and doesn't get to do anything fun anymore. Since I'm only a traffic-cop, I get to talk to you." He looked at her, eyes smiling above sagging, spotted cheeks, hoping for a smile from her. But a lifetime of bad cops hadn't prepared her for a decent one, and she kept her face wooden. "If you have any questions I can't answer after we've looked through this, I'll get the lieutenant in here. All right?" He spoke easily, but earnestly, like he didn't think that Kris was wasting his time.

"OK."

"Why are you interested in this case now?" he asked, opening the file and pushing it in front of her. He smelled of tobacco.

"I only learned I had a brother a couple of days ago."

"Really?" He picked up the top sheet. "Evie Gabriel? Is that your name, Gabriel not Stewart?"

"Gabriel."

He handed her the sheet.

"So you're checking out your roots?"

"I guess."

Hart let her read through the file. There were statements from Evie and Ben. Both said the same thing. On Friday, November 3, 2013, they had both gone to bed around ten. Kris had never seen her in bed that early unless she had a man on top of her. Corvus was asleep on the sofa in the front room. When Ben awoke at 6:30 for work the next morning the sofa was empty. They searched the apartment building, the neighborhood, and talked to the neighbors. No one had seen a thing. It had been about twenty below that day; but Corvus's cold weather gear was still in the closet. When asked why they hadn't gone to the police, Evie hadn't responded, and Ben had said that he'd spent his life tracking; if he couldn't find Corvus then the police couldn't either. But Kris remembered him lying on the floor pissing in a bottle—more likely he wouldn't have asked for help.

There was a form for every person interviewed. Kris read the comments the neighbors had made about Evie and Ben. Evie'd apparently been sober. She doted on Corvus, but was an erratic mother, one minute hugging and kissing him and the next shaking and yelling at him. Ben was quiet and hard working, but, said one neighbor, maybe a little too distant and aloof, especially as Corvus got older. Uncertain of himself around the boy, another said. The boy cried often, sometimes for hours; Evie wouldn't know what to do, and Ben would leave the house, not returning until late, when Corvus had exhausted himself.

Hart showed her how to read the forensic reports, the fingerprint and fiber analyses and the reports made to the state police and the FBI's missing persons bureau.

"All routine," he said, scanning the pages. "All dead ends."

Kris turned back to a sheet that had basic information about Ben and Evie. Evie'd been unemployed; Ben had been working full time at the Great Land Tannery. She borrowed Hart's pen and wrote out its name and address on her palm.

"All set?" he asked.

Kris pushed herself away from the table.

"Must have been pretty grim, losing a kid like that." Hart sighed. "Anything you want to ask the lieutenant?"

Kris shook her head.

"I can't think of anything either. It all looks pretty straightforward. Funny, though, they didn't call the police right away. That could've made a difference."

"Do you know where this is?" Kris held out her palm with the address on it.

"Placer Street? No. Let's take a look at a map."

He gathered up the sheets and stuck them in the folder and led her back out to the front office. A large plastic map of the city hung on a wall. He ran his eyes down the index and then searched south of the city.

"Here it is," he said, tracing a thin black line with his finger.

The sun was up when she came out of the police station. It was too low to the horizon to be seen over the buildings, but in its dull rays the overcast sky had turned gray-white. She drove over to Cushman, stopped at Foodland for some chips and Snickers before driving south into the industrial part of town. Down where she used to live. She slowed, looking for the street she'd last lived in; the yellowed, fog-bound street she'd walked out of nine years ago when she left Alaska. Different buildings lined it now and she'd cruised past before recognizing it. She pulled into the parking lot of a pawnshop and picked at the cracked vinyl dash of the Subaru debating whether to go back. Without being aware of having made a decision, she put the car in reverse, backed out of the parking lot, and continued south.

So Ben and Evie had been together for four years. It'd be the longest Evie'd ever been with the same man. But Kris could see it in Ben—the patience, the self-sufficiency that Evie needed. Maybe even the love. And Ben sobered her up; maybe all she needed to stop drinking was a stable man. Did they split up because Corvus disappeared? It was probably his son that had kept Ben in the relationship; when Corvus was gone, there was no reason to stay.

The Subaru rattled loudly over ridges of ice frozen to the asphalt and Kris tightened her grip on the wheel until the street cleared. And then a chill settled in her belly. Maybe Evie left him. Maybe Ben followed her to Juneau. Maybe he did kill her because she'd moved in with another man. Maybe Justin was right.

Suddenly she couldn't think and she let the Subaru drive itself while scattered facts and thoughts whirled in her head until she remembered the wool fibers on the bushes and came back to Lambale. Ben couldn't have done it. Evie's murderer lay half way down a cliff wrapped around a tree. It had to be Lambale.

She got lost and had to ask for directions before she found the tannery on Placer Street. The parking lot in front of the building had been poorly plowed and there wasn't enough room for the Subaru between the two trucks already parked there. Kris drove down to a body shop and pulled into a corner of its lot and walked back along the road to the factory.

The lobby was deserted. A couple of chairs sat on a carpet spotted with coffee stains and cigarette burns. The walls were flimsy wood paneling that had buckled and warped. A dusty bear pelt sagged on one wall and in the corner were some black and white photographs of men with rifles standing behind dead animals. Behind an empty glass counter was a door; Kris pushed through it into a room lined with barrels of chemicals stacked against the walls, each with a black skull and cross bones stamped on its label. At the opposite end was another door, which opened into a concrete floored room filled with large vats and silent machinery. A sharp, chemical tang spiked the air. Kris unzipped her parka and walked into the room. The first vat she peered into was empty; dust and a crumpled cigarette pack lay at the bottom.

"Damn."

Kris turned, searching the room for the owner of the voice. Something clinked and then there was a sound of scraping metal. She followed the sound through the machinery until she found a man in a faded Carhartt jacket, on his knees leaning into the base of a machine. A bulb hung from a hook over his head. Tools and greasy machine parts were clumped in different piles to one side of him.

"I'm looking for the manager," Kris said.

The man grunted and withdrew his head from the cowling.

"Who the hell are you?" He was bald and wore glasses, which he pushed up his nose with the back of his hand.

"Kris Gabriel. A friend of mine used to work here."

He got off his knees and rose heavily to his feet, looking at her suspiciously. His shirt had been pulled out of his pants and she could see the skin of his stomach sagging over his belt. A socket wrench hung from a hand. "Who's that?"

"Ben Stewart."

The man pulled a rag out of his pocket and wiped his hands slowly. "I know old Ben."

"He and my mother were partners for a while."

"Gabriel," he said. "I thought it sounded familiar." His face eased up. "If you're looking for him, I don't know where he's at." He hitched up his pants, and got awkwardly back down on his knees. "I've got skins coming in here in a week and I'm not ready for them yet." He poked his head back into the opening. His arms tightened and Kris heard him grunt and whatever it was he was unscrewing, gave and his arm worked rapidly. Something clanked inside and a second later he brought his hand out and dropped a bolt into a tin can. The hand groped on the floor until it found the rag, then disappeared back inside with it.

Kris raised her voice. "Ben worked here, right?"

"Yeah," he answered, his voice muffled. "He hated it, but he was a good worker."

"Hated it?"

The man withdrew his head and looked at her. "Nobody who spends forty-fifty years in the bush willingly works for someone else."

"How long did he work for you?"

"Three years, thereabouts." He stuck his head back in the cowling.

"Did he sell you any furs the winter after he quit?" Why else would Ben have been up at his cabin?

"Ben couldn't trap anymore; he was like seventy. He had trouble getting through the day here. And to tell you the truth, I wasn't sorry when he gave his notice. I'm not running a nursing home for old trappers."

"He gave you notice after his boy disappeared?"

"What's that?"

"I said did he quit because his boy disappeared?"

"Who disappeared?" He pulled his head out and looked at her, wrinkling his nose to work his glasses higher.

"Corvus, his son. They woke up one day and he was gone."

"I don't remember that." His brow furrowed, but he was frowning from confusion, not because he was trying to remember.

"That had to be why he quit. Things fell apart for him after that."

"He never told me anything about it."

"What'd he say when he quit, then?"

He looked back in the cowling. "I don't remember. Something about something, I guess." He leaned in again with the wrench.

"So he gave you what, a week's notice?"

"Nope. He gave me plenty of notice. In fact, he trained the man who came in after him."

"But he didn't work past November." Ben hadn't signed his Bonus stub in December, so he had to have left by then.

"I don't remember. I think he left about this time a couple of years ago. Before Thanksgiving anyway."

"So when did he give you notice, then?" Kris said sharply. Ben couldn't have given notice before Corvus disappeared.

"What is this? The Inquisition?"

"Just tell me when he told you he was quitting."

He jerked his head out. "Back off, sister. I don't owe you nothing."

Kris glared at him, then dropped her eyes.

"Corvus was my brother," she said by way of an apology.

"I don't give a damn. I don't answer to assholes." He picked up a Phillips head and went back to work.

He worked quickly. Tools disappeared into the cowling and parts came out. Each was set off to the side in an organized line. Bolts and nuts were dropped into the can beside a pile of cracked wiring. Every once in a while he would glance out to see if she was still there.

Eventually he said. "As near as I can remember he gave me notice at the end of September or the beginning of October."

"You're sure?" Corvus had disappeared on the night of November third.

"Yeah. I hired Hank toward the end of October and that gave Ben two or three weeks to break him in."

Kris was silent again, turning this over in her mind. It didn't make sense.

"Do you know Ezekiel Damon?"

"Uh huh. I bought skins from him too. He trapped off the John east of Ben. But then, three or four years back, he quit showing up. I figured he started selling out of state. You can get better prices Outside. Tanneries there have lower overheard, but a lot of the trappers, especially Natives, don't like dealing with people they can't see. That's the only thing that keeps me alive."

"Do you know where he lives?"

"Not a clue." He pulled his head out, reached around for a cardboard box, and pulled out a part with wires sticking out of it. It was new, the matted steel clear and unblemished. He turned it over in his hand, examining it, before reaching back in with his socket wrench.

"If I wanted to find an old trapper in this town, were would I go?"

"Willy's."

"What's that?"

"Bar, off Cushman a ways."

"Is that all it's called? Just Willy's?"

"That's all anybody I know's ever called it. Ask for Jake Ash."

The sun had set when she got back in the Subaru, but the light was still a dusty gray. It was probably between one and two p.m.. She ripped the bag of chips open with her teeth while she drove back up Cushman. She followed the tanner's directions and found Willy's stuck between a tire store and a machine shop. She parked in front and pushed her way through the door, unzipping her parka as she entered. Miller clock, moose rack, dead TV, a pool table, a few tables and chairs; she'd never been here before, but she'd been in a lot of bars like it. It was empty; not even anyone behind the bar. She lifted herself on top of one of the stools and looked through a line of whiskey bottles at her face reflected in the mirror wall behind them.

A door at the back of the room opened and a scrawny man came out holding a pad and pencil.

"Sorry," he said. "I was doing my ordering. What can I get you?" he asked, walking behind the bar and pushing up his sleeves.

"I'm looking for Jake Ash. I was told I could find him here."

"He does his drinking here. But not till after eight or nine."

Kris glanced up at the Miller clock. A little after two.

"How about Ezekiel Damon? Does he come by?"

"Never heard of him."

"Thanks. I'll be back around eight."

Kris zipped up the parka outside the bar, zipping in cold air. She flinched at its bite but left her hood down and lit a cigarette, smoking it squeezed between her lips, her hands balled in her pockets. This was the Fairbanks she remembered. Gray twilight trapping the city's lights, dirty snow pushed against the sides of buildings, roads cracked and warped, cars and trucks pounding up and down them, banging into the potholes and over black bumps of ice, spewing huge clouds of exhaust that hung in the air until another vehicle plowed through them shredding them into cold, visible whirls.

No one turned to look at her.

■ ■ ■

"No. I'm working."

"I'll come up then."

The line was quiet.

"OK," Justin said without enthusiasm. "Let me see if the conference room is available."

The State's hold music jangled in Barrett's ear. A minute later, Justin came back on and said, flatly, "It's free."

"I'm on my way." Barrett hung up. He stuck a notebook into his blazer pocket and grabbed his raincoat and hat on his way out of his office. Justin had sounded guarded, even a little belligerent. Good signs. He's hiding something, and he's scared.

Barrett stepped into the rain and cut across the small parking lot on the channel side of the station, kicking through the gray-white slop the rain had made of Monday's snow. It had started last night and already the snow line on the mountainsides had retreated up to eight-hundred feet or so. He leapt over a puddle of rainwater backed up over a storm sewer clogged by mushy snow washing down Main Street. Rain spattered against his hat and shoulders as he walked up the hill. At Third, he crossed the street and climbed the short hill by the Spam Can to the state office building loading dock.

The woman behind the reception desk pointed out Justin's cubicle. Barrett walked to it and stood in its opening, dripping water on the carpet, waiting for Justin to turn around. Justin continued typing, ignoring Barrett long enough to register his annoyance, then clicked all his windows closed and said to him as he stood, "Wanted to finished that up."

Barrett let him play his games.

"This way," Justin said. Barrett followed him across the office to a small conference room that must have doubled as a storeroom. Cardboard boxes were piled in one corner, and the bookshelves, which lined the walls, were stacked haphazardly with books, government reports, and three-ringed binders with titles like, "State of Alaska Home Health Care Policy" and "Care Delivery to Geriatric Populations." A table, circled by chairs, crowded the room. At one end of it was a stack of papers and a phone; Justin pulled out a chair at the opposite end—so Barrett couldn't face him directly—and sat down. Barrett circled the table, squeezing between the bookcase and table, and sat facing the door.

Justin leaned back in his chair. "What's up?" he asked.

"How much money did you give Kris?" No point screwing around.

"I didn't give her a thing." His tone was testy.

"You didn't you give her money to fly to Fairbanks?"

"Kris is in Fairbanks?" Justin sat up, looking at Barrett in surprise.

"She flew up yesterday."

"You're joking." Justin said. "She didn't tell me."

"She bought a one-way ticket that cost three hundred and twelve dollars. It will cost her another three hundred and twelve dollars to get back here so that she can fly home. That's a lot of money for someone who stays at the hostel and wears a Princess Tours poncho."

"So she charged it," Justin said.

"She didn't. She doesn't have a credit rating and the Alaska Airlines clerk remembers her paying cash. Where'd she get it?"

"I haven't the faintest idea," he said.

"Did she get it from Lambale?"

"How would I know?"

"You know Lambale's missing." Barrett made it a statement.

"I saw it in the paper yesterday."

Barrett had spent the day before checking every possible route out of Juneau—there weren't many. He'd found no trace of Lambale and was convinced that he hadn't left town. "Do you know where he is?" It was a throwaway; Justin wouldn't know.

"He's in my closet."

"You don't think it strangely coincidental that the morning after Lambale vanishes, Kris skips town on a ticket she can't afford?"

"Where's the connection?" Justin asked. "What could she possibly have to do with Lambale disappearing?"

"I don't know, Justin," Barrett said gently. "But I think you're in trouble."

"Me?" Justin was caught off guard, but not yet worried. "I've never met the man."

"What did you find under the floor at Vern Jones's cabin Sunday?" Hit him from behind.

Justin didn't move, but Barrett saw a wariness fill in behind his eyes.

"Nothing."

He didn't deny lifting the floorboard. Barrett would have enjoyed toying with him. Forensics had found polyester fibers stuck to the plywood: the type of fibers found on the hi-tech, overpriced gloves you bought at Foggy Mountain or REI. Nothing Vern would have owned.

"Pretty sharp, finding that spot. The forensics crew had taken the entire shack apart before they found it."

"It was obvious," Justin said. "Ice on the floor meant the insulation had been ripped out." He relaxed slightly.

"You didn't tell me about it."

"Nothing there, nothing to tell." Justin picked at something on the chair arm.

Barrett watched him trying to look unconcerned. You've got to learn to look a person in the eye when you lie to him. Out loud, he said, "The dust on the shelf below the floor had been scraped aside by something hard. Something metal."

Justin didn't say anything.

"What did you find, Justin?"

"The locks of hair. That was it."

"You know that tampering with material evidence in a murder case is a felony? It can bring five years in this state."

Justin glared at him, looked away.

Barrett circled and came in from another direction. "Where was Kris Monday night?"

"At my place." Confidence trickled back into his voice.

"From when to when?"

"From five until about ten. I walked her back to the hostel."

"You were with her the entire time?"

"No. I got home around eight."

"Eight? How did she get into your house?"

"Apartment. I don't lock it."

"How do you know she was there since five?"

"She told me."

"She told you?" Barrett shaded his tone with sarcasm.

"Yeah. She'd eaten dinner, done a laundry, taken a shower."

"She made herself right at home." More sarcasm.

"She's a friend."

Is he being defensive? "I'm sure."

Justin pressed his lips together.

"How long does it take to take a shower?"

Justin didn't answer.

"Was her hair still wet?"

"I didn't notice." His eyes wandered along the bookcase.

"Was her laundry done when you got home?"

"No," he said, looking from the bookcases to the table.

"No? How many loads did she have?"

"Just her clothes."

"Just her clothes?"

"Yeah."

"One load?"

Justin didn't say anything.

"Three hours to do one load?"

"Maybe it took her a while before she decided to do it." He flared a little.

"Maybe." Come on, fight me. "What did you do with her from eight to ten?"

"We…"

"Did you sleep with her?" Barrett was playing with him; he knew Justin hadn't; Kris was more than he could handle.

"No."

"So what do you do for two hours with a pretty woman?"

"We talked."

"About what?"

"About things."

Barrett let his voice harden. "Quit jerking me around, Justin."

Justin stared at the table.

"Do you want a lawyer?" Drag him back into reality. "Should I read you your Miranda rights?"

"We came down here," he said unexpectedly.

"Here?" That was a hot date.

"Yeah. We wanted to check an inconsistency in something Ben had said."

Barrett pulled out his notebook. The hole in Kris's story looked promising, but this was a twist he hadn't expected. "Start from the beginning," he said and Justin told him about the forged signatures on Ben's Bonus stubs.

Barrett sat back in his chair and pressed his pencil point into his thigh until it hurt. It was an extraordinary piece of detective work. He never would've found it. Stewart. Barrett'd been negligent; he'd forgotten the old trapper in his rush to find Lambale yesterday.

Barrett looked at Justin. Tall, ungainly, and bright. He was slouched in the chair staring blankly at his hands resting in his lap. He'd still not answered the questions Barrett'd come to ask. Why was he covering for Kris? Did he think this was a game? Did he have the hots for her?

"That was good work," Barrett said, leaning forward on the table. Justin's mouth twisted into a rueful smile.

Pause. "Justin, Kris is using you. She's using you for an alibi and she's using you to keep quiet about whatever it is you found at Vern's."

"Up yours," he said.

"So why didn't she tell you she was leaving for Fairbanks?"

"Maybe she tried to."

"You got voice mail?" he asked.

No answer.

"She came by to tell me. Your office is only a couple of blocks out of the way."

Justin stared back at him.

"Justin, dammit. This isn't a game. Lambale may be hurt or dead. If Kris knows—"

"All right," Justin said irritably, sitting up. "We found about twenty-four hundred dollars in twenties in a cookie tin under the floor."

Jackpot. "You took it?"

"Kris did. I tried to talk her out of it. Tampering with evidence, but she wouldn't listen and made me keep quiet."

Made you? "What else?"

"There was a letter from Kris to her mother in there and a card with a number on it."

"Letter?"

"It was the letter Kris wrote to her mother telling her when she was coming up. I think Vern intercepted it before Evie saw it."

"What was the address?"

"Evie, care of the AWARE shelter."

"The AWARE shelter? Then how did Vern get hold of it?"

Justin grinned wickedly. "Maybe they're not as liberated as they make out."

"And the card with the number?"

"It was a five-digit number that started with a nine. I thought it was a valley phone number, but when Kris tried it she got a recording saying the number was not in service."

"Did you hear it?"

"No."

"Do you have the number?"

"Kris took it."

Barrett looked at the phone at the other end of the table and then at the shelves. "Get me a phone book."

Justin left the room. He was back in a second with one, which he handed to Barrett. Barrett flipped through it, found the page he wanted and ran his finger down the "L's."

"Does 789-1378 sound right?" he asked.

"No. It had two sets of double digits in it."

Barrett thumbed through the book again, found the number for the Rain Country Gallery and reached across the table for the phone. He punched it in and waited, listening to the rings. Alvilde Lambale answered.

"This is Barrett. Do you have a second line at home that's unlisted? You do?" He wrote a number on his pad, thanked her, and hung up. He wrote several similar numbers above and below it, spun the pad around and pushed it in front of Justin.

"Is it one of these?"

Justin picked it out immediately.

Barrett hit the speaker button on the phone and keyed the number. After the fourth ring, Alvilde's accented English assured them that their call would be returned promptly. Barrett broke the connection.

"She lied to me," Justin said.

Sunday he's a hero, Wednesday he's a sap. "You better hope your girl-friend is a reasonable girl," he said, "or you're in trouble. Vern had to be blackmailing Lambale, probably for something he did to Evie. Kris is bright enough to figure that out and impulsive enough to do something unpleasant about it."

Barrett's blood began to move—this girl would be one wild ride.

■ ■ ■

"That one there." The bartender partly uncurled his forefinger and point-ed back into the far corner. "The one with the beard."

Kris looked and saw five men seated around a table with glasses of beer in front of them and blue smoke coiling up from cigarettes. "They all got beards," she said, but she knew which one he meant. Ash's beard was thick and gray and squared off a few inches below his chin; it rose in front of his ears in neat lines and merged into a gray fringe that circled his head. His face was lined and leathery like Ben's; he sat quietly, listening to the others.

He spotted her as soon as she started toward them, squeezing around the packed chairs, a beer in her hand. His eyes followed her, but she avoid-ed them, looking down at the chairs she was pushing through. As she approached, he spoke to one of the others, who looked around at her in surprise, then pulled an empty chair from a neighboring table. Kris slipped into it and the men quieted, looking her over.

Ash leaned forward, his hand lifting from his lap and reached across the table. "Jake Ash." He shook her hand. The others in turn stretched out their hands and spoke their names.

Kris introduced herself when she'd shaken the last hand. From Jake, she felt an instant sharpening of interest.

"Ben Stewart used to be friends with a Gabriel," he said.

"Evie, my mother," Kris said.

"Good man, Ben."

And Evie? Kris shouldered out of her parka, letting it flop over the back of the chair.

"Where's Ben been? I've haven't seen him since last winter."

"Isn't he up the Alatna?"

"I thought he threw it in."

"Yeah, when he met Evie and had the kid."

"Did they go Outside?"

"Ben, Outside? It'd be kinder to shoot him."

"Didn't the kid die or something?"

Kris sipped her beer and let them talk around her. As she listened, she realized that they didn't know what to do with her. A stranger, a woman at their table, a break in their routine they didn't know how to handle. It didn't bother her and she sat with her beer listening to the conversation rise and fall. It wandered from Ben, without anybody asking her what she might know about him, or why she'd suddenly appeared at their table, to nights on the trail, makes of snowmobiles, gossip about other trappers, getting ready for the season, the price of furs, Outsiders in the bush—weekend trappers catching each other's dogs, leg hold traps, environmentalists…

"Never seen a wolf kill."

Kris sensed a change of tone. The man speaking was younger, in his mid-thirties, with several layers of gray and blue woolen underwear showing at his neck, under a worn flannel shirt. He turned toward her, his elbow on the table and finger outstretched.

"What do they think? That it's Disneyland out there? Ever see wolves rip the belly out of a living moose? Ever hear a moose scream? A leg hold trap is like dying in your sleep by comparison."

The others had dropped out of the conversation and were watching her. It was clear to Kris that they'd heard this before.

"Fucking greenies don't know what nature is. Got to keep the balance of nature they say. What do they think the wolf do? Say OK, boys, we've eaten enough caribou, time to lay off and eat mice until the herd grows back?

"You know," he whitened around the base of his nose, "once a man could raise a family in the bush. He'd hunt his moose in the fall, trap during the winter, and work a little placer claim in the summer. Now you can't do any of that: the wolf have eaten the moose, the greenies have knocked fur prices too low to make it pay, and they've shut down mining because they're upset about a little dirty water. Have you ever seen the Yukon? What's another ton of dirt going to do to it?"

He pulled into himself, stretching his lower lip and showing his bottom teeth. "It makes me so mad, I could kill somebody."

Kris set her glass on the table, twirled it with her fingers. "Why don't you?" she asked evenly.

"I'm going to," he said, but his bluff had been called and he sat back his chair, quietly fuming. Kris caught hidden smiles on some of the other faces.

Jake looked over their heads to the bar and made a circular motion with his finger.

"Are you looking for Ben?" he asked Kris.

"No. Ezekiel Damon. Do you know where I can find him?"

"Ezekiel," said another. "There's a strange one."

"Is he still out on the Sixtymile?"

"No, he quit a few years ago. Run out by the tourists."

"What he'd do with his team?"

"Still has it. He's off the Elliott, up toward Livengood."

"That was one amazing team. I saw him come into Bettles at the end of the season back in the nineties. He said "whoa" once and the dogs just stopped. He didn't set a brake, tie off. or nothing. He was in the store for half an hour and when he came back they were sitting there waiting for him."

A waitress appeared with a pitcher of beer and fresh glasses. Kris reached for her wallet. Jake caught her eye and shook his head.

When they'd finished pouring the beer, she asked, "What mile on the Elliott?"

They started arguing again until finally one pulled a napkin out of the stack in the center of the table and began drawing a map. When he'd finished, he turned it around in front of Kris. "This is where it takes off from the Steese." He pointed to a branch off the main road. "It's more than twenty, but less than thirty miles after that. Look for a hill. You'll come over the top of it and on the left is an old pit." He drew it in. "Go another half mile or so and his road will take off to the left. He doesn't plow it so his truck will be up by the road. That's as close as we can get you." He pushed the napkin toward her.

"Thanks." She folded the map and stuck it in her pocket.

"You're welcome," he said formally.

They looked at her expectantly, waiting for her to tell her story now. Kris lifted her glass and drank. The silence lingered, but before it grew uncomfortable they turned back to each other and started up their stories of the bush again. When Kris had finished her beer, Jake reached across the table, pointing to the napkin in her pocket. She handed it to him. Borrowing the pen, he wrote his name and number in the corner.

"If you need anything," he said and pushed it back to her.

"Thanks," she said and got up, lifting her parka off the back of the chair. She nodded to the table and left.

THURSDAY, NOVEMBER 19

Kris punched the trip meter.

More than twenty and less than thirty miles. She turned north off the Steese on to the Elliott Highway. The lights of an occasional car raced past her heading into town. Her lane was free and Kris kept the Subaru moving. She'd gotten a later start than she'd hoped for. Ringer'd wanted the truck today and there had been a whispered tiff between him and Annie this morning. In the end Kris had dropped Annie off at the library and promised to be back to pick her up by four. "Don't leave me waiting on a street corner," Annie said. But if Ezekiel wasn't at his cabin, she wasn't going to leave until he came back, even if it meant abandoning Annie and huddling all day in front of the Subaru's heating vents.

The cabin had been dark when she'd gotten back last night. But Wally started barking as she drove in and she'd tripped over some construction of the boys' while groping in the dark for her bed. She felt everyone in the cabin rouse, mutter, and twist around in their sheets. The boys had dropped off again, but rustlings and caught breaths from the curtained bed continued for a long time, leaving her stiff and awake long after Ringer and Annie had quit.

The road bobbed and weaved over the hills. The oncoming yellow lights thinned out to one or two cars every five minutes or so and had disappeared completely by the time she reached twenty mile. She slowed, peering into the trees on the left, looking for the pit after each hill she'd topped. At twenty-seven mile, she found it and a little farther on she saw a pickup parked off the road in a space that had been shoveled out of the snow thrown up by the plows.

Kris turned around in the road and pulled up behind the truck against the snow bank. She got out of the car, leaving it idling—she wanted it to start when she got back—and closed the door quietly. If he still had his team, they'd scent her soon enough. She walked around the truck and found the path. The morning had grayed enough to see it cut through the smooth, unmarked snow. It led down off the road, twisting between the slender, widely-spaced aspen and birch. Footsteps had beaten the path into the snow, and the air was cold enough—maybe ten or fifteen below—that the packed snow squeaked under her feet.

Kris headed down and when the path leveled out, she stopped. Sharp and unmuffled, she heard the rhythmic thwack of an ax striking wood. Farther down the path, something rippled in the dim light. She tensed, ready to run. A white shape the color of the snow jogged toward her. It was a dog. It stopped, not making a sound, and watched her. Then it came forward, its paws flicking in and out at the end of long forelegs, its ears pointed and alert. Ten feet away it leapt off the path and hopped through the deep snow around her, jumping back into the path behind her. Kris stepped forward and it followed, shepherding her into a clearing ringed by the small, leafless trees. It was lighter here, the morning gray unfiltered by the branches. A cabin sat to one side of the clearing and next to it a man stood with his back to her and an ax over his head. He snapped it down, exploding a round of spruce into splinterless halves, which spun off the chopping block into the snow. He reached down, lifted another round from the pile at his feet, set it butt-end on the block and lifted the ax; it fell and the cycle repeated.

Next to the cabin were stacks of split wood; across the clearing were two open sheds, stuffed with scraps of lumber, stacks of old shingles, stove pipes, PVC tubing, a window frame, and other junk. Between the sheds, capped with snow, was a row of fifty-five gallon drums. Littered around them were empty blue Blazo cans. She missed it at first, but when her eyes came back around she saw the dog yard through the trees at the far end of the clearing. The dogs were on top of their houses, staring at her, quivering silently; their tension explosive.

The white dog that had followed her in trotted past her around the pile of split halves and sat in front of Ezekiel. He lowered his ax and twisted around, staring into the trees toward Kris. She moved to give him something to see and with a short swipe he lifted and buried the ax in the chopping block and walked toward her.

He was tall and came closer than a stranger should. Standing over her in the half-light, he looked dried and desiccated, like jerked meat. His face was scarred and pitted; blood vessels had broken in his nose and cheeks, black framed glasses hid his eyes and a grayed, untrimmed beard fell in spikes from his chin. Ice rimmed the mustache under his nose and a ball of frozen breath dangled from the hairs at the corner of his mouth.

Kris looked steeply up at him and, for a moment, she quailed. In him was an authority that his ravaged face and the baleful lenses of his glasses pressed down on her.

"Why are they quiet?" she asked impulsively, nodding to the dogs.

He lifted his fist and opened a finger. The dogs exploded. Their violence unleashed, they charged, surging against their chains, their hind legs thrusting against the snow, front paws flailing the air. Some barked, most howled, their muzzles lifted to the sky. He closed his hand and the dogs stopped instantly.

"My minions," he said.

Kris fought to relax her shoulders. "I'm Kris Gabriel, a friend of Ben's," she said. "You're Ezekiel Damon?"

"I am." He took off his gloves, they were cotton. He didn't offer his hand. "Come in."

Kris followed him into the cabin. It was dark. Ezekiel struck a match, lifted the glass chimney of a kerosene lantern, and lit the wick. He set it on a table by a window—a gray square in the wall. He lifted another lantern off a shelf and lit it, placing it on the other side of the table. But even with two lights, the cabin was buried in shadows. It was small and built by a person whose only interest was utility. The floor was unpainted plywood; the basin and slop bucket in the corner were framed by two-by-fours toe-nailed into the floor and side wall. Shelves made out of peeled spruce poles were fastened onto two of the walls. On them were bottles and cans, loose tools, scraps of tin, spools of thread, coils of string and twine and books. Row and row of books browned and greasy-looking from the soot of winter fires. Under the shelves were open boxes and crates of fabric, dried food, pots and pans, old magazines and clothes and forgotten projects.

In the bush, Kris knew, nothing is thrown away. She sat in a chair made of slab wood, pulled off her mittens, and unzipped her parka, throwing it over the back of the seat. Ezekiel removed his glasses and, with a thumbnail, scraped off the frost that had grown on the lenses when they'd hit the warm and moist indoor air. After they were clear, he opened the damper on the wood stove, lifted the top, and put several sticks of split spruce, fiddling with the logs to get them right. To the side of the stove, was a ladder nailed to the cabin wall leading up to a loft.

Ezekiel pulled a small cook stove from under the plywood counter by the basin and set it on top. He poured Blazo on it and touched a match to the gas. The flame flared high, lighting Ezekiel's face with wild yellow streaks. He was older than Kris had imagined. The skin over his cheeks was sunken and when he spoke again, she saw black gaps between stained teeth.

"Ben is a good man," Ezekiel said, turning on the stove when the flame died down; it roared like a tiny jet engine. He put an enameled pot over the blue flame and reached up to a shelf for mugs.

"Yeah." Kris wasn't sure what to say. "He hurt his back." Ezekiel didn't respond and Kris felt awkward. "They had to take him to the hospital," she added.

"Ben ran a good line," Ezekiel said. "He could skin out a mouse without nicking the hide."

They were quiet, waiting for the water to boil. Ezekiel filled the mugs and dropped in tea bags. Red Rose. They sat at the table by the side window. Behind Ezekiel, the undampened fire took off and Kris could hear the snap of exploding pitch. Ezekiel sat straight in his chair and gazed down at her. The wavering flames of the lanterns reflected in his lenses.

"Evie Gabriel was my mother," Kris said.

Ezekiel didn't respond.

"She was murdered last week."

"It is better that way," Ezekiel said unexpectedly. "The burden that he has had to bear."

"What burden?"

Ezekiel said nothing.

"I'm looking for Corvus."

"He's not here," Ezekiel said.

"I know that. What do you know about him? Do you know how he disappeared?"

"Talk to Ben."

Was Ben still angry at her? If she'd risked another day in Juneau before coming north, would he have calmed down enough to talk to her; would he have known things about Corvus that hadn't been in the police reports?

"Why did you forge Ben's name on his Longevity Bonus stubs?" she asked.

His expression didn't change. "I didn't forge anybody's name."

Kris turned in her chair and searched through the folds of the parka for the inner pocket. She unzipped it and pulled out the copies Justin had made of Ben and Ezekiel's stubs. She found one with Ben's signature on it and another with Ezekiel's forged signature, and one of Ezekiel's own stubs. She placed them before him.

"You signed this." She tapped Ben's stub that Ezekiel had signed.

Ezekiel stared at her.

"The Longevity Bonus check is pretty important to you, isn't it?" she asked, looking around the cabin. Anywhere else but Alaska, it'd be the worst kind of squalor.

Let him think about it. She got up, lifting her teacup and moved away sipping the tea. No sugar. She walked to the sink, but couldn't find any on the shelves. She dumped the tea out; it trickled into the slop bucket below, and rinsed the cup with clean water from a pot and laid it upside down on the plywood counter. A towel hung from a nail; she dried her hands.

It was too soft.

She touched it again and then lifted it off the nail and raised it to the light. It was a diaper. Old and worn, with fraying edges, but a diaper. Who used cloth diapers? Kris wadded it in her fist and walked back to the table, easing into her chair.

The photocopies were lying on the table untouched.

"Why did you forge Ben's signature?" she said, this time with more strength in her voice.

"Who are you?" Ezekiel's voice was low.

"These will get you thrown off the program," she said.

"Do you think you can set me against Ben Stewart?"

"Whatever you tell me, I'll keep quiet. Nothing goes to the cops."

"They don't concern me."

"Ben brought Corvus here, didn't he?"

"Talk to Ben."

"He's my brother, Ezekiel," she said, softly.

"Talk to Ben."

"Why did Ben bring him here?"

"I never saw the boy."

"Explain this, then." Kris placed the diaper in the middle of the table on top of the photocopies. He looked at it, his eyes hidden behind the reflected flame of the lanterns on his lenses.

"It's a diaper," she said.

"I see that."

"Corvus's diaper."

"I buy rags at the Salvation Army. Twenty-five cents a bundle. It came from there."

"You don't buy rags at the Salvation Army. You don't buy anything."

"Suit yourself." Ezekiel stood, blew across the lantern chimneys blowing out the flames, and picked his gloves up from the table. "I have wood to split."

Kris gathered up the diaper and photocopies, and stuffed them in a pocket. She stood, fumbling for the parka's zipper. She was shaking, and she wasn't sure why. Ezekiel stood with his hand on the door latch, looking down at her, the light in the cabin too weak to illuminate his face.

Kris approached him, pushing her hands into her mittens. He didn't move.

"Kris Gabriel," he said. "Go home. This isn't for you to know." Then he was gone, out the door and into the cold air.

Kris pulled the door shut after her. Ezekiel had vanished. When the dogs scented her, they howled, launching themselves against their chains. Their fury followed her to the road.

■ ■ ■

Barrett looked up through the rain at Stewart's house squatting in the black and broken shrubs on the steep hillside above him. The window overlooking the channel stared vacantly into the morning darkness. No light shone in it; the house looked dead. He'd tried to call, but Stewart had no number, listed or unlisted.

He started up the stairs. After his talk with Justin the day before, he'd called the hospital, but Stewart had been sedated. When he called this morning, he learned that Stewart had walked out before six; the staff hadn't been able to stop him. Barrett wondered at the toughness of the old trappers, remembering Huntington's story of the Native elder whose skin was so leathered it turned a hypodermic needle. Life in the bush was a different order of existence.

Stewart was probably back in bed asleep, but Barrett had wanted answers on Monday and today was Thursday; he wasn't going to wait any longer.

It wasn't Stewart, though, who disturbed him; it was Lambale. What the hell could he have done that Vern could blackmail him for? It would be easier to blackmail a Hallmark gift card. Barrett stopped on the stairs, ignoring the rain driving into his back. The question had nagged him all day yesterday. It had to be something to do with Evie. Which meant that there had to be some connection to the AWARE shelter; there was nowhere else that they could've met. But he'd spent all of yesterday afternoon there and learned nothing. Yes, Lambale had been friendly with Evie, but he'd been friendly with many of the women he got to know during the construction of the new wing. No one had seen or suspected anything out of the ordinary.

Did Kris know what Vern Jones had had on Lambale? Justin had convinced him that they hadn't found any pictures or other evidence in the shack, although Kris may have found something in the loft in addition to the leather purse that she hadn't told Justin about. Barrett started up the stairs again. If Lambale had done something to Evie, what would Kris want from him? Money? More likely it would have been blood; vengeance was more her style. But what could she do to him? She'd had only two hours. Lambale logged off his computer at five-sixteen and Justin had guessed that her footprints on his steps had half an hour's worth of new snow in them by the time he'd gotten home at eight. Two hours and fifteen minutes.

Barrett'd had people crawling over the city again yesterday. The airport, the harbor—fishing and pleasure boats—hotels, friends' houses; they hadn't found a single lead. The Mercedes had been towed to the police garage and was being taken apart by forensics. No report yet, but he didn't have much hope. Lambale had vanished.

What did Kris do? What could she do in two hours, in the middle of town, with a man twice her size?

At the house, Barrett took a couple of deep breaths to quiet his breathing and then raised his fist to bang on the door loud enough to wake Stewart. But before he knocked, Stewart called to him from inside and Barrett turned the handle and went in.

A single kerosene lamp sat on a chair close to Stewart and cast a dim glow into the small room's darkness. He sat stiffly in a chair by the wood stove facing the window. Even in the shadowed light, his face looked drawn and sunken. Barrett took off his dripping hat and raincoat and hung them on a nail. Stewart nodded to the chair with the lamp on it and Barrett lifted the glass lantern, setting it between them on the floor, and sat down.

"How are you feeling?" he asked.

Stewart pointed to several bottles of pills on the windowsill.

"I'm surprised to see you sitting up. In fact, I'm surprised to see you at home."

"That was not a good place to be," Stewart said, his voice raspy.

"I'd like to ask you some questions, Mr. Stewart."

Stewart was silent.

"You misled us," Barrett said. "And you have hidden from us facts material to this investigation." Barrett paused, waiting for a response. There was none; he continued. "You were down the Point Bishop trail forty minutes, not twenty as you'd claimed. What were you doing there during those additional twenty minutes?"

Through the shadows, Barrett saw Stewart's lips tremble and then slowly form his words.

"Saying good-bye," he said.

Stewart's simple declaration, so full of pain and loss, momentarily silenced Barrett.

"Why didn't you tell me?" he asked, but when Stewart didn't answer, he didn't press.

"Why didn't you tell us that you and Ms. Gabriel had a son together?"

Again Stewart's lips trembled and it took seconds before he could speak.

"Does Kris …?" he asked.

"Yes. She found her mother's purse with the lock of his hair. That's how we found out."

Stewart's eyes dropped to the floor. An unfelt draft guttered the lantern flame and the shadows on Stewart's face wavered.

"Why didn't you tell me about your son and your relationship with Ms. Gabriel, Mr. Stewart?"

"Do you think I killed her?" Stewart lifted his head and held Barrett's eyes with his own. Even in the dim light the pupils were unnaturally large.

Barrett was irritated and didn't spare him. "The circumstantial evidence is compelling," he said. "Your whereabouts on Tuesday can't be corroborated. Since she knew you, it would have been extremely easy for you to get her down to Thane. It was you, of all people, who discovered the body; you lied about the length of time you were down the trail on Wednesday and you were there long enough to destroy any evidence you might have left the previous day. You attempted to hide your relationship with Gabriel—including the fact that you had a child with her, which suggests jealousy as a motive for the murder, since she had become involved with another man. In fact, your arrival in Juneau only a few weeks after they arrived indicates that you probably followed them here from Fairbanks. No grand jury would have difficulty returning an indictment for murder on this evidence."

Rain, hard as gravel, splattered against the window and Stewart turned to watch the water stream in crooked runnels down the glass. Barrett waited for him to speak; when he didn't, Barrett spoke again, sharply, trying to force answers out of the old man. "Why didn't you tell me about Evie and Corvus?"

"Where's Kris?" Stewart asked.

Barrett straightened in frustration. Stewart had too many painkillers in him.

"She's in Fairbanks," he said.

Stewart's head lumbered around, concern pricking through his stupor.

"She's looking for Corvus," Barrett explained.

"Corvus?" What was that in his voice? Barrett tried to hear it again. Surprise? Fear?

"Yes. She knows about Ezekiel Damon. She knows that you spent the winter Corvus disappeared at your cabin in the Brooks Range and she knows that Damon forged your signature on your Longevity Bonus Stubs."

"She knows?"

Stewart was worried; Barrett could hear it now. Worried for whom? Himself? For Kris?

"Why did you leave Evie and go back into the bush?" Barrett pushed, trying to break through Stewart's haze.

He didn't answer right away.

"We lost Corvus. We...she started drinking. I..." Stewart stumbled, confused. "It was too much," he said. He looked at his hands lying limply in his lap. "There was so much I didn't know," he said at last, defeat naked in his voice.

Barrett was suddenly embarrassed. The old man's soul was exposed, laid open by the painkillers. But he continued to press. "Why did you have

Damon sign your stubs? Why didn't you just go on remote and pick up your checks when you came out?"

Stewart stared into the darkness. Barrett waited him out.

"To pay the rent," he said softly. "Evie's rent."

Barrett sat with him watching the light thicken into the dull gray of pre-dawn. He sat until he could see the mountains across the channel emerge from the dark and the rain falling in cold, unrelieved sheets from clouds sagging from the sky as if tired of lifting their own weight. When it was time to go, he asked Stewart if there were anything he could do for him, knowing beforehand the answer would be no.

Then, as he stood, he said as an aside, "Do you remember Loren Lambale? The man who paid for Evie's funeral?"

Stewart looked up at him.

"He's missing. He disappeared Monday evening." Barrett was going to say more, but decided not to. What could it mean to the old man?

He snugged the door closed and hunched his shoulders against the rain as he started down the long line of steps.

■ ■ ■

From behind the rain-splattered glass, Ben watched Barrett jog downwards through the broken bushes that hid the stairs. He saw him vanish behind the shrubs at the bottom and re-emerge on the street below, walking care-fully, skidding once, down the steep road toward the Baranof Hotel until he merged into the morning gloom.

Ben dropped his eyes into the thick tangle of brambles that covered the hillside below him. Salmonberry, thimbleberry, and the tall growing goat's beard. They lay before him, dead and lifeless, victims of the flatten-ing wind, the pelting rain, and comfortless cold. He could not remember when their stalks and branches, coursing with sap, had stood erect and unbowed—their green leaves lifted to a warm sun. He looked up. Against the muddy gray of the clouds he saw a raven, black as the arctic night, lift to the wind and then fall in wild corkscrews toward the water below.

Before it was seized by the waves, it extended its wings, catching the wind, and was hurled back into the sky.

He turned from the window to the cabinet by the door. Underneath it, on the uncluttered little table, lay a telephone book and the telephone unconnected to the rest of the world. He knew that there was nothing behind the cabinet door. He pushed himself to his feet with the cane they had given him and hobbled, three-legged, to the cabinet. Its knob was above his bowed head and he reached for it without looking up and pulled the door open. The bottom shelf, level with his raised eyes, was empty. He reached his hand in, quivering, leaf-like, and swept it across the unpainted wood. His pistol was gone.

Oh, Kris.

■ ■ ■

Christ, four and a half and still in diapers. Kris lifted her foot off the pedal; the curves were coming too fast. What was going on? She pulled a mitten off with her teeth and shook a cigarette out of the pack. The driver's side window was thick with the frosted moisture of her breath; she cracked it to let the smoke out and shivered when the cold air sliced in. Corvus had been at Ezekiel's and he must have been there after he had disappeared—otherwise Ezekiel wouldn't have denied it.

Did Ben steal his own kid? It looked like he had it all set up: he gave the tannery a month's notice, he had a place to hide him—maybe he even had Ezekiel drive to town that night to pick the boy up so Ben didn't have to leave the apartment. But then what? Why steal your own kid?

Ben couldn't have left Corvus with Ezekiel for long; he didn't look like he'd be into changing diapers. Ben had to have gotten Corvus out of there before going up to his cabin—which would have been by the end of the month, before he got his December Bonus. Kris blew smoke into the windshield. Annie was sure to smell it. The car sped over a rise and Kris glimpsed the top curve of the sun, sharp and pale behind a thin overcast, coming up through the trees.

Did he take Corvus with him into the bush?

What else could he have done? He didn't have any other choice. Kris braked the Subaru and pulled off the road. In the glove compartment, she found a tattered road map of Alaska. Half of the folded panels had frayed off and she hunted through them looking for the pieces she needed. If he'd taken the boy with him, he couldn't have flown in; Corvus'd be seen. She fit the panels together on her lap. So he had to get in another way. The Elliott Highway continued north from Ezekiel's cabin until it reached Livengood where the haul road to the oil fields on the North Slope started. To the west was Allakaket where Ben's river, the Alatna, drained into the Koyukuk. With a mittened hand, she traced the Koyukuk backwards through Bettles to where it forked; both the south and middle forks cut the haul road just below the Brooks Range. Kris measured it off with the edge of the mitten. About fifty miles down the Koyukuk from the haul road to Allakaket. Ezekiel could have run him and a dog team up to one of the forks in his truck and from there it was a straight run by sled to the village. It wouldn't have taken Ben two days.

Then what?

Kris looked through the cracked windshield. Down the road were a couple of ravens picking at some road kill. They hopped on and off the flattened animal tugging at frozen pieces of flesh.

Allakaket—it was a Native village. If Evie couldn't do it, couldn't raise a kid with the alcohol disease, then maybe Ben gave him to a Native friend to raise—and if Evie wanted to keep him—not give him up to a stranger—that would have been why Ben had to sneak him out of the apartment. When Kris was a kid, the state had taken her away from Evie twice—and both times Evie struggled helplessly with the social worker before collapsing on the floor crying. Kris had figured Evie didn't want to lose the welfare money she got when Kris was at home. But she and Ben weren't on welfare, she had nothing to lose if she lost Corvus. Except Corvus.

Kris released the brake and drove back onto the road, accelerating over the road kill and scattering the ravens.

Corvus had to be alive.

When Kris arrived back in Fairbanks, she drove straight to the airport. The parking lot was half-empty; she left the Subaru idling and walked across the lot to the entrance. The counters for the local carriers that flew charters and scheduled routes out to the villages were off to the side. At the Frontier Flying desk, a woman working her way through a stack of forms told her that all the seats for the afternoon flight into Allakaket had been taken by the Venetie basketball team. So Kris bought a ticket for the next morning.

"You're not local, are you?" the woman asked.

Kris shook her head.

"Do you have a place to stay? There's nothing there, no hotels or anything. And they won't let you sleep in the school without prearranging it. The Venetie team has probably taken it over **anyway**."

Kris's face hardened, people were always trying to talk her out of things.

"You know what you want to do," the woman said. "Is talk to Nancy Kestrel at TCC. We fly her in all the time. She might have an idea. Do you know where TCC is? Tanana Chiefs Council?"

Kris vaguely remembered that TCC was a Native organization that worked in the villages. "Is it still downtown by the river?" she asked; she remembered it being close to the youth shelter.

"Yes, around Noble Street." The woman pulled out a business card and wrote Kestrel's name on the back. "Talk to her and if you need to make changes to your ticket let me know by this afternoon."

The receptionist buzzed Kestrel and then pointed Kris down a corridor toward her office. Kestrel was on the phone when she arrived and Kris hovered in the doorway waiting for her to get off. Kestrel was Native, hair permed, wearing a skirt, stockings, and short heels. She waved her hands as she talked and her voice was friendly though with an edge of authority in it. The office was on the south side of the building and on a floor high enough off the street for Kris to be able to see, through the city's haze, the white disk of the sun hovering above the horizon. Tropical plants hung from the ceiling, grew in big pots in the corners, and in smaller ones on top of file cabinets and along the edges of her desk. What would Ringer say about tropical plants a hundred miles south of the Arctic Circle?

Kestrel hung up and beamed at Kris, her arm outstretched.

"What do you think of my plant?" she said, after they'd introduced themselves and Kris had sat down. She picked up a small plant with rubbery leaves and a single red blossom on a short stalk. "I grew it from a seed a friend sent me from Costa Rica."

"Don't think there's much chance of it becoming the kudzu of the north," Kris said, siding with Ringer. Seinfeld'd had a show about kudzu.

Kestrel laughed. "Not a chance. So, what can I do for you?"

"I need to go to Allakaket and the woman down at Frontier Flying said you might know of a place I could stay there."

Kestrel's eyebrows shot up. "I wasn't expecting that," she said. "Why would anybody who doesn't live there want to go to Allakaket at this time of year?"

"I think my brother might be there," Kris said and she told her enough of the story for it to make sense.

Kestrel didn't speak until Kris had finished. "Corvus isn't in Allakaket. If there were a strange boy living there I'd have known about it inside of a day. It's a tiny village, less than three hundred people. Nothing happens there that everybody doesn't know about."

Kris's face went stony.

"But let me give the village office a call and see what they know." Kestrel found the number, punched it in and when someone answered, asked about Ben. She listened, then put her hand over the phone, "No one saw Ben with a boy. In fact, no one saw much of Ben at all that winter. Usually he comes down to the village a couple of times a season to pick up bush orders sent up from Fairbanks, but the last year he was there, he never came down. They don't think he was working his lines either."

Then, as an afterthought, she said, "Remember that the village was pretty chaotic that year; it was still recovering from the flood." Kestrel looked at her questioningly. "Anything else?"

"I want to go up to his cabin," Kris said, impulsively. If Corvus hadn't been seen in Allakaket, the cabin was the only other place Ben could have taken him.

"Whoa, it's getting serious up there, you know," Kestrel said. "Not much light there and colder than here."

"Is there someone who can get me up there from Allakaket?"

Kestrel spoke into the phone again and then hung up. "Beth's gone to get Johnny. He's got a new snow machine and can probably run you up." Kestrel looked concerned. "Corvus is not going to be up there, Kris."

"Maybe I can find out what happened to him. Maybe Ben took him somewhere else."

"I doubt it," she said. "I know all the villages north of here and south of the Brooks. If a strange boy came into one, I'd hear about it."

"Who's Johnny?" Kris asked, changing the subject; she didn't want to be talked out of going up.

"A good kid, eighteen or nineteen. Doesn't talk much. Sober. Lives mostly subsistence, traps some in the winter, knows what he's doing. I'd feel safe going out on a snow machine with him."

"Thanks," Kris said.

"You're part Native?" Kestrel asked.

"My mother was Athabascan. I don't know what my father was." Kris felt uncomfortable. She didn't want any ties pulling her back here.

Kestrel told her stories about life in the villages until the phone rang. She explained what Kris wanted, listened and then said to her. "Johnny will take you up, but he has to get back early—big basketball game tomorrow evening."

"How far is it?" Kris asked.

Kestrel pushed the speaker button and repeated Kris's question.

"Maybe seventy miles," Johnny said. His speech had a heavy Native lilt; Evie'd had a trace of it too. "Harold broke trail up to Mettenpherg Creek last week, he's putting a line in up there. It's probably blown in some and after that we have to break it new. They'll be overflows, but the ice is good. The river closed in a few weeks ago."

"Can you do it in a day?" Kestrel asked.

"Four or five hours up and three coming back. Long day."

Kris raised her voice. "I won't come back with you. I want to stay up there for a while."

Johnny thought about this. "You want me to come get you later?"

"Yes. Four or five days."

"Give her a good price, Johnny," Kestrel said.

"A hundred plus gas for each trip."

Kestrel nodded to Kris.

"OK," said Kris. "I leave here tomorrow at eight-thirty on Frontier. Can you meet me at the airport?"

"I can do that."

"Ready to go?"

"We'll have to gas up, is all."

Kestrel said goodbye and hung up. "Take cash and everything you need up with you. There's a store, but not much in it and it's expensive."

Kris stood, gathering her parka and mittens.

"It's pretty courageous going out in the bush this time of year. There's not a lot of margin for error. Have you got all the gear you need?"

"I can get it." She could borrow stuff from Annie.

Kris wandered the aisles behind her shopping cart without a really good idea of what she needed. Meals at home depended a lot on adding water, stirring and ten or fifteen minutes in her toaster oven. She threw in some cup-of-soups, cans of beans, frozen burritos—if she left them outside to-night they wouldn't thaw—a couple of Rice-a-Roni packages, Kraft macaroni and cheese, frozen lasagna, and coffee. Going through the checkout, she loaded up with candy bars.

It was three-thirty when she pulled into the staff parking at the library. Annie saw her come through the doors and waved.

"How was your day?" she asked, looking up from behind a stack of new kids' books she was pressing bar-code stickers on.

"Good," Kris said. "I'm going up to Allakaket tomorrow." She unzipped the parka and stuffed her mittens in its pockets.

"You're what?"

"I have to be at the airport at eight. I'll just sleep there so you don't have to get up early to drive me in."

"Allakaket? What are you going to do there?"

"Go up to Ben's cabin."

"Honey, it's the middle of the winter."

"I got a ride up on a snowmobile."

Annie settled back in her chair, her eyes on Kris. "You move fast, my friend. Let me get this stuff done and we can talk on the way home. Why don't you check out our mural." She pointed into the kids' reading room. "See if you can find the cheechako."

The painting was in the corner of the room and stretched from the floor to the ceiling. On a hill was a fairy castle and, wending their way toward it with banners rippling in the summer breeze, was a long line of fairy-tale people. Kris examined each one. Near the bottom, lost in the trees, she found a mosquito huddled in a parka. That was the cheechako, she figured, bundled up and shivering in the middle of summer.

Annie wasn't being subtle.

■ ■ ■

"Oatmeal. You got to have oatmeal. The quick-cooking stuff, you can eat it hot or cold."

Oatmeal wasn't something she was likely to eat. Hot or cold.

"And you can load it with calories: butter, honey, raisins, and nuts. You'll need piles of energy." Ringer scooped cupfuls of the cereal out of a red and blue cardboard barrel into a gallon-sized Ziploc bag. It looked like shredded newspaper. "Let's see," he said, squeezing the air out of the bag and sealing it. He reached under the counter and pulled out a red box the size of a suitcase. "Powdered milk."

Evie'd brought powdered milk home from the food bank once on one of her sporadic attempts to improve themselves. Kris had poured it into the toilet the next day while Evie'd pushed the flusher.

Kris looked without interest at the growing line of neatly packed Ziplocs. There was no point in arguing with him; she'd chuck what she didn't want later. The food Kris had bought lay heaped at her feet; half of it rejected. Ringer had pulled out all the cans; "They'll just freeze and burst." It'd pissed off Kris that she'd forgotten that. Christ, she'd grown up with frozen pipes. "You need a microwave for this"—he'd tossed aside her two packages of frozen lasagna—"and even if you cooked it up in a pot, you don't want to lug the plastic containers around with you." He made a face at her Rice-a-Roni and macaroni and cheese but let her have them, taking them out of their packaging and writing the instructions on the inner envelope. "Got to watch your weight."

Annie wandered over and surveyed the food and gear spread out on the table. "Tampons?" she asked. Kris shook her head; she had a week yet.

"Water is a big problem. It freezes in minutes. You keep this"—he lifted a flat plastic bottle—"inside your parka. This one"—it was wrapped in foam fastened with duct tape—"is insulated. If you put boiling water in it, it should stay liquid for a couple of hours. Drink this first, then the other." He put them next to the pile of gear he'd laid out for her. Ringer's enthusiasm was oppressive and she just let him do his thing. He didn't seem to understand that she was going up on a snow machine; she wasn't going to be trucking this shit across any frozen tundra.

FRIDAY, NOVEMBER 20

"Will ya look at that," Ringer said with disgust, pointing through the truck's window at a woman tiptoeing through the inch of snow that had fallen during the night. "Can you believe somebody'd be wearing heels in Fairbanks? In the winter?" The woman stepped into the rut a tire had made in the snow and followed it toward the terminal. Kris remembered Alvilde, who'd come to Evie's funeral in heels, and which had kept sinking into the wet ground as she stood by the grave.

Ringer pulled into an empty slot and popped the clutch. "She needs a good pair of mukluks." He slid out, slamming the door. The back gate screeched when he lowered it to pull out the pack. He slung it on his shoulder while Kris reached in and grabbed her duffle. Last night, the pack had been too heavy for her to lift after Ringer'd finished stuffing it with all the food and gear he thought she'd need, and she'd made him repack half the food into her duffle.

Inside, the terminal was bright and busy. The first Jenny in Alaska still hung motionless from the ceiling. They walked over to Frontier Flying and the woman behind the counter remembered her.

"Did you find Nancy?" she asked.

"Yeah, thanks."

"So you're all set?"

"Yeah, I got someone to meet me there." Kris dropped the duffle on top of the pack, which Ringer had already dropped on the scales.

"Sixty-five pounds. You're over weight."

"You're at minimums," Ringer said. "You can't go any lighter and you're not even packing a tent or cook stove."

"It's a dollar a pound for anything over forty-five pounds. Another twenty."

Kris pulled out a bill.

"Gate C. Have a good flight."

Ringer walked her down to the gate.

"You don't have to hang around," Kris said. She didn't like good-byes and she owed Ringer too much to feel comfortable sitting with him.

"Yah, OK. I got to hop on my chores, anyway." He stuck out his hand. Kris took it.

"It's beautiful country up there," he said, surprising her with a moment of reverence. "It's God's country. Enjoy it." He squeezed her hand. "Later."

Kris brushed aside an unexpected feeling of loneliness as he walked away. She turned and surveyed the waiting area; eyes that had been resting on her dropped as she met them. There were four other people, all Native and certain to be wondering what she was doing, a stranger, going to Allakaket in the winter. They had open faces—one man looked back up and smiled at her—but they were strangers and she looked away. She wanted a cigarette, glanced at the clock, but there wasn't enough time. She sat and waited, fidgeting with her parka zipper.

At twenty after, the woman who had written her ticket came down and opened the door leading onto the tarmac. Cold air rolled into the room. Kris zipped her parka and lined up behind the only other woman on the flight. Framed by the door was the morning's darkness, punctuated by lights that flashed and sped by on low tractors and baggage carts. In the distance, a jet lumbered into the black air. The woman smiled at her and took her boarding pass. Kris filed across the tarmac to a small plane. Standing next to the steps up to the plane's door was a uniformed stewardess in an open parka who looked part Native; a half-breed like Kris. The stewardess pulled her out of the line when Kris approached.

"Wait here a sec," she whispered.

Now what? Kris watched, irritated, as the others climbed into the plane before her. The stewardess greeted each by name. When the last had climbed on, she motioned to Kris.

"Up you go," she said and climbed up behind her. Kris stooped under the plane's low ceiling and started down the narrow aisle for an empty seat in the rear, there were only eight seats in the plane, but the stewardess plucked at her parka and steered her forward into the cockpit, pointing at one of the pilots' seats. Kris sat down uncertainly and stared at the instrument panel in front of her. The stewardess turned back into the main compartment and pulled the plane door closed. She recited her safety lecture and passed around a basket of candy and earplugs. She offered it to Kris, saying, "Take some candy to keep your ears from popping, but you won't need the plugs."

Then she squeezed between the seats and settled into the one on Kris's left. She glanced slyly over at Kris while pulling her arms out of her parka and settling it around her. "First rule. Always be the last one on a bush plane, that way you can sit up front." She stretched behind her shoulders for her seatbelt and clipped herself in and then reached over and pulled Kris's seatbelt over her; it was more complicated than the one on the jet. She showed Kris how to click the different belts into the circular buckle at her waist. Then she handed her a pair of earphones and Kris fitted them over her head.

"I'm Jen," she said, the electronics making her voice sound small and impersonal.

This is the pilot?

"Kris," Kris said into the microphone. Her voice sounded in her own set, but the first letter had been clipped off. 'Ris.

Jen had a checklist open on her thigh and was rapidly going down it, flipping switches and pushing buttons. The cabin lights clicked off and Jen's face was speckled with green and orange lights from the control panel. The plane shuddered and Kris heard the whine of an engine begin to rise in pitch. A few seconds later, the second engine caught and its whine followed the other's up the scale. When the whines were equal, a man in coveralls stood in front of them and signaled. Jen rested her finger on a gauge. When the needle moved into the green, her hands moved across the controls again, then one settled on the steering handle in front of her and the other on buttons labeled "Throttle" and "Feather." She pulled them out slowly and the plane moved forward.

Jen's voice spoke, full of easy authority, in Kris's earphones; someone else responded. The plane moved across the pavement and turned into a lane marked by yellow lines. They taxied alongside the runway. When they reached the end, Jen spoke again, and was answered, "cleared for takeoff." She pulled the throttle out and the plane accelerated as they turned onto the runway. They straightened out and Kris was pushed back into her seat as they raced down the pavement. Jen pulled the steering wheel in front of her and the plane lifted into the air. Two heartbeats later, she spun them in a tight curve to the right and Kris looked down at the airport shrinking away from her.

The plane flattened out of its curve and continued climbing. Jen was punching buttons on a small instrument in the control panel between them; abbreviated names of villages flashed across a tiny display." Allkt" appeared; she locked it in and settled back, her hands off the controls.

"Don't you just love it?" she said, looking at Kris. "Damn. I'd do this for free." She laughed. Kris turned away, uncomfortable with her own smile. The lights of Fairbanks were behind them now, but the ground below was still littered with unwinking white and yellow dots that traced roads branching away in the darkness. Even those lights soon passed beneath them and the darkness that surrounded them took on its own shapes. Hard black hills cut the unfeatured sky and the silver sheen of snow-covered lakes and rivers broke the bottomless black of the forest.

"How'd you get to be a pilot?" Kris asked.

"Not a problem. Just busted ass," Jen said.

"Wasn't it hard being a woman?"

"You mean 'cause of the guys?" She looked over at Kris. "All you got to do is be better than them. That's not a problem either." She laughed.

Jen asked her why she was going to Allakaket and Kris told her briefly.

"Pretty gutsy," she said. "You shouldn't have any problems, though. You know it's going to get cold?"

"How cold?"

"Cold. See that star?" She pointed off to the left. "Betelgeuse. The sky's starting to clear. Once the clouds are gone, the temperature will drop."

"How cold?"

"Forecast is thirty below at Allakaket by this evening. Colder tomorrow as the high settles in. Probably even colder up river." Kris saw Jen's green and orange reflection in the windshield grin. "It's going to be an adventure." She clapped her hand on Kris's knee and shook it. "You excited?"

It was a strange question. Life was something you punched through, something that turned on you if you didn't keep on top of it. Excitement wasn't a choice.

"No?" Jen asked, misreading her silence. "Nervous?"

"No. It's just something I got to do," Kris said. "That's all."

"Yeah, I know," said Jen so quietly that the mike barely picked it up. Then, when Kris was silent, she asked, "For you or for your mother?"

Kris felt uncomfortable. Jen was starting to ask questions like Annie did. It confused her; questions were the bullets fired by social workers and ministers and cops to control or humiliate you: What are you doing here? Do you want to live on the street all your life? Do you know what you're doing to your body? How can you let the devil take your soul?

"I don't know," she said, evasively. "You just got to fight back." Then, more sadly than she realized, she said, "Evie never did."

They flew on. The plane was steady; Jen's hands never touched the controls. Kris looked again for the star, but it had disappeared. The night and the drone of the engines wrapped themselves around her and she relaxed into her seat letting the stress of the last few days fall away. Then, from the darkness, memories she'd pushed out of her head scuttled back into it like roaches. Lambale. How long before they found his body? Could they tie her to it? Her puke, fingerprints left on Lambale, the truck that tailed the Mercedes, its lights blasting the back of her head. What would it take? Scenes from that night began to drive her mind: the explosion, the scream, the inhuman shape charging her, the shots, his eyes in the dying beam of the flashlight. The images rushed at her; Kris pushed herself back in the seat, her eyes wide, too frightened to blink.

"You OK?" Jen asked, looking at her, her face spotted by the instrument lights.

"Yeah," Kris said. "Yeah, I'm fine." She breathed; trying to force the tension out of her. The gun had just gone off. He slapped her hand and it fired. It wasn't what she had wanted to do. But no one would believe her; not with five bullets in him.

Justin had to be wrong. There must've been an hour on Tuesday when Lambale was able to sneak off with Evie. He could've said he was going out for lunch or slipped off in the morning when everyone was scrambling to set things up; no one would have noticed in the confusion. Lambale killed her; it was the only possibility that made sense: the money, the phone number, the connection with AWARE, the woolen fibers in the bushes. Paying for the funeral was a perfect cover; no one would suspect him.

And he'd raped her. He hadn't denied it.

An hour after leaving Fairbanks, the plane began to descend on its own. A little while later, Jen pointed through the windshield and in the distance, Kris saw a tight bundle of lights floating in a motionless sea of blackness. As they neared, the lights separated, but there weren't many. Jen clicked a button several times with her thumb and twin rows of blue lights marking the runway flashed on. They had dropped fairly low before Jen took the controls and brought them down, with focused ease, on a gravel strip. The plane decelerated quickly and they bounced up to a small, spottily lit building. Standing in the light and shadows were small groups of people watching the plane approach.

Jen killed the engine on the side of the plane that had the door. Kris looked out of the window while Jen finished shutting the plane down. Snow crystals, sparkling blue and gold in the electric lights, whirled and flowed in a stream a foot deep across the strip. Jen unclipped, wiggled into her parka, and squeezed between the seats into the passenger compartment. When she opened the door, cold air filled the plane and Kris pulled the parka zipper up to her throat. She struggled with the buckle until she found the release button and when the last of the passengers had climbed down, she followed them out.

The wind wasn't strong, just a breeze, but it bit into her checks and tugged at her hair and she felt her ears and nose begin to sting in the cold. But she left her hood down, not wanting to limit her vision. The steady howl of the far engine blotted the sounds of the people and idling trucks bunched around the plane. The baggage was already piled on a hand-pulled cart and bags from a second cart were being loaded through the cargo hatch in the plane's tail. Jen was off talking to a man with a clipboard. She looked professional and assured and Kris felt a pang of difference. Jen was in her own world. Angry with herself, Kris turned away, scanning the milling people for Johnny. She found him in the distant shadows in front of a chain link fence, leaning his knee on the seat of a purple-black snow machine that looked like a resting cat. He was watching her and when he saw she'd spotted him, he came toward her. They met at the baggage cart.

"Hi," he said.

"Hi, Kris Gabriel." Kris stuck out her mitten and he shook it, shyly.

"This is mine." Kris pointed at the pack on the baggage cart, hoping he'd take it. She pulled her duffle out from the bottom, leaning into the bags stacked on top of it so they wouldn't fall over as she worked it free. Johnny slung the pack over a shoulder and walked back to his machine. A sled was hooked on behind and was already loaded with a couple of red plastic gas jugs and a nylon bag. He pulled an insulated one-piece suit out of the bag and handed it to her.

"Just try this on," he said. He had one on under his parka. It had zippered legs so Kris could step into it without taking off her boots. While she struggled with its zippers in her mittened hands, he lashed her pack and duffle behind the jugs. They finished at the same time. Johnny mounted the machine and turned the ignition key; it started without a cough.

"Kris."

Kris jumped. Jen stood by her.

"Good luck." She wrapped her arm around Kris's shoulders and gave her a sideways hug. "See you in four days, huh?"

"Yeah," said Kris barely louder than the noise of the snow machine. "Thanks."

Jen squeezed her arm and then was gone. Johnny handed her goggles and a neoprene face mask; just holes for the eyes and smaller ones around her nose and mouth to breathe through. She climbed on behind and squeezed the edges of the seat, holding on tightly as he accelerated through the gate and into the snow-covered street. They flashed by small houses, still new-looking, all built, Justin had told her, after the flood. They sped up to a big log cabin with bright lights in the windows. Through them, she saw shelves lined with cans and cartons of food. Johnny stopped in front of a gas pump and filled the jugs. Kris stood off to the side watching; when he'd finished, he nodded at the cabin and she went inside to pay. While she had her money out, she counted off another five twenties and handed them to Johnny when she returned.

He was ready to go. Kris got on behind him and gripped the edges of the seat between her legs. Johnny reached around, loosened her hands, and placed them around his stomach. Kris felt uncomfortable being so close to him and held his sides instead. He gunned the engine and they shot off.

They flew past the last house and into the darkness. The machine's light stretched into the night, illuminating a heavily used trail. It turned and twisted down the riverbank onto the Koyukuk. Across the river she saw the lights of another village and then the lights were behind them and the darkness ahead was unbroken except for a handful of low stars. Ten minutes later Johnny turned left onto a narrower trail, which cut across the river. When the bank closed in on their left, he turned his head over his shoulder and shouted. All Kris could hear was "Alatna."

The wind lanced into her. It drew the warmth out of her hands and feet and the cold stung her knees and butt where her clothes were stretched tight over her body. She pulled the draw cord of her hood as tightly closed as she could and shrank into Johnny's back, pressing her parkaed cheek against his shoulder. The cold could not be escaped and she tried to disengage her mind from her hurting body.

Johnny pushed the machine and it sped over the snow. His body lifted and weaved, always anticipating the bucking and bouncing machine while Kris hung on, lifelessly absorbing the pounding of each bump and dip. The light grayed and soon she could see, through the narrow opening of her hood, the skinny, widely spaced spruce that lined the river. Their branches grew down their sides, barely extending a few inches from their trunks as if they were hugging themselves, shivering in the cold as uncomfortable as she was. And the winter had just begun.

Ringer had showed her the Alatna on a map. It bowed to the west before turning northeast and then north again into the mountains. Following the Alatna north from Mettenpherg Creek, she guessed that Ben's cabin was just at the start of the high foothills of the Brooks Range. Kris'd found the John River, which flowed into the Koyukuk to the east of the Alatna, and the Sixtymile where Ezekiel had his cabin. With her finger she'd traced the route he and Ben would have had to travel on their rare winter visits. It went over a high pass between the Mettenpherg, which flowed into the Alatna and the Sixtymile, which flowed into the John. Ringer couldn't see how they'd gotten a dog sled up the slope on the Mettenpherg side; the contour lines were stacked so tightly together.

When the sun had risen into the treetops behind them, Johnny stopped and unwrapped a thermos from his nylon bag. He poured two cups of coffee, handing her one. Kris wanted a cigarette, but didn't want to pull her mittens off to get the pack out of her pocket. Frustrated, she drank her coffee too fast and held her empty cup, unwilling to ask for more.

"Good time," Johnny said.

"How much farther?" she asked. But he only shrugged.

The sun was a brassy gold; its top edge skimmed above the tips of the spruce. The sky overhead was still whitish with a thin haze, though in the north it was blue. Against the blue, the distant peaks of the snow-covered Brooks shone in the low light. Their summits and ridges were sharp and crystalline against the sky.

The coffee hadn't warmed her and standing without moving hadn't either. She was ready to go. Johnny finished his coffee and wrapped the cups and flask back in the bag, tucking it under the lashes in the sled. When it started, the mutter of the snow machine was a sudden intrusion in the quietness, but she soon lost herself in its whine as they continued north.

Johnny stopped again when they reached the cut-off to Mettenpherg. He pointed up the stream. "My uncle traps up that way," he said. "He set his traps last week." He rooted around in his nylon bag and brought out some candy bars and jerky. Kris's fingers were too weak from cold to pull open the zipper on her duffle and Johnny had to do it for her. Kris dug out a Power Bar that Ringer had given her, but she couldn't get her teeth into it, it was as hard as concrete. She walked up and down the trail hunched in her parka, trying to warm up.

"It's going to be slow now, breaking trail," Johnny said as they got back on the machine. The sky had cleared in the last hour and Kris could feel the temperature dropping.

The snow machine bucked and fought against the unbroken snow. Sometimes the snow was light and fluffy and they powered through it like a boat ripping through quiet seas, shooting the snow into the air like a wake. Other times it had been packed by the wind and Johnny had to wrestle the machine through it. The river began to enter the foothills and then the lower mountains of the Brooks and the ice underneath the snow was pushed up into ridges and hard bumps. They crashed into overflows, and Johnny gunned the machine as he felt it break into the water that had been squeezed up through the ice and, insulated by the snow, had not yet frozen. There were still open leads in the river and when they passed them she could see the waters of the Alatna tumbling south, steaming in the cold air.

The sun had set when Johnny yelled over his shoulder and pointed up into the woods. Kris followed his hand and, in the dusk, saw a cabin set back in the protection of the trees on a high bluff on the right side of the river. Johnny drove past it to a point where the bank dropped closer to the water's surface and muscled the machine up the bank. He turned sharply and followed a path cut through the trees up the small hill to Ben's door.

She didn't have time to look around. Johnny left the machine idling and, wading knee deep in the snow, hurried back to the sled and quickly untied her pack and duffle. He set them by the door, pulled out a gas jug, refilled the tank, and retied the jug in the sled. Kris watched him helplessly, trying to keep feelings she couldn't name at bay.

When he had finished and was scrubbing spilled gasoline off his mittens with loose snow, she asked hesitantly, "Would you like to come in and warm up?" Silently she pleaded for him not to leave yet.

Johnny shook his head. "Game tonight. I'm already late." Basketball, Kris knew, ruled bush villages. Johnny knelt on the seat and revved the engine, thick leather mittens were fastened to the handlebars. Grinning, he looked up at her. "See you next season."

An unimaginable weight of loneliness settled on her. Johnny squeezed the throttle, spun in a tight circle, and shot back down the trail. Kris tracked the whine through the trees and when he appeared on the river below, she followed him through the tiny opening in her hood as he raced back down their trail, disappearing finally behind a bend in the river. The sound of his machine faded slowly until she wasn't sure whether she was just hearing its echo in her ears.

■ ■ ■

The silence closed in on her. It blocked her ears; she swallowed and listened again. Distantly, she heard the murmur of her own pulse. Her breath burst from her in a little gasp and she began to shiver. Her teeth clattered, the muscles in her legs jumped, her feet and toes were wooden blocks, and the piece of skin dividing her nostrils burned beyond belief even when she breathed through her mouth. Her body, clenched and tight for hours, loosened, and the cold sank into it remorselessly.

She clamped her jaw to keep it still, waded through the snow to the door, and lifted the simple wooden latch with the edge of her mittened hand. The door creaked open and the snow piled up against it spilled inside. She forced an arm under a strap, heaved the pack through the door, and kicked the duffle in after it. Both windows were shuttered; the only light fell through the door. She left it open.

Kindling by the stove, Ben had said to Justin.

The wood stove was made from a fifty-five gallon drum with a door cut into one end and the stack coming out of the other. It sat on homemade legs against the back wall. Kris knelt before the door, took off her mitten, and grasped the metal stud, trying to pull the door open; but her fingers, too weak with cold, slipped off. She forced the vee between her thumb and forefinger under the stud and pulled back. It creaked open;

her skin froze to the rusted metal, but when she peeled off her hand, she didn't feel the pain.

Stacked carefully to the side of the stove was a small pile of finely split wood, white in the darkness, and a curved piece of birch bark. She lifted the bark between her palms and ripped it into strips with her teeth. She picked the strips up with her fingers, but they were clumsy and scattered the strips on the floor of the stove. She brushed them into a pile with her hands. The little sticks of split wood would not stay in her fingers and she cupped a palm under her hand to catch ones she dropped. The stove door was in her shadow; she couldn't see into it. Blindly, with trembling hands, she placed the sticks where she guessed the pile of birch bark was. In her concentration, she unclenched her jaw and her teeth chattered wildly.

Lighters were better than matches, Ringer had told her. He'd given her a handful of disposable ones, which she'd dumped into a zippered pocket. She bit the zipper's tang with her teeth and pulled it open, but her thumb was too rubbery with cold to spin the wheel. She forced the snowmobile suit open a few inches and thrust her hands under her shirt into her armpits, but there wasn't enough warmth there to bring her fingers back.

She peered into the gloom; there had to be matches. On the counter against the side wall, she saw the outline of a jar. Stumbling to her feet, her arms crossed on her chest and her hands still pressed into her armpits, she hurried over to it. Kitchen matches. She pulled out her hands, but couldn't unscrew the top. She knelt on the floor again, squeezed the jar between her knees and, pushing her palms on either side of the lid, twisted it. It loosened; she spun it off, letting it rattle across the floor. She spilled the matches in a heap. She picked up two, squeezing the ends between her palms. They sparked and flared when she swiped them against the rough metal of the stove. With both hands, she pushed them through the stove door. By their light, she saw the muddled disarray of her sticks and bark and remembered her failure to light the fire that day with Ben.

Kris dropped the burning matches into the stove and used their light to build a pyramid of sticks over the strips of bark. The matches died and she lit more, dropping them by her little pile. When it was built, she searched for bigger sticks to feed it once it got going. She found, stacked against the wall behind the stove, a day's worth of wood and she loaded up her arms with split lengths and carried them to the front of the stove.

This is it, she thought, and struck another match squeezed between her palms. It flared. Steadying her shaking arms against the side of the stove, she touched it to the bark. It took. A tiny flame and greasy black smoke curled up from its edge. The flame grew, twisting up through the kindling and flickering in the hollow belly of the drum. Kris added sticks and each caught quickly. Smoke began backing out the stove door. She stumbled up and opened the damper on the stack.

The fire grew. Kris fed it larger lengths of wood until it roared and air was visibly sucked into it through the open door. Its heat burned her cheeks and the blood rushed back into her fingers. They burned with a wild, itching pain. Sobbing, she beat them against her legs, then raced into the snow, and buried her hands until they numbed again. Then, pushing hard against the snow that had fallen onto the floor, she shut the cabin door and crept cautiously to the outer edge of the stove's warmth.

Slowly, painfully, the circulation returned to her fingers.

■ ■ ■

Barrett lifted his overnight bag onto the conveyor and watched it disappear into the maw of the x-ray machine. He emptied his pockets onto the plastic tray and walked through the detector. It alarmed. The security guard frisked him with the hand-held unit, which squealed when it passed above the parka slung over his arm. Barrett worked his hands through its pockets and pulled out a cardboard box of nine-millimeter slugs. The security guard looked disgusted, but before he could say anything, Barrett handed him the bullets and pulled out his badge. "I checked my pistol at the front counter," he said.

"You should've checked these too," the guard said.

"Right. I forgot about them. I haven't worn this in years." He indicated the parka.

The guard weighed the package in his hand and looked at the woman behind the monitor. She shrugged. He handed them back to Barrett.

"Thanks."

The plane was already boarding. Barrett got in line.

Kris had been at the Fairbanks PD yesterday looking through the file on Corvus. She'd copied down the address of the tannery where Ben had worked. Barrett called the tannery and talked to the owner. When he asked what Kris had wanted, the owner went silent, then said finally, "You know, Detective. I liked that girl. I'm keeping my mouth shut," and he'd hung up. It didn't really matter; Barrett knew what Kris wanted. She was looking for Ezekiel Damon and all she had was his post office address; she needed his street address. Barrett pulled up Damon's DMV records and copied the address off the computer screen: 27.4 mile Elliott Highway.

It would be his first stop.

SATURDAY, NOVEMBER 21

Only her nose stuck out. Around it was a shaggy circle of frost.

The sleeping bag wasn't worth shit. Kris rolled over. That hip ached too. Her chin was tucked into her knees and her arms hugged her chest. She was still bundled in the snowmobile suit and parka, and her feet were curled up inside two pairs of socks and the shoepack liners. She rolled back, not breaking out of her fetal ball. Both hips ached. No way in hell she was getting out of bed just to take a stinking piss.

She rolled over again, struggling against the pressure in her bladder, but she didn't have much choice; it wouldn't hold out until breakup. She ripped the zipper open. Air, intolerably colder, gripped her as she kicked the bag off her feet and slid over the edge of the high bed, stumbling when she hit the floor. Damn fire must have gone out hours ago. She fumbled for her boots in the dark, and forced her feet into them; the leather uppers had frozen and were rigid as stone. The cabin door was stuck; she tugged it open and scurried into the night, surprised that it could be even colder outside. The outhouse was in the trees off to the side; she'd found it the evening before. It didn't have any Styrofoam insulation around the hole to sit on like Annie's did, just a bare wooden board. She squatted over it, hell if she was going to frostbite her ass, and pissed into the void below.

Cold and shivering, she closed the cabin door behind her and built a fire. It started easily and she thanked Ben for his patience that day at the beach.

In minutes, the stove was drawing and the fire crackling.

Kris bustled around the cabin, singing a Mexican jingle she'd picked up at the shop, returning to the stove every few minutes to rewarm her fingers. She lit the lantern she'd found the previous evening. Its glass reservoir, full of kerosene, had been stoppered off with a wooden plug that Ben had whittled to keep the fuel from evaporating. It amazed her that he was so orderly and thought of such details. She'd pulled the plug out and screwed the wick assembly into the hole, letting the wick soak up the fluid before lighting it. Ringer had made her bring candles and a quart of kerosene in case there were none at the cabin. Winter nights twenty-two hours long, he'd told her, were impossible without light.

She finished unloading her pack and duffle, lining up the bags of food on the counter. Underneath it, she found Ben's few pots and pans neatly stacked. She dug out the largest, packed it with snow, and set it on a metal plate that had been fastened to the curved back of the stove. The snow melted into just a few cups of water and, when it melted down, she added more, using a plastic bucket she'd found in the shadows under the counter to scoop up the dry snow. Every time she opened the door to go out, the cold outside air tumbled over her like avalanching snow. It frosted the moisture in the cabin's air creating a thick mist, which swirled and eddied across the floor.

It took her a while to figure out how Ben cooked. There was no cook stove, but under the counter, she found a grill that fit inside the wood stove, on which she could put Ben's small pots. In L.A., she never ate breakfast, but this morning she was hungry and she sorted through her Ziploc bags, surveying her options. She had one: Oatmeal. Oatmeal and powdered milk. With no instructions. Ringer must figure everyone ate this shit. What's it got to take—water, heat, and oatmeal?

She burned it. Apparently it had to be stirred and for some reason, the powdered milk lumped up when she poured it in. But the honey and raisins were OK. In fact it was all OK, even though it looked like puke.

Out of deference to Ben, she cleaned up, and then she got started. She was convinced he'd brought Corvus here, and she wanted to know what he'd done with him. Kris took the cabin apart. It didn't take long. For a person who had lived here for forty years, he didn't have much, although, like the plug in the lantern reservoir, everything he had was functional and well crafted.

She found nothing, not even a diaper.

Narrow shafts of gray light were squeezing through cracks in the shutters when she'd finished searching the cabin. She suited up and went out to take shutters off. The cabin had three windows and she lifted the shutters off each, leaning them in the snow against the cabin walls.

The woodshed, just a roof supported by poles that kept the rain off several rows of split wood, was on the other side of the small clearing that contained Ben's homestead. She loaded up her arms and replaced the wood in the cabin that she'd burned. Next to the woodshed was a food cache, a tiny cabin supported on poles far enough off the ground to keep bears out of it. Kris had seen pictures of caches on post cards and paintings done for tourists but never thought they really existed. Leaning against a neighboring tree was a ladder. Kris moved it over and propped it against the cache and climbed up. The door was closed with a board stuck between two brackets. She slid it out and pulled the door open. It was empty.

Kris was getting discouraged. Ben was so thorough that even if Corvus had been at the cabin the entire winter, Ben would have destroyed any evidence that she might be able to find.

She plowed through the snow to the remaining shed. Its walls were made from small logs set vertically in the ground like the stockades of forts in old westerns. The shed's roof extended five or six feet past one of the side walls and sheltered a large bundle wrapped in a heavy green canvas. Under it, Kris found Ben's snow machine. It was yellow and blockish, with none of the sleek, cat-like lines that Johnny's had. Hanging from the roof above the snowmobile were two dog sleds. Kris stepped on the snow machine to look at them more closely. One was fastened with rawhide and had a wooden frame that was worn and cracked. The other was fastened with steel bolts and had plastic runners.

The door to the shed was locked with the same type of handmade latch that closed the main cabin. Inside were Ben's tools: axes, saws, hammers, hand drills, and shovels. Dog harnesses hung from nails on one wall.

Some were made from nylon webbing, but most were of leather that he had sewn himself; the seams were hand-stitched, and the edges were not machine-straight. On the facing wall were his traps, maybe a hundred or more hanging from nails by wires. There were different sizes and shapes; some she wouldn't have guessed were traps if they hadn't been with the others. Suspended from the ceiling were two pairs of snowshoes; one pair were small and oval-shaped, the other much longer, with steep up-turned toes and long tails. Both looked as if Ben had made them. Kris rolled out a heavy plastic barrel partly filled with bags of nails and stood on it to unfasten the smaller pair. The bindings were still on; thickly greased and spotted with dead mosquitoes and other bugs that had landed and not been able to escape the goo.

Lined up under a workbench were plastic fuel jugs. Kris shook them all; most were empty, but liquid sloshed in two and a third was full. She carried them outside where the light was better. Two red and a blue. The red ones were marked "premix," but smelled like gasoline to her. The blue one smelled like kerosene. There was about a gallon left in it and Kris was relieved; Ringer's quart wouldn't have lasted long during these twenty-hour nights. She hauled it to the cabin with the snowshoes.

The cabin was warming, but still not warm enough; Kris wanted to sweat. She fed more wood into the stove and stripped down to her long underwear. Ben had a single chair, one he'd made out of willow saplings, and Kris wondered where he sat when Ezekiel came to visit. She pulled it across the floor next to the stove and sat in it trying to figure out the snow-shoe bindings. They were handmade, too, though they had metal buckles and her boots fit them without having to be readjusted; they were, after all, Ben's boots. She buckled the straps and clomped around the cabin. When she had the hang of them, she suited up and went out and waddled in the snow. Where it was deep, the small snowshoes were worthless. They sank so far and so much snow fell on top of them, that she couldn't lift a foot to take another step. But they worked OK where she'd already walked through the snow, and she retraced her trails to the outhouse and sheds, to flatten them out and make them easier to walk on.

The sun was up, but the trees were too high and the sun too low for it to be visible from the clearing. Behind the cabin Kris could see a hill which had a slice of golden light crowning its top. Moving fast, since the sun wouldn't stay in the sky for long, she switched snowshoes, putting on the larger ones and then circling behind the shed and into the woods. A shallow mound of snow snaked through the trees. It looked odd and Kris followed it, realizing after a few minutes that it was a trail. It had been cut through the woods, and Kris noticed that the snow was deeper in it than it was under the trees because there were no branches overhead to catch the snow as it fell.

She walked for a few minutes, struggling through the deep snow with the snowshoes, before she found the dog yard. Twelve doghouses, tiny log cabins set in three orderly rows, faced the trail. In front of each was the stake their chains had been fastened to. It looked like a deserted town; each house was half-buried in gentle drifts of snow unmarked by paw prints.

The trail continued, staying level for a while and moving at an angle away from her hill. Thinking that it led in a different direction, Kris debated leaving the trail and cutting through the trees. Eventually, it turned and climbed a side ridge. Kris toiled up it and sweat started dampening her long underwear. She folded back the tunnel of her hood and unzipped her parka part way, letting in the desert-dry arctic air. Her breath steamed in large clouds, frosting her eyelashes and the hair circling her face.

When the ridge steepened, she zigzagged back and forth to keep the snowshoes from sliding backwards like skis. At the top of the hill, she found a single large spruce tree that had been hidden from the cabin. It was big around for a tree this far north, although not very tall. Under it, facing the river, was a flat area in the snow, which looked like a low table, too flat and too rectangular to be natural. Kris stepped on it and pushed the snow off with her snowshoes. They scraped wood and she stepped off and swept the rest of the snow away with her mittens, uncovering a wooden platform made of seven or eight saplings a foot or so off the ground.

It was Ben's thinking tree, she realized, remembering his story of sitting under an old spruce and watching over his valley. Kris sat on Ben's homemade bench, sitting awkwardly with her feet twisted to the side by the long snowshoes, and leaned back against the tree. The sun was half hidden behind a distant ridge of hills. As she watched, it disappeared behind them, moving quickly. Before her, the Alatna River wound through a thin forest of widely-spaced trees, which were black against the snow, and on the high bank overlooking the river below her Kris could see the cabin's snow-covered roof and smoke from the stove smearing the air.

The cold had clamped into her as soon as she'd stopped moving. She pulled up the zipper and squirreled into the parka, determined to see the first star come out. There weren't any stars in the sky in L.A. Or, if they could be seen through the city's lights and dirt, she couldn't remember ever looking for them.

The sky darkened slowly and Kris scanned it for points of light. Suddenly, she found one, low and bright and not far behind the sun. Did it have a name? She wanted to wait for more, but the bite of the cold had become too painful and uncontrollable fits of shivering shook her. When she slid forward to put the snowshoes flat on the ground before standing up, her parka stuck for an instant to the tree before releasing with a faint ripping sound. She twisted around to see what had snagged her.

Carved into the tree's flesh a couple of feet above the wooden bench was a small cross. Kris touched it with her mitten, then drew out her hand and touched it with her fingers. During the growing season, sap had risen out of the bark and beaded up along the edges of the cut. Her warmth and weight had been enough to soften it and make it stick to the fabric.

Kris knew who the cross was for. She stood and gripped the log seat and tried to wrench it free, but it was anchored solidly in the frozen ground and didn't move. She brushed away the snow in front of it and, bending down, peered beneath. Snow had blown in and she shoveled it out with her hand. When the ground was clear, she could see in the dim light that the sandy soil was smooth and level. Too neat to be natural. Neat like Ben.

Kris stood and stared down at the wooden bench, certain that it covered a grave.

SUNDAY, NOVEMBER 22

By the next morning, Kris knew what she was going to do. She closed the cabin door carefully behind her, the stove inside filled with wood and well damped down so the cabin would be warm when she returned, and walked to the tool shed carrying the snowshoes and kerosene lantern. Its dim light deepened the shadows and they flitted and wavered as she searched for a shovel and pickax. She found both in a corner, leaning against the wall with a sledgehammer, crowbar, and other tools she didn't recognize.

The sky was black and littered with stars that stared down at her without warmth as she snow-shoed up the hill to Ben's tree, the shovel and pickax over her shoulder. When Kris reached the cross she stood quietly before it and hesitated. It was white in the starlight, the frozen sap weeping from the cut; Ben would tell her that it was better to let him alone and maybe he was right, but she had to know.

She got to work.

The snow wasn't as deep at the top of the hill as it was down at the cabin. Kris shoveled out around the log bench, then sat on it to take off her snowshoes. The bench rested on four legs set into the soil, soil so frozen, it rang like stone when she struck it with the shovel. The pickax was too heavy for her to swing well and it only bounced when it hit the ground. She reversed the shovel, sliding the handle under the seat, and pried upwards. A leg broke out. It hadn't been set very deeply and after a struggle, she levered the other legs out as well.

She lifted the bench and moved it out of the way. Framed by the four leg holes was a narrow rectangle of sunken sand and dirt that was free of the rust-red spruce needles that carpeted the ground she'd cleared of snow. One of the roots of the spruce tree that had crossed the sunken area had been cut. It looked like Ben's work: clean and competent. Kris lifted the shovel and slammed the blade into the ground. It hit without loosening a grain of sand. She lifted and dropped it loosely; the ground had to be thawed before it could be dug out. That meant a fire and that meant hauling wood up from the cabin. And that would be a major chore in snowshoes.

Kris looked out over the valley, still lit only by the stars. Counting today, she had three more days before Johnny came back for her. Might as well get started.

When she got back to the cabin, she searched for something she could load with logs and pull over the snow. Too bad there weren't any dogs; she looked up at the sleds hanging from the underside of the roof, too big for her to pull. Below them, sitting under the army tarp, was the snow machine.

Kris pulled off the tarp. It was too stiff and heavy to fold neatly, and so she dragged it into the snow behind the shed, noticing, as she did, that a strip had been cut off one edge. The machine looked old and worn; there were dents and scratches in its yellow cowling, cracks in the vinyl seat, and the headlight was broken. She straddled it, feeling the frozen seat bite into her rear, and looked at the controls. She hadn't driven a snow machine since she was a kid, but she'd been on motorcycles in L.A. She found the throttle, the choke, and the pull cord. The gas cap came off easily, but the tank was empty.

She retrieved the half-empty jug of premix from the shed wondering if gas went bad. It was at least two years old, maybe older. She unscrewed the cap. Reversed in the opening was a pour spout which she screwed onto the threads and filled the machine's tank, slopping gas onto the snow.

With one knee on the seat, she pulled the cord. It caught on something and stopped a few inches out. Grabbing it with both hands, she pulled again, harder. It came all the way out. She pulled the cord again and again until sweat broke her skin and she had to unzip her parka to cool down. The engine never coughed or sputtered.

She sat on the seat, discouraged. It could be broken, old gas, or the engine too cold. She couldn't do anything about the first two, but she could do something about the cold. She got off the machine and looked at it. It was too wide to push through the cabin door. Lighting a fire under it or putting coals on the cylinders might work if it didn't catch fire. She was on her way to the woodpile when she had a better idea. Excited, she jogged back to the cabin, ignoring the cold air cutting her throat, and stoked the fire in the stove. In minutes, it was blazing. Kris packed more snow into the pot sitting on the metal shelf. It disappeared quickly and she dumped in more as it melted. After the pot was full of water, it took forever for it to heat up. The cabin heated faster and Kris cracked open the door to cool it down.

The pot never boiled, and finally Kris gave up trying to get it any hotter. She damped down the stove and carried the pot to the shed. Steam rose out of it in a swirling cloud that blinded her, frosting her eyebrows and eyelashes. She lifted the front cowling and when she poured the hot water over the cylinders it froze in a clear glaze, but as she poured more, it melted and the metal warmed. When the pot was empty, she could put her bare hand on the cylinders.

Quickly she grabbed the cord and began pulling. After the third or fourth pull, she heard a sputter. She pulled again and the sputter lasted a little longer and after a few more pulls, the engine caught. It idled rough and she pressed the throttle and the machine lurched forward and stalled. Kris cranked the cord again and it started on the first pull. More gently this time, she pressed the throttle and the machine moved forward, climbing up the deeper snow outside the shed and into the yard.

Kris shouted as she raced in a tight circle in front of the cabin, but the cold air whipping into her hood lacerated her cheeks and she slowed it to a walk. She parked it in front of the shed and lowered the dog sled with the plastic runners. With rope that she found coiled and hanging on a nail, she tied the sled to the snow machine and towed it to the woodpile.

By the time she'd filled the sled with wood, the sky was gray and the stars had disappeared. The snow machine wasn't strong enough to make it up the final ridge to the top of the hill while towing the wood. She unhooked the sled, broke a trail to the top with the machine alone, and then dumped half the wood and hauled it up in two trips. She started a fire and, when it was large enough to leave, Kris went back for another load. After she'd returned and had unloaded the sled, she took the shovel and scraped the fire to one side of the rectangle and dug out the thawed dirt. The soil was sandy and dry and even though the fire had been burning for thirty minutes or so, only the top few inches had thawed. It took a while, but Kris learned that the thawed ground insulated the frozen soil below and if she moved the fire and dug out the heated earth more frequently, the hole deepened faster.

The day lightened and the sun, cold and distant, drifted into the sky. The fire was hot and Kris stripped off the snowmobile suit and worked with her parka unzipped, moving in and out of the fire's heat. When the bottom edge of the sun rested again on the horizon, the hole was several feet deep, and Kris squatted at its edge, warming herself in the hot air that rose from the flames, wondering how deep it went. Periodically she probed beneath the fire with the shovel, feeling for something that felt different than frozen sand.

The sun was gone and the daylight a darkening gray when she found it. A different vibration traveled up the shovel's wooden handle as she twisted it below the ashes and glowing coals of the fire. Quickly, she shoveled the fire out of the pit, piling the burning logs and glowing coals to one side and adding more wood to it to keep it going. The pit was almost four feet deep, making it difficult to shovel up the loose sand while standing on the lip. Kris brought up what she could and then jumped in. She touched the bottom with an unmittened hand; she didn't want to melt the soles of her boots. The sand was still hot and she shoveled it out. As she scraped with the shovel, a fabric appeared. She knelt, brushing the loose sand away. It was the same green tarp that had covered the snow machine.

Carefully, Kris worked her shovel along the sides, loosening the sand. The bundle was a little more than two feet long. It looked tiny to her. She stepped up the sides of the pit, pressing her feet into the walls to keep from standing on the tarp and forced the shovel's blade underneath it, trying to break it out of the frozen ground. Slowly she worked at it until she'd freed one end and then she squatted, wrapped her arms around it, and heaved upwards. The tarp ripped loose and she cradled the bundle in her arms. It had no weight, no substance; it was too light to be a body.

She lifted it out of the hole and laid it on the bank, scrambling up after it. The fire had shrunk to a few small flames that cast their weak light against the gathering darkness. Kris fed it more wood and pulled the tarp into its glow. She paused for a moment, scared suddenly of what she would find.

Would he look like Evie? Like Ben?

It had only been a week since she'd learned she had a brother. For a few days she'd hoped that she would have someone to touch, someone who needed her. It was a lost hope, she knew it now, maybe she knew it a week ago, but when was the last time she'd hoped for anything—hoped hard?

The tarp was cold and stiff, but dry; no ice sealed it shut. Kris found an edge and forced the rigid canvas apart. It separated with a ripping sound. When at last she pulled it away, his face slipped out of the darkness.

Her heart faltered, caught, and raced. Empty eye cavities stared up at her. His teeth, baby tiny, were clenched and his lips had pulled away in a grimace of pain no four-year-old should know. Trembling, Kris folded the tarp back from his head. Pressed into his scalp was long, rusty-brown hair, the color of the fallen spruce needles that covered the ground circling his grave. Was it Ben's color, or was it a mixture of his and Evie's? She lifted him, cradling him in her arms, and turned him to the fire. His skin was brown and papery like dried grass. She turned him further and the light of the fire flickered over his face.

Then she saw it.

Her breath clogged in her throat and she hugged him in terror. At the edge of an eyebrow, was a bullet hole.

■ ■ ■

Barrett had taken over Ted Osgood's office. Osgood was Outside visiting family for Thanksgiving. Barrett had worked with Osgood on a couple of cases; he was an old Alaskan hand who would have been royally pissed if Barrett hadn't moved in and messed up his desk. The Lambale file and the new one he'd started on Kris Gabriel were open and their papers spread across the desktop between pictures of Osgood's kids on one side and pictures of a fishing trip on the other. On top of the papers was a yellow legal pad with a list of every hotel, motel, bed and breakfast, and name-less dive in Fairbanks that rented a bed. Kris hadn't checked into any of them—under her name or anyone else's. Barrett was certain that she was staying with someone she knew, but trying to track down her old friends would take too long and he wasn't going to try.

Damon had been no help, either. He'd stood there staring down at him, an ax in his hand, his damn dogs howling behind him. But Barrett knew that Kris had been there. It was in his eyes; they were too wary, too instantly hostile when Barrett entered the clearing. Funny how Ezekiel and the man at the tannery had protected her. She was so damn prickly, he hadn't expected she'd make any friends.

But he was stuck; he had no clue what her next move would be. What had Damon told her? Why he'd forged Stewart's signature? Barrett already knew that—so he could pay Evie's rent after Stewart had left. But that wouldn't have gotten her any closer to her brother. What else did she have?

He stared at the papers littering Osgood's desk.

The Alatna.

Stewart had gone up to his cabin on the Alatna after Corvus had disappeared. That's what she had. Barrett signed into his cell phone and searched for flights into Allekaket.

There were two. He started with the first.

■ ■ ■

Kris sat on a spruce round in front of the cabin, her back resting against the door. The sun had set hours ago. She'd returned the snow machine to the shed, stoked the fire in the wood stove, watching for hours the flames consume the wood that gave them life, and then she ate one of the spaghetti dinners that Ringer had made up for her. When she'd finished washing the dishes and refilled the pot on the stove with fresh snow, there'd been nothing else to do. The tiny cabin and the darkness lurking at the edges of the weak lamplight pushed in on her until finally she'd suited up and had come back outside. The cold bored through her arctic gear and the sleeping bag wrapped tightly around her body. She couldn't stay long.

How did Ben stand it, the endless nights? Day after day. The shortest day of the year was still a month away, yet the sun wasn't above the horizon for more than two hours now. Two hours of feeble sunlight, four hours of grayness and eighteen of black night. Why did he come back, year after year?

She exhaled; her breath froze into a cloud of mist that moved slowly across the clearing toward the trees. Above her, the stars were brilliant, like silvered dust tossed against the sky. Beneath the stars, pulsing faintly in a green ribbon, the northern lights curved down from the mountains behind the cabin, arced across the night and curved north again, disappearing over the trees. The night air was crystal-still. When she listened, Kris heard the blood pulse in her ears. Nothing could be more different from Los Angeles: from its hard, unwinking lights; the ceaseless, restless movement of cars and people; the background rumble of engines and brakes and tires rolling on hot pavement; and the city's grit blown against your skin, plugging your nose, coating your mouth, and sticking to your sweat.

She ached; a hollow longing for something she didn't understand burned in her gut. What was it she missed? Was it the bustle of strangers—people passing her in the streets—handing her things over counters, or standing before her in line? That was all she had in L.A., and she never ached there. She worked, sometimes late, and when the day ended she went home, ate dinner, watched TV, and did it again the next day. The guys at work spoke Spanish to each other and, except for the company Christmas party; she didn't do anything with them. Save Our Sisters would invite her to special events—she was one of their success stories—but she'd stand to the side, watching the others laugh and drink, and slip away when no one was looking.

Kris pulled the sleeping bag around her, burrowing deeper, trying to ease the ache. Suddenly, she realized that she was as isolated as Ben; except he had his dogs and his bears and weasels; his mountains and streams and his thinking tree.

And he'd had Evie.

Then Kris understood: Ben would have died here; sore joints hadn't run him out of the bush. He would have been content feeling the life drain out of him, sitting under his tree watching the ravens and whiskey jacks— but a bigger love, Evie and Corvus, had pulled him into the dust and dirt of Fairbanks, into a miserable apartment, and the job at the tannery. He went happy, and it was most likely his love for Evie that had taken him to Juneau, following her, hoping. ...

Why did he kill Corvus?

There had been no blood around the wound. Ben had wiped it clean once it had stopped bleeding. Not believing he could shoot his son in the face, she turned the feather-light body over and found the entry hole in his hair under the bulge of his head. It too, had been cleaned of blood, although Kris didn't look closely.

She unwound the rest of the tarp. He looked tiny, Ben had curled him up, his knees at his chest, though Kris didn't know how big a four-and-a-half-year old should be. He was wearing woolen pants with a leather belt circled with bear and caribou carvings, something Ben had made, several heavy shirts, and little, hand-stitched mukluks. The police report had said that Corvus's cold weather clothes were still in the apartment; did Ben make the mukluks and the belt before burying him?

Before she rewound the tarp, she noticed that the fingers of one hand were clenched in a fist. Clasped in his fingers was a small ball. The fingers were frozen and brittle; Kris tugged, but was afraid they would break if she pried them open. She pushed her finger down the hollow of his fist and forced the ball out. It was hard and, in the firelight, milky white. On an impulse, she put it to her nose and inhaled. Spruce sap. Involuntarily, Kris looked up at Ben's tree, searching for a wound he could have taken the sap from.

Had he cut the cross yet?

Kris pushed the ball of sap back into Corvus's hand and rewrapped him tightly in the tarp, before lowering him into his grave and filling it back in. She dug shallow holes for the legs of the bench, leveling it as best she could. There were a few unburnt logs left, which she reloaded onto the sled along with the pickax and shovel. The coals of the fire steamed and hissed when she kicked snow on them and the darkness filled in as the last embers were smothered.

The snow machine engine had cooled and it needed a few tugs of the cord until it fired. Kris put her knee on the seat and surveyed the hilltop before leaving. It was a mess, but the first snowfall would cover everything, returning it to the undisturbed whiteness it had been before she'd come. Kris didn't know how to say good-bye and so she just left, carefully working the machine down the steep sections of the ridge until she was on the level path leading back to the cabin.

The vast curve of northern lights had grown. The lights were starting to lift, rising high into the sky in green sheets. When she'd lived in Fairbanks, the lights had been part of the winter night, but since moving to L.A., she'd forgotten them and now they seemed strange and unreal.

You killed my brother, Ben. Are you a monster? Or is there something I don't know?

Alone. The name for the ache she felt bloomed in her mind. She was alone. Evie was gone, Corvus was gone. There was no one else. Her father. Maybe he was still alive, maybe he'd changed. If he knew about her . . . A spark of hope flashed, but spent itself and she turned away from it—twenty-five years had passed and no way to find him. He'd blown through their lives like trash blowing in the street.

Kris folded the tunnel of her hood back and gazed again at the sky. The lights were tinged with red now and starting to writhe, rippling curtains reaching unimaginable miles into space. How could they be so violent and so silent? It was as if they were screaming—screaming in terror of the blackness and of the emptiness—and there was no air to carry their cries.

Mom. You didn't get my letter. You never knew I was coming.

Kris gazed down the snow-covered river, bright in the starlight. *Ben thinks I deserted you.* She squeezed her hands into fists in the parka's pockets and pushed against the fabric.

I couldn't come back. I . . . It hurt so much.

She slumped, then loosened her parka, unzipping it and pulling it away from herself. The sleeping bag fell off her shoulders and, with bare hands, she opened the snowmobile suit letting the warmth it held flee into the night. The air ground into her exposed skin like broken glass, cutting between her breasts and searing her belly. Blood withdrew from her feet and hands and they began to throb in cold too remorseless for life to withstand. Kris shuddered as if struck and began to shake.

Mom. Did you love Corvus?

Did you love me?

MONDAY, NOVEMBER 23

The snow in the snow machine track had set up hard like Styrofoam and Kris hiked back to the hill without snowshoes. On the steep section, where the trail followed the ridge to the top, Kris kicked steps in the hardened snow to keep from skidding backwards. From one hand dangled a cushion she'd found hanging from a rafter, out of the reach of mice, and in the other she carried a broom made from stiff grasses, which Ben must have cut one fall before they had been softened by the snow. Curled up in her sleeping bag the night before, waiting for sleep, Kris had decided that she didn't want to leave Corvus's grave so dirtied, even though it would soon be covered with fresh snow.

The snowmobile and her own feet had torn and trampled the snow in front of the spruce tree. Ash and soot from the fire had blackened it and it was pocked with the sandy dirt she'd dug from his grave. Kris braced the cushion against the bench and began to sweep fresh snow over the ashes, her footprints, and snow machine tracks. The broom's grasses kinked and broke as she swept and she realized that the shovel would have done a better job. Throwing back her hood and letting her hair swing free, she warmed as she worked and overhead the sky lightened, turning a pale cloudless blue.

When she'd finished, and the dirt and charcoal had been covered, and new snow spread around the tree, she dropped the cushion in front of the bench and sat down, leaning back against its rough wood, beside Corvus. The valley fell away before her, opening onto a sea of black trees, white snow-covered lakes, and hills that rolled toward the red-orange glow spilling into the predawn sky. Slowly, the colors turned gold and, as she watched, the sun slid above the horizon and its light, weak and heatless, splashed across her face. Without squinting, she watched it curve into the sky.

She heard a sudden wiffling sound and a raven, its wing feathers pushing hard against the air, flew past her. It soared out over the river, and a second raven rose from below to join it. They spiraled around each other, cawing as they climbed. It was the first sound on the river Kris had heard that she hadn't made. The birds played in the icy air. In the distance beyond them, flew another, a black speck against the blue. The two over the river plunged into the trees and vanished from sight. She waited for them to rise again, then searched the sky for the third, found it and watched, waiting for it to wheel from its rigid path as the others had.

Instead, it arrowed toward her, never wavering. It grew wings and landing gear and turned from black to white and came noiselessly toward her. For one excited moment, Kris thought Jen was coming to visit. But it couldn't be; no one she would want would come for her.

The plane's drone slowly penetrated the silence. Kris crouched, ready to spring down the slope and into the trees. It swerved; the pilot had spotted the cabin, or the smoke rising from its stovepipe. It banked hard and flew in a tight circle. The lower wing pivoted in space above the clearing and a pair of dim faces floated behind the windshield. The single prop thrashed the air. It was a small bush plane, a tail-dragger, and under its wheels were short, fat skis.

The plane broke out of its circle and dropped down over the river behind the trees. Between the branches, Kris saw flashes of aluminum speeding down river until it emerged into the open only feet above the snow. It rose steeply, banked, reversed direction, and came in slow, its flaps lowered and the noise of its engine dropping in pitch.

Kris jumped up, grabbing the broom and cushion, and raced back down the hill, her shoepacks punching through the hardened snow, until she was halfway back to the cabin. She cut off the trail, dropping the broom and cushion behind a tree, and pushed through the snow toward the river. Without snowshoes she was slowed to an awkward walk, stumbling over branches and downed trees hidden in the snow. Before she reached the riverbank, the plane's engine quit and the silence flooded back.

When she broke through the trees, she was on the high bluff down river a short ways from Ben's cabin. The plane was farther up; it'd stopped where the snow machine trail climbed the bank and took off into the woods up to the clearing. Two people were fitting a covering over the engine cowling. One was wearing a blue parka that looked like a uniform. A state trooper, she was certain, but the plane wasn't marked. The other's parka looked normal, but when his hood fell back, as he was stretching a bungee from the engine cover to a wing strut, Kris saw a pink circle of scalp.

Barrett.

He must have found Lambale; he must know she'd killed him.

After they'd gotten the engine covering on, they clambered up the bank and disappeared into the woods. Neither had snowshoes. Would they be able to track her? She looked back at her footprints in the snow. Her prints were all around the cabin; it'd take them a while to find the fresh ones heading out from behind the tool shed.

How long could they let the engine cool before it wouldn't start in the cold?

She heard a shout. Through the trees, the cabin was less than a hundred yards away. The shout came again, indistinct, but it sounded like "Kris." They shouted together the third time and she heard her name clearly. Kris crept along the top of the bank, ready to duck into the woods if they appeared again on the path to the plane. The bluff lowered and flattened out as it approached the opening in the trees through which the cabin looked down the river. She could hear a voice talking now. It was Barrett's. He shouted again.

"Kris, I just want to talk to you."

They came all the way out here to talk to her?

A pistol fired; she jumped. Assholes. A gun wasn't going to bring her in. It fired again and then was silent. Kris waited, hunched in the snow, balling her hands in her mittens and wiggling her toes; she'd have to get inside soon.

It was quiet. They were probably in the cabin warming up and going through her stuff. She dug the snow out from under a tree and squatted in the hole fastening her eyes on her trail behind her. If they tracked her, she wanted to see them coming.

The sun had set and the sky had become a bluish-gray when she heard their voices again. The sounds vanished into the woods and Kris watched the point where the trail came out onto the river. They appeared, walking awkwardly, trying to step in the foot holes they'd made going up. Kris was close enough now to see their breaths fog the air. The blue parka took off the engine cover while Barrett rooted around inside the plane. He dumped a red rubber bag into the snow, jumped down after it, and dragged it up the path a ways. The two shook mittened hands and the blue parka got in and started the engine. The prop kicked once or twice before the engine caught and it accelerated into a blur.

"No," she said out loud. The plane skidded around in a tight arc, accelerated and raced down river; in seconds it lifted into the air and the noise of its prop faded quickly into the arctic silence. Barrett hefted the red bag onto his shoulder and climbed back up the bank into the woods.

Two minutes later she heard the cabin door close behind him.

■ ■ ■

Justin took a late lunch. He marked himself out on the staff board, scribbling in 3:30 for the time he expected to be back. Unless someone's computer blew up, no one would miss him for a couple of hours. He stopped on the loading dock to zipper his jacket and squint through the rain at the flanks of Mount Juneau. The snow line was still below the clouds, about fifteen hundred feet: low enough to be adding snow at Eaglecrest, but he didn't think it'd add enough to open the ski area before Thanksgiving.

He jumped off the loading dock and headed up Main Street to Chicken Ridge. Justin had gone up to Eaglecrest the day before, Sunday, hoping to blow the crud out of his head that had been plugging it since

Barrett had forced him to tell what he and Kris had found at Vern's shack. The last few days had been rough. He'd alternated between humiliation and self-recrimination for caving into Barrett so quickly, anger at Kris for not telling Barrett herself, and hurt that she'd lied to him and taken off to Fairbanks without saying good-bye. The whole sour mess had stewed in his head and he'd spent Thursday and Friday staring uselessly at his computer during the day and twisting in his sheets at night.

Saturday, when he went into the office to try and catch up, was no better and he realized that he needed to beat himself sore in order to clear his mind. So yesterday he'd loaded his gear into the car and driven up to the ski lodge. He fitted skins onto his skis and hiked up to the ridges. Fat, wet flakes were falling; the snow on the ground was thick and pasty; mashed potatoes would have been easier to ski, and he stuck to the steeper runs in the west bowl to have enough momentum to crank his boards through the turns. The exercise helped. By the time he came down, sloppy wet, cold, and tired, an intracranial truce had been called and the demons in his head were stilled. Barrett, he knew, was just doing his job and, realistically, Justin should've told him every-thing from the start. Kris, whatever her feelings toward him might be, was chasing things more important to her—Evie and Corvus—than he was. Christ, he thought when he'd reached the end of the skiable snow and bent to release his bindings, her mother had just been murdered. What did Kübler-Ross figure? Eighteen months for the grieving pro-cess. It hadn't been two weeks yet; romance wouldn't be on her agenda for a while.

At the top of Chicken Ridge, he searched Seventh until he found his Subaru parked with the driver's side against the guardrail. He opened the door, knocking it against the metal, and squeezed in, catching a pocket zipper on the door. He turned the car around in the street and drove down Goldbelt, letting it coast the hills and around the curves until it slowed where Twelfth leveled out; he touched the gas pedal to keep it moving. At Glacier Avenue he turned right, splashing through puddles backed up against the curb, and a few minutes later pulled off onto the shoulder and killed the engine.

Below him sat the AWARE shelter, a blocky concrete structure that looked like an army barracks. To the left was Lambale's new wing; rain had eroded gullies in the muddy hillside where the contractor had stripped away the grass.

Kris.

An embarrassed breath escaped through his teeth, fogging the windshield. He'd thought the fight with Vern had brought them closer together. And when she'd shown up at his apartment Monday and seemed so comfortable with him, he'd been certain.

But nope; he was just the best available patsy. Someone to use for an alibi.

Enough, he said to himself, irritated. Let's not get started again.

Justin shivered; the car was cooling down. He wiped the fog off his side window and peered again through the rain at the AWARE building, its hard angles warped by the water running down the window. Yesterday evening, after warming up in the shower and eating dinner, he flow-charted everything he knew about Evie's murder on old report layouts—large sheets of graph paper he used when he was designing a new system. It didn't take long before the sheets were covered with an unintelligible spaghetti of different possibilities as he drew lines between different people, events, and evidence. Late in the evening, tired and frustrated, he pushed them away. Sherlock Holmes had said that speculating without data was like racing an engine without its transmission engaged: it produces lots of heat and noise but no forward progress.

But the charts had identified the key piece of data that he lacked: The route Kris's letter to Evie had taken after it arrived at AWARE. Justin was convinced that it was too coincidental for Evie's murder to have happened the day before Kris showed up in Juneau; the day before Vern tried to kill Kris. "There are no coincidences in life," Ross Macdonald had once said. "The web of causality is almost infinitely exact."

Clearly someone wanted them both dead. Justin was now convinced it was Vern. It wasn't Ben because Ben hadn't even known Kris was alive, much less that she was coming back to Alaska. Vern, however, since he'd read Kris's letter to Evie, had known.

So, the question was: How did Vern get Kris's letter? If Justin could answer that, he might be able to tell if someone other than Vern had read it; if not, then Vern was the murderer because the coincidence of Evie's murder and Kris's arrival and his attack on her happening all in the same twenty-four period was simply too great otherwise.

Justin opened the door. Holding the hood of his raincoat by its visor to keep it from blowing off, he splashed through the water coursing in chevrons down the drive. He was nervous; there didn't seem to be a tactful way to ask how the letter had gotten into Vern's hands without sounding like he was accusing them of violating feminism PC by giving a letter addressed to a woman to a man.

The front door was locked. He pushed the bell and waited. It opened and a young woman, in her early twenties, with dusty blonde hair and a colony of studs in one ear, looked out at him expectantly. He gave her his name and asked to see a manager or supervisor. She let him in and he stood inside the door, letting himself drip while she went to a desk and spoke into the phone. After she hung up, she told him that someone would be in in a minute and then, looking at the puddles around his feet, made an unappreciative comment about the weather, which, in November, is the only kind of comment one can make about it.

A side door opened and a woman of medium height, blue eyes, and gray hair pulled back into a ponytail walked toward him with a questioning look. "Margie Shaker." She held out her hand.

"Justin Palmer," he said. "I'm a friend of Kris Gabriel's whose mother, Evie Gabriel, stayed here a couple times in the last few months." Justin had decided to be straightforward, telling her exactly what he wanted. AWARE was certain to have confidentiality rules they wouldn't break without a good reason.

Shaker's face didn't register Evie's name. Don't ask, don't tell.

"AWARE may have a piece of information that might point to Evie's killer," he said. Shaker's eyes became guarded and Justin quickly told her about the letter and how he'd found it.

"How do you know Evie didn't pick it up here and show it to Vern?" she asked.

"Because there was no reason to hide the letter except to hide it from her," he said. "And I'm certain she didn't know about the hiding place under the floor because Vern was sure to keep control of the money—he was hiding it from her too."

Shaker nodded; Justin figured she knew well enough about men controlling money. He watched her carefully, gauging her reaction.

"I would feel more comfortable talking to the police about this," she said.

"I understand. I called Barrett this morning, but he's in Fairbanks."

"Maybe it's not important then."

"No, it's important," Justin said, too emphatically. "He just didn't think of it."

Shaker's expression grew impatient.

"I could call him in Fairbanks and if he thought—" Justin started.

"I would need to talk to my board," Shaker said.

Liability. Or just an ugly mess if the letter had gotten out of their hands and into Vern's in the wrong way. "Fine. I'll call him and let him get in touch with you if he thinks it's an issue." Justin shook her hand and then fumbled with his zipper and hood, while Shaker left through the door she'd entered. Once his hood was on, he walked over to the desk and, reaching out his hand, said to the woman with the studs, "I didn't get your name."

"Kelly Lamoreau."

"French-Irish?" he asked.

"French-Canadian. No Irish." She smiled back.

He waited until seven-thirty that evening before calling both Lamoreaus in the phone book. He got Kelly's mother, who gave him Kelly's phone number, which was listed in her housemate's name.

"Kelly," he said when he recognized her hello. "Justin Palmer."

"I knew you would call," she said right away.

"I wasn't too subtle?" Justin asked.

"No," Kelly said.

"I understand that Ms. Shaker has to be cautious, but it's not really a big deal for the shelter," Justin started.

"It's not me you want to talk to," Kelly interrupted, trying to brush him off. "It's Sheridy Bunker. She was volunteering when Ms. Gabriel was in the shelter. She's got a paying job now and doesn't come in anymore."

"Do you—"

"Yes," and she gave him the number.

"Thanks."

"It's OK."

Justin punched in Sheridy's number. When she answered, he told her what it was he wanted without mentioning Shaker's worries.

"I gave the letter to Mrs. Lambale," she said.

"Alvilde Lambale?" Justin was startled.

"She asked me to call her when it came so she could take it to Ms. Gabriel, who'd left the shelter by then and was living somewhere out in the Valley."

"You can do that? Give a letter to some else?" Justin asked.

"Not usually. But the Lambales were like gods there. And they were pretty good friends with her."

"Friends with Evie?" Justin asked, surprised again.

"Oh yeah. They didn't make it too obvious and Mrs. Lambale was a little stand-offish, but that's just her."

Justin squinted at the blank screen of his TV, thinking. Friends? Of course, the blackmail had to be something sexual. Christ, what a slime: a battered woman.

"So you gave it to Mrs. Lambale?" he asked.

"Yes, she picked it up the day it arrived."

"Do you remember about when that was?"

The line was silent. "I'd guess the third week of October," she said slowly.

That made sense. Evie had left the shelter in September and Kris had said that Vern had gotten out of Lemon Creek Prison in early October.

"Thanks, I appreciate it." Justin hung up and slumped back on the couch, quietly triumphant. Alvilde must have handed the letter to Vern when she dropped it off, or he pulled it out of Evie's hands after Alvilde left. No one else knew Kris was coming to town, so Vern murdered Evie.

Assuming, he caught himself, assuming that the timing of Evie's murder and the attack on Kris was not some ungodly coincidence.

■ ■ ■

Kris was in trouble.

She rose and hiked back through the snow to the snow machine trail and re-climbed the hill. It put some warmth back into her, but the bite of the air was more menacing now. Barrett had her trapped. She could not survive the night outside. By morning, she'd be frozen as solid as her grandfather had been when he'd rolled his truck and couldn't break out.

The sun had set and the light was fading; in another hour it would be dark. It wasn't likely that Barrett would come looking for her. All he had to do was wait and she'd come to him. She had nothing. Not a candy bar; not a match. The lighters that Ringer had given her were heaped on the counter next to her oatmeal and powdered milk.

Damn, it was cold.

She walked down the hill, turned around, walked back up it. She did it again. By the time the last light had faded from the sky, she'd packed hard steps into the snow and her feet could find them in the dark. The movement didn't warm her, but it slowed the cold creeping into her hands and feet. The tip of her nose stung like it was being squeezed by pliers. When she breathed through her mouth, the air burned her lungs. When the pain of breathing became too much, she turned her head sideways in the hood and breathed into the padded fabric. The warm air she exhaled blew back against her face, but when she turned again to look out of the hood's tiny opening, the moisture that had condensed on her face evaporated, freezing her skin.

She walked up and down. The familiar knot of hunger twisted her stomach. How many nights had she gone to sleep with it? Not for years now. Not since she'd started working. Manuel, jeez, how are you all doing? Have you got the dispatching figured out? What day is it—it must be getting close to Thanksgiving. I'll be back soon. A few more days is all.

Up and down. She wobbled, fell to her knees, her mind fogged; when it cleared she dragged herself to her feet without pulling her hands from her pockets. Her snow steps had worn away and now she climbed up and down on rocks and frozen soil.

God, she was cold.

She was shivering now. It's when you stop shivering that you worry: Ringer again. She clamped her jaw to still it and the muscles on the side of her face twitched and jumped until they broke it free and her teeth clacked uncontrollably. Now, every time she re-climbed the hill, she fell to her knees. Sometimes her feet shot out from under her and she pitched forward, landing on a shoulder she twisted around to take her fall.

At some point in the night, she knew she couldn't go on. She fell and did not get up, lying in the snow and shivering beyond control. How many hours until daylight? Five? Ten? And then what? It wouldn't warm. Barrett wouldn't leave. She'd still be cold. She rolled, labored to her feet, which were senseless in her boots, and staggered down the hill back to the cabin. The window was dark and nothing moved inside when she peeked in. Barely felt, the inner warmth of the cabin leaked through the glass. She pressed against it, unwilling to leave the frail heat. Unwilling to give in to Barrett.

She heard the single snap of a pocket of sap exploding in the wood stove and when she ignored the cold and focused, she could smell the smoke coming out of the stovepipe.

Smoke.

Moving quietly around the cabin, her jaw clenched, she found the stovepipe where it emerged horizontally from the logs of the back wall. It stuck out more than a foot before it turned upwards again, ending two or three feet above the roof. Wires, looped around the pipe and tacked into the wall, supported it. Kris grasped the vertical section above the elbow and gently tried to turn it. Nothing happened. She leaned her weight into it and gently pushed and pulled until the joint began to loosen. Patiently, and desperately quiet, she worked it back and forth, hoping the sound wouldn't carry down the pipe and resonate in the cabin. When it was fully loose, she lifted as she twisted. The pipe edges, rusted with age, rasped as she pulled them apart. Every few turns, she stopped and listened, but heard no sound from Barrett.

When it came off, hot smoke drifted slowly out of the open end, stinging her eyes and filling her nose with the warm scent of spruce and the acrid bite of creosote. The stove was banked way down. Working quickly, Kris packed the pipe-elbow with snow. She stuffed it down the bend and packed the dry, talcum-like powder as hard as she could. When it was full, she reconnected the pipes, not bothering to push them as tightly together as they'd been before. Then she ran around the cabin and hid in the trees across the clearing from the front door.

The cold, which her excitement had held off, set back into her. She squatted under a tree wrapped into a tight ball, watching the door, which was clouded every few seconds by her breath. Maybe he would die of smoke inhalation before he woke up. That would solve a lot of problems. Nobody could pin his death on her and it might confuse the hunt for Lambale's murderer long enough for her to get out of state.

She waited.

Suddenly the door burst open and Barrett, without his parka, dashed out, hacking viciously and sucking in the clear air. He grabbed a double handful of snow and rubbed it in his eyes. Behind him, thick smoke floated out of the cabin and up into the night, dimming the stars above the roof. When he'd gotten control of his coughing, he covered his mouth with his shirt and vanished back inside. Kris heard the stove door open and Barrett curse. A second later he was outside again, coughing and shouldering into his parka. Stepping in her footprints in the snow, he disappeared around the corner of the cabin, heading for the stack.

Kris sprinted across the clearing and into the open door. The smoke inside was thick; her eyes teared and burned. She stooped below it and beelined for the back corner where the kitchen counter hooked into the back wall. Her heart beating, she moved the pots and plastic barrels away from the wall and squeezed into the space under the counter. She hugged her knees and listened; Barrett was still fiddling with the pipes. She uncoiled and crawled out. Keeping low, in the fresher air, she searched for her pack, then noticed that her gear was lined out on the counter. The assholes had gone through her stuff. Her fingers picked around the bags of food until she felt the candy bars. She grabbed a handful and stuffed them in a pocket. Barrett passed the side window; she saw his shadow, cast by the starlight, against the wall. Silently and stifling a cough, she scurried back into her corner under the counter and shrank into the shadows.

Barrett stepped through the door and closed it behind him.

"Kris," he said. He clicked on a flashlight and probed the darkness with the brilliant beam. The light bounced off her boots and kept on going. He reopened the door and yelled into the night. "Kris, come in and get warm." He stood in the door; the cold air sinking to the floor, misting, and wrapping itself around her. She didn't move.

Barrett yelled again, listened, and then came back in, closing the door. The stove was drawing now, but the cabin had cooled down. He put the flashlight on the counter, pointing it at the stove, and came back by Kris to gather an armful of the split spruce stacked against the wall. Kris counted the eyelets on his boots. Fancy, fake ruffed, Sorels. He loaded up the stove and in minutes the fire was roaring. It drew the last smoke out of the room and waves of heat rolled over her and her blood begin to throb in her cheeks and fingers.

She bit her knee to keep from crying.

■ ■ ■

Kris awoke. The cabin had cooled down. Her legs ached; she stretched them out on the floor in front of her and dozed off again.

Barrett was awake. She felt him come alive in his bag. Quietly, she folded her legs, tucking her heels against her butt, and pushed herself deeper into her corner. His feet thumped softly on the floor, the grate of the stove squeaked open, and then suddenly he was in front of her, his hands pale in the darkness lit only by the starlight falling through the windows. His body radiated a warm moistness; sweat from sleeping too warm. The stack of wood against the back of the cabin was low; Barrett squatted and loaded an arm with spruce; he reached to the right, groping for sticks. Kris lowered her face against her knees to hide the whiteness of her skin.

She felt him stop moving.

"You had me worried," he said, "I thought you were outside."

Kris lifted her head. His face, a dim blur, the eyes hidden, was looking at her.

"Come on out. You must be stiff." He rose and took the wood to the stove and began rebuilding the fire.

Kris hesitated, then crawled out.

The wood caught and the orange light of the flames danced on his face.

Kris stood by the stove, little heat came from it yet, and watched Barrett looking intently into its belly. The wood began to crackle.

"I cooked up a couple of your macaroni and cheeses," he said. "Looked better than the barley sugar and C-rations in the survival gear. Let me heat up the left-overs." He used a stick of wood to push the fire deeper into the stove and set up Ben's cooking grill. He dipped a small pan into the large pot of snowmelt on the stovetop, testing the water with his finger before placing it on the grill. He stirred water into the pot with macaroni and set it in the stove next to the other. His movements were quiet and assured; nothing rattled or clattered as he searched for spoons and lids in the dark.

The cabin warmed and she slipped out of the parka, dropping it on the floor and, a minute later, still too warm, she unzipped the snowmobile suit, pulling her arms and legs free and laid it on top of the parka. She untied the shoepacks and pulled the liners out with her feet, leaving the liners on as slippers. Unprotected by her arctic gear, the heat radiating from the stove pushed through her clothes and rubbed, hot and dry against her skin.

Barrett wrapped a bandanna around his hand to protect it from the fire and tended the pots, pulling the one with the macaroni out frequently to stir its contents. When dinner was ready, he gathered up his clothes, flashlight, pistol, wallet, keys and other hardware off Ben's only chair and lay the bundle on the kitchen counter. He pulled the chair in front of the fire and gently guided her into it. He poured water from the small pan into a mug, found Kris's coffee among the Ziplocs on the counter and mixed it in adding sugar and then put the mug into her hands. He scraped the macaroni into a bowl, added a spoon, and set it at her feet. Then he pulled the plastic bucket from under the counter, turned it upside down, and sat it next to her in front of the fire, his head at her shoulder.

Kris sipped the coffee; he'd made it sweet. She sipped again, wrapping her hands around the cup's warmth. The fire crackled, casting its light against their legs and into their laps. Barrett lifted her bowl of macaroni from the floor and balanced it on top of the stove to keep it warm. The stove was beginning to shed heat like the hot California sun.

"We'll have to bank it down soon, or it'll cook us out of here," he said. It meant losing its light and muffling its sound. He shifted forward, his knee brushed her thigh, and peered into the stove, then poked at the fire with a stick, breaking it apart, spreading the logs and coals around the stove's interior to cool it. He was in his long underwear; the synthetics had absorbed his odor and it swirled around him when he moved.

The coffee was gone; she set the mug down and reached for the bowl. The macaroni was hot and thick with cheese. She ate it all, running a finger around the bowl and sucking it clean. He took the bowl from her and set it on the floor in the darkness. His body moved like a cat's; when he stood to fill her mug the fist of his cock pressed against the fabric stretched tight over his thighs and hips.

Her heart began to thud slow and hard against her chest. Years ago, when Save Our Sisters was dusting the street off her and primping her for a job, Kris had hung out with Mariah, who'd had a rabbit named Dyke. It ran loose in her apartment, dropping hard pellets of shit wherever it hopped. Mariah would pick them up and jump shoot them into bowls she had set up on the bookcases and refrigerator. One night, when Kris was sitting cross-legged on the floor, Dyke started humping her knee.

"I thought it was a she," she said. The rabbit, its eyes murky-gray and unblinking in their intensity, gripped her thigh with its forepaws and pumped her knee like a toy jackhammer.

"Yeah, she's just asserting her dominance," Mariah said.

Kris had slapped it away.

"More?" Barrett asked.

She reached down for her mug on the floor by her feet and when she turned to hand it to him, she brushed her breasts against his arm. He made her another cup, moving silently and with animal-like assurance in the darkness. When he handed her the mug, she waited until he had seated himself on the bucket before sliding off her chair and on to her knees at his side. He turned his head; she pushed it away with her chin, sucked the lobe of his ear between her teeth, and bit hard, exhaling into his ear, tasting blood. She slid her hand down his belly and under the waistband of his long underwear. When she touched him, he shuddered as if he'd been hit.

Kris freed him from the tangled fabric, he raised his hips and she pushed the underwear down his legs, letting them fall around his ankles. He reached to touch her; she pushed his hand away.

"Hang on," she whispered. "I got to take a leak." She stood, picked her parka off the floor and put it on and then swept the floor with her feet until she found her shoepacks, which she stepped into but didn't bother to tie. She shuffled to the counter, kicking over her pack, which had been leaning against a counter support and started rifling through the Ziplocs, hidden by the darkness. As she felt through the bags, Kris glanced through her hair at Barrett, who, outlined by the flickering glow of the fire, had turned to watch her. He looked comical sitting on the bucket, his long johns puddled around his ankles.

"Tissues," she said to herself, but loud enough for Barrett to hear. She pulled his long metal flashlight out from under the heap of his clothes and pointed it at him. "Where's the switch?" She pushed it and the white beam shot out and hit him in the face. "Oh."

Barrett squeezed his eyes shut and turned his head away. Before he could recover, she swept the plastic food bags off the counter and into her pack and then tucked the pack under her parka.

"Got them," she said. She shuffled to the door in the loose shoepacks and opened it. Next to it, were his boots.

"Back in a bit," she said and swept the beam across the plastic bucket he was still sitting on so he couldn't see her kick his boots into the snow. She pulled the door shut, yanked her shoelaces tight, picked up his boots and switched off the flashlight before running to the tool shed, where she dropped the pack next to the snow machine and heaved the boots into the trees behind it. Inside the shed, she waved her hands in the darkness until they bumped into the large snowshoes that she'd rehung from the ceiling the day before. She pulled them free. Under the workbench, she found the plastic jug of gasoline and dragged it and the shoes outside, dumping them by the pack. She fought the frozen tarp off the snow machine and, as quickly and as tightly as she could with mittened hands, she lashed the pack, jug, and snowshoes onto the back of the seat. When the load didn't shift when she tugged on it, she hauled the tarp back over the snow machine. She cut over to the woodpile, gathered up an armload of wood, and jogged back to the cabin, flicking on the light as she approached.

Cold air came in with her, sank to the floor, and, in the flashlight's beam, swirled in a mist towards Barrett, who was sitting in the chair now facing the open stove.

"Monumental piss," he said.

Kris dropped the wood on the floor next to him and turned off the flashlight. He'd pulled his long underwear back up. She took off her parka and pulled her feet out of her boots, ignoring him. She knelt in front of the stove and fed more wood to the fire. It grew and warmed the outside air that had come in through the door with her.

"Where's my sleeping bag?" she asked after a while, watching the flames.

"Under the bunk."

"Would you set it up, please?"

Barrett stood and rummaged under the bunk, which was high—only a few feet below the slant of the roof. Hot air rose in cabins, sleeping close to the floor was chilly. She heard the sound of the nylon fabric being pulled out of its stuff sack and then a zipper being opened. Barrett arranged the bag on the bunk and then pulled off his long underwear and climbed up.

When she was warm again, she took off her clothes, laying them on the counter next to the flashlight and the pile of Barrett's clothes. She stood naked before the fire, feeling its heat and watching the pattern of shadow and light play across her legs. The light didn't touch her breasts, but the lumpy bandage over her nipple was silhouetted against the firelight that bathed the cabin floor. She worked it free and threw it into the fire and thought of the lonely nights listening to Evie keeping a man happy.

She closed the stove door and turned the damper, then climbed up and kneeled on the bed, straddling Barrett.

He reached up and traced the curve of her thigh with a finger.

TUESDAY, NOVEMBER 24

Kris slid quietly off the bed, pulling the sleeping bag with her and wrapping it around her body. The floor was cold, her feet bare, she padded over to the counter and felt for Barrett's pistol under the pile of his clothes and slipped it into her sleeping bag. She gathered the last of the wood she'd dumped by the stove and fed it to the coals left from last night's fire and, as the fire came to life, she stood on her sleeping bag to keep her feet off the floor and dressed. She stepped into her shoepacks, put on her parka and, carrying the plastic bucket by its bail, slipped outdoors with her sleeping bag and snowmobile suit. She groped in the bag for the pistol, stuffed it into a pocket and then rolled the suit up in the bag and stuffed them into the snow against the cabin wall opposite the sheds. She filled the bucket with snow.

"'Morning," Barrett said when Kris reentered the cabin. He spoke from the dark; no light reached the bed from the fire.

Kris hung the parka by the door, carried the bucket to the stove, and stuck a finger into the pot of snowmelt; the water was hot, but half had evaporated during the night. She dumped the snow into the pot, mounding it high. The fire was drawing and the stove was beginning to radiate heat.

"Bath water?" Barrett asked. "Enough for two?"

"Plenty of snow," Kris said. She stood in front of the open stove warming her hands. She'd packed the snow into the bucket without her mittens. The fabric of the Barrett's sleeping bag rustled and Kris felt a gathering of purpose come from the bed.

"What happened to Loren Lambale, Kris?" Barrett asked.

He'd had his fuck, now it was back to work. Then the significance of his question jolted into her: he hadn't found the body. What the hell was he chasing her for? She stood motionless in front of the stove, her mind scrambling for her next move.

She shook her head; then, because he couldn't see it, she said, "Don't know."

"You thought Vern was blackmailing him."

So Justin had talked.

"Which made it reasonable to conclude that he killed Evie," he said. "So what did you do to him?"

Kris watched the fire build through the open door, then said, "Nothing. I waited for him at the parking garage and we talked in his car."

Barrett waited.

"He told me he'd raped her."

"Raped her? He admitted to it?"

"I guessed and he didn't say no. But that's what Vern was blackmailing him for and that's why Lambale killed her." The mound of snow slumped below the lip of the pot. Kris put the lid on.

"Then what did you do?"

"By then I was screaming at him. He couldn't take it and got out of the car and ran down the emergency stairs."

"Why didn't you come and get me?"

"You're a prick." The fire was roaring now, the heat forced her to step back.

"Didn't stop you last night." When she didn't reply, he asked, "You wanted him to get away?"

"Where was he going to go? I needed to find Corvus."

"That's why you came up here?"

"Ben spent that winter here. I thought he may have brought Corvus up with him."

"Kidnap his own child?"

"It was all I had."

"And?"

"Nothing." Kris lifted the lid and touched the water. If Barrett bought her story about Lambale, maybe she wouldn't have to run.

"Lambale didn't kill your mother," he said.

Kris heard the sleeping bag rustle and tensed. If he got out of bed, he'd miss his boots right away. The rustling stopped and when he spoke again, his voice came from higher in the corner. He'd sat up to lecture her.

"He drove in with Alvilde that morning and was at the bank for a two hour executive meeting at eight. A little after ten, Alvilde picked him up in the Mercedes and they went over to the shelter to help set up for the ceremonies. Alvilde stayed about an hour then drove back to her gallery. She parked in the city garage, which is more than a mile from AWARE. He could've used someone else's car to take Evie down to Thane, but it still would've taken a minimum of forty-five minutes there and back—assuming he knew where to find her. She'd been invited to the dedication but never showed. But it's immaterial, he never left; between ten and four, there was never a moment when someone at AWARE wasn't working with him.

"Alvilde arrived with the car after four; the dedication had already started; she'd had an accident and had returned home to change. Afterwards, they ate dinner with the mayor and most of AWARE's board. They left the dinner at ten and arrived home at ten-thirty. The ME put the time of death between nine a.m. and four p.m.

"He's clear; he had no opportunity to kill her."

So Justin had been right.

"I also don't think he raped Evie. You misinterpreted his silence. Plenty of lawyers, doctors, and bank presidents abuse, murder and rape, but not Lambale. It's not in him."

Kris felt the water again. Close enough. She lifted the pot, felt in the darkness with her foot for the plastic bucket, and poured the water into it.

"And I don't believe, not for a second, that you'd let a man you thought had killed your mother get away from you."

Kris set the bucket on the floor between the stove and the door, leaving the handle up.

"Lucky you got your fuck before you decided I was a killer," Kris said. She lifted her parka off the peg by the door and put it on.

"Did you kill him, Kris?"

Kris walked to the bed and looked up at Barrett. In the light from the open stove, she could see the whiteness of his body outlined against the dark. He was sitting naked, leaning against the wall, his legs drawn up, both forearms resting on his knees, looking down at her, supremely confident.

"I did not kill him." She held his hidden gaze, then turned and walked away. As she passed the stove, she closed its door, cutting off the only light in the cabin. Without slowing, she lifted the bucket and, reaching the cabin door, lifted the latch and pulled it open.

"I got to take a leak," she said.

"Again? Have you got a urinary infection?" he asked.

"The clap," she said and pulled the door closed.

The hot water steamed in the cold, frosting her sleeve and hair. She set the bucket in the snow and put on her mittens; picked it up again, grabbed her sleeping bag as she rounded the corner, tucked it under her other arm, and ran awkwardly to the tool shed. Barrett wouldn't wait in the bed for his bath and she had maybe two minutes before he figured out she'd taken his boots.

The tarp was stiff and heavy; she dropped it behind the snow machine and stuffed the sleeping bag with the snowmobile suit under the rope lashing the gas jug and snowshoes. In the cabin the flashlight snapped on, its beam lit the window; Barrett was searching for his boots. She pulled out the gun and pushed the safety off and levered a round into the chamber, then transferred it to her left pocket; her right hand would be on the throttle. She took off her left-hand mitten, stuffed it in the pocket underneath the gun, and pushed the parka hood off her head, feeling her ears instantly sting in the cold.

The bucket of water steamed. Resting it on her knee, she tipped it over the cylinders, pouring the water in a steady stream. When it was gone, she flung it aside and yanked on the cord. The engine cranked, violently loud in the stillness. She yanked again, pulling the cord with her entire body. Again. Nothing. Again. It sputtered. Again. It sputtered and caught.

Barrett came pelting around the corner of the cabin. Kris gunned the engine and shot out of the shed, racing toward him. He was hidden behind the flashlight; it shone at her like the headlight on a locomotive. She hurtled towards it, blinded; it was all she could see. Then it swung back; he was winding up to knock her off the snow machine. The gun was in her hand; she pointed it to the side and fired. She pointed it over his head and fired. She pointed it at him and he dove into the snow. The machine screamed past him, raced around the cabin, across the clearing, and down the trail.

■ ■ ■

The wind sliced into her face. It blasted into her hood, flattening the fur ruff and stunning the breath out of her. The throttle was pressed flat out; the machine bucked and swerved on the edge of control and she struggled to keep it in Johnny's track with a single hand on the handlebars. Her other hand was jammed in a pocket wrapped around the pistol barrel trying to absorb its heat; she'd used both hands to muscle the machine down the hill and onto the river and her left hand had been naked to the air slicing into it. The high points of her cheeks, her nose, and the ridge of her brow grew heavy, freezing solid and sagging on her face like lead weights. But she didn't stop—she felt Barrett standing on the bluff behind her, in his bare feet, watching her disappear down the river and she didn't want him to see her hurt.

The river curved behind a bank; it curved again. When she was out of sight and could no longer withstand the pain, Kris stopped, leaving the engine idling. She pulled off her other mitten and, pressing both hands open against her face, pumped her breath, ragged with pain and the shock of the cold, into them. Warmed by her body, the air spread over her frozen skin, but it took a long time before the frostbite in her cheeks and nose thawed, and the returning blood made her face itch and burn. She turned her head inside the hood to wipe off the moisture her breath had left on her face before it froze, then she pulled the sleeping bag out from under the ropes lashing the gear and climbed into the snowmobile suit still warm from the heat of the cabin.

She wrapped the sleeping bag around herself, opened the snow machine's cowling and draped herself over the engine, wrapping her hands around the cylinders. When her fingers had warmed enough to be used, she put on the mittens and fumbled at the lashings on the gear. She needed Johnny's face mask; the wind in her face would be painful without goggles, but without a mask, it would be almost impossible, unless she drove at a walk. When she'd freed the pack she began pulling things out and laying them on the seat, careful not to lose anything in the dark. She had about half of her food, two days' worth, although there was a lot of oatmeal; all of her cigarette lighters, no cigarettes, a big metal cup, both water bottles—empty, some clothes, her duffle, and the sleeping bag. No toothbrush, but searching again she found the face mask in one of the duffle's side pockets.

Kris kept out a bag of nuts and dried fruit, stuffed the sleeping bag back into the pack, and retied everything on the rear of the seat. With the face mask on, she pressed the throttle and moved slowly forward. She wasn't interested in speed now; it was too cold.

The trail was hard and clear; there had been no wind since she and Johnny had driven north, and the going was easy. Kris tried to figure when she would get to Allakaket. She had five gallons of fuel, minus whatever she'd burned the day before hauling wood up the hill. If Ben's machine got ten miles to the gallon, that was fifty miles, and it was seventy to Allakaket. A twenty-mile hike. She could do that, though she'd probably run into another snow machine she could hitch a ride into the village with. But if this thing got fifteen miles to a gallon, she recalculated, she could be in Allakaket in four to five hours, early enough to catch Frontier's afternoon flight back to Fairbanks and maybe the last flight out of Fairbanks to Juneau.

It sounded good, but after thinking about it she changed her mind. She had no place to hide in Juneau; it would be safer to spend the night in Fairbanks with Annie again; Barrett couldn't have found Annie, Kris'd never mentioned her to Justin. Justin. Barrett probably leaned on him and he caved like a junkie begging for a hit. If she stayed at Annie's tonight, she could get Ringer's gear back to him, then blast through Juneau tomorrow— not even leave the airport—and be in L.A. by tomorrow evening.

L.A. Kris leaned into a curve. It sounded very nice. Warmth, light, sun, warmth, food, warmth, her own bed. It wouldn't take Barrett long to track her down, but she'd have a few days to get organized. Fake IDs were cheap in L.A. and she'd have about a thousand dollars left over from Vern's stash—enough to set her up on a beach in Mexico while she figured out what to do next.

Kris lost herself in the engine's whine, maneuvering the snowmobile easily over Johnny's trail, which was lit by the stars overhead. She motored past animal tracks left in the snow, past the dark silent trees, and past the leads they'd seen on the way up, still open after three days of serious cold.

And then she realized she couldn't leave right away; she had to see Ben. She needed to find out why he'd shot Corvus; it would nag her forever, not knowing. Screw Barrett; she'd get around him. Bet he thinks a lot of himself now, sitting alone in that little cabin—without her, or his gun, or his boots. Kris laughed. It rolled up from her belly and out the holes in the face mask. God, he has to be really pissed off. How long is he going to have to stew there until his plane shows up?

Damn.

If it came today, he'd beat her to Allakaket. Kris let go of the throttle and the machine stopped. She got off and walked behind it and into its track, where she didn't sink into the snow, and tried to think. The noise of the idling engine confused her and she went back and turned it off. The absoluteness of the arctic silence settled over her.

She could wait until Barrett cleared out and then go back to the cabin. Then what? If he hadn't taken the food she'd left, she'd still have only a few days' worth and the cops would still be waiting for her in Allakaket. Kris's pacing became more agitated. There had to be another way out other than through Allakaket. Kris tried to picture Ringer's maps. There wasn't a whole lot out here. She couldn't remember what was down the Koyukuk from Allakaket. Up river was Bettles and then the haul road. The road was fifty miles from Allakaket, one hundred twenty from the cabin; it would take more than five gallons to get her there and no way could she get past Allakaket or up the Koyukuk, without being seen—there would be way too much snow machine traffic on the river around Allakaket.

How was she going to get out without getting caught? A rut was forming in the trail behind the snow machine as she stomped her feet in the packed snow trying to stay warm. Then she had it. If she could get over the pass between Mettenpherg Creek and the Sixtymile, the route Ben and Ezekiel used when they visited each other, she could get onto the John River, which runs into the Koyukuk just below Bettles. No one on the John would know who she was, and Bettles was big enough that she could sneak into it without anyone noticing her. That would fix Barrett. She'd disappear, and he'd think that she'd died on the trail, fallen into an overflow or something.

She looked at the snow machine. Five gallons wouldn't do it and it'd be a long hike into Bettles if someone didn't come by and give her a ride. So what was her choice—a long walk or meeting Barrett in Allakaket. Kris started the engine.

The cutoff up the Mettenpherg was sharp and clear in the starlight. Kris turned up the trail as carefully as she could, trying not to make her tracks too obvious. She got off the machine to brush fresh snow over the track the machine had cut making the turn. When it looked good enough to fool someone in a plane, she sped up the trail broken by Johnny's Uncle Harold when he'd laid out his trap line the week before.

Mettenpherg Creek was narrower than the Alatna and Harold's trail wound and twisted between rocks and falls in the stream. Sometimes it left the stream all together and went along a bank or cut across wide expanses of treeless snow, to pick it up farther along. Kris learned to rock and weave with the machine, rising and falling as it climbed and fell over the bumps and dips, and her movement kept her warm enough not to shiver. She kept her eyes on the wall of mountains to her right, looking for the pass over to the Sixtymile. Ringer's map had not been very detailed; only a single page covering hundreds of miles of the northern section of the state and she had no idea how far up the Mettenpherg she had to go, or how far it was over the pass to the Sixtymile, or how far it was from there to Bettles.

Sunlight was shining on the mountain peaks to the north when she found the pass. The ridge that she'd been following on her right dipped low and opened wide. The stream, too, had narrowed and rose more steeply and Kris didn't think that Harold's trail could go that much farther unless he'd left his snow machine and gone on foot. She stopped and stood on the seat, surveying a route up to the pass. There were a few scrawny and widely-spaced trees between the stream and the mountains; they wouldn't be difficult to get around, but the slope to the pass was steep, steeper than the hill to Corvus's grave and no obvious route led to the top.

At a low point in the bank, Kris gunned the snow machine; its belt spun for second, unable to grip the loose snow, then it caught and thrust the machine over the rim. It was easy picking her way through the trees; enough snow lay on the ground to cover dead falls and fallen branches. When she reached the start of the slope, she turned and cruised slowly along its base looking for a route up. She couldn't see how Ben got a dogsled, much less a snow machine, up it. Then, at one end, Kris noticed a fold that ran like a ramp across the face of the slope. It was steep, and she couldn't tell how far up it went, but there was a chance that she could power the old machine up it. She circled around and opened the throttle as far as it would go. The machine blasted through the snow and launched itself up the ramp. As soon as it hit the incline, it started struggling and the belt began kicking out snow behind it. Less than fifty feet up, it quit.

To lighten the load, Kris kicked a shelf in the snow and put the pack, gas jug, and snowshoes on it. She drove off the ramp onto the steep hillside to turn around; leaning into the slope, her shoulder brushing the snow, as she turned it out of the fall line, anxiously trying to keep it from rolling over. She motored back down to the bottom, turned around, and raced back up. Each time she ran it up, she punched another ten or twenty feet higher on the ramp, but she was a long way from the top when the ramp vanished into the hillside and the machine could go no farther.

She ran the snow machine down to the bottom again, turned, and came up to where she'd left the gear. Lashing it loosely, she hauled everything to the top of the ramp, dumped the gear in the snow, and sat limply on the seat, the machine idling quietly. There was a comfort to its heat and noise and she didn't want to leave it. It could cover in an hour what would take her a long day to do on snowshoes. How had Ben and Ezekiel gotten up this? She scanned the snow above her, but saw no way up.

There was no choice. Kris killed the engine, knowing that if she came back in an hour, she'd never be able to restart it. Then, with a snowshoe, she shoveled snow over it, hiding it, even though her trail up the slope was obvious. She pushed her boots into the snowshoe bindings and buckled them tightly. The pack wasn't as heavy as it had been in Fairbanks, but now she wished there were more in it. She heaved it onto her shoulders and cinched the waist belt tight, pulling down on the parka skirt so it covered her rear.

Ready. She glanced around to be sure she had everything and then stepped into the snow above the trail. When she put her weight on it, the snowshoe shot out behind her like a ski, throwing her face down in the snow. The pack pinned her and for a second she panicked, breathing snow into her mouth and nose and thrashing her arms in the bottomless powder, trying to push her face up for air. Forcing herself calm, she unclipped the waist belt and twisted out from under the pack and lay, panting in the snow.

The cold air she was gasping into her chest began to frost her lips and freeze her lungs. She closed them and, quieting her breathing, breathed through her nose. She shook the snow out of her mittens, lifted and re-settled the pack on her shoulders and started again, this time at an angle to the slope. It was hard, her uphill leg had to do most of the work and loose snow fell on top of the snowshoes doubling their weight.

Within minutes, her chest was heaving and the arctic air tore at her throat, but she began to overheat, an unexpected luxury, and, when she turned to cut across the slope in the other direction, she stripped off the snowmobile suit and left her parka open. Every few feet she had to rest, her throat sore, her heart thumping madly, and the pile of snow covering the snow machine never seeming to get farther away.

The sun had set when the slope leveled out and she could walk up the pass without traversing. She stopped, dropped the pack in the snow, and sat on it to rest. Her heart took a long time to settle down, and before it had quieted the cold had cut into her again. The height of the pass was still in front of her, how far away she couldn't tell, but the way toward it was clear; mountains rose on both sides and no trees or scrub blocked her way. The snow machine would've screamed up this part of it.

Swinging each foot wide so that the snowshoes didn't bump into the other leg, she headed into the narrow valley. Even with the pack on her back, her feet did not sink far into the snow. It was denser here, packed and scoured by the wind, and the snowshoes rode near its surface. She trudged forward, her eyes on her feet, her mittened hands crossed on her chest. When she raised her eyes to look at the top of the pass, it never seemed any closer. And when she finally reached what had looked like the top, she found higher ground beyond. The first miles were difficult. Every few hundred feet she would stop and rest, hitching her pack high on her shoulders and leaning her hands on her knees, and look back down her tracks at the confused snow where she'd last stopped not far behind her. The pack straps rubbed her shoulders raw, and the waist belt bunched up the bulky parka and rode painfully on the seams of her fleece pants. The muscles in her calves ached, and the tendon anchoring her heel stung every time she lifted a snowshoe to move it forward.

If she did one mile an hour, and it was one hundred miles to Bettles, that was one hundred hours—four straight days—eight if she walked only half a day. Maybe she was doing two miles an hour. That meant four half days to Bettles. Maybe Bettles is only... She reworked the calculation over and over, but the conclusion stayed the same: She couldn't do it. She'd die if she didn't go back and give herself up. They'd probably catch her anyway. All Barrett had to do was tell Alaska Airlines to call the cops when she bought a ticket in Fairbanks. Then she put one foot in front of the other and slogged on.

Kris's pace didn't slow when the gray light turned black and the snow glowed in the light of the stars. The slow, rhythmic crunch of her snowshoes breaking into the wind-crusted snow and the rasping sound of her breath lulled her into a stupor that dulled the pain of the pack sores on her shoulders and hips, the ache of her thigh and calf muscles, and the bite of the cold in her unmoving fingers clenched tightly in her mittens. The snowshoes, heaped with snow, became stones she struggled to lift with each step. The air was harsh and dry as desert sand, and every breath she exhaled spewed a cloud of moisture that she could not replace, and her throat felt rough and scaly like spruce bark on an old tree. The water bottles were empty, and there were no trees, no brush to make a fire to melt snow, and the snow was so cold and so dry that when she put a handful into her mouth it had numbed her lips and tongue and had melted into a trickle too small to swallow. Her stomach twisted with hunger and, without water, her nuts and raisins mucked up and stuck in her throat.

She couldn't stop until she got out of the pass, until she dropped into a valley with trees where she could build a fire. Without warmth, she would die if she stopped moving. How many miles had she walked up and down Ben's hill the night before, trying to keep warm before she gave up and went back to the cabin? One—maybe two? And she hadn't had a pack or snowshoes. But then, she'd had a choice of jail or death by exposure. Now, she didn't even have that.

Kris didn't notice when the ground started sloping away, the change was too slight when she crossed over the pass. She just trudged on. Every mile or two, she'd stop and dig her socks out of the shoepacks and pull them back up her legs; her feet were loose in the boots and the socks worked their way around her heel and bunched up at her toes. Her nose ran, a steady trickle of clear fluid which she wiped on the back of her mittens, until they were coated with an ice sheet of frozen snot, which she'd rub against her pants to scour off.

Maybe an hour, maybe two hours later, the parka zipped to the end of the hood now, her body too exhausted to warm itself even as she walked, the tip of a snowshoe stepped into silver light. Kris took several more steps before faltering to a stop. In front of her, through the tiny opening of her hood, the snow sparkled as if dusted with diamonds. She circled at the waist, moving the hood, and found a break in the mountains overlooking a valley; and floating over the distant horizon below her was the moon. Its light shone up the valley and into the pass, reflecting off the snow crystals and casting her shadow so far into the depths behind her that it merged with the night.

Bright and full, it felt, for a moment, like a friend who'd come to walk by her; to accompany her over the snow and through the darkness. But as she watched, the horizon bit into its lower edge, and she knew that it would leave her; that it shone for other reasons and not for her. Unbidden, the memory of Justin's touch, of his finger on her cheek, suddenly came to her, and, like the moon, it lifted her for an instant, as if she weren't alone, and then she remembered how she'd turned away from it and the feeling vanished. Cold, exhausted, uncertain of the miles she had yet to go, she dropped her head, lifted a foot, and continued on.

Hours later, Kris noticed that her snowshoes sank deeper with each step and that more snow tumbled on top of them before she lifted her foot to move it forward. She kept moving, too weary to turn and see how far she'd dropped out of the pass. After another mile, she walked through the leafless tips of willow bushes sticking out of the snow. She trudged on, her feet falling forward, helped by the steeper slope. She passed more brush, then a warped and barkless tree; and then scattered trees, all stunted, half buried in the snow, and she walked faster, trying to outrun her exhaustion.

The frozen stream began in a shallow, narrow chasm that she couldn't get through. She hiked a ways up the side of the mountain, her snowshoes slipping on the slope, and paralleled the stream until the stream bottom below widened out. Standing in the small patches of level ground bordering the snow-covered stream were a few wind-twisted spruce; enough for firewood.

Too tired to be careful, she skidded down the slope until she reached the stream bottom. In the starlight, she found a tree whose lower limbs had shed the snow out from its trunk, making a deep well under it. She tugged at the buckle on the pack's waist belt, but her fingers were too weak with cold to pull it open. Frantic with frustration, she tore at it with both hands, then gave up and walked into the tree, branches breaking against her face, and, hugging the skinny trunk, pressed the buckle against it and twisted her hips to snag it open. The full weight of the pack fell on her shoulders. She shrugged it off, letting it fall behind her in the snow.

Shaking now, she broke dead branches off the spruce, dropped them onto the pack, and then snowshoed to the surrounding trees for more. The snowshoe bindings were frozen; she knew she wouldn't be able to get them off until she had warmed her hands. Moving fast, she scraped the snow out from around the tree with the snowshoes still on her feet and, kneeling awkwardly in them, built a fire. She'd put one of the lighters in an unzipped pocket so she could get to it with cold hands. She pulled it out, dropped the mitten, and sucked her thumb to warm it, counting to sixty, then took it out of her mouth and spun the wheel; it flamed.

And again she cursed Ringer. When she pushed the lighter under the pile of twigs, the flame curled up and seared her thumb. Ignoring the pain, she forced the flame under the kindling, feeling her skin blister, smelling, just before the spruce caught, burning flesh.

WEDNESDAY, NOVEMBER 25

Barrett didn't have a pistol to check, and when he approached the security post he tossed the package of slugs into a trash can.

So who screwed who last night?

The attendant took his boarding pass and he stepped down the jet way to the plane.

Had she manipulated him from the start? She couldn't fake those juices; but if she came last night, she kept it to herself, as if it was war and she wasn't going to give him anything.

He showed the steward his seat assignment and was pointed down the aisle.

She hadn't let him on top, and he'd humored her, thinking he'd have her in cuffs in the morning and Lambale's disappearance solved. Instead she had played him.

Got too cocky on that one, grunt.

He squeezed into the center seat; two big people surged over the armrests on either side of him. So he'd have to share his seat; his penance for buying a ticket at the last minute.

So she killed Lambale; she wouldn't have run otherwise. He'd been operating on suspicions when he followed her north. He'd had no evidence: no weapon, no means, no body, and until she'd fired at him, he'd had nothing to write a warrant on. Now he had a charge: assault with a dangerous weapon, and it was the troopers' problem to track her out of the bush. Better their budget than his, although it would have been fun to tag along since they wouldn't take her seriously until she'd made fools of them once or twice.

The jet rolled down the taxiway, accelerated into the turn onto the runway, and powered into the dark sky. Barrett sat back, his arms forced into his lap by the riot of flesh on either side of him. If the guy in the window seat gets up to take a leak it'll upset the plane's trim.

It was impressive how she'd disappeared. They had flown the river at treetop down to Allakaket. It was possible she got there before they did, but no one in the village saw her come in. He'd talked to the VSPO and alerted the air services, warning them to notify the troopers if she tried to book a flight out. He'd also found the kid who'd taken her up river and told him to let the VSPO know if she contacted him. There was no possibility that Kris could get into or out of Allakaket without Barrett finding out about it.

But something nagged him. Like gristle stuck between his teeth. It nagged him all the way to Juneau, and it wasn't until the plane made its dog-leg turn over Spuhn Island that he admitted it to himself. Kris Gabriel wasn't going to walk into any trap. She'd outsmarted him every step of the way.

And she'd do it again.

■ ■ ■

She was shivering. Most of the night she'd only been able to doze, waking every twenty or thirty minutes in a chilly stupor, to shift a hip, an elbow, or a foot that the cold had gripped through the sleeping bag. Where she touched the ground she was always cold, and, for most of the night, she'd slept shivering on her forearms and knees, her forehead cradled in her hands. The little energy she'd put back into her body before collapsing the night before had leaked into the darkness and now her body no longer had the strength to warm the bag.

She needed hot water and hot food and the longer she waited, the colder she would get and the harder it would be to make her hands and feet work building the fire. But the semi-cold inside the bag was heaven to the bone-crunching cold on the other side of it and she coiled into a knot, fighting the warning voice in her head, until blindly, without thinking, she pulled down the zipper and rolled out. She groped in the tangled fabric for her boots, which she'd slept with so they wouldn't freeze, and pushed her feet into them, lacing them quickly, her fingers already numbing.

It was darker than she'd remembered it being coming over the pass and she couldn't make out the branches of the tree she'd slept under. She hunted with her feet for the path through the snow to the tree where she'd cooked dinner the night before and hurried over to it. Working quickly, she found the kindling and the pile of sticks she'd saved for the morning, started a fire, and stuffed her cup with snow. While the snow melted, she collected another armful of wood and then organized the Ziplocs of instant coffee, oatmeal, and powdered milk. The raisins were gone; she'd finished them crossing the pass. The honey was as hard as concrete and Kris put the plastic container in the heating water to thaw.

The sky was starting to gray when she repacked the pack and put out the fire. Both water bottles were full and hot, the one inside her parka flooding it with warmth. The oatmeal felt solid and bulky in her stomach, and the sky was clouding over. Clouds meant it would warm up and most likely snow, which would make it harder going, but would cover her tracks over the pass.

The little stream she'd camped by entered the Sixtymile after an hour's snowshoe. It was a difficult hour, her muscles were stiff and crippling sore, her scorched thumb throbbed, and the tendons up the back of her ankles burned like they were on fire. The Sixtymile was narrower than the Mettenpherg and it fell faster. Kris often had to climb around rocks and hike up the hillside to circle around sections of the stream squeezed by rocky walls. There were many overflows; slushy water invisibly sandwiched between the river ice and the snow. Twice water welled up between the lacings of her snowshoes. She'd jumped backwards, but the slush froze immediately to the frame and rawhide lacings, doubling their weight. No amount of hacking with Ringer's knife would get all the ice off and she just had to lift the extra load.

But she made good time. Her muscles warmed, and the soreness she'd awakened with, eased, the snowshoes worked better for her, and she was going downstream, and she knew she would survive. Even if it were eight days to Bettles, she'd get there. She looked up from her feet more frequently as she walked, watching the peaks of the mountains to the north shine in the light of the sun, which was hidden behind the ridge on her right, and she scanned the trees on either side of the stream hoping to spot Ezekiel's cabin. If he had food cached there, she could burrow in for a couple of weeks until Barrett figured she was dead. All she needed was snow to cover her tracks and no one would suspect that she'd hiked across the pass.

The valley widened and the frozen surface of the stream smoothed, making the walking easier. Overhead, the clouds thickened and the temperature warmed, and Kris opened her parka. Her mind began to clear, but as it relaxed, the screams and shots of the night down at Thane crept in. Barrett was wrong about the rape; Lambale had denied everything else, but not the rape.

But if not him, who'd killed Evie?

It was in the afternoon, the invisible winter sun no longer shone on the peaks, when she heard the airplane. Its drone snuck up on her, inserting itself into her world before she was aware of it. Without thinking, without turning to look, she picked her feet up high and ran as fast as she could toward the trees, the pack beating hard against her back. She was in them when the plane banked in a sudden burst of noise around the curve in the stream behind her and flew past at the treetops.

She flattened herself against a tree and listened to the engine. It faded, then grew again. Looking up through the trees, she watched it approach. It found the spot where Kris had cut for the woods and began circling. The center of its circle drifted toward her as it followed her tracks; it was a trooper plane; AST was written on the fuselage.

The woods were too thin and the branches tucked too close to the trunks to hide her. And what the hell, who else would be out on the river at this time of year? She broke cover and hiked back to the stream. It was too narrow and rock-strewn for the plane to land; with any luck it would have to land on the John, and by the time she reached the larger river, it would be dark. She paid no attention to it, not even looking up, and kept moving downstream.

The plane circled overhead several more times and then headed off toward the John. Kris stopped to listen. Its drone diminished steadily, then rose in pitch and intensity and suddenly went silent. It had landed. Kris surveyed the trees. She couldn't hide; they'd just follow her tracks. And with the pack, she couldn't outrun them. If she went back upstream, all she had to do was stay in front of them until dark; it wasn't likely that they were set up for a night chase through the bush.

But Kris wasn't going back. It'd taken too much to get this far, and she wasn't going to do it twice. She cut into the woods, hiking away from the river until the ground began to rise and the trees stopped; this far north, trees only grew in the stream bottoms; the mountainsides were bare. At the edge of the trees, she turned and paralleled the stream, hiking toward the John. It wasn't easy walking. The snow was uneven and the tips of her snowshoes caught branches and brush buried in the snow. The Sixtymile was about a hundred feet away, but the woods were so thin, she could see big patches of it through the trees.

After she'd walked for half an hour, she slowed and moved more cautiously, dodging from tree to tree only when she was certain no one was watching. It was another fifteen minutes before she saw the first trooper, pressed close to the far bank, searching the trees methodically every few steps he took. He wore a blue parka, with the hood up, mittens that reached to his elbows and white bunny boots lashed into metal snowshoes. In one hand, he held a rifle.

She was being hunted.

She scooped out a hole in the snow and buried her pack. Then, crawling under a tree with branches low to the snow, she dug out a second hole and squatted in it. A few minutes later another trooper, with only his head showing above the bank, crept past on her side of the stream. He moved cautiously, always keeping in cover. Every few steps, he searched the trees, scanning carefully. He didn't see Kris. She waited five minutes, in case more were following, before slinging the pack onto her shoulders, and, as silently as she could, continuing downstream through the uneven snow. The valley began to widen and she left the edge of the trees, cutting closer to the stream to keep it in sight; she didn't want to miss the plane.

Had they reached the spot where she'd cut into the woods yet? If they guessed what she was going to do, they'd be back this way fast. Slowly, she crept to the bank and looked upstream. Two lines of snowshoe prints followed each bank until they disappeared around a bend. No one was in sight. Turning downstream, Kris saw the plane. It pointed away from her at the end of a parallel set of ski tracks. There was no movement; it looked deserted, but if anyone were there, they'd be inside and out of sight.

Moving fast, Kris slid down the bank and jogged awkwardly downstream, picking up the plane's tracks since she could move faster on the packed snow. Ten feet from its tail, she dropped her pack and snuck up along the left side. She stood still, listening. Cooling metal tinked, it was the only sound. Pressing against the side of the fuselage, delicately stepping over each snowshoe so she wouldn't trip, she crept forward to the side window. Its bottom edge was above her head. She crouched below and looked up. Nothing. She rose slowly, keeping her eyes fastened on the inside of the cabin. Still nothing. When she stood on her tiptoes, she still could not see fully into the cabin; someone could be slumped over sleeping.

Screw it. She reached up to the handle and threw the door open, tensed to run. The plane was empty. She pulled herself sideways into the pilot's seat, her feet dangled outside, the snowshoes knocking against the hull. She scanned the instrument panel. What did she need to do to keep this thing from flying? The panel looked similar to Jen's, though not as new, and it amazed her there were so many gauges and buttons.

"Holy shit," she spoke out loud. The keys were in the ignition switch.

She pulled them out and wrapped her mitten around them. If she dropped them in the snow they'd never find them. She hesitated. It couldn't be that easy; they probably had a spare set or could hot-wire it or something. While she searched again for a way to disable the plane, an idea bloomed in her head. What did it take to drive one of these things? Just to move it. She had the key in her hand, the steering wheel in front of her, and the throttle in the center of the panel was even labeled.

Excitement grew in her.

She dropped out of the plane, ran back for her pack, dragged it through the snow, and shoved it behind the pilot's seat. Then she unhooked the bungees holding the engine cover to the wing struts, ripped the Velcro closures open, pulling the cover off the cowling, and threw it into the cabin. She peeled off her mittens and knelt to unfasten the snowshoes. For a second she hesitated. If this didn't work, they'd grab her before she could get the shoes back on and out of there. "It's do or die, girl," she whispered. She unbuckled the lashings and pushed the snowshoes behind the seat. Before climbing into the plane, she ducked her head under the wing and looked back upstream. No sign of them yet, but they'd be on her trail in the woods by now, they knew which direction she was headed and they might be getting worried. She hauled herself in and slammed the door.

The ignition lock had "Left," "Off," "Right" and "Both" written around it. It made no sense; the plane had only one engine. She pushed the key in and twisted it to the "Both" setting. Two green lights blinked on. Nothing else happened. Maybe it needed gas. She turned the key to "Off" and pulled the throttle out a few inches. She turned the key to "Both" then to "Right" and then to "Left." Nothing.

Shit.

Kris stared at the panel thinking hard. What did Jen do? But Jen did so much; her hands were all over the cabin, flipping switches and pulling levers, none of it made sense.

Checklist.

She had a checklist. The cops had to have one; they ate and shat Standard Operating Procedure. She looked frantically around the cabin. On the lower right of the panel was a glove compartment. Maps, gum, and an empty cigarette package. She slid the seat back and looked underneath it. Life preserver.

Where was that list?

She found it in a door pocket. It was big, with big metal rings holding the plastic pages together. Ignition. Ignition. Kris paged through it. She was running out of time. Last page. Damn. She started over from the beginning. Slow down. There it was. Page Two. Turn key to Left and Right, check indicator lights. Turn to "Both." Kris turned the key. Push "Start" button. Kris scanned the panel carefully looking at each button. She found it; it was neatly labeled. She pushed it. The engine coughed and the prop jolted around until all cylinders were firing and it spun into a blur. Next on the list was throttle and operating temperature. Kris had it. She pulled the throttle, the engine roared, the prop vanished.

The plane didn't move.

She pulled the throttle all the way out. The engine howled, the plane shook, but still didn't move.

She pushed the throttle back in and flipped frantically through the checklist. There was nothing in it about moving the plane. It figured you knew how to fly. Kris tossed it on the floor. Jen, help me. Kris wracked her brain. How did she get us to move? She put her hand on the wheel and pulled out the throttle. That was all. The throttle was half out; Kris stared at it. The prop was screaming and they were dead. Next to the throttle was another lever. "Feather." What the hell was that?

Kris pulled it out; the plane shuddered and broke out of the snow. It began to move forward, picking up speed.

"Yes!" Kris yelled.

The plane skimmed across the snow; too fast. Kris pushed the throttle in until plane bounced along at a fast walk. Easy until she got the hang of it.

Won't the pigs be pissed.

Oh, shit. They'll die. They had nothing with them to survive the night unless they carried matches. If she killed a cop, even God would be after her. It was worse than killing a white man. She could leave them food and some lighters. No sleeping bag; that stayed with her.

She stopped the plane, letting the engine idle, the prop visible as it spun, and reached over the back of her seat to pull food out of her pack. But her eyes caught a red bag stuffed in the back of the plane. It was rubber and the same color that Barrett had pulled out when he stayed behind at Ben's. She climbed over the seat and crawled into the back of the fuselage. It was labeled "Emergency Survival Gear." Below was a list of the things inside. Kris scanned it. Food, bivy sacks, fire starters, everything they needed. She dragged it forward, clicked open the door and hauled it over the folded back of the seat, letting it drop onto the plane's ski.

She looked back. Far up stream, the cops burst out of the woods and raced toward her. They were still several hundred yards away and Kris watched them without concern. One dropped to his knee, unslung his rifle, and leveled it. Kris didn't move. Even with a scope, he was too far away and his heart and lungs were pumping too hard. Any shot would be wild. He aimed. There must have been a shot, because he worked the bolt, but she'd heard nothing, the noise of the plane drowned out any sound. She let him take another, then calmly ducked under the wing and climbed back into the plane.

It started up smoothly and raced down the river, toward the next bend. As it approached, Kris turned the wheel to stay in the middle of the stream. The plane didn't respond. She turned it harder, then cranked it all the way over. The plane shot straight for the bank and Kris slapped in the throttle to stop before running into it.

She twisted the handle back and forth. The one on the right side turned in sync. Jen had turned this handle every time they had made a turn. Kris remembered the steep bank out of the Fairbanks airport; Jen'd cranked the handle way over. She opened the door and looked down at the ski while she turned the handle. It didn't move. She looked closer; it didn't look like it could turn. Fat lot of good it would do in the air if the wheels turned. Kris leapt into the snow sinking to her knees and looked out from under the wing. The cops were racing toward her, the one with the rifle far behind, but the one in front kicking up snow and coming fast.

Not the wheels, not the wings, what was it that turned this thing? She walked quickly around the plane looking for something that turned it. She stared at the tail. That was it; it turned like a boat. It made sense to her as soon as she saw the rudder. But it was flat even with the tail and she'd left the wheel turned hard over. There had to be another button she had to push.

Kris set her shoulder against the rudder and shoved. It moved easily. Which way? The stream turned left; she shoved it hard right, you push an outboard the opposite way you want to go. She let it go and the rudder came back to center. Shit. She had to jam something between the rudder and the fin to keep it angled.

The survival gear. She high-stepped through the deep snow and tore open the red rubber bag, pulling things out of it. She found a package of barley sugar. Taking it back to the rudder, pulled it right and stuffed the sugar in the crack to keep it in position.

She raced back into the plane. She pulled out the throttle; the plane jumped forward, gathered speed, and curved to the right.

Damn!

The trees and bushes on the bank of the stream were a plane length away.

Kris mashed the throttle lever in and dashed back to the rudder. She pushed it left as far as it would go and restuffed the sugar in the crack. Hopping in her foot holes, she raced back to the door. Before ducking under the wing, she looked upstream. The nearest cop was only a hundred yards away and blowing hard. His face was blood red and his snowshoes were kicking up clods of snow.

She wasn't going to make it.

Kris climbed into the seat and as she swung her feet under the dash they hit something that hadn't been there before. She ignored it and pulled out the throttle. The plane sped toward the bank before the rudder caught the wind and it skittered to the left, the inside ski catching the snow on its edge instead of under its tip. Kris accelerated into the turn; the right wing crashed through the leafless bushes on the bank and cracked the trunk of a spruce sapling. When the plane was aimed down the next stretch of the river, Kris stopped it and opened the door to leap out. Again when she twisted in her seat, her foot stubbed on something on the floor. This time, she looked under the panel. Pedals. At once, she remembered Jen working her feet as they turned. Kris rammed her foot against the one closest to her and pulled the throttle. The plane surged forward and at the same instant there was a crash at the rear of the plane; the tail sank, dragging into the snow. She ignored it and pressed her feet onto the pedals and wiggled them. The plane fishtailed. Sluggishly.

She accelerated. Scraping and thumping sounds came from the tail, reverberating inside the cabin. Then came a rhythmic banging.

It was the cop. He was hanging onto the tail of the plane. The banging stopped; then there was a sharp whoosh at her ear and a hole materialized in the windshield. Frigid air lanced her face.

He was shooting at her. Through the fuselage.

Kris sat on the edge of her seat to get a better grip on the pedals and pulled the throttle out. The plane accelerated and began to bounce hard over the snow. She felt the tail lift. How fast before this thing took off? She pumped the pedals; the tail swayed back and forth; too slow to shake him off, but enough to screw with his aim.

The trees raced by. The stream began to narrow; the banks closed in. The wind coming through the bullet hole knifed into her eyes, blinding her with tears. She put a hand up to deflect it. The plane hit a rock, bounced, was airborne, then hit the ground hard, slamming Kris into the steering handle, when she straightened, she pulled it back toward her.

The plane staggered into the air.

Terrified, she hammered the throttle lever into the control panel. The plane fell, hitting hard, bounced, and hit again. The weight on the tail vanished and the plane was at once responsive to the pedals. Kris pulled the throttle out again and accelerated fast, aiming for the next turn. If the cop was still alive, she didn't want to take any more bullets. She whipped around the bend, cut the speed enough to stay on the ground and raced for the next curve ahead.

When she was around the turn, she slowed; her hands shaking; her head aching with cold like it'd been dunked into ice water. She let the plane take care of itself and reached behind the seat for her pack, rooting around in it for her bandanna. She twisted it into a cylinder and, leaning over the high dash, stuffed it through the bullet hole. Next she looked for the cabin heater, but when she found it, it was already on. Nothing works when it was this cold.

The outside end of the bandanna flattened back against the glass and fluttered madly in the wind. Were the bruises on her neck gone? She hadn't looked in a mirror since Annie's, hadn't taken a shower since Juneau, and had been living in the same clothes for the last five days, with a few more days likely. By the time she got back to town she'd look as chewed up as when she was sleeping on the streets.

Two more gentle curves and the Sixtymile merged into the snow-covered John.

Damn, she'd missed Ezekiel's cabin.

The John was broad, the bordering mountains farther away and they disappeared completely in the distance in front of her. The river had impassable pressure ridges worming through the ice and often Kris had to zig zag the plane across the river, looking for ways through the folds of ice. After a while, the river began to swing through big looping curves, and Kris lost all sense of direction.

The light was still gray, but the darkness of night wasn't far away, and Kris was searching for the switch to turn on the plane's headlights when the left ski dropped violently and the plane swerved around. She slammed the right pedal to counter the swerve and pulled the throttle out to get the left ski back on top of the snow.

The plane screamed forward, crashed into something that didn't give, and flipped.

■ ■ ■

Where was Kris? Ben twisted his spoon in his soup, the bowl cold in his hands.

Had he run her off, like he'd run off Evie?

Ben remembered the day he'd set the dogs free. He fed them the last of the food and when they finished, he unclipped them one by one, starting with Doonerak, the lead dog, from the chains in front of their doghouses. The first ones freed didn't wait for the others, but shot into the dark morning, racing back down the trail they'd struggled to break a few days before. The ones still shackled, howled and leaped against the chains, berserk with frenzy, their forelegs pawing at the air, their breath steaming in the blackness like the breath of demons. When the last one was set free, she howled in pursuit, trying to overtake the others. In seconds they were gone, galloping without stop the three hundred miles down the Alatna, up the Koyukuk, and down the haul road back to Ezekiel.

That morning, when the last dog had gone and the arctic silence closed in around him, he'd been protected by his anger; the silence wouldn't start to tear at him for another month—when he realized what he'd done.

Are you back in L.A., Kris?

How many nights had he fed himself this stuff? He looked at the green soup setting up like concrete in the cooling bowl. All those nights on the trail, sustained by hot bowls of split peas, the steam frosting his eyebrows and lashes.

Why hadn't Lambale told her? The question seared him. Had he been scared? Had Alvilde silenced him? With Evie gone, no one else knew; Lambale had nothing to drive him but his own soul.

Ben put the bowl of congealing soup on the wood stove behind him and sank his head into his hands.

Forgiveness must be easier bought than asked for. Evie hadn't even let him buy it.

It hadn't been his regular bar, the one he'd walked into seven years ago late in the spring, leaving behind the soft light of the late evening and the sweet air, flavored, even in the city, with cottonwood pollen. He was standing inside the bar, letting his eyes adjust to the gloom, when the room was filled by a laugh, which bubbled, rich and smoky, out of an unseen throat. Peering into the back, Ben saw her, leaning a hip on a table in the dim light, finger under the chin of one of the men sitting around her. She said something too low for Ben to hear; the men circling the table laughed, but the one whose chin was lifted by her finger swatted at it. She flicked it out of reach, rocked her head back, black hair swinging away from her cheeks; her throat, white in the dark, lifted and opened, releasing laughter that rustled like the wind in a grove of aspens.

It wasn't that long ago, that late evening, but he had stood taller then and wove easily between the packed tables and chairs, to an empty one in the shadows back by hers.

She saw him coming, saw his hairless head and called, "Hey, old man. What happened to the pelt?"

The others at the table turned to look at him.

"Skinned it out a couple seasons back," Ben said. He pulled out a chair and nursed beers that evening, watching her laughter slowly dissolve in whiskey. She lasted longer than he, and he turned before exiting into the night and looked again at her sitting at the back table, her throat hidden now in the shadows of her chin.

The night he first took her to the room he rented when he came into town, she was weeping. He helped her up the stairs and down the hall with the buckling wall panels to the last door. He laid her on the bed, removed her shoes, and, returning from the bathroom with a dampened towel, wiped her face and hands. She wasn't very drunk, not as drunk as some evenings he'd seen her, but something had been said at the table that had ended her laughter, and Ben, who sat with them sometimes, saw her slink into herself. Without asking, he'd touched her arm, lifting her from the chair, and they'd walked into the soft light of midnight, the sun skimming below the northern horizon.

She asked what he was going to do to her. Ben, uncertain of her meaning, sat on the floor and leaned against the bed frame, his back to her. He said he'd never seen her sad before. Evie turned on her side, pillowing her head with her palms pressed prayer-like under her cheek and looked at him and told him that she was always sad, that her laughter hid it for a while, but it never left her. And that night someone at the table, a friend who'd known her since the days when she hadn't had to laugh so hard, had, thoughtlessly, pushed her back into memories she tried to bury.

She slid her head closer to the edge of the bed and studied him. He watched her from the corner of his eye, not comfortable enough yet to look fully at her. Strands of black hair that shimmered with blue slipped off her cheek and fell over the edge of the bed, hanging an inch above the floor. Ben lifted a finger to touch them.

"I had a girl once," she told him. Smart and tough. Even when she was young, she was as headstrong and fierce as a wolverine on a kill. She told him of the time they'd played tag in Foodland, racing down the aisles, the girl screaming with laughter, knocking things off the shelves when she spun around the corners; and the times they snuck into the movies, pushing against the folks streaming out the exit doors and hiding behind the seats until people showed up for the next show. And the snow angels they rushed to make in fresh-fallen snow before the city's dirt turned it gray.

The next spring, when he'd come out of the bush, earlier than usual, though the sun was high and warm and the mud thick as the frost came out of the ground, he found her in a cramped room that smelled not of whiskey, but of bleach and fresh laundry. She was sitting in a low chair and when she looked up at him, her eyes innocent and resolute, he saw a baby in her arms.

"It's going to be different this time," she murmured and had handed him his child.

Ben stood, leaning heavily on his cane, and, lifting the bowl off the wood stove, carried it back to the kitchen. He scraped the uneaten soup back into the pot and stuck the pot in the refrigerator.

Where was Kris? Had he run her off when he yelled at her?

Had she found Corvus?

Evie, I miss you.

■ ■ ■

Kris was hurled into the steering wheel and then bounced hard against the cabin ceiling as the plane flipped over. The engine grunted, quit. Metal groaned. Kris lay on her back, stunned, her breath knocked out of her, blood trickling from her nose.

The cold revived her. It muscled in through the windows and the cabin's thin metal skin as if they weren't there. She gasped, the air knocked out of her lungs, pain searing her side. She groaned, swore, and, turning over, pushed herself up. The overhead lights and radio jacks jabbed into her butt. She wiggled off them and sagged against an upside-down door, battered and confused.

It was almost dark; some green and orange lights, still lit on the instrument panel, were bright enough to cast shadows around the cabin. In the gloom, it looked like the front windshield was buried in snow, but she could see out the side windows. The door opened easily when she twisted the handle and pushed it open. She crawled out onto the wing and, with both hands grasping the landing strut, hauled herself unsteadily to her feet. The plane's skis stuck into the air like the legs of a dead rat. The prop was a tangled mess. The tail stuck into the air, the tip of the rudder a foot off the snow. Leading away from the propeller back up the John, was a dark blue scar ripped into the snow. The ski had broken through into an overflow and the plane flipped when the ski strut hit solid ice.

She crawled back into the cabin and gathered up her things. When she had the pack cinched up, she backed out onto the wing dragging it and snowshoes behind her. She stood on the wing, the pack leaning against her thigh, looking at the river wind away from her, not wanting to buckle on the snowshoes and start hiking again. The plane hadn't bought her twenty miles.

She carried her gear to the wing tip. With the tail of a snowshoe, she probed for water beneath the snow. It came up dry. She sat on the pack and began buckling on the snowshoes; then hesitated. In the distance, she heard the bee-like whine of snow machines. The sound was coming toward her from up river. She looked through the dusk, tracking the noise, finally spotting their lights when they broke through the trees on the far bank, a mile or so from the river. There were two, moving too fast to be breaking trail; they skirted the side of a low hill and then cut across treeless flats.

They didn't see her, sitting on an upside-down plane in the middle of the river. She knew the drivers were each huddled in their little worlds, deafened by engine noise, light-blinded by the headlamp, trying to ignore the icy wind, and longing for the end of the trail. They sped past, their red taillights winking between the widely-spaced trees until, finally, they disappeared.

Kris stepped carefully off the wing tip, feeling the snowshoe settle solidly into the snow, and cut across the river toward the trail. The bank was too steep for her to struggle up; the big snowshoes slid backwards unable to grip the snow. Farther downriver, she found some willows she could pull on to hoist herself up the bank. The snow in the trees was deep and dry and the big shoes sank into it, snagging the underbrush. When she found the snowmobile trail, she was warm and sweaty again.

The trail was hard packed and the snowshoes were pointless. Kris lashed them to the pack. The last dim light had drained from the sky and nothing penetrated the clouds. The snow, so bright under the stars, was barely visible and, other than trees, which sometimes loomed, darker than the night; in front of her, she could see almost nothing. At times, she'd step off the trail, plunging knee-deep in unpacked powder. But as she grew accustomed to it, her feet learned to keep to the trail, and she moved easily through the darkness, her feet crunching on the hard snow.

This must be the trail that had run Ezekiel out of his cabin. Too many people, too much civilization. But there was a comfort in it for Kris; it meant she was getting somewhere, that she was close to people and less alone. She made good time, maybe twice the speed she could on snowshoes. The soreness of her muscles and the bruise on her ribs where she'd hit the plane's steering handle numbed into a background ache. And the pack felt lighter, her hips and shoulders broken to it, and her breath came easy when she hiked up the hills.

Two days running without a cigarette, some kind of record for her.

The air was warming up, and she walked with the parka open and hood thrown back for several hours, until her hunger grew too painful to ignore. She quickly built a fire and reheated the remaining macaroni and cheese she'd saved from the night before. One dinner left; a Rice-a-Roni. She cleaned her cup, melted snow, and refilled her water bottles before moving on.

When those two cops were rescued, Barrett would know she was headed to Bettles. Kris guessed they'd be picked up tomorrow; search and rescue would be swarming up the John and Alatna at first light. Which meant that she'd have to be undercover during the day and she'd have to sneak around Bettles and try to make the haul road by night.

Forty, fifty miles on one Rice-a-Roni and a bag of oatmeal.

The macaroni and cheese hadn't filled her and though the air was warming she began to shiver as she tired. She pushed herself for another hour before searching for a tree to dig a hole under and throw her sleeping bag in. She was off the trail, knee deep in snow when she heard the snow machines. Moving fast, she waded back to the trail, the pack hanging loosely from a shoulder. They were coming from upriver; she turned to meet them.

It took longer than she'd expected for them to appear. When the three machines barreled around the last curve, their lights grew without slowing and for a frightened moment she tensed, ready to leap out of their way. They finally cut their engines so close, she could see isolated hairs on the ruff of the lead man haloed by the lights behind him. The machines slowed, creeping the last few feet toward her, pinioning her in their beams. Dark shapes, silhouetted in the light, rose from seats and approached her.

They pulled off their goggles or slid them up under their hoods, but left their face masks on. Black and demonic, their machines rumbled like beasts behind them, shafts of brilliant light shot over their shoulders and between their legs. They turned their shadowed, faceless hoods toward her.

"We've been watching your tracks," one said. Native lilt.

"Could I get a ride into Bettles?"

Words spoken between them that Kris didn't understand and then the same one answered, "We're not going to Bettles."

Which was weird; there was nowhere else to go, unless they went down the Koyukuk to Allakaket.

"Can you get me down the trail then," she pushed. "I need to get to Fairbanks."

There was quiet hissing as they argued in whispers. They didn't want anything to do with her. If this were Los Angeles, it'd make sense; people would pass a kid bleeding on the sidewalk without stopping to help. But not in the bush; no one was left on the trail.

Then Kris realized that they were doing something illegal. They were struggling between not wanting to get caught and their traditions.

She approached them, pulling back her hood so that she was less impersonal. They fell silent. "Listen," she said over the noise of the machines. "I'm from Los Angeles. The day I'm back in Fairbanks, I'm on a plane to California. No one will ever know how I got off the John."

"What the hell are you doing up here then?" Surprise overcame caution.

"Best we keep our stories to ourselves," Kris said.

There was a silence, which tensed as it stretched.

Finally. "We can take you to the haul road." The voice wasn't welcoming.

"Thanks. I won't see a thing."

THURSDAY, NOVEMBER 26

A pickup with a cap over the bed was waiting for them when they reached the road. Except for a few times when they'd stopped to take a leak, they'd driven straight through. The trails were good and they'd howled through the night faster than Johnny had. Kris never saw Bettles, but she'd seen lights reflecting off the clouds when they'd crossed up river of it.

She lifted her pack and snowshoes out of the sled and stood in the darkness watching the figures pull boxes out of the back of the pickup. Occasionally they clinked and Kris knew they were running liquor into a dry village. The boxes were stacked and then lashed in each of the sleds. Someone went around and filled the snow machines with gas and the empty gas jugs they'd been carrying were exchanged for full ones the driver pulled out of the truck. Accounts were settled in front of the truck's headlights, and then the machines were mounted, each man resting a knee on the seat, and skimmed along the road until they picked up the trail and dropped off the high shoulder into the trees.

The driver of the pickup walked over to her.

"Like a ride into town?"

"Yeah, thanks," Kris said, relieved it'd been so easy. He lifted her pack and snowshoes with a grunt and heaved them into the back, closing the gate and door of the cap afterwards. When Kris hoisted herself into the cab, the warm air almost overwhelmed her. She shed her parka and mittens and opened the zipper on the snowmobile suit.

The driver did a U-turn and quickly worked the transmission up through the gears until they were speeding over the graveled road. It was wide and well plowed. He glanced over at her. "No names, right?" Kris nodded. He laughed. "They take themselves so seriously. Hoods in the woods." He laughed again, then said, "Six hours to town if we don't blow a tire."

Kris couldn't fight the warmth any longer; she slumped against the door and fell asleep.

The truck clattered violently and Kris felt the rear wheels lose traction and fishtail. Her eyes flew open and she sat up. They were speeding through the night. Big chunks of gravel in the road, almost small rocks, cast long shadows, which shrank rapidly as the truck approached and its headlights raced over them. Static-ridden music ebbed and flowed from the radio as they sped up and down hills, and a blue wraith of tobacco smoke drifted across the cab.

"Sorry," he said, noticing that she was awake. "Got going too fast back there."

"It's a long drive," she said.

"Yeah." He pointed at a pack of Camels on the dash. "Help yourself."

Kris sucked hard and felt the smoke jet into her lungs. "How much farther?"

"Couple more hours. We'll be on pavement soon. Livengood's just ahead."

They continued on in silence for a while; the berms of snow, piled along the side of the road by the plows, raced out of the night and vanished behind them. A semi snorted past, not lowering his hi-beams and kicking up stones that ricocheted off the windshield.

"Couple of troopers had their plane stolen from them yesterday," the driver said.

Kris felt a spike of fear. "Yeah?" She took another drag.

"Seems like they were running down some girl up on the Sixtymile. She got around them and ran off with their plane. Flipped it when she hit an overflow on the John."

Kris stared woodenly out the window, feeling the world closing in around her. She couldn't run fast enough. The reflected glow of the driver's cigarette brightened in the windshield. He held the smoke for a second and then spewed it out in rapid mucus-laden hacks. He choked, struggling for fresh air and coughed again. This time the coughs were mixed with a bark of laughter. When he got control of himself, he squashed his half-smoked cigarette in the ashtray and said matter-of-factly, "That's very funny."

He glanced over at her, his eyes alive in the dash lights. "Not often we Indians get to dick the cavalry anymore."

After a while, Kris asked, "How do you know this?"

He uncurled a finger from the wheel and pointed at the radio. "It's been on a couple of times already."

"If it happened yesterday," Kris said carefully, "how'd they find the cops so fast?"

"Beacons. The girl left them the plane's survival gear and there was a radio beacon in it. And the beacon in the plane was triggered when it flipped. AST scrambled a plane out of Fairbanks and the troopers were home in time for dinner."

Kris finished her cigarette and stubbed it out in the tray. Home in time for dinner. They were overwhelming; she didn't have a chance.

The truck hit the pavement and the hum of the tires on the road put her back to sleep.

She was shaken awake.

"We're here," he said. "Where do you want to be left off?"

The truck was pulled off on the side of the road opposite a mall; its lights lit up the predawn gray and cars raced by with the thoughtless determination of ants. It was snowing. She didn't feel the relief she thought she would feel to be back in a city where hunger and death by exposure weren't much of a concern.

"Airport, I guess," she said, sitting up.

"OK." He drove down through the center of town instead of taking the new road that cut across the city's northern edge. This was the part of Fairbanks that looked the most familiar to her. What was left of home. The truck sped down Barnette with the rush of other cars, each trailing almost normal clouds of exhaust. She saw the bank thermometer before they turned onto Airport Way. Five above zero, practically summer.

When she saw the sign for Cowles Street she changed her mind.

"Could you drop me off at the library?"

"You're joking," he said.

"It's on Cowles." She pointed through the windshield. He turned right and then right again into the library's parking lot.

"Funny place to head after getting off the trail," he said, teasing her while he pulled her pack out of the truck. "I always go straight for a beer." He set the snowshoes on top of the pack.

"Good luck." He stuck out his hand and Kris, mittenless, shook it. She shouldered her pack, watching the truck drive away, and then hiked up the walk to the library door and pushed into it. It rattled against its lock. Kris backed up and looked inside. No lights were on. Then she saw the printed sign taped to the door. "The Library will be closed for Thanksgiving."

Thanksgiving? It was their busiest day at the shop. Trucks going everywhere trying to get last minute inventory to shops before Friday, the biggest shopping day of the year. It was a crazy time and they all worked; none of the Mexicans had any interest in the American holiday and it meant nothing to her. In Fairbanks, when she was a kid, Thanksgiving had meant dinner at the shelter or the Salvation Army. It had meant sitting next to her mother, hating the charity, pretending she wasn't interested in the turkey and jellied cranberries while watching other kids play between the rows of packed tables.

She rattled the door again, frustrated. Then she decided to blow-off Annie; she'd give her a call and say good-bye over the phone and get out of town. Kris began pulling stuff out of the pack in front of the library doors, separating her clothes into one pile and Ringer's gear into another. Flattened at the bottom of the pack was her duffle and under it was

Barrett's gun. She felt its weight in her hand, thinking what a fool she'd been to carry it over the pass.

She stripped off Johnny's suit and tucked his mask in a pocket. The suit had been used hard; there were rips in it that she didn't remember being there when he'd given it to her. She hoped he hadn't gone back up to the cabin for her; everyone in the village must have known that the cops were after her, but he might have gone up anyway to check for her. She stuffed five twenties in the suit's inner pocket, rolled it up, and stuck it on top of Ringer's gear in the pack. Then she carried the pack behind the evergreen shrubs alongside the building and pushed it into the snow. The snowshoes were leaning on their tails against the library doors; she debated taking them down to Ben. Then decided they'd just be in her way. She walked back and tucked them beside the pack; maybe Ringer could use a pair.

The library's dumpsters were around the back of the building. She lifted the top and pulled out a black plastic garbage bag heavy with trash. After wiping the pistol with a T-shirt, she stuffed it into the bag and heaved it back in. Maybe she should've taken the slug out of the chamber, but she didn't want to go digging for it and so she lifted her duffle and headed back towards Airport Way.

At the corner of Cowles she stuck out a mittened thumb. There was no shoulder, no good place for a car to turn off, but a clunker stopped almost immediately, square in the right-hand lane, backing up traffic behind it. The blocked cars began honking and Kris hopped in, dragging the door shut after her, the duffle on her lap.

"Let 'em honk," the driver said and flipped the bird in his rearview mirror. With slow deliberation he put the car in gear and drove off. "You wouldn't know it was turkey day except for the ads," he said, looking at her and shifting into another gear. As the car accelerated, Kris felt cold air blowing up her legs. She kicked some folded newspapers that were on the floor to the side and saw, beneath them, the asphalt skimming by under her feet.

"It's important to have good air circulation," he said laconically. Kris recovered the hole with the papers and clamped her foot on them.

"Robin," he said and reached a hand across to Kris.

"Kris." They shook mittens.

"Where're you going?"

"Airport."

"That's not too far out of my way; I can take you down there."

"Thanks." Kris considered him out of the corner of her eye. Fortyish, he had long hair, half in a ponytail, the other half floating around his head, and a shaggy beard. Wrinkles and lines broke up his face, no ring on his finger, clothes were old, mostly woolens and not fancy synthetics. His feet were in floppy leather boots. Not even insulated. Counter-culture type. She was going to need him.

"I've a friend who says you can't hitchhike in Fairbanks anymore," she said, being friendly.

"Not since the pipeline, at least," he said. "Money changes things. Now this place is just like America." He swept his arm through the air, taking in the shopping malls and fast food places lining the street. "Used to be Alaska here."

"You sound like him, too."

"Who?"

"Ringer." Kris couldn't remember Ringer's last name.

"Ringer, Annie, and their muppets? Yeah, same species. Good folk, though Annie's a little heavy. Can't be stoned around her without feeling like you're breaking her heart."

"They were good to me," Kris said.

"I don't know why people want to make Alaska just like the place they left," he said. "It's like going to Japan and eating at McDonalds. If you don't like what they've got, stay home." He sounded resigned, as if he'd already given up this fight.

"Yeah," Kris said, wanting to keep him happy. "Ringer bitched about a BMW that passed him on his way to work and he came unglued when he saw a woman in heels tip-toeing through the snow at the airport." As she finished, something broke loose inside her head and rattled out of sight into the crevices of her mind.

"...years in Alaska and have never been out to any of the villages," Robin was saying while leaning into the long turn that brought them up to the entrance of the terminal. He stopped in front of the doors. "Here we be," he said.

Kris took a breath. "I need a favor," she said.

"Shoot."

"I need someone to buy a ticket to Juneau for me in their name."

The old hippie regarded her silently. Through his skimpy beard, she could see his Adam's apple bob. "What's going down?" he asked, unenthusiastically.

"I don't want anybody to know that I'm going to Juneau."

"The cops, you mean."

Kris stayed silent.

"Are you carrying?"

"No." She pushed her duffle toward him.

He unzipped it and stirred through her clothes.

"Oatmeal?" he asked, lifting out the Ziploc.

"Yeah. Tell Ringer next time you see him."

He stuffed it back in the duffle and zipped it closed. "I can't ask why?"

"Better not to."

"What do you want me to do?"

Kris pulled out her remaining cash and counted off three hundred and twenty dollars. "Buy the ticket in your name," she said handing him the bills. "Get your boarding pass and stuff. They'll ask for picture ID." He nodded. "You give me the ticket and split."

"TSA'll get you going through security," he said.

"I'll buy a ticket to Seattle and get through security on that. I'll get on the Juneau plane with your ticket—they don't check ID again when you're boarding, and Robin works for a girl's name."

Robin dropped the clutch back in and drove around to the parking lot. They got out and Kris wandered over to the tourist board advertising Fairbanks hotels while he stood in line. Fifteen minutes later, he handed her the ticket.

"Plane leaves in two hours. I got you a window seat."

"Thanks. Say hi to Ringer and Annie for me."

"Will do," he said dourly and left.

He wasn't real happy about that, but screw him. In the end, all these counter-culture types were self-righteous farts who didn't have the balls to do anything but whine.

Kris had things to do before the plane took off, but she searched for a window that looked out on the airport and stood before it, vacantly watching the planes, fuel trucks, and baggage carts scurry, in unquestioning certainty, through the predawn light. Something Robin had said bugged her; it slithered in the shadows of her mind with the slippery frustration of a dream.

McDonalds in Japan? Never being in the bush?

No; something else.

Kris rapped a knuckle against the thick glass. It was cold. A flat white truck trundled by.

Was it something she'd said?

BMW?

No.

Heels.

■ ■ ■

A stewardess came on the PA system and told them they were fifteen minutes out of Juneau. The nose of the jet was pointed down.

There was a clarity of purpose in Kris now. There were things she still didn't understand, but she knew what she had to do.

The seatbelt sign came on and, as she turned to grope for the loose end from between the seats, her side ached. If she'd been wearing a belt when that plane flipped...

Her left side had a brutal-looking bruise where she'd hit the wheel, which looked like it should hurt more than it did. In an out-of-the-way women's room she'd found at the Fairbanks airport, she changed her clothes and sponged herself clean with a damp T-shirt as best she could. Her hair was still a mess; twigs and needles had fallen out of it with each pull of a comb she'd bought from the airport store. She remembered her mother checking her ends and brushing her hair every morning before the spotted, desilvered mirror in their bathroom. Kris tied her hair back, glad that it was black so the remaining pieces of the northern forest hiding in it were invisible.

The phone call to Annie was more difficult and she wavered in front of a bank of phones, gathering her courage. When Annie's recorded voice came on the line she was relieved. There was too much to explain, and Annie wouldn't like what she was going to do. After the beep, Kris explained where the pack was hidden at the library, asked them to send Johnny's stuff up to him, and then said good-bye. It was too abrupt, but she'd call again when she got to L.A.

The plane broke through the clouds and rain streamed across the window. Kris could see the line of lights that fronted the shore and the disembodied lights of cars moving across the blackened hillside above them. The plane made its strange turn and the flaps whined out from the wing. It flew over the salt marsh, and Kris realized that she still did not know why her mother had written her the letter asking her to come back to Alaska or even how, after nine years, she'd found her. It was something lost with Evie; she'd never know.

Kris stood with the others and filed out of the plane. She cut down to the baggage area and walked up to the Hertz desk. It was a different woman, older, than the kid who'd given her directions to AWARE the night she'd arrived in Juneau.

"I'd like to rent a car, please." Kris was asked what kind and handed a form to fill out. When she was done, she pushed the form across the counter and pulled her bills out of her pocket. The woman shook her head.

"We don't take cash. Credit cards only."

"What's wrong with cash?" Kris asked.

"You've got to have credit to rent—" Kris turned away and walked angrily down the line of rental agencies. They all said the same thing.

Kris pushed out the doors and looked at the line of cabs. Most had people climbing into them, but someone at the end of the line waved, and Kris walked down and got in.

"First and Main," she said and didn't respond to any of his prattle about the lousy weather they'd been having, lousy even for November.

Rain fell from black clouds that lumbered up the channel and smothered the peaks of the black mountains that pressed against Juneau. The cab pulled up to the curb by the Sealaska Building. Kris paid him, pushed the door shut, and hiked up the hill to Seventh Street trying to ignore the rain blowing into the parka and dripping from its hem onto her pants.

Justin was the last person she wanted to see, but if she could sneak his car away for an hour, it'd work just fine. It wasn't on Seventh and she walked down to Sixth. It wasn't there either. She tried Fifth and then all the cross streets. There were plenty of parking spaces; he was probably at a friend's for dinner.

Ben had a truck, but he didn't leave his keys in it, and she wasn't ready to see Ben yet. Kris hiked back up to Seventh and climbed down the steps to Justin's apartment. A light was on. She knocked and then, impatient, turned the knob and pushed it open.

Justin was half out of his chair when she walked in. His mouth dropped open in a little O. On the kitchen counter behind him, was a plate with a stripped drumstick on it.

"Relax," Kris said. "I know you told Barrett everything. Forget it."

Justin dropped back into the chair.

"Where's your car? I need it."

He was still digesting her arrival. Kris waited.

"I don't think you should use it, Kris."

"I only need it for an hour."

"Barrett's looking for you," he said.

"Yeah, me, and not the person who killed my mother."

Justin paused then said unexpectedly, "Vern Jones killed her. I left a message at the station for Barrett, but he hasn't gotten back to me yet."

"Not even close," she said.

"No, listen to this," Justin said, a little too eagerly. "It was too much of a coincidence for your mother to be murdered the day before you arrived unless the killer knew you were coming. The only person who knew was Vern because no one else had read your letter to Evie. I traced it from AWARE to Montana Creek. A volunteer at the shelter gave it to Alvilde Lambale to give to Evie. I called Alvilde and she said she'd given the letter to your mother, but she saw Vern take it out of Evie's hands before she'd opened it."

"You're forgetting the wool fibers and the leaves you found."

"I found?"

"The twisted-up leaves by the stream—the ones with the holes in them." Kris could see his mind engage and then he looked at her sharply.

"Do you know who did it?" he asked.

"Where's the car?"

"What are you going to do?"

"I'm going to have a talk with Evie's murderer. Then I'll call Barrett." Justin was silent.

"Justin, it's no big deal. Let me use the car."

"It's at the subport," he said.

"The what?"

"The free parking down by the Coast Guard station, across Egan from Centennial Hall. "

"I'll be back in an hour."

"Kris," he said as she opened the door. She turned impatiently.

He started to say something, then stopped. His eyes held hers for a second, then she closed the door, and ran up Justin's steps, down Main to Fifth, took the stairs down to Willoughby, cut through the parking lots that were scattered around the office buildings there, and jogged across the highway into the subport. Justin's car was easy to find; the lot was almost empty.

Rain splatted on the windshield. The road out to the valley was black, rain-slicked, and without cars. There was a pair of taillights way ahead of her and nothing in her mirror. Would she be there? Or would she be out for Thanksgiving dinner?

The highway veered left after it passed the industrial valley. Would Justin go to the cops? Barrett was probably still in Fairbanks looking for her, but if Justin called the station, they'd send someone after her.

Give me a break, Justin.

All she needed was an hour.

■ ■ ■

Barrett's daughter was in bed. His wife sat stiffly in front of her computer, silently and petulantly protesting his distraction, which had deadened Thanksgiving dinner. Barrett sat in an easy chair staring at her rigid back; spread on his lap was the forensic report on Lambale's Mercedes and the auditor's report of Lambale's accounts both of which he'd found on his desk when he got back from Fairbanks yesterday evening.

The techs had found nothing unusual about the car except more dirt and dried mud on the driver's side floor carpet than one would expect of a man who wore smooth-soled shoes and several dog hairs on the driver's head rest and nowhere else. The Lambales didn't have a dog, and dogs tend not to sit on headrests. The hairs could have come from a ruff, but it was too warm to be wearing parkas yet.

The auditor claimed that all the money in Lambale's accounts was accounted for. When Barrett had called the auditor at home this morning, telling him that he didn't believe the report—Lambale was a banker and could hide anything—the auditor had been unequivocal: Lambale's financial records, which included his wife's except for her gallery, were meticulous and transparent; it was not possible that he had made an unrecorded payment of between two to three thousand dollars in the last six months.

Barrett dropped his eyes from his wife's unyielding back, to the reports in his lap. He leafed through the financial statements. If Lambale hadn't given Vern the money, who had?

And why—his mind had stubbed against this again and again since he'd first read the report—why had Lambale written a check for thirty-five hundred dollars to a detective agency in Seattle?

His cell rang.

"Kris is here," Justin said. "She took my car. She says she knows who killed Evie."

■ ■ ■

Except for a token light, the Lambale house was dark. Both outside doors and the sliding glass doors opening onto the deck were locked. Kris leaned against the handle on the glass door; the lock couldn't be that substantial. She braced her back against the rock retaining wall at the side of the house, put her foot against the handle, and pushed. Her body vibrated as she forced her leg straight. The lock gave with hardly a sound and Kris ducked inside, sliding the window shut again. Lights were on at the neighboring houses, but they were screened by trees. No one could have seen her.

Kris searched the house. It didn't take long to find the gun.

She checked the light switches by the front door, unscrewed the bulb in a floor lamp, and sat down on the sofa in the living room to wait.

■ ■ ■

Twisted leaves.

Barrett pushed the loose pages of the Gabriel file away from him. Without asking, Justin reached over his desk and scooped the papers into the manila folder and set it on his lap. Barrett suppressed his irritation. If forensics had found any twisted-up leaves at the site, they hadn't put it in the report. Justin said he had found three different sets on what he thought was the path Evie and her killer had taken through the brush from the trail to the stream. Justin had been clued in by the footprint with the crepe sole—obviously not a police print. It had been Stewart's, who'd shown the police his boots and his path down and back from the stream.

"Twisted?" Barrett asked.

Justin nodded, his head bent over the file.

"Screwed-up like someone was putting out a cigarette butt?"

Justin looked up.

"Or like someone was trying to destroy something?" Was it Stewart covering his tracks?

"A couple of leaves had holes in them," Justin said.

"Holes?" Barrett repeated, perplexed. "Were there holes in the soil underneath?"

"I didn't look, but somebody twisting his foot back and forth would have plugged them up anyway."

"I need to talk to Stewart." Barrett rose.

"Kris didn't go there," Justin said, "she wouldn't have needed my car."

"I know that." Barrett was testy. "But Stewart's hiding something, and I want to know what it is." He started out from behind his desk, then stopped. "Lambales," he breathed. "She'd have to drive out there."

Justin closed the file. "Oh yeah, I found out how Vern got Kris's letter. Alvilde picked it up at the shelter to give to Evie and Vern took it from her."

"Jesus shit! How long have you been sitting on that?" Barrett leaned over his desk glaring at Justin. Before Justin could open his mouth, Barrett added sarcastically, "Do you think Alvilde'd run out to Montana Creek in her fucking Mercedes to drop off a letter for a drunk?" He stared at Justin, his mind churning. What the hell was Alvilde doing in this? Vern needed to kill Kris to keep control of Evie. That made sense. But was it Alvilde who'd told him when Kris was flying in? Did she know that Vern would kill Kris? Did she want Kris dead, too? For God's sake, why?

Barrett sat, stunned. Nothing made sense.

Then he got a piece of it.

"Holes?" he said, softly.

Justin didn't answer; he looked sullen.

"Give me the file." Barrett reached over his desk and pulled it out of Justin's hands. He ransacked it, sliding the papers and reports across his desk until he found the sheet he was looking for. At the top of the page was the number; he punched it in. The phone rang four times and voice mail picked up. Barrett slammed the receiver down and ran for the door, grabbing his pistol and coat off the hook as he passed.

"Where're you going?" Justin was right behind him.

"You stay here," Barrett said without slowing. He pushed through the station's doors and ran through the rain to his car.

"I'm coming with you," Justin said, panting, catching up with him in the parking lot.

"No." Barrett pulled the car door open.

Justin ignored him and ran around the hood, splashing through a puddle backed up against the curb, and pulled the passenger door open and climbed in.

Barrett didn't argue. He squealed onto Marine Way. It was the family car. No lights or siren, but it had a police radio slung under the dash. He keyed the mike and reported into the dispatcher. Rehooking the mike, he turned to Justin, his face grotesquely yellowed by the sodium streetlights racing past.

"You do everything I say. Understood?"

"Of course."

■ ■ ■

Upstairs the phone rang four times and quit.

Kris felt sweat prick through her skin.

The blackened windows opening onto the deck reflected a blinking green, reversed "12:00" from a DVD display in another room.

Alvilde wanted Kris dead. That was the only reason why she'd have given Kris's letter to Vern. She knew that Vern would kill her. Kris knew why Vern had wanted her out of the way. But why would Alvilde? What difference could Kris make to Alvilde?

Kris stared at the blinking clock. How did Alvilde even know Kris existed? Evie, Ben, and Vern were the only people in Juneau who had ever heard of her.

The heavy weather seals of the outer door sucked against the doorjamb as it was pushed open. Someone entered the outer entryway. Kris heard the quiet unconcerned scrape and click of shoes on the tiles. The person moved as if she felt at home. There was a clink of hangers from the closet.

Kris rose quietly from the sofa, propped the shotgun against the armrest, and pressed herself against the wall behind a floor lamp wondering if it were Alvilde and what she would do if it weren't. She touched the paring knife that she'd taken from the kitchen and stuck in her back pocket, and then pushed her palms down the sides of her pants to wipe off the sweat.

A key slid into the lock on the inner door and turned. The door pulled back into the entry and light fell onto the carpet in a crooked rectangle. Into it stepped a woman in a long skirt, loose blouse, and heels. The light was at her back and her face was hidden in her own shadow, but Kris knew it was Alvilde. Erect and contained, she stepped into the room. Tucked in one hand was a small purse and in the other an empty salad bowl. Alvilde touched the light panel on the wall and the light in the entryway went off, but the living room remained dark. She rocked the light switch several times, then pulled the door closed behind her, and strode across the room toward a lamp on a low table in the far corner.

Kris stepped away from the wall. She heard fabric rustle as Alvilde bent down to reach for the switch. The lamp clicked on, flooding the corner of the room with a cone of light. Alvilde turned, pulling off a thin pair of gloves, and spotted her standing in the shadows.

Alvilde regarded her without surprise and in the second that she stood watching her; Kris felt her shift from distant appraisal to expectation, as if she were demanding better service of a waiter.

"Yes, dear?"

"We have some things to talk about," Kris said.

"Not this evening, Kris. It's late."

"You killed Evie."

Alvilde regarded Kris coolly. There was no concern, no agitation, no fear in her face. "I think you'd better go," she said.

"We're going to talk."

Alvilde picked up her purse and the salad bowl, which she had placed by the lamp, and walked across the carpet toward the kitchen. Kris followed.

Over her shoulder, Alvilde said, "I've asked you to leave, Kris."

Kris pulled the paring knife out of her pocket, grabbed Alvilde's arm, spun her around, and pricked the point of the knife into the hand holding the dish. A drop of blood welled out, beading on her skin.

"We're going to talk." Kris stepped back to the sofa, picked up the shotgun, and tucked the stock loosely under her left arm. It was old and heavy; the name of the manufacturer, engraved on both barrels in an old style of lettering, wasn't English.

"You shot her with this." Kris lifted the barrels slightly.

Alvilde had transferred the bowl to her other hand and was looking at the drop of blood, turning her hand in the light. She glanced up, looked at the shotgun and then at Kris.

"That was my grandfather's. I brought it back from Denmark after he passed away and gave it to Loren. It hasn't been used in years. Never in this country."

"Then you won't mind if Barrett takes a look at it. And he'll want to see the Italian shoe you had repaired; the one you broke the heel off of when you were climbing out of the creek. He'll also be interested in the blue woolen suit you were wearing that day, to see if the fibers he found on the bushes match it. And I have the money you gave Vern and the card you wrote your number on. Barrett'll get those too."

"Do as you wish, child. May I put my dish in the sink without being attacked?" she asked. She stepped out of her heels.

Kris moved toward her, the gun under her arm, the knife still in her right hand, frustrated at Alvilde's cool.

"I know why you killed her," she said. "Loren raped her. Your husband raped my mother, and you didn't want anybody to know. It's kind of tough being on the board of this and the board of that when you're married to a rapist." Kris lifted the knife and pressed it gently under Alvilde's chin.

Alvilde looked down at her, her eyes clear. "Puts you in an awkward position, doesn't it Kris?"

Kris had no warning.

Alvilde dropped the dish and with both hands grabbed the barrel of the shotgun, wrenching it out from under Kris's arm. Without pausing, she stepped back, swinging the heavy gun over her shoulder, and then down at Kris. Kris, stalled for an instant in surprise, ducked to her right. The stock glanced off her shoulder and slammed into the side of her head. She stumbled across the floor, stunned. Alvilde swung again and hit her in the back, crashing her into a wall. Kris fell, rolled, tried to push herself up but her shoulder gave out and she collapsed on the floor, gasping for air.

Alvilde raced up the stairs, her stocking feet padding noiselessly. Kris panted, dragged herself to her hands and knees, fumbled on the floor for the knife, and picked herself up. The blood drained from her head and her vision clouded. She fell against the wall, breathing hard, then pushed herself off, her vision clearing as she moved to the stairway. She looked up; light from an open door lit the ceiling of the upstairs hall. Grasping the railing, she pulled herself up the stairs, ran down the hall and into the lighted room at the back of the house.

Alvilde was standing by a wooden desk. A box of shotgun shells was dumped on the desktop. In one hand, she held the gun, open at the breech, and with the other, she slid two cartridges into the barrels, snapped the gun shut, and turned smoothly to face Kris.

Kris stopped, her brain still reeling from the blow, and stared at the gun barrels leveled at her.

"Come in," Alvilde said, her breathing already under control. She pointed the gun to the center of the room.

Kris walked in. Against the far wall was a twin bed set under a narrow window, at its foot a clothes drawer. It was her bedroom, Kris realized, and she slept alone, Lambale wouldn't have fit in the bed. Kris looked back at the gun, the shells on the desk, and then back at Alvilde.

"Pretty cocky keeping all that in the house," she said.

"No one would suspect me," Alvilde said. "You were very clever to work it out." She held the gun in both hands, the stock resting on her hip; the barrels steady. "It wasn't Loren's fault when he attacked your mother. He was young. They were drunk, the others pushed him on."

"It was his dick," Kris said. "No one made him put it anywhere he didn't want it to go."

Alvilde waited for her to finish. "It was a long time ago, and Loren has spent most of our married life helping poor women like you. Those new rooms at the AWARE shelter are only there because of him."

"Made him famous; he's the big man in town," Kris said.

Alvilde looked at her levelly. "I wouldn't expect you to understand. He has done more than any normal man would have done to atone for it."

Kris snorted.

Alvilde ignored her. "Then your mother came, out of nowhere, after all these years, because she saw his picture in the paper. She wanted money, from me, because she knew Loren would have confessed, publicly. That thing he did, it rotted in his soul. And I gave her money—"

"It was Vern wanting the money. It wasn't Evie."

"Of course not," Alvilde said. "She wasn't competent to do it herself. But Vern couldn't do it without her, she was his only evidence, and I wasn't going to let a drunk destroy my family. The rape just wasn't that important."

"She was my mother," Kris said.

"And who are you?" Alvilde asked without malice. "An uneducated girl working for Mexicans? Be reasonable, Kris, you are nothing."

Alvilde straightened and lifted the gun. "I will claim self defense," she said. "You broke into my house and attacked me. You should have gone home; there was nothing you could have done here."

Kris looked at Alvilde's finger on the triggers, then into Alvilde's eyes—there was no doubt or hesitation in them.

"Shooting me with the same gun that shot Evie's going to be difficult to explain."

"You brought it into the house. I don't know where you found it." Alvilde's eyes narrowed slightly as her finger tightened on the triggers.

Up on the road, a car door slammed and feet pounded on the wooden stairs. Alvilde tilted her head slightly to listen. Kris threw herself to the side, out the line of fire, bounced off the wall, pushing hard, and hurtled back at Alvilde.

Alvilde whipped the gun around and fired.

■ ■ ■

Barrett was ten steps down the staircase when he heard the shotgun blast.

"Shit." He spun around and ran back up the stairs, shoving Justin against the railing as he passed him. "Back here with me," he shouted. He pitched open the car door and grabbed the radio mike.

"Barrett. 10-69. Shotgun fire from private residence. Casualties unknown." He gave the Lambale address.

Barrett rehooked the mike. Backup was minutes away. He wasn't going to wait. He flipped off the safety on his revolver, the .38 he'd used before buying the automatic, and glanced through the windshield looking for Justin. The stairs down to the house were directly in front of him.

They were empty.

■ ■ ■

The barrel exploded; the powder blast scorched her cheek and shot sliced through her jacket sleeve. Deafened, ears thundering, Kris lunged past the shotgun and into Alvilde, crashing her into the desk. She wrapped her arms around Alvilde's waist, her head pressed against the silk smoothness of Alvilde's blouse, and hung on. Her right eye burned; she squeezed both shut. The blast roared inside her head, her breath burned like acid in her throat; she clutched Alvilde desperately, trying to recover.

She was hit. The force of it stunned her. Alvilde stretched again and contracted convulsively, driving the shotgun's stock into Kris's back. Again. Kris shuddered; pain exploded in her upper back, an arm went numb. She heaved, lifting Alvilde, spun and threw her across the room. Kris forced her eyes open, the one blurred and weeping, and saw Alvilde hop, and stagger across the floor trying to stay upright in her tight skirt. It ripped to her waist, and a pale stockinged leg thrust out struggling for balance; it missed, and Alvilde sprawled violently on the floor, her head snapping back as she hit, the shotgun tight in her hands.

Kris, still deafened, half-blinded, ran toward her. From the floor, Alvilde snapped the gun up and aimed. Kris dove to the floor, rolling hard. The gun tracked her. She hit the wall and struggled frantically to her feet. The door—she wasn't going to make it.

"Kris!"

Holy shit, Justin.

"Kris!" It came from the ocean side of the house, the glass doors.

Kris froze against the wall, five feet from the door. The barrels steadied.

"Up here," she yelled, fear and relief shaking her voice.

"It's Justin," she said, turning to Alvilde. "He knows, too. He knows about the shoes and the rape, he's the one who found the money." Kris gulped air. Don't sound desperate.

Lithe and controlled, Alvilde climbed to her feet.

Justin's feet sounded on the stairs.

"Shoot me, and you still get nailed for Evie." Kris struggled to keep her voice even.

Feet ran down the hall. Justin burst through the door and stood there, chest heaving, and stared at Alvilde.

"Drop it, Alvilde," he said. "There's nowhere for you—."

Alvilde turned, lifted the barrels, and pulled the second trigger.

The gun fired again, and Justin disappeared as if he were plucked from the room.

The door was empty. Kris stared, stunned. The blast reverberated in her ears. A foot in a white Nike slid slowly back through the door and into the room. It didn't twitch.

Alvilde was back at the desk, the gun open, pulling out the spent shells and ramming fresh cartridges into the barrels. She didn't have a chance.

Kris charged across the room and wrenched the gun from her hands and hurled it under the bed. She grabbed the belt of Alvilde's skirt, pitched her around, and tripped her. Alvilde landed on her back, rolled, and Kris fell on her, pinning her face-down on the floor. Unable to move, Alvilde went limp.

Kris let her breathing slow, then locked her fingers in Alvilde's hair, and pulled her head back. She pressed her elbow into the joint of Alvilde's jaw and levered her weight into her forearm, forcing Alvilde's face into the carpet. Alvilde's mouth puckered open like a fish's and her breath whistled faintly between her teeth.

Leaning on her arm, Kris looked down at her. Alvilde's eyes stared forward along the line of the floor toward the far wall. They blinked when they needed to blink; there was no fear in them. A line of saliva hung from her lower lip. Kris looked at the whiteness of her scalp through her yellow hair and then at her ear with the small gold earring hanging from the lobe and the tiny hairs in the ear hole. The ear hole was clean. Under the skin on her neck a vein pulsed. Slow, steady, rhythmic.

Kris reached down and pulled the paring knife from her back pocket and traced its steel point along the soft rise of the beating vein.

What did she want? Justice? Vengeance?

Alvilde lay quietly, waiting.

What was this woman to her? So certain, so superior. Who had killed Evie and Justin. She pressed the steel into Alvilde's neck and then released it, watching the pocked skin smooth out. She had killed to protect her family, her kids, like Ben's old grizzly sow, the one he had to shoot to…

Ben.

Kris went cold, as if ice water had surged into her chest. He knew.

Alvilde heaved, tore her head out from under Kris's forearm, and, twisting her body, tried to bring her hands up. Shocked back to awareness, Kris pushed the knife against Alvilde's throat. A line of blood rolled down the white skin and dripped onto the floor. Defeated, Alvilde went limp again.

"I'm not going to kill you," Kris said quietly. "Just mark you." Without pressure, she drew a line with the tip of the knife from her eye down to her jaw, then lifted the blade, and crossed it with a second line. "When people see these scars, they will know you for what you are, a murderer married to a rapist."

Alvilde's eyes shifted, and she blinked fast, once. Kris lowered her head in front of Alvilde's face and looked into her eyes, but Alvilde focused into the distance, ignoring her, and Kris knew that Alvilde would never acknowledge her.

From the first floor, she heard the glass door slide in its track. Startled, she caught her breath and listened. It was quiet, but she could feel someone else in the house.

Moving fast, Kris shifted her elbow above Alvilde's ear and, extending her forefinger along the spine of the knife, pressed it hard into the skin below the corner of Alvilde's eye. Alvilde stiffened, but stayed quiet as Kris drew the knife down her cheek. The skin parted easily and blood welled up and flowed from the line of the cut and onto her nose. The flare of her nostril dammed the flow for a moment before it spilled over and ran down her upper lip.

She started the second cut –

The Nike twitched.

Adrenaline jolted into her; she jerked the blade from Alvilde's cheek and stared at the foot. It twitched again. Then Justin whimpered, faintly and full of pain.

Savagely, Kris finished the cut, slicing the skin from jaw to cheek bone. Kris felt a tremor. Alvilde gasped once, sucking blood into her mouth. Her lips stayed open; blood and saliva ran onto the carpet. Kris rolled off her and ran softly across the room to the door, stepping over Justin's leg into the hallway. He was sprawled across the floor, head and shoulders half propped against the opposite wall. Bone, filmed by blood, glistened in the light from Alvilde's room. His right shoulder looked like it'd been chewed by dogs; blood trickled down his jacket and soaked into the carpet. She stepped on it and the carpet squished.

"Justin," she whispered, kneeling at his side and putting her lips to his ear. "Who's in the house?"

His face was dirty white, like glacier snow, and his breath caught on shit in his chest. "Barrett," he breathed.

Kris could barely hear him.

"How the fuck did you get in front of him?" Suddenly she was furious; as angry as she'd ever been at anybody in her life.

He turned his head, grimaced, his eyes not focusing. "Get you."

"Bullshit." She struggled to keep her anger, felt it drain, then surge away, like spring floodwaters blowing through an ice dam.

He closed his eyes, moaned. Sweat beaded on his forehead.

"You want to get laid that bad?" Kris said, her sarcasm empty, not able to hide the concern in her voice.

"I guess." The corner of his mouth tightened.

"Shit, Justin," she said.

He took a breath. "'S OK. I can work a computer with one hand."

She touched it, the fingers sickly warm and lifeless.

"Not bra hooks," she said.

"Don't be too easy."

A stair squeaked. Kris tensed, looking down the hall.

"Got to go?" he asked.

"Yeah." She mouthed the words and let go of his hand. Leaning into his ear, she whispered, "I'll be there when you wake up." Crawling carefully over his legs, she hurried back into the bedroom. Alvilde was sitting up, leaning on an arm propped against the floor, her stockinged legs splayed to her side, the ripped skirt bunched up underneath her.

Kris squatted in front of her. Blood ran out of the cuts and dripped off her jaw and onto her blouse. Alvilde looked at her now, but her eyes were blank. "Barrett's coming up the stairs," she whispered. "He knows, too. Leave Justin alone." She hesitated. Had Ben shielded Alvilde because he thought she was protecting her kids? Was that Ben's law? The law of nature—whatever it takes to stay alive. It was one Kris understood. Or was Ben protecting the kids—to stop the pain from spreading, like a disease, outward from Evie?

Or was there something else?

Kris didn't know, but she had no anger left. She lifted her hand and touched Alvilde's bloody cheek. "She was my mother," she said, gently.

Kris heard another creak on the stairs and looked up in alarm. Justin moaned. Was he giving her time? Quickly, she crossed the room to the bed, dropped the knife onto the white covering, and climbed onto it to reach the window. It was tall and narrow and opened sideways like a door. She wiped the blood on her hands on the curtain and then pulled the window open. There was a bug screen across it; she found the fasteners, popped them, and pitched the screen into the night. Kris sat on the sill, stuck both feet through the window and flipped around, supporting herself with her arms, facing back into the room. Alvilde, still sitting on the floor, lifted her eyes and looked at her. She was crying silently, her face expressionless, the tears on her left cheek turning watery red as they mixed with blood. Through the door, Kris saw Justin, slumped against the hall wall, his skin chalky gray, watching her. She nodded.

Kris slid down the outside of the house, but it was set deeply into the mountainside and her feet touched ground before her head dropped below the bottom edge of the window. In the distance, she heard sirens. She turned and looked again into the room. Alvilde was on her hands and knees crawling across the floor. Except for Justin, the doorway was empty. The sirens wailed closer. Alvilde crawled behind the bed, out of sight, and Kris waited for her to re-emerge. When she did, she stood, rising slowly, the shotgun in her hand.

Kris opened her mouth to scream a warning to Barrett, but Alvilde, her short hair wild, her blouse ripped at the throat and pulled out of the waist of her skirt, turned away from the open door and walked to the desk, lifted the chair, which had been knocked over, and set it on its feet. The chair faced into the room. She sat in it, moving slowly, as if her arms and legs were stiff and heavy. She planted the gun on the floor between her knees, shuffling the butt a little farther out from the chair, bent at the waist, and rested her chin on the barrels. Her hand fell blindly down the gun to the triggers.

Alvilde's eyes shifted, focused.

Kris followed them and saw Barrett standing in the door, a pistol in his hand dropping slowly to his side, his mouth opening.

Alvilde pulled the triggers.

■ ■ ■

Kris staggered away from the window. Alvilde's head—Kris slipped on the wet grass, fell to her hands and knees—had exploded.

The sirens were screaming above her now. Up on the road cars pulled off braking hard, doors slammed and the sirens died, their howls winding down into the night's background clutter. Trees stood massive and shadowy on the mountainside behind the house. Kris scrambled into them and crouched behind a trunk, clinging with both hands to the deeply-ridged bark as feet thundered down the wooden steps. Between the trees, she saw legs flash by the knee-high lights that lit the stairway. A voice barked orders.

Grasping roots and rocks, Kris pulled herself up the slope through the trees, angling sideways away from the stairs. It wasn't as steep as the hillside at the end of Thane, but it was wet, heavy with the smell of earth; spruce needles and bits of twigs and dirt clung to her hands and knees. When she reached the pavement, rain-slickened and glistening black under a single street light, she peered around a tree back up the road to the Lambale turnout. Two squad cars, the Mercedes, and an SUV sat at the head of the stairs, deserted. She crept onto the pavement and ran down to where she'd left Justin's car. A pickup raced around the curve in front of her, catching her in its lights; she turned her head. A thin drizzle wet her hair.

At the Subaru, she searched the ashtray for the keys, then her pockets; her hands shook and they felt clumsy and swollen. She found the keys and fumbled the correct one into the ignition; the engine ground, started on the second try, and she wheeled into the road back toward town. Kris gripped the steering wheel with both hands, trying to still them.

She stared out the window, her eyes not registering the oncoming headlights; Justin's bloodied shoulder and lifeless hand lit up in her brain. She drove by instinct, unaware when she passed the ferry dock and the boat harbor at Auke Bay. It was the second time he'd saved her. She remembered his touch again, at the state office building, his finger on her cheek. It had felt like an intrusion, just his prick calling to him. Now she felt its tenderness and knew that he'd been trying to bridge the same gulf that separated him from the world that she'd stared into the night she dug up Corvus.

The car swept around a long curve; a pair of headlights pushed her tail, bouncing off the rearview mirror into her eyes. When the road straightened, the car behind pulled out and a kid, hanging out the passenger window, flipped her off as they accelerated past.

How did Barrett know she'd be at the Lambale's? Was it Justin who figured out it was Alvilde? Kris'd never told him about Alvilde having her shoes repaired. And it was Ringer who'd clued her in when he'd pointed at the woman in heels picking her way through the snow at the Fairbanks airport. Jesus, Ringer'd crow when she told him that Alvilde's heels had given her away. It had been her remaining heel that had poked the holes through the leaves that Justin had found by the stream. If she'd been wearing rubber boots like an Alaskan, instead of hanging on to her snotty Outside elegance, no one would've guessed.

The windshield wipers swept back and forth, alternately sharpening and blurring the lights of the city in front of her. On her right, like a hole in space, were the black waters of the channel. Nervous juices pooled in her stomach; she lifted her foot from the pedal, slowing. Did Ben know she was coming? Did he know why? Cars passed her, and she pressed the pedal again, letting the cars in front of her drag her toward the city.

If Ben had noticed that his pistol was missing, he'd know that she'd taken it and, if he knew that Lambale was missing—he'd put it together. For a moment, Kris was buoyed by a flash of anger: If Ben had told her that it had been Alvilde who had killed Evie, Lambale would still be alive and she wouldn't be running from a life in prison.

She passed the lights of the AWARE shelter blinking through the screen of trees on her left. Had Lambale really built the new wing to make up for the rape? Weird he felt so guilty about it; in Evie's world, there wasn't a big difference between rape and straight sex. Men took what they wanted; sometimes someone bothered to ask first.

The road curved around the downtown boat harbor; below her, the boats floated in their stalls, patient and dumb as cows. She wouldn't have much time. Barrett would be after her as soon as he got things under control at Lambale's. He could've called ahead and had a cop waiting for her; but she didn't think so. Barrett would want her for himself.

It was raining harder in town; the water spilled from the sky, cold and lifeless and as empty of drama as a dead TV. Kris parked in the lot behind the Bergman Hotel and, carrying Ben's parka in her arms, walked up the hill to the foot of his staircase. She hesitated and looked up at his window, letting the rain fall on her. Smeared by the water, a dim light glowed behind the blank square of glass. He'd see her coming up. Or hear her. Did he know that she knew about Corvus? And about the four years he spent with Evie?

Kris started up the steps. When she reached Ben's door, she rapped gently and opened it without waiting for him to let her in. He was sitting in his chair by the window; the flame of a kerosene lantern on a chair next to him flickered in the breath of damp air that followed her in. Their gazes touched, then Kris looked down while she levered her feet out of the shoepacks and hung the parka on the peg, the mittens stuffed in the pockets.

"Came by to return these," she said, looking around for the sneakers she'd left two weeks ago. They were under the little table with the telephone, heels set neatly against the wall.

Ben was quiet. He looked wary. Kris lifted a chair out of the corner and set it in front of the window angled toward his, the lantern between them.

"You knew, Ben," Kris said, quietly. "You knew it was Alvilde who killed Evie."

"Yes," he said.

"Why didn't you tell me?" Kris asked. "Why did you feed me that fucking bear story?" Then suddenly, as she asked him, she knew the answer, and the heat of her anger vanished, like the warmth of a dying fire vanishing into the arctic night. She slumped in the chair; her energy drained out of her, and the hollowness of exhaustion opened in its place.

Ben's eyes, as hard as she'd ever seen them, locked onto hers. "Evie didn't need to have you, her own daughter, the police, the papers, proving to yourselves what you already believed, the only thing you could see— that she was just another drunk Indian."

He breathed, shallowly, like it hurt. "Evie didn't need vengeance," he said.

He looked away. "She needed your love."

"Bullshit, Ben," Kris said, softly. "You didn't tell me because you didn't want anyone to find out you'd killed Corvus."

"Corvus," he said his voice airless.

"Yeah, Corvus."

Ben looked stunned, as if he'd walked into a wall he couldn't see.

"You were up the Alatna?" he asked, sounding distant, as far away as the river and the mountains he'd never return to. "At the cabin?"

"I dug up his grave," she said.

Ben stared at her, his expression unreadable. Then he turned his head and looked out the window. Kris followed his stare. The night hadn't changed: the darkness rent by the city's lights, the ceaseless rain that dribbled down the blackened glass, the sea black and quiet in the channel.

"She missed you so much," he said, lost in the night.

"Why did you shoot him, Ben?"

Ben pulled his gaze from the night as if he knew he could no longer run from his boy. His bald head, glossy in the low light, bent forward hiding his face.

"He wasn't right in his head," he said, not looking up. "He was almost five, still in diapers, wobbly, like a newborn caribou, just hanging onto my leg. He'd have to be taken care of all his life."

His head rose. The wrinkles that nested his eyes had deepened and sagged. "He didn't know my name."

"You thought killing him was better than letting him live?" Kris asked. She waited, but he didn't answer. "What did you think it would do to Evie?"

"I knew it would be better this way." He looked at Kris again, his eyes threaded with red lines. "I was angry. Angry that she couldn't let him go. I…" He took a breath. "Nothing I said could change her; make her see that it was what we needed to do. That he was better gone."

"So you kidnapped him."

"Nothing in the wild lives if it isn't right. A wolf bitch will abandon a deformed pup; a grouse won't feed a chick that ignores her call. Evie . . . she loved him anyway.

"And I took him from her." Ben looked at her, his eyes, empty as glass, asked for nothing: not sympathy, not understanding, not pity. "I didn't want to stay up the Alatna that winter, but I had nowhere to go. Evie was gone to me. She'd guessed that I'd taken Corvus and turned on me before I left.

"I had to come out before breakup. When I got to Fairbanks, Evie was drinking again and wouldn't talk to me. Once, when I tried, she screamed and screamed until I had to leave."

He squeezed his hands shut. "I never got to tell her I was sorry."

"So you followed her down here," Kris said.

"There was nothing else for me to do."

Kris understood then that this man, who'd spent fifty years alive and happy in his world of mountains and forests, had had his heart opened by her mother and then, the law of nature, the law of the weak and the strong, the only law he knew, destroyed the little human joy he had made for himself. Now he was lost to both worlds, the human and the wild: Evie was gone, and he could never go back to the Alatna. Even if he were still young, his heart expected too much from life for the hills and trees ever to fill it by themselves again.

Kris let him be. She looked out his window at the lights of Juneau. A car was climbing the steep hump of the bridge over to Douglas Island and the lights across the channel burned without warmth.

Barrett would be there soon.

After a while, Ben lifted his head and looked out the window, too. He sat still, but Kris felt a tension building in him. A muscle in his cheek jumped like it was being jerked by a string.

"What?" she asked.

"It wasn't because of Corvus," he said, his voice tight. "It was because of you."

"What was because of me?"

A hand fidgeted, his lip trembled, and Kris felt the fear in him.

"When I looked at the tracks," he said, speaking again to the night. "I saw a woman pushing Evie through the brush, rushing to get it over with, frightened, so nervous she'd forgotten to change her shoes. I saw Evie trip, grab a stalk of devil's club, not feeling the thorns stab into her skin; I heard her wailing; like she'd wailed the morning Corvus disappeared and I saw her lift her hands to protect her face, and I saw her blown backwards by the shot, her dress snagging on a branch as she fell into the stream.

"Since she was a girl, everything she loved had been taken from her: her father, her mother to whiskey." He paused. "You. And Corvus and, when she was happy with Vern, her life." He spread his hands. "She'd had too much pain, and I was too tired, too guilty myself to care who killed her. I wanted her left alone.

"Then you came. And you wanted to know. And I knew I couldn't keep you from it, but—"

"What?"

"Oh, Kris," Ben groaned in a whisper so choked with pain that she looked at him in surprise. "At the funeral, when he handed you the card, I saw it in his nose and the line of his chin. And his walk, his left leg lifts high and circles out when he walks. Like yours."

"Like my what?" Her ears popped and filled with static. The rain clicked on the windowpane, the lantern flame skittered and shrank, drawing the shadows out of the darkness.

"He was your father."

The noise swelled in her head; she saw his lips move, but couldn't hear him. She grasped for something to cling to, something to shield her from his words.

"He raped her," she said. Her heart pumped air through her body.

Ben looked stricken.

"He told me he did."

"Twenty-five years ago," Ben said. His eyes, bloodshot, pleaded with her, wanting her to understand without him having to say more.

Kris felt like she'd stepped off a cliff. She opened her mouth; her eyes widened slowly as Ben's words penetrated her, penetrated years of crusted anger and hidden loneliness.

"No." She buckled. A sense of bitter loss and fear blew through her and she slipped out of time and place. She saw her mother, a teenager on the street with a little kid, she saw her collapsed on their apartment rug her hair fanned across her cheek, she saw the lonely bundle at the bottom of an arctic grave, and she saw Lambale crumpled around the big spruce tree, whispering as he died, trying to tell her he was her father.

Her next breath was ragged, her chest burned, and she struggled for control. "Why didn't you tell me?"

"Lambale was going to—"

"No, he wasn't," she said. "I was in the car with him. He never . . ."

His face had been speckled green by the dash lights, his gloved hands tight and nervous on the wheel, his lips struggling for words. And she'd beaten him into silence.

"It was Lambale who found you," Ben said, his eyes lighted with fear and pity. "No one else could have. And he wouldn't have searched for you unless he was going to tell you. That's why Evie wrote you, that's why she wanted you to come home. To meet your father."

"Ben." She gasped.

"But Alvilde fought it." He pushed on. "I saw it at the funeral. She stood so cold, so angry at him. When she looked at you, I knew it was because of you." Ben bowed his head.

"Ben." Kris desperately wanted him to look at her. "You don't understand."

"I couldn't tell you Alvilde killed Evie. It would've taken her from Lambale. And if it broke him, you would have lost him." And then quietly, like wind rustling dead leaves, "Like I lost Evie."

"Ben." *Look at me!* "I shot him." Her voice sounded outside her skin, empty and far away. "It was an accident." She was pleading with him, wanting him to understand. "I thought he killed her, killed my mother."

Ben didn't move. He didn't look up. His fingers stiffened against each other and then lay limp in his lap. In the lamplight, Kris saw a flash of silver drop from his hidden face and vanish into his open hands. Trembling, she stumbled out of the chair and knelt by his side and laid her head in his gnarled fingers.

"Ben," she whispered. "Hold me."

In his teens, Russell Heath hitchhiked to Alaska and lived in a cabin on the banks of the Tanana River: in his twenties, he lived in Italy and then traveled overland across the Sahara, through the jungles and over the savannas of Africa and into southern Asia: in his thirties, he sailed alone around the world in a 25 foot wooden boat; in his forties, he wrote novels; and in his fifties he bicycled the spine of the Rockies from Alaska to Mexico. He's worked on the Alaska Pipeline, as an environmental lobbyist in the Alaska Legislature, and run a storied environmental organization fighting to protect Alaska's coastal rainforests. Several years ago, he moved to New York City to dig deep into leadership development and coaching. He now coaches business and non-profit leaders intent on making big things happen in the world.

Leadership Unleashed
www.russellheath.net

Made in the USA
Middletown, DE
24 July 2015